# MAD, BAD AND DANGEROUS TO KNOW

"Do I want you?" He moved in one rough lunge to haul her up against him, her face smothered against his chest, her legs tangled with his. "I've wanted you for four years, baby. That's how long you've been under my skin."

She flushed deeply, as shy suddenly as if he'd never touched her before. His lips on hers were warm—the kiss sweet—his mouth nearly chaste.

This kiss was a vow, a serious, reverent one.

Then she drew breath and looked down, away from his brilliant gaze.

"I'm coming to get you tomorrow, Shiloh." His words were steady and determined. "Get your things ready."

———

Harper
Monogram

# BILLY BOB WALKER GOT MARRIED

## LISA G. BROWN

HarperPaperbacks
*A Division of HarperCollinsPublishers*

HarperPaperbacks  *A Division of* HarperCollins*Publishers*
10 East 53rd Street, New York, N.Y. 10022

Copyright © 1993 by Lisa G. Brown
All rights reserved. No part of this book may be used or
reproduced in any manner whatsoever without written
permission of the publisher, except in the case of brief
quotations embodied in critical articles and reviews. For
information address HarperCollins*Publishers*,
10 East 53rd Street, New York, N.Y. 10022.

Cover illustration by Jacqueline Goldstein

First printing: April 1993

Printed in the United States of America

HarperPaperbacks, HarperMonogram, and colophon are
trademarks of HarperCollins*Publishers*

10 9 8 7 6 5 4 3 2 1

#### For Lee

Even though you firmly believe that most red-blooded men would rather be shot than say some of the things that romance heroes say, and even though I don't think this book is good enough, it's still dedicated to you . . . for all the years of love.

# Acknowledgments

Thanks to Darlene Grisham, who listened and then listened some more; to Karen Lewallen, who helped me prepare the manuscript and was always generous with her praise and kind with her comments; and to Carolyn Marino, who gave me a second chance.

I also need to thank Florence Crawford, court recorder, and Glenna Sullivan from Mississippi State University for their expertise.

And to a neighbor, Mississippi—thanks for the setting of the story and forgive me for the liberties I took when I crammed the geography of your entire northern section into two fictional counties.

# 1

*Some fool had* made an awful mistake.

Clancy Green, the bailiff, knew it the minute his watery blue eyes slid down over the paper he held in his hand, the docket that listed all the cases to be heard that day by the Honorable Judge Robert Sewell. Right there, dead at the top of the list, was the name "Walker."

Actually, the first line said, "Allen vs. Walker," but Clancy already knew.

It was Billy Bob himself.

What in blazes was the boy thinking of, to let his case come up before Sewell, of all people?

There was going to be trouble, trouble, trouble. Just thinking about it made Clancy sweat; he could feel little wet rivulets trickling down his bony back under the new shirt he'd just bought at the Wal-Mart over in Martinsville a week or two ago. He had a perfect right to sweat, he told himself. It was scorching hot to be just the first of May, and besides, this morning when they'd tried to turn on the central air-conditioning unit that was supposed to cool Sweetwater's courthouse, nothing had happened. Zilch. Sue Ellen Terry, the county court clerk, finally took matters in her own hands (she liked to do that) and sent to Turner's Small Engine Shop to get B. J. Turner to come and try to fix the thing.

So far, he'd had no luck, and now here they all sat, sweltering away together in this tinderbox of a courtroom—Clancy; Vinia Thompson, the court recorder; eighteen plaintiffs; and numerous defendants and witnesses. The only two missing as of yet were the judge himself . . . and William Robert Walker.

Clancy swallowed again, sweated some more, and finally swore viciously to himself, staring once again at the devilish paper.

"Well, I never, Clancy Green," an offended voice said somewhere near his elbow, and he jumped, startled. Vinia Thompson had settled herself into her customary chair, the one reserved for the court recorder, apparently while he'd been deep in apprehensive thought, and now glared up at him indignantly from near his elbow.

Too late Clancy recalled just what he'd muttered to himself and flushed a little in embarrassment.

"Sorry, Vinia," he muttered. "I didn't see you sit down."

"I should hope not," she told him repressively. "I never heard the like of such vulgarity. Don't you ever go to church?"

Vinia's mouth was as prim as the old maid she was, and her movements were precise and proper. Although they were of the same age—both fifty-two—Vinia had hardly changed one iota from the thin, toothpicky girl she'd been as a student at Briskin County High School. Even her straight, short, carefully molded hair had remained the same—except that now and then it looked suspiciously darker, as if it had just been doused with Loving Care.

But even to have hinted at such a thing as the possibility of Vinia coloring her hair on the sly would have embarrassed and offended her nearly as much as Clancy's profanity had.

Remembering exactly what he'd said, Clancy thought that he had indeed been rather . . . well, profane.

"You'd swear, too, if you'd seen this list," he told her defensively.

"Swearing is the sign of a lack of control and discipline that I—oh, *my!*" Vinia's sentence broke off abruptly as Clancy shoved the paper under her long nose and pointed with one quivering finger at the name on the top of the list. "Oh, my!" she repeated with dismay.

Then she looked up at Clancy. "What will we do?"

"Do?" Clancy exclaimed, staring at her as if she were crazy. "I don't know 'bout you, woman, but I don't reckon I'll do a dam—I mean, a single thing."

"Does—does the judge know?"

"How could he? He's been out of town for weeks. Just got back this mornin'. But you can bet Billy Bob knows. Why'n the he—Sam Hill he'd let this thing happen is anybody's guess. Surely he could'a stopped it. He could'a told 'em—" Clancy broke off. He wasn't sure exactly what Billy Bob Walker could have said, after all.

"He's out to make trouble," Vinia predicted dismally.

"Well, this oughta make enough for even him," Clancy returned.

At that moment, a buzzing fly entered the room by way of the windows they'd pushed and shoved up to ventilate the place—and Judge Robert Sewell took a more dignified route and entered through the door from his chambers off to the side.

His entrance was as striking as always. He was a big, tall man, and unlike many of the judges in this rural section of northern Mississippi, insisted upon formality. Even in the heat of this early spring day, Robert Sewell had on a crisp white shirt and a dark tie that showed above his flowing black robes.

He wore the robes on every courtroom occasion, no matter how slight, and on the occasions he was called upon to marry a couple, he even wore them then. People who admired him said it was his way of making it clear that the law of the land deserved respect.

Those who despised him said it just showed he was a stuck-up snob whose family had been among the very few in the area to have the money to send their son to law school at Ole Miss. The robes made sure nobody forgot just who he was.

A few of the female persuasion whispered that the black garment emphasized his tremendous height and threw the fading blond of his hair into icy relief. He was undeniably handsome; his looks had helped him catch the eye of the daughter of another well-to-do-family, this one from Biloxi. His wife, Lydia, was nearly as smoothly perfect as Sewell himself was.

But nobody ever said any of those things to Judge Sewell, because the robes did one more thing—they set him apart, and his distinguished, aesthetic face finished the job, marking physically some sort of fence between him and the farmers and workers and laborers that made up most of Sweetwater and the rest of Briskin County.

A good judge, most said.

An elegant, fine figure, the women added.

A mighty cold fish, Clancy thought miserably, and hastened to drop the paper with its disastrous name down by his side.

The judge grimaced as he settled himself into his seat on the raised dais. "I thought somebody was coming to turn on the air-conditioning," he said in the general direction of Clancy.

Clancy clutched the paper and swallowed once, the Adam's apple in his long, skinny neck bobbing deeply, and his answer was meek. "B. J. Turner's down there tryin', sir. There's something wrong with it."

The judge looked up. "I think we're all aware of that." There was a trace of mild irritation in his voice as he reached into an inner pocket for his glasses. The gold wire frames gave just the right touch of somber intellectuality to his features. "Tell Turner to fix it."

Clancy was not normally a tenacious man, but today he was grasping at straws. Anything to delay the evil hour when the judge realized exactly to whom the first name on his list belonged.

"Yes sir, I will, but you know, some of the council members think that since we had a shortfall in taxes anyway, and since this May's mighty mild and pretty, we'd be doin' well to leave these windows open." Clancy gestured grandly toward the wide open apertures, the ones that had let in the adventuresome fly that was just now buzzing around his head.

Sewell stared at Clancy. "I beg your pardon?"

"You know, just take advantage of God's good mood and save the county money in the electricity department, to boot . . ." Clancy trailed off, weakly.

Most of the courtroom had gotten quiet when the

judge walked in; now the rest of it fell silent at the byplay between Sewell and the usually taciturn bailiff. Sewell himself was staring at Clancy as if the latter had lost his mind. Then he leaned forward, locking his fingers together with care.

"Mr. Green," he said, his voice silky, "when I am six feet under the Mississippi soil, I will have an eternity to admire the elements. The flies, the heat, the dirt that God has made. But until then, my courtroom will not be turned into some example of primitive living. More than flies and dust, I find the odor of sweat repugnant." Sewell released his fingers and leaned back in his chair, which creaked under his weight. "The minute Turner gets that unit fixed, I want it turned on. Is that clear?"

Clancy nodded. This diversion had not been a good idea.

"The council can cut corners someplace else. Not in my courtroom. And if they don't like that"—he looked out idly at the listening audience and added humorously, suggestively—"then we might look into *their* finances to find out where our taxes are going. Maybe we could cut *their* budgets."

There was a moment's pause, then as the crowd caught what Sewell was saying, a startled cheer of approval went up, as well as a smattering of laughter and a shrill whistle from the throat of Toy Baker, who stood leaning against a side wall.

Clancy had time to think resentfully that even while most of the general redneck populace was a little wary of Sewell, he had an uncanny knack for working them— when he chose to lower himself to do so.

It was true—Robert Sewell might even be governor someday, especially if he got Sam Pennington's money and power on his side.

And if things like William Robert Walker didn't crop up to cause trouble.

"Where's the docket?" the judge questioned abruptly, searching through the papers on his desk. "Here, Mr. Green, who's the first case?"

Clancy glanced wildly at Vinia, whose head stayed bent determinedly over her keyboard. He cleared his throat. There was no help for it.

"The case of Bud Allen and the Country Palace versus William Robert Walker." Clancy said it quickly, hoping the three words would slide together innocuously.

The judge had been scribbling something on a note-pad, and it took a second or so for the name to register. His hand jerked an infinitesimal bit, then stopped all movement.

"I beg your pardon?" he repeated again. His voice was deadly calm, but his blue eyes were steely behind the lenses of his glasses.

"Bud Allen and the Country Palace vs. William Robert Walker," Clancy answered. This time his voice was firm, and just maybe there was a trace of defiant, malicious knowledge in it.

There was a long, startled stillness in the too-warm, too-crowded little courtroom while Sewell breathed. That was all he did, just took a few deep breaths, while the skin that was stretched tautly across his cheeks mottled scarlet.

"And who—" the judge stopped a moment, suddenly flexing his hands as if they'd gone stiff, "who is responsible for this case being on my docket?" He might have appeared calm, and his words might have been distinct, but there was a rich fury running through his voice, outrage and temper mingling.

Nobody moved. Nobody answered.

Sewell took a long, deep breath. "Who is the attorney representing Bud Allen?" he demanded at last in the tense silence.

Finally, a throat cleared, and J. C. Hayes came reluctantly off the back wall a few steps.

"I reckon I am, sir." On any normal day, J. C. looked and acted more like a loud used-car salesman than he did a lawyer, but this morning he was subdued. Even his lacquered brown pompadour was a little flatter.

Sewell stared at him in distaste. "Why is this case on my docket?" he demanded.

J. C. squirmed under Sewell's unflinching stare. "I don't know what you mean, Your Honor." To Clancy's ears, his voice had a slight whine to it.

Sewell sucked in his breath sharply. "I've got no use for either you or your client, Mr. Hayes," he told the lawyer, his voice harsh. "But you know that. Bud Allen is in this courtroom just every few months or so over that— that so-called business of his. I've put up with that. But dragging this man Walker into it . . . he's a—a—"

"A what?" came a drawling, half-amused voice from the doorway.

The absorbed crowd gasped as if they were one unit, and all eyes turned toward the voice.

Clancy did the same—then groaned.

The man leaning lazily on the doorjamb, completely filling the opening, had both hands shoved nonchalantly down in the front pockets of skin-tight Wranglers. His shirt was opened carelessly down three buttons, and he had a green battered John Deere cap pushed back on his head.

Everything about the newcomer said clearly that he just didn't give a damn, not about the courtroom, not about this case, and most of all, not about Robert Sewell.

Sewell, on the other hand, was notching steadily upward on the fury scale. His nostrils were spread, his lips thin.

"I'll not hear this case," he said, thickly.

Both J. C. and the man in the doorway—William Robert himself—straightened.

"I don't know why not," J. C. interjected quickly. "You're the judge who's supposed to hear it, Your Honor. My client's got no complaints. And Billy Bob—" J. C. looked toward the other man, his face bland and guileless as a baby's.

Walker laughed, his laugh as careless as the rest of him. "Billy Bob's got no objections, either." The three men faced each other over the heads of the people in the courtroom in a triangle of contention. The man in the doorway was putting on a good act, Clancy thought in quick-born pity, but tension suddenly emanated from him with an electrical force in spite of his casual stance.

"This . . . is a travesty," Sewell finally rasped out, and he stood, his movements jerky and disjointed.

"You have to give a reason if you refuse to hear a case, Your Honor," J. C. told Sewell quickly, too quickly.

"I'm aware of the law," Sewell answered icily. His composure was coming back to him, Clancy thought, as the shock of Billy Bob's presence wore off.

"I don't know any reason for you not to hear the case, Your Judgeship," Walker put in, crossing his arms over his chest. "But maybe you do." His voice was challenging, suggestive.

Billy Bob's sheer audacity nearly knocked Clancy off his feet; he was afraid to look at Sewell, to see his reaction.

In a rush of fury, Sewell snatched up the gavel. "How dare you," he demanded, then he caught himself, and slowly sat back down. After an instant's pause, he said distinctly, through tight lips, "Very well. You're right. I'm quite sure, Mr. Walker, that I can administer justice to you, for once in your life. You'll get just what you deserve in my courtroom."

"I figured that," Billy Bob answered, his voice cheerful, his face innocent and angelic.

But there was a palpable strain quivering between the two of them as they eyed one another in a fleeting, heavy silence.

Old enemies, Clancy thought.

Through the open windows drifted clearly the words of Sue Ellen Terry as she called cheerfully to someone across the courthouse lawn, "How you doing, honey? We heard you were in the hospital having your tubes tied. You should'a let some of us know, just for moral support. Why, there's not a whole set of Fallopian tubes in town except Lou Talley's, and you'd think after she'd had those five wild boys, even she would have the good sense—"

There was a rippling burst of nervous laughter in the room, and it jarred Sewell into turning away from Walker's blue stare.

"Close that window," he told Clancy sharply. "And make sure Turner gets the air-conditioning fixed. I'll hear this case. The defendant and the plaintiff may step forward."

J. C. and his client, a rather stout young man in blindingly green slacks and a matching checked shirt, hastened to do as they were bid. They were seated at the tiny table in front of Sewell's bench even before the other man pulled himself off the door facing and began his leisurely, insolent stroll up the aisle. The wooden floor under his feet creaked loudly as he moved; even those creaks had a defiant, rude sound to them.

He threw up a hand once or twice at friends who spoke as he passed.

William Robert Walker was fairly awesome, no matter where he stood. He was six feet, three inches tall, and that was before he pulled on his Justin boots every morning. Long-limbed and lanky, Billy Bob—as most of the county knew him—was dominated by a pair of square shoulders that looked too big for the rest of his body, even covered by a pale blue shirt, as they were today. The sleeves were rolled up to his elbows.

It would have helped matters if he had had the good sense to get his hair cut before he kept his court date, Clancy thought aggrievedly, instead of letting it hang to his shoulders, its blond thickness curling under just a little as it brushed the back of his shirt.

But worst of all was that cap, the old, beat-up cap he insisted on wearing. Every day since he was thirteen, he'd worn one similar to it, and they all wound up looking the same, their edges curled down toward his face.

Some folks claimed Billy Bob slept in the hat, and at least one of his old girlfriends, Angie down at the Cut and Curl beauty shop, swore he did one other thing in it as well.

Clancy quickly straightened his face, hoping the judge hadn't noticed his brief grin.

But, no, Sewell's every molecule was focused in fury on the advancing man.

"Aren't you missing something, Mr. Walker?" Sewell asked icily.

Billy Bob looked around himself blankly and played dumb. "Nope," he said at last. "I don't reckon I am."

"When you address the court, you will do so respectfully," Sewell said, his voice tight and implacable. "No, *sir.*"

"No," Billy Bob said promptly, and then dragged out in another show of insolence, "sir."

A muscle twitched in Sewell's jaw. "Where is your attorney?"

"My what?"

"Your lawyer. Your defense. Your counsel. Do I need to explain it in elementary terms for you, Mr. Walker?"

"Oh. You mean like J. C. over there," Billy Bob said calmly. "Well, Bud got to him first, so I guess I'll be my own lawyer."

"I see. Well, it's your neck," Sewell said, and there was a hint of satisfaction in his voice. "Bailiff, swear in these people."

It didn't take long to hear the case. It concerned a fight and a female, things Sweetwater and Briskin County just associated with Billy Bob Walker. They were to him what breathing was to the rest of humanity.

J. C. got right to the point. "Judge, my client Bud here is prepared to testify that Billy Bob got into a fistfight with him down at his club, the Country Palace, and in the process—"

"His club?" Sewell interrupted, and there was a hint of scorn in his voice. "You're referring to that run-down old honky-tonk close to the county line?"

"Now just a minute," Bud protested, rising a little. J. C. pushed him back down in the chair hastily.

"That's the one, Your Honor," the lawyer said agreeably. "Anyhow, Billy Bob here busted it up to the tune of—" J. C. fumbled for a memo on the table before him and held it up to read off painstakingly, "2431.64. Bud's demanding repayment of that, plus another five hundred dollars for pain and suffering because he got two fingers broke when Billy Bob stepped on 'em."

There was a ripple of laughter before Toy called out from his position on the side wall, "That ain't it. All that pain and sufferin' he went through was 'cause Billy took his girl that night, and then Bud didn't have nobody to warm his bed. Ain't that right, Bud?"

In the shout of laughter that arose, and across Vinia's shocked, "Well, I never, I never," Bud called pugnaciously, his face even redder than usual, "You shut up, Toy. You hear me?"

Judge Sewell's gavel slammed down viciously, and his voice rang across the room. "That will be enough. From all of you."

When things subsided, Sewell said in a more controlled tone, "Toy Baker, you may leave the room."

"But, sir, he's one of Bud's witnesses," J. C. put in quickly.

"I should have known as much," Sewell answered in disgust. "All right. Call him. But I want everyone here to know that I consider everything about this case tawdry."

"Tawdry?" Bud whispered questioningly to J. C., who brushed it aside.

"Never mind, Bud, never mind."

So Toy told his story, remembering with relish that it had been one of the best fights he'd seen in years.

Bud aired his grievance and showed the splints still on his broken fingers.

J. C. presented a stack of repair bills both to Bud and the Country Palace.

Through it all, Sewell sat stone-faced.

"All right, Mr. Walker," he said at last. "Let's hear this

argument of yours that's so marvelous you don't even need an attorney to present it."

Billy Bob rose to his full height.

Sewell pointed the gavel at him as if it were a gun. "Take that cap off."

Billy did as he was instructed, raking his fingers through the heavy blond mass. The front of it was cut and layered, as short there as it was long in back.

"Me, I'm not arguing anything," he said peacefully, in the waiting silence.

There was an even longer pause.

"Would you care to explain, then, why you have taken up this Court's valuable time?" Sewell demanded dangerously at last.

"Oh, I guess I just wanted to take a real close look at you," Billy Bob returned, and there was a lick of fire through his otherwise calm voice.

The room hushed again; Sewell's face flushed furiously.

"Since you have no argument—"

"Oh, well, now"—Billy motioned outward with his cap—"I reckon I do need to say that I didn't step on Bud's fingers. I just knocked over a table, and it fell on 'em. Oh, and I didn't start the fight. He took the first swing at me because his girlfriend preferred my company to his."

"That's a damn lie!" This time Bud exploded from his seat like a fat green stick of dynamite. "You put a rush on her, Billy. I told you the next time you did it to one of my lady friends, I'd punch your face in. If you—"

"*Sit down!*" The judge's voice was a roar.

Bud subsided again, still muttering low, dire threats.

"No one—do you understand me?—no one will make a mockery or a three-ring circus out of my courtroom,"

Sewell told the room furiously. "And I don't care to hear even one more detail of this case."

His pale blue eyes met the darker blue ones of the younger man across from him.

"How old are you, Mr. Walker?"

Billy Bob's chin came up, and for the first time, there was a touch of surprised wariness in his face and voice.

"You know," he said at last, flatly.

"If I knew, I wouldn't be asking, now, would I? I said, how old?"

"Twenty-seven."

"Is that all? It seems to me that you should be at least a hundred," Sewell snapped. "You've done enough in this town, in this county, to make trouble for a man four times your age."

"Thank you," Billy drawled laconically.

"How many fights have you been in? Just since you hit adulthood?" Sewell demanded, relish creeping into his voice. The judge was clearly settling down to a satisfying enjoyment of his task.

"I don't know."

"No, I'm sure you don't. But your reputation precedes you into the courtroom. My fellow judges know you well, because you've been in front of many of them."

Billy Bob shrugged. "It's good to know you've been keepin' track of me—Your Honor."

Sewell flushed. "It's not hard for any judge to do, with somebody like you. And I guess it's all pretty funny to you, all the hell-raising you've become known for. You've run wild over this county for the last few years, with little or no respect for the law or decency."

Each of Billy Bob's cheeks had a hot red stain on it, but when he spoke, his voice was taut and controlled.

"You don't know the first thing about me," he retorted. "You've got no call to act like you do, either, nor to judge me on decency. You least of all."

"Stay silent until I tell you to speak. I'm going to sentence you to exactly what you deserve in this case against Allen. You will pay him every penny of what he is asking, plus court costs."

Billy Bob stood stiff as a ramrod, a nerve jerking in his jaw.

"Is that all?" he managed at last, and Clancy had to give him credit—Billy Bob was hanging tough, each word an insolent slap in the face to Sewell.

The judge let a flash of temper show, then said smoothly, "No, it is not, now that I think about it. I sentence you additionally to spend the next fifteen days in Sweetwater's jail for disturbing the peace and fighting in a public place."

There was pure, undiluted triumph in Sewell's countenance for the split second before he controlled it, and in the quick murmur of surprised sound that washed over the court, even J. C.'s mouth dropped open.

He half rose to protest, "Your Honor, we're not askin' that Billy Bob go to jail."

"Sit down, J. C.," interrupted Sewell. "Everyone agreed that I should hear this case. Now I intend to sentence Walker as I see fit."

"But this is not—" Billy Bob said involuntarily, then forced himself to cut off the words. His neck was stained with red now, as well as his cheeks.

"You have something else you want to say?" Sewell stood up behind the bench so that he was taller than Billy Bob across from him, and his voice dared the other man to challenge him again. Billy Bob never flinched from Sewell's stare but he swallowed harshly.

"No," he got out finally, his hands clenching and un-clenching, mutilating the brim of the cap. "Except . . . I should have expected it from you."

Judge Robert Sewell was not in control of himself. As if the words were dragged from him, as the courtroom sat transfixed, he asked hoarsely, "And what does that mean?"

Billy Bob got the last shot. "There's not a whole lot of mercy in you, is there? It's what my mama always said. You remember her, don't you? Ellen Walker."

"Fifteen more days," Sewell gasped out harshly, his nearly translucent skin gone as white as Billy's had red. "Fifteen more or another five hundred dollars in fines—for contempt. And you say one more word and you will rot in jail, and no amount of money will get you out."

After a stark hiatus of sound and movement, Billy put his cap back on, and his hand shook when he lowered it to his pocket again. "Yes . . . sir."

They faced each other like ancient gladiators, and the likeness between the two of them was undeniable.

In profile, they had the same straight noses, the same jutting chins, the same firm lips.

Past the turmoil, outside the courtroom, Bud said un-willingly to J. C., "This ain't right, this deal you set up. I got plenty mad at Billy Bob, but hell, it wasn't nothing to warrant this."

J. C. answered with his own tinge of regret, "It's too late now. Look at it this way—Billy Bob was asking for it. He could have had another judge if he'd fussed a little. He wanted to get next to Sewell. To get his attention. And he did. Maybe it was worth it to him."

"Yeah, but I feel—"

J. C. didn't believe in having scruples; it wasn't good

for his chosen profession. So he straightened his paisley tie and interrupted with a brisk dismissiveness, "Look, Bud, just take the money and run. After you pay me. Forget this whole mess. None of it had anything to do with you. It was personal, between the judge and Billy Bob. A family thing that's been brewing for years."

He swatted the fly that had been buzzing around his head ever since it had quit bothering Clancy, and wiped the sweat off his face.

"You want to blame something for all this, Bud, blame the weather. It's hot."

# 2

*That same too-warm,* early heat wave blew the cherry-red Porsche right up to the stop sign on the east side of the square, where the car sat throbbing for the tiny space of three heartbeats before its tires squealed to the left as it pulled out. But the screaming, impetuous path the Porsche blazed was hardly worth the effort because halfway up the quiet little block, it stopped abruptly, then pulled into the narrow entrance of the tunnellike road that separated the bank from Boyd's Drugstore.

Three men watched the car's flamboyant display before it settled down to a deceptive meekness, just as its red rear end disappeared jauntily down the road beside the bank. Two of the men—one white, one black, but both old, both overalled, and both open-mouthed—stared after it with mild interest.

The red Porsche and its comings and goings always made their day that much more interesting out on the bench in the courthouse yard.

But the third, a tall, balding man whose slight paunch disrupted the neatness of the brown uniform he wore, was not so amused. He came up off the bench in one slow surge, frowning fiercely at the vanishing vehicle, and the way he stood—arms akimbo, hands on hips, feet spread aggressively—made one of the old farmers punch the other one in the ribs and give him a sly wink.

"Girl drives too fast," remarked Cotton Jones, the farmer who'd winked. He sat whittling down a fat, round piece of walnut into a pile of nothingness. Just a heap of worthless slivers that would eventually cover his Red Man workboots completely, that was what the thick brown cord of wood would become before the day was over.

The man standing, the one who wore the badge and the uniform that proclaimed him to be Sweetwater's version of law and order, didn't answer Cotton, but his frown deepened, and his right ear twitched—once, twice.

Yep, he was aggravated.

"She's got brass, you gotta give her that," Cotton went on casually, and his bone-handled knife took another long, slow, smooth-as-butter strip off the walnut stick. He paused to eject a quick stream of amber toward the old tin can that sat beside him. It had once been a large container of Van Camp's Pork'n'Beans; now it made a handy, personal spittoon—on the rare occasion that Cotton hit it when he aimed for it. "She's that much like her old man." He wiped his whiskery mouth with the back of his hand. "But you never would'a knowed it until lately. She used to be quiet as a mouse."

"Wonder what she's been up to this time?" the other old man speculated idly; then he tilted up the Coke can he'd been holding on his knee to pull a burning draft of sugar and carbonation into his throat, one that made his

eyes water. He said *aa-hh* loud and long before he spoke.
"My granddaughter Marie—y'know, the one that works
there"—he jerked his head toward the white-columned
building up the road from them, the one whose brick
facade was broken halfway up with a New Orleans–style
balcony and a heavy, gold-lettered sign that read People's
Bank of Sweetwater—"she says Sam Pennington made
that girl start as a cashier at his little branch bank in
Dover, and he don't call her home to this'n during workin' hours 'less he's madder'n hell about something."

Both the old men waited expectantly for the sheriff to
put in his two cents. He didn't.

"Seems like a waste of all them years she was off at
college, if you ask me," Cotton told Jackson, the one
enjoying the Coke. "He's give her ever'thing else.
Clothes, car, that big education off in Tennessee, like
Mississippi wudn't good enough for her. He might as well
go ahead and make her a big shot at his bank. He means
to, anyway, someday. I reckon she gets just about what
she pleases."

"He'd better let up on her, that's what."

The words came at last in a frustrated growl from the
throat of the man Cotton had been verbally gouging—the
sheriff. His name was T-Tommy Farley—and he had the
added distinction of being related to the driver of the red
Porsche. He was a second cousin to her father.

"What's he on to her about this time?" Cotton asked
innocently, squinting at the end of his stick.

"Does he need anything new?" T-Tommy turned away
from the bank, shifting instead to face the ugly yellow
brick of the courthouse. Its square, four-sided, three-
story body sat like an aging, passive Buddha there in the
dead-center of Sweetwater, softened by the sprawling

trees that wrapped their limbs about its corners. Spring lent beauty to the lawns. Just now, the grass was green and growing; hot pink azaleas blazed along the edges of the sidewalks, mingling with the purples and reds and whites of newly planted petunias; and rich green shadows lay all around them, compliments of the ancient, shiny-leaved southern magnolia tree under which the old wooden slat-backed bench sat.

T-Tommy said flatly, "Shiloh's getting too old to keep on taking it, or his orders. She's twenty-one. Or is it twenty-two?"

"Never live to see thirty if she keeps on drivin' like a bat out of hell," Cotton commented pointedly. "Some-body's gonna have to say somethin' to her."

T-Tommy glared at the cherubic face of his potbellied adviser. "I reckon that means me."

"You're the law. You're the only relative she's got be-sides the old man and Laura. So you better speak up, even if Sam Pennington might chop you off at the knees for interferin'," Cotton answered matter-of-factly. " 'Course, we all figure you do pretty much what he tells you to do. I reckon that's just being smart."

"Don't push me, Cotton. I ain't afraid of Sam, if that's what you mean," T-Tommy snapped defensively, and his fingers fumbled about his left breast pocket, trying to unhook the aviator sunglasses hanging there.

"I reckon I am," remarked Jackson mildly. "Scared of Sam, I mean."

"What d'you say he was mad at her about this time?" Cotton returned to his original purpose with the ques-tion.

T-Tommy gave him a smug, satisfied smirk. "I didn't." He didn't see any point in telling them that he didn't know what had brought the Porsche in to town.

Then he slid on the sunglasses. "Well, I got things to do. And it's gettin' along toward lunch. I better head on over to the jail and see what's cookin'. Besides, I got Billy Bob for nearly three more weeks, and he's already gettin' mighty restless all cooped up like that. He might need my company for a while, just to stay straight. I'll see you boys."

Just as the sheriff turned to leave, Cotton took another shot at the tin can, and T-Tommy paused, grinning.

"Hey, Cotton, you're gonna have to get a better aim, or I'm gonna lock you up for defacing public property."

The two old men watched T-Tommy stroll off whistling, the midmorning sunshine glinting off his silver badge, the rims of his glasses, and his bald spot all at the same time.

"Smart aleck," Cotton muttered, for once laying down his knife.

"Yep," agreed Jackson amiably, one big, weathered black hand scratching his jaw. "But you know what? I ain't never seen a cop yet that didn't have a streak of it somewhere in him. Must be in that uniform."

Just past the bank and the drugstore, the little narrow road suddenly turned into a square paved parking lot with a big red-and-white sign that said authoritatively, Bank Employees Only. The red Porsche nosed along inquiringly, but every spot along the front row was full.

The car seemed to hesitate for a second at the place where a long, sleek, creamy white Coupe de Ville Cadillac sat, right where another sign indicated in bold black letters that this prime piece of parking real estate belonged exclusively to Sam Pennington, Pres.

Then the Porsche made a quick, dicing, on-a-dime

right turn and headed for the only available parking spots, all along the back row, finally maneuvering into a tight little area down at the end.

Inside the car, Shiloh Pennington sat gripping the steering wheel, trying hard to fight down nerves and apprehension and the little licks of rebelliousness that were springing up inside her. On the phone when Sam had ordered her to leave the bank at Dover and get to Sweetwater, he'd said it had something to do with paperwork she'd failed to complete.

And that was an out-and-out lie, she told herself fiercely.

This was about Michael. She knew it already. The weasel had come crawling to Sam; it had taken him twelve hours to do his worst. She should have beat him to it, she told herself in angry self-recrimination, instead of hiding in her room and dreading the confrontation. And say what? she jeered back at herself. Even if she'd had the nerve, Sam wouldn't have believed her.

He thought the sun rose and set in Michael.

But it had come down to this: Now she had to tell the truth and face the music, like it or not.

Thrusting herself out of the car in one violent rush, she winced as her left side brushed roughly against the door frame, and her fingers went in sudden remembrance to the top of her left breast. She shuddered with a wave of revulsion as memory swept over her, and shut her eyes for a moment to block out an internal vision of strong white teeth.

*It wasn't her fault.*

On the thought, her eyes abruptly opened and she looked around at the bright day and the sunshine sparkling hotly off the multicolored cars here in the parking lot. She was fine. She was safe. She was *right*.

There was no reason to shake in her shoes—her white, ridiculously high-heeled designer shoes—as if she were a scared kid again, trying to please and soothe an impossible man who had the roar of a bull ape when he was angry—or hurting.

If he were just angry, she could stand firm.

But if he got that you've-hurt-me-more-than-you'll-ever-know look, the one that said she'd disappointed him (again), she'd have a lot harder time holding her ground.

Oh, God, let him be furious, she prayed.

Smoothing a nervous hand down over her navy skirt, she hit bare skin before she meant to—and then remembered just how short the skirt was. She had put it on this morning as a measure of defiance; she'd realized some time before a sleepless dawn that Michael would go to Sam and she'd be called to account before the day was over. She was glad—*glad*—she was wearing the skirt. If nothing else, it alone would send Sam's blood pressure skyrocketing.

Okay—maybe it was too short. Seeing her reflection in the curved red side of the car, Shiloh winced at exactly how much of her figure it did reveal, and she tugged at it a little nervously.

And maybe the square neck of the boxy, white waist-length jacket was too low. And her huge square earrings too flashy. Sam would have plenty to distract his attention, enough to keep him through the roof for twenty or thirty minutes. He might even forget about Michael.

Ha. Dream on, honey, she told herself with a grimace, then turned to enter the bank and beard the lion in his den.

Marie Watson was her father's personal secretary; she was the first thing people saw if they ever got taken up to the second floor of the People's Bank, as she sat at a three-sided desk in the middle of a spacious office area upon which both the elevator and a set of stairs opened.

Three other women sat at three other desks scattered about the area, Marie's "office girls" they were called, although one was a grandmother who looked her age and generally acted it. She was the first to see Shiloh as she got off the elevator, and she smiled familiarly at the girl who'd been in and out of Sam's office for all of her life.

Then Marie glanced up, and for one minute, her brown eyes held a wry sympathy.

"How are things in Dover, Shiloh?" she asked, smiling.

"Fine. Great. With any luck at all, I'll be back at work there within the next hour or two," Shiloh muttered. She thought bitterly that there wasn't much use for pretense; everybody apparently already knew Sam had yanked her to Sweetwater for some kind of chastisement.

"Sam sent for me," she announced anyway, her words as crisp and sure as she could make them.

Marie glanced down at the big telephone with its buttons and flashing lights. "He's on the phone, but I'm sure you can just go on in. He won't be much longer."

Permission granted to see the king—to face judgment, Shiloh thought fleetingly as she headed for his closed door.

Once inside the big office, she let her gaze wander over the room, doing her best to ignore the man behind the big cherry desk, the one with the telephone at his ear. It was a cool, calm office with a silver carpet that ran right into gray-blue walls. The heavy Austrian drapes were a rich cranberry red, and the same color formed the matting around each one of the grouped trio of pictures on the far wall.

One was of Sam's brother David, who had once been a partner but was long since dead.

Another was of Sam himself.

The third was of a little girl, one with huge, solemn brown pools for eyes and sherry-colored hair, rich with wine tints. That oil had been done of her when she was seven; maybe Sam would have liked it better if she'd stayed that malleable little girl.

But things change.

He was deliberately making her wait. The phone conversation had ended, and in the silence of the room, the sound of his pen scratching out some notation was the only one in the place. Well, she wasn't going to let him intimidate her before this discussion ever started.

With a jerk, Shiloh moved loudly, taking big steps over to the far wall, where a long narrow window looked out on the blue sky and, down below, the parking lot, where her car sat nosed against the rear of another building, the county jail, which actually faced the next street over.

Shiloh made a funny, snorting sound in the back of her throat. It was just like Sam to thumb his nose at the world and build a bank not fifty yards from a jail, as if daring somebody to cross him.

Looking down at the neat little boxed-in square of concrete where the cars sat, she thought suddenly that the parking lot was like her life: closed in. Tight quarters. It had been that way for a long time, but somehow, she hadn't realized it until she came home from the university. No, not even then. She'd not really noticed it until Michael began to talk about marriage.

"Well."

The one word from her father made her twist to see Sam, turned toward her now in the big leather swivel chair, surveying her with displeasure, his thin face under the heavy gray hair nearly delicate in appearance, almost saintlike.

They were a lie, those looks and that refined bone structure. He was bossy, hard nosed, outspoken, a man who'd risen from a job in a tiny mill to become one of the controlling powers in this section of Mississippi.

"I thought I had asked you to call me before you left Dover so I'd know when to expect you," he said at last.

She shrugged. "Mr. Parsons said I could come immediately, so I did—there didn't seem to be any reason to call." Or to keep myself on edge the rest of the day, putting off this discussion, she thought to herself.

"I didn't see you this morning before I left the house," he said consideringly, eyeing the clothes she had on, "which is a shame, because I could have told you then that those clothes might be the rage with some magazine, but around here, in a small-town bank, they look trashy."

"It's the style."

"Where? Out in some damned fruity place like California?"

"I bought these in Memphis."

"Good God, what's the South coming to?" he said. Then he stood abruptly, a pencil-thin man in a smooth, well-tailored gray suit. Like the room, he seemed calm.

But Shiloh knew exactly what it would take to blow that cover; she figured he could maintain it about fifteen more minutes—until they got around to the real reason she was here.

"Aren't you responsible for Ledbetter's mortgages and loans?" Sam asked abruptly, and his right hand shot out to find the short stack of papers that had been stapled together and laid on his desk.

"Ledbetter . . . oh, you mean Noah Ledbetter out at the mill. Yes, I am."

"You want to explain why his notes haven't been renewed yet?" Sam flipped several pages, then held out the papers to her.

Hesitantly, Shiloh came forward, glancing first at her father's still face, then reaching to take the papers, searching for the place where he was pointing.

"Do you see the date? Ledbetter should have been in to sign this form nearly two months ago. He has to do it every year in March. He knows that," Sam told her.

"I know, too," Shiloh returned, calmly. "But he asked me to do some research for him, to see if the loan could somehow be refinanced for better terms."

"And did you?"

"He asked me, so—yes, I did."

"And could it be?"

"No, not considering the amount of money he's borrowed and the way it's being invested," Shiloh answered steadily, then flipped the papers shut.

"And have you told him that?"

"Yes."

"When?"

"Last month."

"Last month." Sam repeated her words, then rubbed his open palm down the side of his left cheek thoughtfully. "So he's had at least four weeks to come in and renew this loan. And that means Ledbetter's had two months where he got out of making his monthly payment."

"So? We'll still get it in the end."

"That's right. We will. But the point is"—and Sam leaned over the desk to tap the papers lightly with his forefinger—"Ledbetter thinks he's conning us. He's used the bank's own paperwork—this yearly finance statement—and the bank's own employee—my daughter—to buy himself two months of free time. He's pulled this stunt before, y'see, but not with me. Only with a gullible loan officer I once had."

"I'm not a fool," Shiloh retorted. "I know what he's doing. I called him two weeks ago and advised him he had to come in and sign the yearly statement, so the payments could begin again."

"Or?"

"I didn't give him an 'or.' He said he'd be in before the month was out. If he's not, then I can pull the rug out from under him, I guess, stop payment on his checks, or something like that. But I won't have to. He knows the signature every year is just a technicality, a nicety. Legally, he still has to pay the bank. You know it, too."

Sam stacked the papers on his desk carefully, making one neat pile of paper. Deliberately, he laid his two gold pens side by side.

"Noah Ledbetter's father was my first boss," he told his daughter, his eyes holding hers. "Stingy. Mean. He worked men until they dropped, for little or no wages because he could get away with doing it around here forty years ago. If he'd had his way, I'd have died workin' in that mill of his. But I got out. It liked to have killed him the first time he had to send Noah to me to ask for money. I gave him what he needed. At the time, me and my bank, we were all that saved his hide."

"I've heard the story before, Papa," Shiloh told him, putting the papers back down on his desk, on top of his stack.

"So you have." Sam slid both hands into the pockets of his pants, his actions crumpling up the sides of the coat and marring its sleek, chic lines. He evidently had no loose change today; if he had, he would have jingled it restlessly, in spite of all his best efforts not to. It was a habit he'd tried repeatedly to stop, mostly because he thought it took away from the image of the uptown banker he liked to promote.

It was the same reason he smoked his cigars on the sly, the same reason he kept a dictionary hidden in his desk drawer, to look up any new words he should know but didn't.

"But I'm telling you that Ledbetter resents like hell me having a hold over him. I'm fair. I play by the rules. And he's going to, too, even if he has to be made to do it. I may have been a dirt-poor worker and he may have been the boss's son, but things have changed. Even after all these years, I want him to remember that, whether he likes it or not. His business is in good shape, so you don't let him slide, Shiloh. You call him today—tell him he comes in and signs the note and makes this month's payment within the next twenty-four hours, or else."

"Or else what?"

He pulled his hands out of his pockets and said sharply, "You just tell him Sam Pennington says for him to get his butt down there. You're my daughter, Shiloh. I want to see some of me in you. I want to see you doing the right things. For once."

There was a long, stark pause while they glared at each other, then Shiloh broke away.

"It's too bad," she told him, her voice low and a little shaky, "that you just can't be me. Or make me what you want. Maybe then I could go ahead and marry Michael Sewell. That's what this conversation is all about—not Noah Ledbetter."

Behind her, Sam sucked in his breath sharply. "All right, let's just wade into the whole damn mess. What in the hell do you mean, breaking off an engagement two months—just two *months*, for God's sake—before you're set to marry the man?"

Shiloh turned so quickly she knocked a pen off his desk and she faced her father furiously. "He didn't waste any time crying to you, did he? I bet he got to the office this morning before you did."

"What have you got against him all of a sudden? You were happy enough when he started courting you. You wanted to marry him then. You know how I feel about him."

"About him . . . or his bloodline? He's one of the Sewells—that's what's important, isn't it?"

Sam's blue eyes were snapping with frustration. "I never pretended that wasn't part of it. I want that for you. I want you to be more than the daughter of a one-time mill worker and a—a—"

"Don't say it," Shiloh cut in sharply. "Don't say it!"

There was a short, gasping silence while both of them breathed harshly, then she spoke more calmly.

"These aren't the Dark Ages, Papa. You can't make me marry him."

Sam's face shadowed as he moved out from behind the desk. "Maybe we'd be better off if they were. Then I'd just chain you up and hand you over. Hell, it must be a real hardship to marry Michael Sewell. He's handsome, he comes from a fine old family, he's a head engineer for the TVA, he's going places."

"I don't love him," Shiloh said desperately, walking over to the window to clutch at its drapes.

"You're finding that out eight weeks before the wedding?" Sam snapped.

"I thought I could. Love him, I mean. But I was really

trying to . . . to please you." Her last words were so low they were nearly whispered, but her father caught them.

"Please me!" he returned incredulously. "When have you ever tried to please me? Was it when you were seven and broke a whole set of dishes because I wouldn't let you keep a mongrel puppy?

"Or maybe you've tried to please me with the men you've been interested in—like the summer you were eighteen and decided you were going to run wild with Billy Bob Walker. Was that when it was, Shiloh?"

She said nothing, her face flushing, just staring out the window.

Then Sam drew another long, deep breath, and continued, more calmly, "I want what's best for you. I won't let you ruin your life out of sheer nerves, or last-minute jitters, or pure contrariness, whichever it is. Michael loves you. He called me half out of his mind this morning. He said you gave his ring back."

"I threw it back," Shiloh corrected. "And what did he say was my reason?"

Her father's thin cheeks flushed a little.

"He blamed me, as I recall. Said I'd pushed you too hard, that you were nearly hysterical last night."

Shiloh gave a short, choked laugh. "Oh, that's good. I was hysterical and it was your doing." Then she turned sharply, her eyes pleading. "Tell me—please tell me—you'll believe me when I give you the truth about what really happened."

Sam stared at her hard a minute. "Are you about to tell me that Michael, the man I've known for years, who's the son of one of my closest business associates, is a liar?"

Shiloh let the curtain fall silently behind her as she hoisted away from the confrontation with her father, bitterness in her face. "You've already answered my question."

"Dammit, Shiloh—"

"I won't marry him," she said flatly. Just keep saying it, she told herself. He couldn't *make* her.

"You can't stand a man up eight weeks before the wedding unless you have a hell of a good reason. I'm waiting to hear—"

A sharp buzzing sound cut across his words as Marie signaled him on the intercom, and muttering to himself, Sam took three giant strides to the desk, pushed a button, and barked, "Yes? What? What is it?"

"It's nearly noon, sir. You can't wait any longer if you mean to be at your afternoon meeting in Tupelo with Mr. Griffin and his partners," Marie offered, a little apologetically.

"All right. Thank you." He straightened, glancing in irritation at his own wristwatch. "We can finish this talk tonight. I'll be home for supper. Laura said this morning you were planning on being there, too. We'll talk then. This is not over, d'you hear?"

He was already on his way out the door, saying something to Marie as he went. Suddenly furious, Shiloh went to the door to call after him, "Sam."

He stopped, turning warily. She took a deep breath.

"I won't marry him. Don't get to thinking that I'll change my mind between now and suppertime." There— it was said again, and this time, as if to confirm it, there were witnesses.

He shot a warning, shocked glance over at Marie, who sat frozen between the two of them, trying to pretend she had gone deaf on the instant.

"I said we'd discuss it tonight, Shiloh. And wear something decent for supper. I can't stand to see much more of that—that thing you've got on."

Nobody said a word in the still office area as Sam got on the elevator and its door closed silently behind him. Shiloh watched the shut door a minute before turning to the four quiet women. Marie's wide eyes were locked on her face.

"He took that rather well, don't you . . . th-think?" Shiloh tried to say jokingly, but the words hung and sobbed in her throat, and terrified that she might cry, she slung her purse—the one she'd never put down—high on her shoulder and rushed out the door that led to the stairs. No time to wait for elevators.

Alone at the bottom of the steps, in the quiet well, she stood drawing deep breaths and fighting down the tears. Nobody—Sam, least of all—comprehended how hard it was for her to stand and fight.

She didn't want to; she wanted to please her father, just as she'd always wanted to. But this time, she *knew*. She would never be happy with Michael Sewell. Why couldn't she make her father understand that? It was her life; when would he realize that and be happy to let her live it?

But so far, she'd kept saying no. She might have given in before, but this time she had to keep fighting. This time, she had a cause so serious she couldn't quit—she hated Michael's guts.

The thought was so defiant and so strong that it made her feel that way, too, burning away her worries over displeasing Sam. She pushed open the back entrance door and emerged into the parking area. The early spring breeze that brushed her face with a clean welcome carried on it the yeasty smell of baking bread, compliments of Danny Joe Yearling's bakery two buildings down from the bank. Maybe she was hungry. Maybe she needed to eat. Maybe then she'd feel better.

Flinging the purse into the open door of the Porsche, Shiloh was about to follow it in when the whistle cut across the fragrant air and arrested her motion. Shrill and rednecky, it was a blatant, wolfy sound that startled her into looking up.

"I got to tell you, honey, this is the best view I've had from this window in days. It makes up for all the other times I've been deprived of the creature comforts since I've been in here."

The sun's rays blinded her for a second or two, but even before Shiloh put up a hand to shield her eyes and clear her vision, she knew to whom the lazy, husky, drawling voice belonged.

Billy Bob Walker leaned carelessly against the bars of the opened window, the one in the back of Sweetwater's ancient jail. She had glimpsed him only a few times around town after her return from college and then, deliberately, she'd kept her distance. She'd learned her lesson once about the tall man who stood propped in the window facing, his blond, tousled hair shining like glinting gold in the sun.

Let sleeping dogs lie, that's what Laura always said, so Shiloh ignored him, turning away. But this dog had a different plan.

"What's the matter? Cat got your tongue? That'd be a shame—I can think of better things to do with it. Things I bet that boyfriend of yours never heard of. Things I didn't get around to showing you all those summers ago when you—"

Flushing, she twisted back to him. "Will you hush?"

she told him furiously. Then she stopped short. For all the taunting, teasing edge to his words, his face was intense and unamused.

"So, you can talk, after all," he said, a hint of mock amazement in his voice. "Even to me, the lowdown jail-bird."

"I always knew you'd come to a bad end, Billy Bob," Shiloh retorted.

His eyes widened as he clutched the bars. "And she knows my name. Miss Shiloh Pennington knows my name."

"Oh, never mind," she murmured irritably, starting once again to slide in the car, but he spoke again, raising his voice, halting her.

"See, I was scared to death I'd gone invisible or something. Because ever' time I've been around you—which ain't often these days—you keep looking right through me. It's a weird feeling, like I've just died and nobody told me yet."

"Well, you can take my word for it—you're alive and kicking," she answered shortly. "And in as much trouble as always. What are you in jail for? General insolence?"

"You mean you don't know?" he asked in mock amazement. "Everybody else in Sweetwater does."

"I've been busy."

"Yeah, I bet. You and the judge's little boy."

His voice had a sudden quiet, harsh edge, the hint of a jeer in his words. Shiloh swallowed, remembering in a flash what she'd tried to forget—Billy's relationship to Michael.

Maybe he read the emotion in her face, for his suddenly went blank. Then he laughed. "You two look perfect together. The golden boy and the little daddy's girl."

"You never change, do you?" she got out at last, pushing her words past the sudden, unexpected hurt that his had brought.

"I get older. I'm not so crazy about doing stupid things anymore—a few weeks in here are making it real clear that they're never worth what you have to pay. I should already have known that. Guess I was supposed to learn it from you three or four years ago. Me, I'm dumb and slow. I even used to believe in angels with big brown eyes."

A slow, hot flush seeped up Shiloh's cheeks at his pointed words. "You're right. That was dumb. I can't imagine an angel wanting you. You'd have to reform first, and I don't think that's possible."

He leaned into the bars, resting his forehead on them as he looked down at her and retorted, "Oh, I don't know. You're not one—we both know that—but you still look pretty angelic. You're sure preachy enough to make a man reform, and there was a time, Shiloh Pennington, when *you* wanted me."

A flaming red wave of color washed clear to her hairline, and she gasped at his sheer audacity as if she'd been struck. "You—you—oh! I was eighteen and too stupid to know better."

"And now you're all grown up?" He looked her over again, then grinned before answering his own question. "Yes, ma'am, you surely are."

"But at least this time I'm not stupid enough to keep on talking to you," Shiloh snapped back furiously.

"It's not my fault that you quit the first time," he returned.

"It must have been your technique. Like wolf-whistling at every girl that goes by. Aren't you getting too old for that?" she returned, sliding in the open door of the car.

"Maybe I was whistling at the Porsche," Billy Bob answered. "As for you, you looked tired. Too much night life with the judge's little boy?"

"Drop dead," she muttered. It wasn't exactly a scintillating return, but she was too burned up to think of a better one.

As she reached out to pull the door closed, he called, "Hey, Miss Shiloh Pennington. I'm a lot of things, but I ain't no liar. I wasn't whistling at a car. I couldn't see anything but legs. Honey, that dress is too damn short."

She slammed the door furiously, twisted the key in the ignition, and the motor roared into instant, surprised life. Spinning out of the bank's parking lot, Shiloh left Billy Bob Walker and his laughter somewhere behind her.

# 3

*So that was* the big conversation he'd been waiting all these years to have.

Billy Bob laughed under his breath, a touch of wryness in the sound. It hadn't quite lived up to billing, but nevertheless, he'd had his chance to take potshots at the high-and-mighty Shiloh Pennington, and he'd taken them.

She'd given them back, too; somehow he'd known she would. They hadn't parted on the best of terms. She'd proven where her loyalty lay and it hadn't been with him. And if the knowledge had made him furious—at least at the time—it had to make her defensive now when he was around.

He'd worn out his emotions for her; now the only thing that fueled his desire to get back at Shiloh was just the sense of satisfaction that he'd at last forced her to face him and had wrung deep-gut, honest anger from her— that, and the outrage that ran through him every time he remembered that she was about to marry the one man with whom he most hated to see her: his half brother, Michael.

Moving from the window that still held a lingering memory of the girl and the red car, Billy Bob slumped down on the edge of the narrow bunk, where he propped his elbows on his worn jeans and dropped his face into his hands, trying to forget.

Robert Sewell was there, in his head, where he had been ever since Billy Bob was six years old and some kid out at tiny Seven Knobs Elementary had called him "bastard," repeating exactly what an adult had no doubt said. He'd gone home crying, demanding to know what it meant—and he'd made Mama cry, too.

He hadn't understood all of the truth when she told it to him, but between the shame in her face and the anger in Grandpa's, he'd realized enough to at least understand why he didn't have a father at home.

As he grew older, he came to accept and even see what lay behind Sewell's total denial of everything. The man had always completely ignored the illegitimate son growing up on the farm fifteen miles north of Sweetwater, twenty-eight miles from Laurel Hill, the Sewell estate. It was the only way Sewell could cope with the fact that he'd once forgotten himself and his place enough to have seduced a backward, shy little country girl like Ellen Walker and then walked away from her.

It must have been gall to the judge when Billy Bob began to look more and more like him and his legitimate son every passing day; it had been bitter enough for Billy to take when he looked in his own mirror.

And to watch Michael have everything Billy couldn't just made it worse. One son was the canker in his father's life; the other was the apple of his eye.

Now Shiloh was with Michael. It didn't matter, Billy told himself firmly. He didn't love her anymore; in fact, he hated her. But the knowledge didn't help. Seeing her—her, of all people—in the local newspaper's wedding announcement section a few weeks ago with Michael had burned like salt in an open sore.

Maybe Billy's fury had led him to clash headlong at last with Robert in the courtroom.

Which brought him back full-circle to the judge, he thought in frustrated anger, pushing himself restlessly up off the bunk.

"Hey, you got a visitor," Davis McKee, the young, redheaded deputy, called back to him from the open door which led from the dingy cell area out to the offices.

"Yeah? Who?"

"Your grandpa, that's who. Go on in, Mr. Walker."

Billy went slowly to the bars as Willie Walker entered, approaching stiffly with the aid of a dark, heavy cane. The stroke the old man had suffered more than two years ago wouldn't quite turn loose of him no matter how he fought; the doctors had decided he would be crippled for the rest of his life.

But then, they didn't know Willie Walker, Billy thought with an unexpected surge of affection as he watched the white-haired man in the faded overalls and carefully starched high-buttoned white shirt—his "town" shirt—advance slowly toward him. Those same doctors had once said he'd never walk at all.

He halted in front of the bars and looked up at the grandson who stood a full head taller. "Well," he drawled at last, "I see you ain't gone nowhere since the last time I was here."

"Gone stir-crazy, that's about all," Billy Bob retorted

unevenly, and he tried to ignore the feelings of guilt the old man's presence stirred inside him. He should be on the farm, helping him.

"It'll do it to you," Willie agreed, looking around at the three cells that stood in a row, each with a hard cot, a chipped, stained urinal and sink, and a little barred window. "It sure ain't home."

"I guess the peach trees have all quit blooming by now," Billy said, wistfully.

"Just about. It looks like it's gonna be a good year. Your mama cleaned the fruit stand and gave it a new paint job. I reckon we'll be ready to open next week, just like we always do." Willie braced both hands on the top of the cane, leaning his bulk onto it.

"I was supposed to do the painting. I promised," Billy answered regretfully. "And who'd you get to go pick up the out-of-state produce?"

"Jimmy Mabrey, he's helping, and one of the Allred boys. Maybe you'll think about what it is that's important, and what you need to be doing, the next time you take it in your head to pull a fool stunt like breaking up Bud's honky-tonk. Or tellin' off a judge." Willie's face got a little darker, but it didn't show much emotion where Sewell was concerned. He'd learned to keep it hidden, but it was there, his dislike of the man, tamped down deep inside, just like Billy's.

"Don't you think I've told myself a thousand times I should have stayed home and stayed quiet?" There was a long silence after Billy's desperate words, then he asked awkwardly, "How're you getting along, moneywise?" It might not do any good to ask—Willie didn't believe in telling about money woes. But sometimes, if Billy Bob watched closely enough, Willie's face gave things away.

Not today.

"We're makin' it," the old man said shortly. "When produce starts sellin', things will get a whole lot better. And when I get off this high-priced medicine and away from those so-called therapists that charge an arm and a leg when they're s'posed to be helpin' me get mine back, there won't be any money problems at all."

Billy Bob didn't remind the old man that he'd be on the medicine and probably with the therapists for the rest of his life; keeping his mouth shut was a small price to pay for his grandfather's pride.

"Fact is," Willie continued, "I've come to offer *you* some money."

Billy Bob stared.

"That's right. I hear you need thirty-five hundred just to get out of this mess."

"What did you do, Grandpa?" Billy asked warily. "You didn't sell something, did you?"

"Not me. Don't reckon I got anything worth that much. But you—you got something Harold Bell up at Bell Farm wants."

Billy locked his hands around the bars so tightly his knuckles went white. "He wants Chase. That's what he's always wanted."

Willie nodded, and in an uncharacteristic show of sympathy, he reached out his old, rough hand and wrapped it around his grandson's on the bars. "He knows how it is, that you wouldn't sell that horse come hell or high water. But he figures a few weeks in here will change your mind, and if you do, you won't have to work all summer just to pay Bud Allen. You can put your money toward that other thing you've got goin'. So I told him I'd come and ask, anyway. Not on account of I want you to sell Chase—but because I know you. You're gonna go crazy locked up in this little room, Billy. It ain't right."

"You tell Bell the answer's the same as always. I raised Chase. He's always been mine, and a month or two in jail won't make me decide different."

Willie hesitated. "I already told him that was what you'd say. It's all right with me. But Billy, your mama hates what's happened with you and that judge. She's dyin' 'cause you're in here. It might do her some good if we could find a fast way to—to get you out."

The throat of the younger man worked convulsively, then he turned his back to the bars to lean on them. "Tell her it's my own fault, like always. Not hers. That I'm okay. And . . . and I'll think about Bell's offer, much as I hate it."

Willie nodded wordlessly, then turned away. "Well, I reckon I'll go get a haircut over at Leland's before I head home. Ellen keeps telling me I need it, and I hate to waste a trip to town on just comin' to see you." His words held a joking tone that forced Billy to turn around to look at him as he stood leaning on his cane. In the quiet stillness that lay between them a moment, Willie said at last to his grandson, "You come on home soon as you can, Billy Bob."

Nodding wordlessly, Billy watched the old man maneuver his body and his cane toward the outside, calling as he did, "Davis! I'm through talkin' to your prisoner."

Then Billy Bob looked at the four walls around him, the ones pressing in on him and collapsing down against him. He was in a big mess—and he deserved every bit of it.

◆ ◆ ◆

Weeping cherry trees lined the side of the paved drive that led through the carefully manicured lawn of 618 Dixie Avenue. The sprawling house at that address occupied three acres of land, acres full of fat spreading oaks and tall, reaching-for-the-sky hickory trees so old that they had twisted and gnarled in places. And scattered here and there, where sunlight struck, there were rose beds and carefully pruned dogwoods that bloomed pink every spring.

Now all that was left of the blooms were bits of rosy, lacy froth clinging here and there on stray limbs, and occasionally dusting the dark green of the bermuda grass as they reluctantly fell.

The house was not a white-columned southern mansion; Sam Pennington touted his mill roots with enough defiance that he refused to look like the established gentry. Or maybe he'd been afraid his neighbors would have laughed at his ambitions if he'd built a modern-day Tara.

So instead, the house was a soft, glowing almond shade, and rather than brick, it was made of a warm, textured stucco. Wide, stretching porches made of flagstone extended from both sides, each under a balconied roof supported by delicate arches. The curved tops of the tall windows echoed the arches and blended the gentle southwestern look with the traditional southern gothic with grace and dignity.

White wicker chairs and heavy rockers sat on the porches, and a handyman was just now putting out a swing on the one porch that was hidden from the road by distance and by big-leafed magnolias and thorny hawthorns, all in preparation for the hot Mississippi summer.

Shiloh could hear Laura instructing the handyman even from the drive, where she left the Porsche.

"I tol' you once, Clarence—that's too close to those windows. The wind blows around this corner so hard sometimes in a storm it sounds like a baby crying, so move that swing over some. No—no—there. Right there."

"Anybody'd think this was a big project," Clarence French, the handyman, muttered. "If you'll just let me hang it where—"

"Shiloh! What are you doin' home?" Laura cut across his complaints in surprise as she caught sight of the girl coming up the two long, shallow steps that climbed to the porch.

"Taking the day off," Shiloh answered the little woman who waited. Laura Kershaw at fifty looked forty from a distance, mostly because she was barely five feet two inches tall, and her shape was trim and youthful. But in her face were lines, and in her eyes was age, the same age that the gray which streaked her dark brown hair proclaimed.

She could be sharp and outspoken, but under it all was a fierce protective instinct that extended to the people she loved. There weren't many of them—her dead husband; her brother, T-Tommy Farley; her cousin and employer for twenty-four years, Sam Pennington; and Shiloh. Laura had been a widow since before Shiloh was born; for as long as Shiloh could remember, the older woman had lived in the little brick house a hundred yards over and behind her own house, separated from them mostly by a lawn and a few pines. Sam had built the house for her.

"Taking the day off!" Laura echoed. "Well, that's a first. All I've heard from you since you got home last fall was how you were gonna work harder than any of 'em.

You were gonna show them that you got your job for more reasons than just being Sam's daughter."

"Maybe I'm tired," Shiloh told her without much emotion as she opened the screened door into the big kitchen, Laura's pride and joy. Across the polished cream tiles of the floor was a big refrigerator with an ice and water dispenser set into its black glass door, and that was where she headed.

Laura followed, her problems with Clarence forgotten.

"Tired of the work?"

"Tired of being Sam's daughter," Shiloh returned. The ice water was cold and soothing, taking away the tears that had burned her throat ever since she left the bank.

"I don't reckon this would have anything to do with Michael Sewell, would it?" Laura asked, her eyes sharp.

"How did you—what are you talking about?" Shiloh hastily substituted.

"Something's going on. He's called every day for nearly two weeks from Memphis, near frantic to talk to you. Best as I can tell, you're not answering. Then I see his car leaving here last night as I'm coming home from the revival—" Laura hesitated, the light skin of her face flushing a little, "and this morning, maybe you don't want me to tell this, but I found your blouse in your wastebasket. Torn to pieces. I been worried sick. A woman wouldn't do that to her own clothes, but a man would. Especially a mad one, like Michael was the last time he called here."

Shiloh didn't move, clutching the empty water glass to her heart as she and Laura looked at each other, but her face went as white as the dough the housekeeper used for her fancy Parkerhouse dinner rolls.

Laura took a step closer.

"What'd he do?"

"Sam's determined for me to marry him. I let him—Michael—think I would. I thought I loved him a little. But I can't . . . And last night, he tried to—"

"He tried to force you, didn't he?" Laura asked knowingly, and she reached out to pull the goblet from the white-knuckled grasp Shiloh had on it. "Here, you're about to break my good glass."

Her prosaic, matter-of-fact voice made everything Shiloh was trying to say seem normal, and the words came spilling out.

"He knows everything about a woman, and everywhere we go, people like him. Especially the women. But I never worried about that because he never noticed them. I think he . . . he loves me. But Laura . . ." Shiloh slid into the antique wild-cherry rocker that sat in front of the big open fireplace in one wall of the kitchen. "He's not a good person. He's not strong, or something. There's no backbone. Whenever something happens, it's always somebody else's fault. And he drinks . . . and drinks. Not at work, but when we're alone together. That's when it scares me."

"And he was drinking when he tore that blouse off your back last night when you two were here by yourselves?" Laura demanded, coming up behind the rocker.

"A little. Maybe . . . more. I don't know for sure, but I"—she shuddered—"tasted it. He . . . tried to—" Shiloh stood hastily, her face twisting. "I can't talk about it, and anyway, Sam won't believe me. Nobody will."

"I'm listening," Laura told her quietly.

"He meant to rape me," Shiloh burst out.

The words rang in the kitchen, ugly and stark.

"You're gonna have to tell Sam," Laura said at last.

"He won't believe. Nobody will. Don't you think I went through this over and over last night? Michael Sewell couldn't be a rapist. And there's Caroline to remember. Like mother, like daughter, that's what Sam would say. So will all of Sweetwater. Remember Caroline?" Shiloh's voice broke as she stared down at the chair she was clutching. "Couldn't get enough men."

Laura's hand rested briefly on Shiloh's back; beneath the navy jacket she wore, Shiloh was hot to the touch, shaking from emotion. She'd always been strung tighter than most, Laura thought, always trying too hard to be perfect. There was laughter and passion in her; it was too bad she kept it beaten down most of the time trying to prove something to her father.

"I believe you do need a rest," was all the housekeeper said. "You go upstairs, have a warm bath, a nap. Tonight, when you and Sam sit down over my supper, you'll get a chance to tell him. I'm fixing creamed breast of chicken. That'll soften him up."

Shiloh didn't smile. In fact, it angered her that Laura should baby her and pamper her, as if one hot meal, one warm bath, and the promise of her father's coming home should pacify her. She was twenty-two, and the world treated her like some kind of brainless infant.

Without a word, though, she turned out of the kitchen. What was she supposed to do? Tell Laura off for her kindness? She was so exhausted she might have finished the speech by falling at her feet.

The oak treads of the back staircase led directly to her big bedroom. Its creamy carpet swept to the delicate, tall posts of the Queen Anne cherry bed under myriad rose and moss-green pillows, the ones that Shiloh scattered

wide as she threw herself across the heavy ruffled cover-
let.

Here, through the French door she pushed open onto
the little balcony, came the sounds of peace: a mocking-
bird chirping, the muffled, distant crack of Clarence's
hammer.

A world so calm that her memories had no place in it,
but the minute she was still, they came washing over
her. . . .

"Come on, let me in, Shiloh," Michael said quietly as
she stared at him through the crack in the door. "What's
going on with you?"

"I don't want to talk to you. I've said all I'm going to,"
she answered steadily.

"Well, good for you. But maybe I haven't," he retorted
angrily and all of a sudden, he gave the door a hard shove,
his movement so unexpected it jerked it out of her hand
and sent her stumbling back.

Then he was inside, pushing the door shut behind him,
but his bright blue eyes were focused intently on her.

For a minute they just stood there, facing each other.
"You've got no right to come shoving in here," Shiloh told
him unsteadily.

"No right?" he asked incredulously. "What's got into
you? I've been coming in here off and on for the last four
years."

But he didn't move away from the door, and standing
there in his expensive sweater and linen slacks, Michael
was so calm, so smoothly sophisticated, that she felt flustered at her own childishness.

And the white-hot tingle of fear that had shot through
her like electricity at his abrupt movement faded into an
embarrassed nothing.

"Oh, all right," she muttered ungraciously, turning her back on him to walk away. "Come on in. Say what you have to say and get it over with. None of it will change my mind."

She didn't really hear him follow her across the wooden floor of the foyer into the family room, where his feet made little or no sound on the carpet. But when she flung herself down on the peach, blue and green striped couch and faced the elaborate fireplace, empty and cold now, Michael was standing there.

Just watching her.

His strange stillness should have been her first warning.

"You want to tell me what this means?" he asked abruptly, tossing a small, square box to her. "I got it out of my mailbox day before yesterday. It's the reason I drove all the way from Memphis as soon as I could."

Shiloh set the package carefully out of her lap, onto the couch, before she looked back at him.

"I think it's pretty self-explanatory. It's my engagement ring. I tried to give it back to you two weeks ago. Finally, I mailed it."

He slid both hands into his pockets as if to keep from strangling her. "You mean to say that you actually meant all that wild stuff you told me after we left the club?"

"Hard to believe, isn't it? But the answer's yes—I did."

"Why? Why all of a sudden just break it off?" he demanded furiously, glaring at her.

Make it clean and quick, Shiloh, she told herself, and she stood, counting off the reasons on her fingers.

"I don't love you, I don't like the way you run over people, I don't like the way you use your looks and your money to get everybody from waitresses to me to do what you want, I don't like the way you just assume I'm yours, or just an extension of you, and most of all"—Shiloh drew a deep breath and looked right at him—"I don't like the way you drink. The way you have no self-control."

Michael's body jerked as if she'd touched a live nerve, and his face mottled red. "The way I drink!" he repeated incredulously. "What in hell are you talking about?"

"Don't treat me like I'm a half-wit. I know what I see. And what's so scary is the way you keep it from everybody until you've got them right where you want them and you think they won't tell," Shiloh retorted, but her voice was unsteady. She knew instinctively that this was dangerous ground. "I'm even surprised that you remember we had an argument two weeks ago. You'd been getting drunker and drunker while we sat there in the corner of the club. I had to drive, remember? And it hit me that I didn't want to be with you anymore. Something . . . something in me isn't satisfied with—with us. I took you to the judge's house. Your parents weren't home, but I used their phone to call a taxi while you were passed out in the car. Did it ever cross your mind to wonder how I got home?"

He never looked away from her face, but his own darkened guiltily.

"That's what I thought," she told him steadily. "You need to get help, Michael, no matter what your parents think. So there's the door, and you can take this with you when you go." She caught up the ring box and stepped briefly toward him, shoving it at him.

He looked down at it for one dazed minute, and suddenly, she felt almost sorry for him. Smooth, beautiful Michael. He'd never been rejected in his life; he was the darling of his parents, the envy of most of the male population of Sweetwater.

Failure came hard for him.

"Here," Shiloh said, more gently, offering the ring again. "I'm sorry."

His hand, already tanned from the two weeks he'd spent in the gulf scuba-diving with friends last month, reached out slowly for it—and then he had her, his grasp on her wrist furious and tight.

"You think you can just walk away from me after stringing me along all this time?" he hissed, his hot face nearly against hers. "You think *I* need help? How about what *you* need?"

"Michael, stop—"

But he ignored her shocked whimper of sound as he grabbed her other arm above the elbow and bent both of them behind her at a painful angle, forcing her into an arching backward stance.

Shiloh stared up in sudden, full-bloomed fright at his face right above hers, and the heat from his body swirled around her. So did the fleeting scent of whiskey.

"I love you. We're engaged. You don't walk out on me. You'll marry me when I say, or when Sam says. Remember him? You haven't told him about breaking it off yet, now, have you?"

His grasp on her arms tightened painfully; both that and his words forced a sharp cry from her.

"That's what I thought. You mean to marry me—this is just some little game you decided to play," he gasped out, his words coming in heavy explosions on her face that made her stomach churn. "This marriage is too important to Sam—to my father—to *everybody* for you to end it."

"No . . . no, I mean it," she whispered, pushing the words out in spite of his crushing embrace around her. "Turn loose, Michael."

"You've made me ache and beg to make love to you,

and I've let you say no and walk away. How many times? How many times, Shiloh?" he demanded harshly, shaking her.

"I . . . I don't know," Shiloh finally gasped out painfully. "Please, you're hurting me—"

"Well, no more. *No more.*" In the sudden heavy stillness, she caught the hot flame that suddenly flared in his eyes, felt the deliberate thrust of his body against her thighs. Bending her arms that he still held behind her, he forced her to her knees, and her heart stopped.

Everything stopped.

She was in a nightmare, darkness all around her, blood throbbing in her ears, as her senses opened wide to take in a terrible, agonizing realization: he was going to rape her.

Right here, in her own house.

"My . . . God . . . no . . . Michael . . . no . . ." The words were only tiny sparks of sound that ignited him into sudden, violent, triumphant action. "I don't want to. *Please.*"

"It's exactly what you're wanting, what you've been pushing me for," he panted heavily, shoving her to the smooth carpet without ever releasing her, following her down like a swooping eagle, pinioning her beneath his tall body and heavy weight.

Smothered—she was being smothered under him, under his scent and his clothes, and she screamed once as she began a violent, twisting, bucking, writhing motion under him, frantic to dislodge his strength and his hold—and finding him immovable and implacable.

Fury shot through her for one blessed moment. "I—I'll *kill* you for this," she blazed up at him, her teeth biting and snapping like an animal. "Sam—Sam will kill you."

Michael watched her struggle for a second before he

replied, "No, he won't. Nobody will believe one word of your crazy story. Not about me. We're engaged. Half the town expects we've been doing this for months, and, by God, we should have been."

He bruised her lips, covering them with his, and when she twisted furiously away, he let his weight press her body painfully down on her arms, still bent behind her, until she made a choking sound in her throat in protest, her face twisted, and her body went limp.

"Now, be good," he commanded thickly. His tongue traced her lips, finally licking across them. "Shiloh," he groaned, then he kissed her again, his tongue pushing past her teeth.

She might vomit, she thought in revulsion, then instead, she bit him—as hard as she could, and she tasted blood.

He jerked away as if he'd been set on fire, a red stain on his lip. "You little bitch!" he said, and they glared at each other, each breathing harshly.

"All right, if you want to play hard ball," he muttered, and he released her arm, still keeping it caught under her, and with one swift jerk, he tore open the white blouse she wore.

She screamed; he stared down at her, his eyes bright and hot, almost as if he didn't see her at all, then slowly, deliberately ran his hand tenderly down her throat to the tops of her breasts, his fingers sliding under the lacy silk of her bra, touching her.

"Beautiful. Just relax, Shiloh. It'll be over soon. You'll see you love me. That's all I want," he whispered. Then, abruptly, he gave another sudden, hard jerk, one that pulled her body off the carpet roughly for a second, and stripped the rest of the blouse away, except for the tattered pieces that clung to her arms. He made no effort to remove them.

Her teeth were chattering; he really meant to do it, and she couldn't remember . . . What was she supposed to do? Let it happen? Fight—if she could? What . . . what?

"Don't hurt me. Please, don't. I'll hate you—I'll hate you—" She couldn't stop the words; they kept rattling through her teeth.

"You're going to love me," he whispered in return, his voice husky and thick. "And then there'll be no more talk about breaking this engagement, Shiloh." He made a husky sound, a murmur of appreciation, as he bent to kiss her right above her left breast. Then his white, perfect teeth suddenly snapped, and he bit her sharply, laughing a little in wild excitement.

She was so numb she only jerked. Then he raised up and reached for his belt buckle, fumbling with it. His weight lifted from her right side and her hand found an escape.

As she yanked it free, her brain flooded with an instant memory of what somebody had instructed rape victims to do—maybe it had been Donahue, she thought hysterically, the thought inconsequential but clear—and she hit him as hard as she could with her fist in his Adam's apple.

He choked, gagged, grabbed at his throat. Then she poked him in both of his eyes with her fingers. He crumpled to the side, and with a strength born of terror, she yanked and jerked herself out from under him.

But she wasn't through: just as he was staggering to his feet, she kicked him solidly right between the legs with every ounce of strength she had.

He gave a strangled cry of agony and crumpled back

to the carpet, clutching himself, making a retching sound in his throat.

The ring box lay right at her hand as she rolled away a second time, and in a blaze of glory she threw it at him.

"Take it—and get out!" she screamed, then she herself ran for the door and escape.

Once outside, the fragrant night air hit her bare skin. Realizing too late her state of undress, she plunged into the dark garage, locking herself inside the Porsche, lying flat in the darkness, shaking, crying, and sick.

His own car had been standing in the drive in the front of the house; maybe it was minutes, or maybe it was hours, before she heard it pull off into the night.

All she knew was that Michael Sewell was gone, and she hated him.

Then she crept back inside the house and threw up in the downstairs bathroom.

When Shiloh awoke, the sun was sinking behind the heavy stand of pines at the far end of the yard, and a slightly chilly twilight breeze brushed across her bare arms from the French door.

Michael was with her for a flashing instant as she struggled up out of sleep, and she gave a hard, frightened jerk that knocked pillows onto the floor.

Shiloh sat up abruptly and shivered. How long would it be before she forgot what happened last night?

Putting her hand to her mouth to stifle the moan, she came up off the bed in one quick motion.

Laura was right: she had to tell Sam. He wasn't heartless, and he was her father; surely she could make him understand. She would tell him tonight at supper.

In the shower, the warm, soothing water sluiced over her, washing away the memories she'd spent the afternoon with, and she toweled herself dry roughly.

When she sat down in front of the mirror, she could find no trace of fear or anger in her face. It looked like always: smooth skin, with a touch of brown rather than pink in it; wide brown eyes above high cheekbones; a nose that wasn't quite perfect—it had a tiny tilt at the bottom instead of being elegantly classic; a wide mouth; and a wild cloud of wine-brown hair that nearly—but not quite—touched her shoulders.

Nothing, absolutely nothing, to inspire passionate love nor ugly lust that she could see.

They said that she looked like Caroline, all the people of Sweetwater, and that Caroline had been a raving beauty when she was young. Shiloh could barely remember her then; her mother had left when she was five. Once, though, she had seen a picture in the attic and she'd stared at it with all the hungry fascination of a twelve-year-old. It had lasted until she realized what she was doing. Then she'd dropped the picture like a scorching coal and had gone running out of the attic.

She remembered enough about Caroline and her leaving to want no part of her.

The girl in the mirror swallowed. Her mother had had an effect, even gone. Shiloh had stayed away from men. She'd never even flirted with one until she was eighteen, and then it had started so easily and felt so right she'd been involved with him before she knew it.

Billy Bob Walker.

Shiloh winced and closed her eyes as his face floated into her mind. It was Michael's face—but no, not quite. Funny, but when she'd first started dating Michael last fall, his resemblance to Billy Bob had only enhanced his appeal.

Now just the opposite happened.

Billy had brown streaks in his hair, hair too shaggy and too long. Michael was more purely blond, his hair clipped close to his head and styled neatly. Billy's face was thinner, one tooth was slightly out of line, his eyebrows were brown, the planes of his cheekbones high and smooth beneath his long blue eyes. He had a beautiful nose, straighter and more exact than Michael's. And where Michael was square and muscular, Billy was lankier and longer. He looked like what he was—a farmhand.

She could remember Sam's fury when he found out, although she never knew who'd seen her and Billy Bob together and told him.

"You're a kid. He's five years older than you and he's got nothing. Not one red cent. No future. And if that's not enough, he's—" Sam broke off his words.

Shiloh remembered that she'd been crying, terrified of her father's anger and hurting because she was about to lose Billy Bob. "What? What is he, Papa?" she had asked him pleadingly. "I know he's not mean. He hasn't done anything to hurt me."

"Exactly what has he done?" Sam asked at last, more quietly. "You've apparently been slipping off to meet him all summer. How far has he gone, Shiloh?"

She had flushed and mumbled, "Not that. I—we didn't do that, Papa. I promise."

He had finally let out his breath in an expulsion of relief, then reached out to touch her face. "Good. You're too young. You've got college and your whole life ahead of you. Don't get mixed up with any man yet. As for Walker," Sam continued, oblivious to her emotions, "he's just not like you. He's not going anywhere. He'll marry some girl from out at Seven Knobs, have a pack of kids, and die a poor man."

"He loves me," Shiloh said steadily.

"He'll find somebody else who's available when you're gone," Sam told her bluntly.

And he had been right: Billy Bob had.

It had hurt, but it had been four years ago. And Sam had been so pleased with her that summer that she had pushed Billy out of her mind and out of her heart. Maybe it had been—up until now—her one and only real spurt of rebellion.

But she didn't hate Billy Bob. Dislike him, maybe, when he was as obnoxious as he'd been this afternoon. But most of her memories, dim and hazy though they were, were pleasant enough.

She doubted she would ever have a pleasant memory of Michael, and she shuddered before she went to the closet to get dressed.


For all its stylish cut, the black dress was meant to soothe Sam's feathers. He liked the somber color, and he would like the simplicity of the nearly straight sheath that curved in around Shiloh's narrow waist.

She twisted once in front of the mirror, her hair swinging richly, brushing the tops of her shoulders. Almost unconsciously, she raised her fingers to brush the same place on her left breast that she'd brushed a thousand times in the last day, and her throat knotted.

In the kitchen, Laura hovered anxiously over the oven. The chicken smelled like heaven, and Shiloh remembered that she hadn't eaten since breakfast.

Leaning over a silver tray to steal a cream cheese tart, she told the housekeeper, "I'm starving. What'd we do to deserve these"—she waved the tart—"in the middle of the week?"

Laura avoided looking directly at her. "There's hors d'oeuvres out, too," she offered. "Miniature broccoli quiches."

Shiloh stopped eating and stared. "Miniature broc— are you sick, Laura? All this for me and Sam?"

"And his company," Laura told her, meaningfully.

"He brought somebody home with him?" she asked in surprise, frowning. "I thought he was set to rake me over the coals. I guess I'm relieved. What can he do to me with company watching? But I don't—"

"You'd better go on out and get it over with," Laura interrupted, "or else there won't be any quiches left. The judge always eats a ton of them." She glanced carefully over at Shiloh as she removed a dish from the oven.

Her words froze Shiloh in motion, and her eyes came up to Laura's sympathetic ones, wide and startled. "What? What did you say?"

"Judge Sewell's here," Laura answered flatly.

At last temper seeped over Shiloh's face, replacing the near-terror of an instant before. "How could he? He didn't even give me a chance before he called Michael's father over. Just like always, he rides roughshod over what I want, and when it's too late, I'm right where he wants me to be. But it—it can't be that way this time, Laura."

The housekeeper looked at the pleading face in front of her. "So go tell them that," she advised bluntly, and as the other woman went out the swinging door on a wave of anger and light perfume, Laura asked nobody in general, "Wonder if I should have mentioned who was with the judge?"

His elegant wife, Lydia. That was who stood by the side of Robert Sewell. Always dainty, always fashionable, she looked undersized and overdressed as she stood by the big, broad-shouldered judge in his subdued navy suit. Only two things gave away his lurking vanity—the carefully waved, lacquered hair and the diamond ring that sparkled on his right hand in the light of a nearby lamp.

Shiloh did what she always did when she was scared senseless: She talked to herself. Be calm, she said; act natural. So you won't marry his son. They can't make you, no matter how cold their eyes. She met her father's warning look as he turned from his conversation with the couple.

"Judge Sewell," she said steadily. Good, she thought, that's it—calm, unruffled. "And Mrs. Sewell."

A movement in the flame-stitched wingback chair that faced away from her caught her peripheral vision. It stopped Shiloh's words like a hand around her heart; she knew intuitively who it was even before the gilt-blond head rose.

"Hello, Shiloh."

Michael's words were as calm as hers, his face emotionless as he turned to face her. He was dressed for the evening, too, in his own well-cut navy suit, crisp white shirt, and striped tie. He looked like a Bill Blass version of a young blond sun god.

She couldn't speak, that clutch of emotions still strangling her. She could see the two of them on the carpet again, right here, nearly where he stood now.

Him, ripping and tearing and hurting.

Her, shivering and begging and crying.

"I like your dress. It suits you," he said at last into the silence. His voice was low, husky, and for one crazy minute, Shiloh saw Billy Bob Walker standing there. His face had worn the same intense look that Michael's had now.

She got her breath all at once, in a rush that nearly floored her. "It's good to see you. But I have to run. I have a—a date tonight."

"Shiloh!" Sam's voice was disbelieving and hard. "I asked you to be home for supper. You agreed. So even if you have made other plans"—and his voice said clearly he didn't believe a word of it—"you can just unmake them."

"Look, I'm not going to be civilized about this," she told him desperately. "Everybody here already knows I broke the engagement with Michael. So either he leaves, or I do."

Her father's gasped outrage was only slightly louder than Lydia Sewell's.

"I mean it," she said stubbornly.

"Let me talk to her, sir," Michael asked pleadingly. "She's got to listen to me sometime. She's got to explain to me why—"

"No," she cut in, panicky that they might really leave her with him. "And if you don't stay away from me, I'll tell them right now what happened between us."

His white teeth flashed in a sort of pleading half smile. "Shiloh, please, listen. I love you."

"You *will* listen to him, Shiloh," Sam said firmly.

"Just like I *will* marry him? I don't have to do anything if I don't want to. And I want to leave." Never in a million years could she have imagined talking like this to Sam, but fear forced her to it. She twisted away, out the door and down the hall. Heavy footsteps sounded behind her; she knew them even before Michael's hand clamped over her shoulder and the same terror that had loosened her tongue poured down her body like a cold drench of water.

She jerked frantically away as he pulled her around. "Don't touch me!"

Michael's eyes burned like blue fire as he stared down at her, but Sam's voice over his shoulder cut off any words he intended to speak.

"You're not going anywhere, Shiloh. You and Michael need to sit down and talk about this."

Shiloh looked from Michael's set face to her father's, then she reached behind herself and flung open the door.

Sam swore. "Dammit, girl, what's got into you? Whatever it is, if you take out of here in that hell-on-wheels car you drive, I'll put T-Tommy on you. He'll get you back even if he has to drag you."

"He'll have to catch me first," she cried over her shoulder; then she ran, heels, black dress, and all, out into the night.


The Porsche burned the wind down the long, stretching road, flying past dark, flat cotton and rice fields and the squat, shadowy little shacks that lay along Highway 25 as it ran west, leading to the delta, miles away.

They wouldn't make her face Michael tonight. She pressed down on the gas pedal, shooting through Mississippi—at least her piece of it—at ninety miles an hour.

# 4

*A revival was* going on at the Church of God on the corner, two buildings down the dark, quiet street from the jail. The preacher was loud and long and not half bad—and Billy Bob ought to know. He'd been hearing the man's sermons drift in on the night air for most of the week, ringing out the raised windows of the old clapboard church and floating down the road and through the open, but barred, ones of the jail, bringing salvation right to the only sinner T-Tommy had in custody these days—himself.

The crowd down at the little steepled building, with their shouts of "amen" and their loud music, was nearly as rowdy as the one at the Country Palace, Billy Bob thought wryly, but at least their enthusiasm was taking them to heaven, not to accommodations provided by Briskin County.

He leaned backward against the cool, gray-painted concrete blocks of the wall beside the window and watched a huge luna moth flutter inquiringly around the distant yellow glow of the naked bulb in the ceiling. In this old jail, the ceilings were twelve feet high, so that the light got lost long before it could reach down to find him. It cast only a sort of dim glow over the bars and the narrow cot where Billy Bob slept.

Eleven days he'd been here. Nineteen more to go, if he could just grit his teeth and bear it. To some people, the inactivity and the monotony might have been nothing.

They were about to kill Billy Bob.

He would have begged if that would make them let him go. Fifteen days for fighting. He had to serve that. And another fifteen if, by next Monday, he couldn't come up with the additional five-hundred-dollar fine Sewell had slapped on him at the last minute for shooting off his mouth.

Fat chance.

Any money Billy got hold of would have to go to Bud, to pay for the damage at the Palace.

Just where was he supposed to get money, anyway? He couldn't work and earn it, not stuck here in jail—but nobody wanted to think about that. And what happened the day he was supposed to be released and they discovered he still couldn't pay Bud? Were they going to give him time to make the money, or was he going to wind up spending the rest of his life in jail?

Surely he didn't deserve all this just because he'd let a streak of contrariness land him in front of Robert Sewell.

His father, the judge.

Billy Bob fought down the wave of bitterness that threatened to swamp him. He wouldn't let it have him; it was the kind of searing, dark emotion that could bring a man down and cripple him for life, and he had the sense to know it.

He kept making himself look the truth in the face: It was his own fault he was in here, just as he'd told Grandpa.

And he must never let the judge have the satisfaction of knowing how much all of this hurt him.

Billy Bob came restlessly to his bare feet, his open shirt flapping carelessly around the bare skin of his sides above his blue jeans as he stared out the window again.

A bass voice in the distant church congregation filled out the chorus of a hymn with exuberance. Resting with his forehead against the chilly metal bars, Billy concentrated on the music, trying to pick out individual voices, wondering if he knew any of them.

"I wasn't going a hundred miles an hour. And I wasn't running from him, T-Tommy. I just thought he was you, trying to drag me back home. I didn't know he was a real cop!"

He knew that voice in a heartbeat. It was clear and angry as it cut across the room, and so distinctly Shiloh Pennington's that for an instant, Billy thought it must be his imagination that had called it up, the result of some subconscious memory from this afternoon when she'd stood free in the sunshine outside his window.

But there was a commotion behind him that made him twist to see what had caused the racket, and his mouth dropped nearly to his knees.

T-Tommy, flustered, was arguing with an angry, red-faced state trooper, who had Shiloh in a firm grasp above the elbow. The policeman meant to pull her forcibly into the cell area; he'd pushed open the door between it and the office, and he, Shiloh, and T-Tommy stood framed there as they argued.

"You act like you know this girl," the trooper was saying angrily. "That's real good, because she's gonna need friends. I clocked her at ninety-eight miles an hour out on Highway 25. That's fifty-three miles above the speed limit. *Fifty-three,*" he nearly shouted, flapping his free hand in T-Tommy's face, which paled considerably as he faced Shiloh.

"Good Lord," he said to her piteously, "tell me you wudn't makin' no such speed as that, Shiloh."

But before the flushed girl—she was shaking in the cop's grasp, Billy realized—could open her mouth to answer, the trooper added, "She's got no license, either."

"I told you—I left home in a hurry."

"I noticed." Furious sarcasm hardened the cop's voice.

"It's in my purse, but I didn't remember to get it before I left."

"I can tell you who she is—" T-Tommy began.

"I don't care who the hell she is," the other man said loudly; then, through clenched teeth, he added distinctly, *"she wrecked the damn car."*

T-Tommy gave a violent jerk. "What?"

"And she better be down on her knees thanking God she ran off in a ditch instead of into a telephone pole, which would have killed her. She was able to walk away— or I should say, run. I had to chase her down on foot, across a cotton field. Then she *kicked* me," the trooper said in painful remembrance, reaching a hand down toward his left shin.

Shiloh struggled briefly in his hard grasp. "I—he scared me, yelling and swearing. He came after me like a . . . a mad dog. When I ran, he jumped me—grabbed me from the back. Of course I fought—what else was I supposed to do?" she asked T-Tommy, half furious, half pleading.

"Reckless driving, no license, wrecked car, attacking an officer," the cop reeled off. "I want her locked up. *Now.*"

"Shiloh, what's got into you?" T-Tommy demanded in desperation.

She took a quick, shuddering breath. "I—I had a fight with Sam. I thought he'd sent you after me, T-Tommy. Then this—this man—"

"Who in the hell is Sam?" the trooper demanded in a rush of frustration. "I hope he's her keeper, because she needs one. This girl's a lunatic."

"Her father," T-Tommy returned mournfully. "Sam Pennington."

The trooper stared. "Sam Pen—" he got out in shock. Then he looked wildly at the girl and made haste to drop her arm, which Shiloh rubbed painfully. "I don't care if her old man does own three counties," he began bravely, but his voice was already more subdued. "She ought not get out of this. It's—it's gonna cost her a bundle, this little joyride. And Pennington ought to be grateful she's getting away so easy. Wait till you see what she did to that car—she could be dead right now."

There was a long silence while the three of them looked at each other. The trooper was just a kid, Billy Bob thought, and getting younger every minute.

T-Tommy took a deep, resigned breath.

"You're right," he told the officer. "She pays. Write up the accident. Give her a ticket, and make it stiff. And I've got an empty cell," he added, pulling the huge jangling clump of keys up from his belt.

Shiloh's face flushed and her chin came up in surprised defiance. "You can't lock me up, surely. I didn't hurt anybody except maybe myself."

"You kicked this man," T-Tommy pointed out.

"I'm—I'm willing to forget that," the trooper put in hastily. "And I'll settle for a heavy fine and a wreck going on her driving record. No need for jail. I was pretty mad when I—"

"She knows better than to run a car at any such speed," T-Tommy cut in flatly. "Don't get your badge all heated up, son. I'm the one that's lockin' her up, and I'm the one who'll be takin' the blame if there is any."

"But—" Shiloh began.

"But nothin'," the sheriff interrupted. "I got no desire to see you dead, Shiloh. So you can just take your medicine. You'll spend the rest of the night right here, thinkin' about why. A'course, you got a phone call comin'. You could go right now and call Sam. Tell him what's happened," T-Tommy added shrewdly.

Shiloh stared at him wide-eyed, then swallowed heavily before she shook her head without a word.

"That's what I thought," T-Tommy said with a sigh. "He's what you're running from, all right, in more ways than one. Look at you—you're a bundle of nerves. You ain't fit to drive, nor fit to face him, either."

Then he fumbled for one of the keys and walked to the cell beside Billy Bob's, where he unlocked the door and flung it wide.

"Come on. And then I'll call Laura—just to let her know you're safe. She can tell Sam that much."

Shiloh tossed back her head defiantly and turned toward the row of three cells. For the first time, she caught a glimpse of Billy Bob as he stood in silence in the shadows, leaning indolently against the window, his elbows propped up in it, his long brown fingers locked together over his flat, bare stomach, and she jumped just a little, whether in surprise or apprehension he couldn't tell.

But she sucked in a deep breath and with a sort of if-you-don't-like-it-you-can-lump-it    movement,    she limped into the cell. Limped, because one heel was broken off of a shoe—the one she'd kicked the trooper with, Billy assumed.

T-Tommy moved with a heavy finality to shut the door behind her, then hesitated at the last minute and didn't quite push it all the way closed.

The watching trooper made a weak protest. "Looks to me like you're babying her."

T-Tommy eyed him, then answered dryly, "She ain't goin' nowhere. And for all your fussin', you're the calm before the storm. You ain't nothin' to what Sam Pennington's gonna be." Then he switched his attention back to the girl and said gravely, "This is for your own good, Shiloh."

He watched the girl who'd sunk onto the edge of the cot as her long, delicate fingers nervously smoothed the white sheet once or twice. She avoided both his gaze and that of her fellow prisoner.

T-Tommy, who suddenly seemed to remember that Billy existed, frowned at him and shook his keys in his general direction. "You watch yourself, Billy Bob. Don't give her a hard time."

His male prisoner lifted his hands in a mocking, silent surrender, then T-Tommy followed the trooper into the outside office, closing the door behind them.

That left the two of them alone in the dusky silence; even the church service had ended.

It had been four years since he'd been alone with Shiloh Pennington, and her unexpected presence here tonight just might make his thirty days in jail worthwhile. Excitement and pure devilment seeped into him as he looked her over.

She was wearing a sleek black nothing of a dress, and her matching hose had been torn up one side. The wild thickness of her shoulder-length hair had bushed out into a wavy, short mane, and she had a scratch along one cheek.

For the first time in years, she looked . . . touchable. Maybe even a little forlorn.

He pushed himself off the wall and as her wary brown eyes swung to find him, he drawled in a weak imitation of a gangster film, "So, Lefty, it's just me and you in the slammer tonight."

"If you say one more word, I'll—"

"Do what? Call the law? Well, don't look now, but somebody beat you to it, honey."

"Don't 'honey' me. I'm not in the mood for it."

His voice went dead serious as he stepped closer to the bars that separated them. "So you wrecked your car, just because you felt like speeding."

"And the worst part is—I lived through it. Right?" she asked defiantly, staring up at him. "Well, don't worry. I'll get a new car."

"Yeah, I guess you will. But what I want to know is, why were you running?"

"None of your business," Shiloh retorted, as she slid off her shoes and wiggled her toes. "If this is a game of twenty questions, two can play. What did you do that you're in here?"

"Nothing."

She made a funny huffing sound.

"It's the truth. I got fined three thousand dollars and two weeks' jail time for being in a fight. But the judge didn't like the way I answered his questions. So he tacked on two more weeks—or five hundred more dollars. And since I don't have the money . . ." Billy's voice trailed off as he looked around himself at the four walls and shrugged. "I guess I'll be in here the whole month."

"All that in one swoop? What did you do, set fire to his robe?"

"I took a dislike to his name. It was Sewell," Billy Bob told her flatly. "Your future father-in-law."

She couldn't contain the shudder that passed over her, nor the flash of understanding that lit her face. "Oh." Then she looked around the cell. "This place is a dive."

"I've been in worse," he said, his voice careless.

Unwillingly, she smiled a little, and the tiny dimple in her left cheek appeared. "Like Farmer John's?" Then she shut her lips tightly, as if she regretted letting him know the memory was in her head, one they had shared.

His head lifted sharply in surprise, and suddenly he recalled things about that long-ago night, too, things he didn't want to remember. A flash of anger swept over him—he hadn't been with her but a few minutes and she was already getting to him.

He said stoically, "We left when things got too rough, then we went parking at Seven Knobs, out on a dark road so quiet I could hear your heart beating—"

She came up off the narrow bed like a shot, cheeks flaming, her hands going up to her ears, and he heard her gasp of breath.

He got a rush of satisfaction from her reaction and he finished inexorably, "—beating like a scared rabbit's."

"Don't, Billy."

"That's what you said that night, too. And I'm sure that's all *you* remember," he told her ironically.

But he knew better—the vivid memory he'd pulled up from the past lay between them now like a quivering, living thing.

He had pushed away from her that night all those years ago, fighting down every instinct that told him to go further.

After all, she'd said, "Don't," and he was trying desperately to obey.

Then she'd suddenly caught at him, kissing his face and lips there in the dark, her hands fumbling at his shirt. He could still remember how hard it had been to breathe, with shock and passion both threatening to strangle him. It was nearly too late when he'd realized the truth—she wanted to please him, but she was scared to death.

He remembered how he'd made himself catch her hands, whispering no to her, telling her they'd wait. And he'd brought her home aching all over, trying to remember she was eighteen, the most innocent eighteen he'd ever seen.

Which showed just how naive he'd been at twenty-three, he thought now, wryly. That same eighteen-year-old had dumped him two weeks later.

But Shiloh in the cell beside his was recalling more than just the way he'd stopped things. She'd been embarrassed when he'd brought her home; she could almost hear the angry words they'd had just before she slammed out of his truck.

Maybe she really was just a tease, like Michael said, because she'd been furious with herself *and* Billy Bob the night he'd been the one to say no.

Was she the same girl who'd kicked and clawed Michael last night?

She stumbled back to the cot and collapsed on it, her head against the wall. She was tired, and confused, and sick with the excessive emotions of the day; that was why she wanted to hide somewhere and cry, why Billy Bob Walker's words had brought both such a flood of half-forgotten memories.

Unwillingly, Billy began to take in things about the girl opposite him that he didn't want to see: her hands were still shaking; a bruise was appearing on her arm where that bully of a policeman had hauled her around; and the shadows under her eyes made her look exhausted.

Why had he said anything? It had been four years ago. He should have played it cool—he should have forgotten everything instead of dwelling on the memory of the one night she'd come on to him.

The door to the office area opened, and T-Tommy entered again, this time alone. His face was apprehensive as he entered the cell where Shiloh sat.

Billy watched, biting back his protest. She'd just got here—he had a whole lot he still wanted to say. So much for being cool and quiet.

Shiloh herself looked surprised as she opened her eyes. "You're letting me go?" she asked hopefully, straightening.

"No, ma'am," T-Tommy answered decisively. "I just got to thinkin' you might need to . . . to wash your hands or somethin'." His thin, leathery cheeks flushed a little; so did hers as she caught his meaning. "I'm gonna take you to the bathroom in the office just in case. You do what you need to do before she gets back, Billy Bob. They ain't no privacy in here, but she'll be gone awhile. I got some things to say to her."

"Yes, sir," Billy Bob said lazily. "I'll get my hands washed real quick." But inside, relief spread. Shiloh would be back.

"You watch your mouth, boy," T-Tommy said without a lot of heat as he ushered Shiloh out, and he began grievously even before they left the cell, "What got into you, Shiloh? Randy just radioed in from the wrecker—he says that car is totaled. The whole frame's bent."

"Well, I wasn't trying to wreck it, T-Tommy," she retorted. "I was scared half out of my mind. Why didn't he just lay off chasing me for a few minutes? I was too scared to—"

The door closed on her words.

Billy Bob took T-Tommy's instructions to heart, then lay back on the cot, punching the pillow up underneath his head, waiting . . . and thinking.

She had changed.

He'd already seen the physical changes when he'd caught glimpses of her around town since her return home last fall. Her eyes looked bigger, her figure was more slender, her lips were more vulnerable.

Up until tonight, he'd thought she was quieter, more contained than ever, at least in public. Shiloh at eighteen had been almost shy, slow to anger, but quick to burn when she finally did get upset.

And sweet . . . Lord, she'd been so sweet.

Billy moved restlessly. The sweetness had been the hardest part to forget.

But now there was an edge to her—she knew how to bite back. She'd learned sarcasm somewhere, just as she'd picked up a gloss of sophistication. The girl with whom he'd spent a summer had worn shorts and jeans and cotton dresses; half the time she'd had her long hair, nearly to her waist back then, looped in a loose braid.

He didn't recognize the girl in the black dress.

But most of all, this Shiloh didn't laugh and tease and sparkle the way his had.

This girl was serious and sad and angry.

Fifteen minutes later, when the door opened again, T-Tommy was still fussing like an old hen, but this time about something new. "—can't go without supper. How long's it been since you ate?"

"I don't know," she said indifferently, sliding down on the hard cot with a sigh of relief. "I'm just tired. Not hungry."

T-Tommy took a deep, aggravated breath. "I'm gonna get you a Coke, and I got a moon pie out in the desk."

"I hate moon pies—but I'll eat it," she added hastily as T-Tommy opened his mouth to fuss some more. When the deputy returned, he waited until she opened the package and took a bite before he moved.

"You understand, Shiloh," he began apologetically, "that I'm doin' this—"

"—for my own good," she intoned, and took another bite.

T-Tommy hesitated.

She said at last, looking up at him, "I'll think about all you said. No more speeding."

T-Tommy left, satisfied, and neither Shiloh nor Billy Bob said a word for a long time. He just straightened up, then sat propped in a corner, one arm wrapped around his raised knee; she finished every crumb of the pie and polished it off with a deep draft from the red can.

In the long waiting stillness that followed, a car went past on the quiet street of the little town, its headlights reflecting briefly on the wall opposite the row of cells; somewhere out in the office area, a phone rang several times, its sound muffled by distance; and at last, Shiloh set the empty Coke can down on the concrete floor at her feet. Then she asked offhandedly, "Wonder what time it is?"

His voice was startling after the quietness. "Getting close to midnight, I'd say."

"That explains why I'm tired."

He could sense her nerves, the edginess in her that seemed to intensify at his immobility, and he got even more silent.

"It seems like forever since I went to work this morning," she offered at last, unwillingly.

"Where do you work?" he asked, knowing good and well where Sam Pennington had sent his daughter.

"At the branch bank in Dover."

"So, you're a banker," he said, flatly. He didn't like the image the word conjured up; it called up visions of her stiff-necked father.

"Not hardly," she returned, and laughed a little. He didn't think she liked the word either. "I'm a lowly assistant to Mr. Parsons, the bank VP who's in charge over there. That's all."

"I thought," he said carefully, because this was getting into a too-personal knowledge and remembrance again, "that you wanted to be a teacher. It's what you used to talk about."

"Oh, that," she said dismissively, "I was a kid."

He kept his voice neutral. "And your daddy wanted you to be in banking."

She said nothing—but he'd hit home. He knew it. When at last she spoke again, there was a trace of anger in her voice. "And you? You were dying to leave the farm and the greenhouse to be a vet. So—why didn't you?"

"Big dreams in a little town," he answered with a shrug.

"They didn't seem big to me," she told him slowly, with reluctance. She didn't want to get too familiar again, either. "You were good with animals. I remember that colt you worked with all summer. What was it you named him?"

"Chase," he answered.

"Have you still got him?"

"Yeah."

"And you're still at the farm? Still landscaping?"

"I don't landscape anymore," he said quietly. "You meet too many dangerous people that way."

There was a moment's pause.

Then Shiloh slid her hand down to her ankle carefully, feeling across the bone. "I think I twisted something," she said with rue as she rubbed her foot. "It must have been when I kicked the state trooper."

"He bruised your arm," Billy Bob said shortly.

Shiloh looked in surprise at the mark above her elbow, then laughed. "It's not really his fault. He thought I was an escaped maniac."

The thought of Shiloh grappling with the policeman didn't do much for Billy Bob. "He turned loose fast enough when he found out who your daddy was," he said harshly. "He's a smart man."

The bitterness in his words ended their carefully neutral conversation. They sat breathing in the dim cells, neither speaking, then Shiloh said politely, "I think I need to sleep. I'm really—"

"The way I see it, wrecking the car and kicking the cop, those were real stupid. I heard you tell T-Tommy you thought Pennington was coming after you. Why run? Why fight? You'll do what he wants in the end."

"I don't really care what you think," she answered hotly.

"I know. I found that much out the night you let your daddy talk you out of me," Billy Bob said, his words utterly emotionless.

"Please. I don't want to hear this again. We said it all four years ago. Why can't we just—"

"No, we didn't." Billy sat up slowly, his anger rising. The misery was gone; he'd suffered through its demise, but the temper was still there. "You talked, and Sam Pennington talked—and swore—and threatened, but me, I mostly got talked at. And talked about. And talked down to."

He stood suddenly, and even in the dim light, the gold in his hair glistened when he raked his hand with its long fingers and big knuckles back through it. Sam had hated Billy Bob's hair, Shiloh remembered just before he spoke.

"I came to get you. I can still see where you always waited for me, there beside the magnolias. Where nobody could see you sneak off after dark to meet me—and that was my first mistake." He took a step closer, his hands on his hips, his open shirt swinging.

"From the very beginning, from the day I first saw you out on the porch when Grandpa sent me to landscape your yard, I should either have run or gone right up to your dad and said, 'Here I am. I'm the grandson of the fruit stand man. Sometimes I work as a landscaper when my grandpa tells me to. That's who I am, Sam Pennington, and I mean to see your daughter.'"

"It wouldn't have worked," Shiloh told him pleadingly, looking up at him.

"Yeah, it would've," Billy Bob corrected. " 'Cause then he would've thrown me out from the start, and I wouldn't have spent the summer runnin' after you only to find out too late that you didn't mean a word of it. You were a damn cheat, Shiloh Pennington," he finished hotly.

Two red flags burned in the girl's cheeks, and she, too, came up off the cot, her eyes snapping. "I'm tired of being called names, d'you hear me? I never cheated you of anything. You talked about Farmer John's—well, you were the one who stopped, remember?"

"And it was a good thing—two weeks later you went to Mexico with your old man."

"You know why," she answered his angry words in desperation.

"Yeah," he returned after a long pause while he struggled with his anger and calmed his words. "Sam Pennington found out, and by the time he got through, there wasn't anything left of us."

He'd gone to meet her that last night—and when he walked up the shadowy little path, Shiloh had been waiting at the magnolias, just like always— but so had her father. One look at the man's stern face and Billy had felt as if he'd been kicked in the stomach.

But in a way it had almost been a relief to face him, to come out in the open with the truth: "I love her," he'd said steadily after they'd gone inside the big house.

Shiloh had been clutching at his hand with both of hers, facing Sam across the room. For a few minutes, he'd actually thought everything was going to be all right. That was before Sam started to speak—slowly, calmly, even kindly.

"So you love her. Do you know how old she is?"

"Eighteen."

"And you're twenty-three. Just what do the two of you plan to do about this 'love'?"

Billy looked down at Shiloh, but he had no fears about his answer: he meant to do—wanted to do—the right thing. "We want to get married," he'd said simply, with a touch of pride, and his fingers tightened around Shiloh's, his mind registering her little gasp of surprise.

Sam was silent a minute before he laughed. It had been a tiny, incredulous sound. "Get married," he repeated. "Yes, I'm sure you do, Mr. Walker. You've got no big plans for your life. No pressing career. No ambition. No money. Shiloh has all of that. You'd do very well to marry my daughter."

The older man's voice had been so deceptively soft that it had taken a few seconds for his words to register. Then Billy Bob's face flamed red as both he and Shiloh broke into protest.

"He's not like that, Papa! And you've—"

"I love her," Billy repeated hotly, and he put his arms around Shiloh to hold her tightly against him, to reassure himself that she was really his, not this hard-eyed man's across the room from him.

"Then I hope you love her enough to let her go," Pennington shot back, turning to fumble in a box on the big mahogany desk for a fat cigar, as if he couldn't stand to see the two of them together. He put the brown tube of tobacco to his lips, then removed it to add, "because you can't afford her. You can't send her to college, or buy her clothes, or make the payments on the kind of car that's being delivered here next week. She's out of your league."

"Papa, I don't care about any of that," Shiloh protested, twisting in Billy's arms to face her father.

"Yes, you do. Or you will when you get a little older. You'll learn to hate this plowboy when you see all that he costs you. Maybe you're too young to know that, but he's not."

"We'll do all right," he'd told Pennington stubbornly.

"How? By living on that old farm of your grandpa's? It might be productive if you had the money to invest in it, but you don't." The older man never even lit the cigar; instead, he broke it into two pieces in his fingers. "And tell me," he'd said silkily, "whose last name are you gonna give my girl? Because the only one you've got belongs to your mother. No man's ever claimed you."

Something exploded in Billy's brain as he stared in an incredulous rage at Shiloh's father. He'd heard the man was a bare-knuckles, down-and-dirty fighter when he wanted to be, and neither he nor Shiloh had dared to hope for his blessing, but Billy hadn't expected this.

"Billy?" Shiloh strained upward from his painful grasp to gaze at his too-white face above hers. "What's he—"

"He's a bastard. Didn't he tell you that?" Sam interrupted, his voice calm. "No father. Doesn't even know who he is."

"You know damn well who fathered me," Billy got out, strangled. Then he looked down into Shiloh's shocked face, and he turned her loose. "It's him—Sam Pennington—who's the bastard," he said, bitterly.

"It doesn't matter to me about your not having a father," she said, but her voice was shaken. "But there's no need to call Papa names. He's just trying to protect me."

"You don't need protection from me—" Billy began.

"Shiloh, listen to me," Pennington cut in. "I'm not asking you to give up this boy. I can see you care about him. But at least give me a little time to get used to the idea. Come with me to Mexico on this next business trip so we can talk this through. At least let me have a chance to—to adjust before you marry him."

Pennington's words were entreating, and as he spoke, he advanced on his daughter, his hand open palmed and outstretched in front of him, making a silent plea for him.

She stared at him, at his hand, as she stood indecisively between the two of them.

"If I can't talk you out of this thing with Walker," he told his daughter quietly, "I'll learn to accept it. Come to Mexico."

"No," Billy said in quick, panicky protest, and then he made a fatal mistake out of pure desperation. "You can't have both of us. Choose, Shiloh. It's either me—or it's him." What else was he to do? He couldn't compete with a glamorous trip, where Sam Pennington was going to spend his time pointing out Billy's shortcomings. He'd suddenly become painfully aware himself of his old clothes—the tan shirt, the faded Wranglers—and the less-than-mint condition of his Ford truck. How could she help but disdain him? He knew right then that she'd have to be crazy to choose him for anything, let alone a husband.

"All I can say is—I love you," Sam told his daughter quietly. "And unlike him, I'm not asking you to give anything up. I just need time." There were tears in his eyes—Billy himself saw them—before Sam turned away from them. Shiloh saw them, too.

"Papa," she'd whispered, and the one word was choked with emotion.

When she hesitantly put her hand in Sam's, Billy turned and stalked out.

Shiloh called his name, then ran after him to catch him outside on the porch. He could still remember how the low-cut white cotton top had accented the smooth, tanned hollow between her breasts where her heart beat as he looked down at her.

"Don't grab at me," he blazed at her, shaking off her hand. "Not unless you're comin' with me."

"I love you, Billy," she said pleadingly.

"What difference does that make now? You love him, too, but he means to see that there's no room for me in your life. And you'll let him."

"He needs me, Billy. I'm all he has. It's been that way ever since my mother left. Let me talk to him. It won't hurt to give him the time. We'll have the rest—"

He interrupted her harshly. "We'll have nothin'. Didn't you hear him? I reckon I'm not good enough for you, and he's not gonna let me try to be. That's okay. There's other girls. And their daddies, they're not so particular."

She looked stricken, then she flushed with anger. "You so much as touch another woman, Billy Walker, and we're through."

"That's what I'm tryin' to tell you, baby," he retorted. "You chose Daddy, remember? And you had a lucky escape, because he's right—I'm going nowhere much, and I *was* born on the wrong side of the blanket. Now, get out of my way."

She had not said another word as he walked away, his shoulders squared. But he'd seen her face as he drove off, and she had looked then much as she did right now, across the jail cell from him—angry and hurt.

But she had learned to conceal her emotions better in their years apart, and her face smoothed even as he stared at her.

"I didn't understand why you were so angry that night," Shiloh said haltingly, and her huge brown eyes looked right up into his. "It knocked me off balance when you told Sam you meant for us to marry. We hadn't talked about it much, but it was all you could say when he jumped you about things. You must have been scared, too, like I was when he caught us."

Billy Bob didn't answer.

"And there was more," she said haltingly. "Sam hurt your pride. And somehow, so did I. I didn't know that then, but I do now."

"You don't know anything," he answered shortly.

"I'm sorry," she whispered.

"I'm not," he returned, his voice flat. "Because if you let Sam Pennington talk you out of me in thirty minutes, we never stood a chance, anyway."

"I called you," she said suddenly, as if it made a difference after all this time. "I'd been in Acapulco three weeks before I finally . . . got over being mad. Your mother answered. I didn't tell her who I was. I didn't know if she knew about me. She said you were in Tupelo."

He stared at her, his eyes bright blue even in the dusky shadows. "I left town. Took a job on the road for the summer. You didn't come back."

"No," she answered, looking down at her hands. "Things—business—kept us down there until September. I came home for a day or two before I left for college. You weren't here. And . . . things had changed."

"I saw you once in town at Christmas. You never spoke," he remembered.

"I'd seen you before then. Maybe when I was home for Thanksgiving," she said, so low he had to strain to hear her. "But I knew it was over. There wasn't any point in talking to you."

"And then Michael Sewell started hanging around," he said starkly. She would never know how difficult it was for him to get that simple sentence out.

Shiloh didn't try to answer him, just watching him mutely. Then he pulled away from the bars and turned his back to her.

"Damn you, Shiloh." There was absolutely no emotion in his voice.

He lay down on the narrow cot again, turning his face to the wall. Even if he already knew it, it hurt to hear how easy it had been for her to forget him.

She lay on her own cot, silent too. When T-Tommy came in a few minutes later, he must have thought his two prisoners were asleep. He snapped off the light, and the cells lay in darkness.

Billy Bob stared at the patterns of light that the moon outside cast on the distant walls, hating the girl who lay not twelve feet from him. The breeze that blew in his window was cold on his arms, so he fumbled for the rough blanket and dragged it half over him, and his movement seemed to shatter the stillness around them.

"I saw you with another girl," she said suddenly, in the darkness.

He froze. "What?"

"I hadn't been back in town a good day that November when I saw you in a car with another girl. She was driving, and she let you out in front of the courthouse. You kissed her, and she was all over you."

Slowly, Billy twisted on the cot, dragging the blanket with him. "And that made a difference?"

"No. *No.* Not to me, not then. It just proved Sam was right, that's all. We weren't supposed to be together."

"I see."

This time the silence seemed eternal. In the darkness, he struggled with himself. It didn't matter, not now, what had happened then. It was over, in the past. He didn't love her anymore; most of the time he hated her. Especially when he remembered that in a few weeks' time, she was set to marry Michael.

His own brother.

But . . . *it didn't matter*. They deserved each other.

Still, he couldn't stop the explanation that tumbled from his lips at last.

"The only reason I was with Angie was that you were gone." He said it suddenly, shattering the long silence. He didn't turn from the wall.

But there was nothing from her.

"Shiloh?"

At last he sat up. She lay sideways, facing him with the light of the big moon falling over her shoulders—sound asleep.

"Really tearing your heart out over this, aren't you?" he asked the sleeping girl fiercely. "I think I'm sorry for Michael."

She woke him up just before dawn, crying in her sleep and calling Michael's name. The word froze his sudden, startled, awakening movements and an old, better-forgotten jealousy stabbed him.

But that was before his mind registered the fear in her voice.

"No—no," she was whimpering, over and over, twisting on the bed. "Michael—"

"Shiloh!" he said it sharply, rising to go to the bars. "Wake up. Shiloh!"

She stilled, then gasped.

"Shiloh, are you awake?"

The moonlight touched his face this time, coming in

from a different angle, and she gave a short, choked cry that was full of fear.

"Wake up, Shiloh, you're having a bad dream."

He could hear her breathing change as she tried to orient herself, then she asked tentatively, "Billy?"

"What?"

"I thought you were—"

"I know what you thought."

She sat up abruptly. "I'm . . . I'm sorry." But her teeth chattered.

"What for?" he asked dismissively. "Just forget it. Try to go back to sleep."

But instead she stood up, moving away from the tangled cot as if she were afraid of it, and she came hesitantly across the cold concrete floor toward the bars that separated them.

He stilled, watching her warily as she advanced, her bare, silk-stockinged feet making only a slight wisping sound.

"Did you ever think that God does funny things? You ask Him for help, and there's no telling where you'll wind up," Shiloh whispered, putting her hands on the bars between them. Another moth circling another light, that was what she reminded him of as she gravitated unwillingly toward him.

"What are you talking about?" he asked suspiciously.

"Things have been going wrong ever since I came home from college. I want to please Sam, but I can't. And this past week"—she laughed a little—"it's been like something out of a horror story. Here I am now, in jail, with the one person who doesn't want to see me, the one person I never meant to speak to again."

"Let me guess," he said ironically. "You're not talking about T-Tommy."

"So help me, Billy Bob," she choked out, and she was crying—crying, for God's sakes. "I must be in here for a reason."

"What's the matter? *What?*" he demanded, and he rose, too, and went to the bars where she stood. He could feel the warmth from her body this close—it was too close—and smell the rich scent of her perfume. It, too, was different from the one he remembered.

This was not the girl he'd once loved, he reminded himself, but whoever she was, she was hurting.

"Billy," she whispered at last, her voice dark with heavy emotion, and she slid her hand up the bars to touch his, where it clenched the bar above hers.

He felt the touch. It shocked him, but he didn't move.

"I'm in trouble," she gasped out at last.

His hand jerked. "Trouble? What does that mean?"

"I don't want to be Michael Sewell's wife. I told him. And I told Sam."

His heart nearly stopped, and finally, he tested his hearing with caution. "You don't want to marry Sewell," he repeated.

"No, I don't."

"Is he the reason you were running?"

"He—and Sam. I'm scared that one morning, I'm going to wake up and find that I am married to him, no matter what. Sam will make it happen. He always makes it seem right."

"What did Michael do to you?"

"Do! *Nothing.*"

"Don't lie. You were scared to death when you woke up and thought I was him."

"I said, nothing."

Billy took a deep breath of pure frustration. "I could shake you, did you know that? You're so sure until your father gets mentioned. Then you're weak-kneed and spineless."

She tried to jerk away, but his hands flashed out, catching hers. "Don't marry him. Hell, you walked out on me. You can do it to him."

"I don't want to hurt Papa. He's had so many hurts—"

"Dammit, he's a bitter old man. So he fell for a woman twenty years his junior. He married her and she made a fool out of him with every man in town. He's not the first one it ever happened to. He's been feeding his pride and building his ego ever since at your expense. Your mother was gone for most of your life. She's dead now. *Dead.* Just because they screwed it up, you don't have to pay."

His hands were hurting her, nearly bruising her fingers.

"I know all that," she said resentfully, "but it's not that easy."

"Yes, it is. Just say no. Run to Mexico again. Shoot both of them. *Do* something, Shiloh."

They stared at each other a long moment, then she swallowed and whispered, "You look like Michael."

He shoved away from her as if her presence burned him, taking two steps back. Then he said tautly, "No. Michael looks like *me.*"

Back at the cot again, he wondered why he'd ever tried. Her words hurt.

"I didn't mean it the way it sounded," she protested, then laughed a little in frustration. "I don't know how this happened. I haven't seen you in ages. But here you are— here I am. And I'm telling you things I didn't mean to say. You always did that to me." Her voice held a trace of resentment.

"Yeah, well, the feeling's mutual."

At last she, too, moved back to the cot in her cell, but she was restless. He could feel it even across the space that lay between them.

"So, are you still seeing that girl?" she asked at last.

"If you're talking about Angie Blake, sometimes."

"And—somebody else?"

"Sometimes."

"You're still living at home, too."

So she knew something about him after all.

"I kept telling myself I'd leave," he answered, slowly. "And I did once in a while, but I always came back. I kept remembering that peach orchards take a lot of work. So do pecan groves. And he's an old man. Then there were all those acres of trees the two of us planted—dogwoods and pines and more peach and pecan. He kept saying, 'Hold on, Billy. They'll be worth something one day.' He had a lot of hope for them. So I just kept planting and tending, but I didn't mean it. I was thinking about other things, working on other things. Then he had a stroke, and I had to stay. Mama couldn't run the place by herself, and we had to live."

Why tell Shiloh all this? It didn't matter to her. But he'd said it without thought, just another truth dragged out of one of them by the isolated intimacy of the dark cells.

"But you don't get to work with animals, like you wanted."

He hoped to God that wasn't pity in her voice, and he answered brusquely, "Yeah, I do. I train horses for Harold Bell." He'd give her no more than that; he'd told too much about himself already.

"The man who does the traveling rodeos?" she asked.

"That's the one. I used to travel with him once in a

while, taking care of his stock. Mostly in the summer. That's why I was in Tupelo when you called."

"Is that what you're going to do when you get out of here?"

"*If* I get out of here, you mean," he corrected. "But I don't have the fine, so I'll be here the rest of the month. At the best, I'll work all summer—somewhere—to pay Bud back. At the worst, they'll put me in here again because I can't come up with it."

"Why do you fight all the time? And hang out at all those places and stay in trouble? You never used to do that."

"Because I want to."

"Was the fight over a girl?"

He didn't answer.

"That's what I thought," she said flatly.

"It's nothing to you," he shot back. "At least I'm not running around town with somebody I don't even like, wearing their ring. Look—just go back to sleep, okay?"

"I can't," she said at last, her voice apologetic. "I might dream again. This jail is too quiet. It's lonesome, too."

He meant to shut her up with some insolent, rude remark, but there it was again, the lost-little-girl quality in her voice that made him go weak at the knees.

Some impulse made him stand, then drag his cot over to the bars between them. She heard his movement, saw what he was doing in the barely discernible light of dawn.

He stretched out on it, then let his hand linger on the bars.

"Well? I thought you were lonely," he questioned at last.

In one sudden, decisive movement, she stood, then copied his movements. They lay there on their separate cots, just the bars between them. Then he reached his fingers through, and she slowly caught them in hers.

There were no words between them. He watched her a long time in the gray light as she slept, clutching his hand like a child instead of the ultrachic Miss Shiloh Pennington. Her lashes lay like heavy fans on her cheeks, her lips were barely open as she breathed. But her long, shapely legs belonged to a woman.

It was easy to remember now the hold she'd once had on him—and why he had to keep hating her for what she'd done.

He fell asleep himself on the thought, and didn't wake until T-Tommy aroused him with a loud exclamation, staring through the bars at the cots so close together, at the entwined hands. Billy's was cramping, his fingers half asleep.

"Good God a'mighty, Billy Bob. What do you think you're doin'?"

# 5

*He got no* answer from either of his two prisoners; Billy moved hastily, pulling his hand free of Shiloh's and rolling off the other side of the cot. The rude movement woke her up.

"What's wrong?" she asked groggily, sitting up painfully.

"You tell me," T-Tommy muttered, glaring at Billy Bob as he leaned one shoulder against the wall and yawned.

"Is it—Sam? Did he come after me?" Shiloh asked hesitantly.

"No, leastways, not yet," T-Tommy answered, diverted for the moment from his suspicions. "I just got in myself. But I gotta call him, Shiloh. If he ain't already mad and worried, he will be when he comes through town and sees what's left of your car over at the body shop."

"Do it, then," Shiloh told him quietly, although her

heart had already started a rabbity jumping motion at the thought of what Sam was going to say. "Call him."

"And besides, you gotta get a way home," T-Tommy added, rationalizing a little more. But still he hung around the door of the cell which he'd swung wide, jingling the keys that hung from his belt, before he asked anxiously, "Reckon you'll be all right when he gets here, Shiloh?"

"Good Lord, T-Tommy, he won't beat me," Shiloh answered, laughing a little.

"You hope," Billy murmured, then fell into silence when T-Tommy shot a glance at him.

"Come on, then, let's go," the sheriff said to Shiloh, standing back and motioning her out the door ahead of him. "No sense in you hangin' around back here any longer."

Shiloh hesitated. She wanted to say something to Billy Bob; there had to be some explanation from her as to why she'd spent four years treating him like a stranger, and then last night just lost it and told him everything.

She felt the heat that crawled up into her face as she remembered that emotional breakdown this morning after the dream she'd had. What in the world had possessed her to tell him about Michael?

Her eyes were beseeching as she looked over at him. He was no fool; he knew exactly what she wanted.

"Don't worry," he said brusquely, as he straightened off the wall and began buttoning his shirt. "Your little secrets are safe with me. And if we ever run into each other again, we'll be strangers."

"Did he do something?" T-Tommy demanded of the girl. "I wouldn't have thought it of him, in spite of everything. But if he—"

"No. I had a bad dream," Shiloh cut in. "I—I used to know him. He worked on the yard. That's why he was holding my hand. So don't say anything to him—there's nothing else to say, anyway."

She meant the pointed words for Billy Bob, and she was sure he knew it.

"Then come on, Shiloh. Let's go call Sam and get it over with," T-Tommy said reluctantly.

Her father was at the jail within thirty minutes. To a stranger, he might have looked normal. But there was a white line around his lips, and the pearl tie tack that he used every morning was not in place.

Shiloh faced him squarely when he walked in the sheriff's office, trying to act her age. Now was a fine time to start, she thought wryly.

"Now, Sam," T-Tommy began placatingly, but the other man was in no mood for small talk.

"Is she charged with anything? Can she go?"

"Yeah, she can go. The trooper wrote up this ticket, and there's a fine." He held out the slip of paper toward Sam, but Shiloh stepped up, trying to balance on her broken heel, and pulled it out of his hand first.

"It's my fine. I'll pay it," she said quickly.

"You damn well will," Sam said angrily. "And you can buy the next car you drive, too. I don't suppose you've seen what damage you did to the other one yet."

She didn't answer, just going to the door, where she stood waiting for him.

"I thought it might do her some good if she stayed here last night," T-Tommy announced, a little belligerently.

"You mean you thought I'd kill her if you brought her home," Sam corrected him tersely. "Well, don't worry. She'll live. Laura told me she was safe—that was all—so I've had time to cool down. I *think*," he snapped as he turned to follow his daughter.

Neither of them said a word as they sank into the cream leather seats of Sam's Cadillac, but he turned purposely, not toward home, but toward Randy Tate's body shop.

Shiloh knew why; she didn't move a muscle until he pulled up alongside the garage—and there sat what was left of her red Porsche. She couldn't stop the wince of regret and dismay before she climbed out of Sam's car and limped over to it.

Randy himself came out to greet them. "You sure made a mess out'a this one, Miss Pennington," he said cheerfully as he tucked a pencil behind his ear. All three of them gazed at the crumpled left side of the car. Both the front windshield and the window were shattered, and the fender was nearly touching the door. The right door—the one Shiloh had scrambled out of to safety—wouldn't shut.

Randy touched the open door regretfully. "Frame's all bent up," he said. "I might could fix it, but I doubt it. And it'd cost way yonder too much. You'd be better off just buyin' a new one."

"The next new car she gets," Sam interpolated grimly, "it'll do well to make sixty miles an hour. No more speed cars for her."

Randy glanced from one to the other. "Oh," he said at last. "Well, your insurance will total it. But if you should want to sell it to me, I might could use parts of it. I couldn't pay much, of course. It ain't worth much anymore. But I might come up with more than you'd expect."

"I'll think about it," Shiloh said, feeling a little sick at the sight of the damage.

"Are you ready to go? Now that you've seen your handiwork?" Sam asked.

Without a word, she got in the Cadillac again.

His silence lasted until they got into the house. Then she spoke, to forestall him.

"I want to take a shower. I have to get ready for work," she announced.

"Oh, no, you don't," Sam snapped, pushing open the door to the study. "We're going to talk, me and you. You need to see a doctor to make sure you're not hurt. And don't even start about work. You've got no way to get there unless I loan you a car, and right now, that's not something that strikes me as real smart. Sit down, Shiloh."

She wanted to remind him that she was no child to be ordered around, but she was too tired and the effort seemed too great. She might as well get it over with, so she followed him reluctantly into the room, defying him only by going to the window instead of sitting down as he motioned her to do.

Neither of them said a word for a long moment, then he spoke harshly, "You could have been killed."

"But I wasn't."

"And if you think I like coming to the jail—the Briskin County Jail, of all places—to get my daughter, then you can think again." He made an angry gesture. "What is it with you? You've never given me much trouble, Shiloh, until now. You wait until you're twenty-two and then rebel, like some snot-nosed kid."

"I didn't rebel," she objected "I only said no. Maybe you're just not used to hearing it."

"I can't stand by and let you mess up your life, girl. You're throwing away Michael and a chance to be a part of the most respected family in this section of the state."

"Sam," she said bluntly, turning toward him, "the judge is all for this marriage because of your money. Because of your pull."

"What's wrong with 'Papa,' like you used to call me?" he asked irritably. "And as for the judge, I know that. Both of us want something that the other one's got, so we join. That's good business."

"But I'm not business," she answered passionately.

"Nobody ever said you were. But if you and Michael hit it off—and you did—there's that much more to the good."

He was as stubborn as a brick wall, and she felt as if she'd run full-tilt into one. Taking a deep breath, she put out her arm to try to hold off the force of his personality while she explained one more time that she couldn't marry Michael. Right here in the bright light of this spring morning, she would have to tell her father what he'd done.

But he caught sight of the same marks that Billy Bob had seen the night before. "Who grabbed you?" he demanded, his face darkening.

"Nobody."

"I know the marks of a man's hand when I see them," he answered.

"Oh, those," she said, glancing down at them. "The policeman had me by the arm last night."

"And just what was his name?" Sam demanded dangerously.

Shiloh covered the marks with her own hand. "And if I tell you, you'll do what? Have his job?"

"Any man that roughs up a woman—"

"He didn't rough me up. He tried to catch me, that's all. And you know what's so funny? You're all up in the air about a cop who grabbed me, but I'm scared to death that you won't believe me when I tell you about Michael."

Sam stopped all movement, arrested. The bright morning sun was merciless as it streamed through the windows on him; Shiloh saw the deep lines around his eyes and mouth, the way the silver that had taken over his hair was encroaching now into his eyebrows. He was sixty-two—and he looked it. But she couldn't afford to be merciful now.

"Michael tried to rape me."

She just said it, then looked away, out the window on to the sunshiny front lawn.

Sam never showed a flicker of emotion.

"Because he lost his temper and tried to anticipate his wedding vows here at the house the night he tried to make you take his ring back?"

Her face paled. "He told you," she said breathlessly. "You knew all along, and you didn't do anything."

"Did you think he wouldn't tell me? He confessed it like a man the morning after it happened—Lord, was that just yesterday?—and he didn't like saying it. He said you ran, and he couldn't find you."

"I'm telling you—begging you to believe me. Michael didn't just try to anticipate—he attacked me like an animal. He . . . he *bit* me."

His face flushed a little. "Oh, come on, Shiloh. You're claiming that, then saying you got away?"

"He did—I did!"

"Do you really think if he'd been serious, you'd have escaped? As big as he is?"

"You don't believe me."

"I do to a reasonable extent. I think he got mad, but he's sorry. And the fact is, he didn't—didn't—"

"No." Her voice was dull and colorless.

"And what do you expect men to think of you, anyway, the way you dress sometimes these days?"

"It wasn't my fault!"

"Nothing happened. How could I lay fault on anybody?" he asked patiently.

And then her temper broke. "I want out. I have to get away. From him, and mostly, from *you,* Sam Pennington."

He winced—actually winced. She'd scored a hit there, but it didn't matter anymore.

"I want you to calm down and quit acting like a hysterical teenager," he said at last.

"No name that you can call me will change the truth about what he did. I'm leaving both of you."

"Don't be a fool, Shiloh," Sam said in anger. "He'll come after you. And if he doesn't, I will. Every time."

The certainty of his words, the memory of the steely determination in Michael's hands, made Shiloh's stomach shake.

"Neither of you will find me."

"Try running, Shiloh. I'll cut you off at the bank. Without a car, without money, with me blocking you at every turn—you're not going anywhere."

She looked around the study blindly, then asked with deliberate cruelty, "Is this the way you tried to keep Caroline?"

He took a sharp breath, shock and pain spreading over

his face. "How could you bring that up, after all this time?"

"I'm your daughter, I regret to say. And I've got a point to make. You couldn't hold her, no matter how many times you brought her back."

"I stopped trying, dammit."

"You loved her. You cried for her. I heard you the day after she left. And the next day, and the next. I hated her for what she did. I was nearly five years old, and I told myself I'd never make you cry."

A red line of blood was seeping up his cheeks as Sam returned, "So do as I ask. Marry Michael. You gave your word, Shiloh. Now I intend to see you keep it. Like it or not right now, you'll thank me someday, when Michael's a success and you've got the world at your feet. No mill life for you. And I won't let you be like—"

He broke off his impassioned words, but she knew already.

"Like who?" she demanded. "My mother? Isn't that it? I'm like Caroline?"

He flung up his head and his words were harsh. "I hope not, Shiloh. Because if you are, you're nothing but a whore."

It hit her like a slap in the face, the agony so old she recognized it, so new that it was a fresh bleeding wound. She didn't do anything dramatic, just stood looking at her father's shuttered eyes, at the set face with its distinct cheekbones, at the thin, implacable line of his mouth.

Then she twisted to walk away, barely able to breathe from the pain.

"Shiloh."

Her name on Sam's lips stopped her before she was halfway across the room; she never turned to face him.

"Make up your mind to it. You're going to marry the judge's son if I have to drag you up the aisle kicking and screaming. You'll make something of your life no matter what—or who—Caroline was, or where I came from. I swear it."

She didn't go to work: Laura and Sam won that round.

But she refused to go to the doctor, so she figured she broke even in the battle.

There was no time to contemplate wins or losses, however; Shiloh shut herself in her silent, shadowy room and licked her wounds, trying to stop herself from bleeding to death.

There'd been so much misery, so much dislike in her father when he talked of her mother, Shiloh's flesh and blood. How could he love the daughter when he despised Caroline, the other half of her, so much?

She thought about the net that was closing around her. She'd been right, and Sam's heart was set on the marriage to Michael.

She was trapped.

She should have hated Michael; instead, she was so angry with her father that the memory of him held little or no sting anymore.

Sam had been telling the truth about one thing: Running was no way out. Besides, she didn't want to run. Her temper was up now. Sweetwater was her place in the world, where she belonged. She wanted life here, on her terms. Sam couldn't shove her out any more than he could shove her around. She wouldn't let him. She was as tough as he was. She would stand right here and fight.

But how?

There had to be some way to block Michael, to stop Sam, to give herself breathing space.

Something that would leave her safe, but make her independence clear.

If she hurt Sam, he'd just have to be hurt. She had to show no more concern for his wants than he'd shown for hers.

What had he said, his voice as hard as a diamond? "You're going to marry the judge's son if I have to drag you down the aisle. . . ."

Shiloh thought about that for a long time, sitting on the high four-poster bed and staring out the French doors at the red ball of the sun as it sank that afternoon behind Pine Ridge, the dark, high line of trees that lay to the northwest of Sweetwater.

And by the time it set and the last pink lights had faded into dusk, she knew exactly what to do. Then she went to the telephone to see if Randy Tate was still at the garage.

Sweetwater had a weekly newspaper that was churned out every Friday; a copy was delivered to the jail at noon. By the time it made the rounds and got to Billy Bob, it was crumpled and out of order. But it was reading, and it was from the real world, so he took it when it was offered along toward suppertime.

He'd picked it back up a third time, deciding he could stand to read even the obituaries, when the door opened to the outside office and T-Tommy ushered in Shiloh.

Billy lowered the bare foot he had propped up on the bed and let the newspaper fall, surprise written on his face.

"Don't tell me she's wrecked another car," he said to T-Tommy.

The sheriff's face was dark. "She claims she came to see you. Now I don't know what's goin' on here, but I don't like it."

"I just wanted to thank him for being kind night before last," Shiloh said casually. Today she looked like a rising young executive in her red suit.

"So thank him," T-Tommy snapped.

"I want to talk to him *alone*," Shiloh said pointedly.

"Sam won't like you coming to the jail to talk to somebody as wild as Billy Walker, and I—"

"He'll never know if you don't tell him," she interrupted.

T-Tommy hesitated, then threw up both hands. "Okay. Okay. What can happen with him behind bars?"

Neither Shiloh nor Billy Bob answered that provocative question. But when he was gone, Billy rose slowly to his feet.

Shiloh didn't remember, even two nights ago, that he'd been this tall.

"You—you need a shave," she offered unnecessarily.

He ran a hand down the side of his face, almost in surprise. "I didn't know I was havin' such particular company this Friday night. Came back to gloat over less fortunate convicts, did you?"

"I told T-Tommy—"

"I heard what you told him. So, now you can tell me the truth. But if this is for another talk about your—your boyfriend—"

"No, it's not that."

"Then what?" He braced his palms against the bars, leaning his shoulders in toward her.

There was a lot of Billy Walker, Shiloh thought, a little panicky now that she was here. Tonight he had on just a white T-shirt with the tight jeans, and despite his tall, lanky build, there were muscles visible in all the right places, especially in his arms and shoulders. He looked dangerous, but then, there had always been a wild, half-tamed air about him. Maybe it was the comparison to Billy that had always made Michael seem civilized and too smooth.

She looked away, hoping she could do this.

"I went back to work today," she offered. "I'm driving one of Sam's cars. At least the trooper didn't pull my license. That's the reason I'm here so late. Because of work, I mean. The bank doesn't close until six on Fridays." Stop rambling, Shiloh, she told herself—even if you are nervous.

Billy Bob eyed her quizzically. "You can visit me anytime, honey," he answered humorously. "I don't have a real full social life these days."

"Yes, well, this is not exactly a social visit," Shiloh answered, and her cheeks flushed a little.

"Then what is it?" he asked, interested despite himself.

In answer, she unzipped the little alligator bag that hung over her shoulder and pulled out a sealed envelope, which she held out to him.

Billy looked down at it, then at her. "I think you're supposed to put the saw in a cake you've baked," he advised with a glint of laughter.

"Would you stop being funny and open it?" Shiloh snapped, exasperated.

So he pulled it from her hand, obligingly tore one end open, and let the contents spill out into his hand.

"My God," he breathed at last, staring down at the green bills that covered his palm.

"You can count it if you want to. But I can tell you,

there's thirty-five hundred dollars there," Shiloh said, offhandedly.

His eyes, nearly black with shock, lifted to stare at her. "What's this for?"

"You said you needed this much to pay your fine—and get out. Wasn't it thirty-five hundred?" she asked anxiously.

His face darkened, and he frowned as he crumpled up the bills by closing his hand over them, and crammed them, helter-skelter, back down into the envelope. Then he shoved it at her. "I'm not your charity case," he said fiercely. "I don't need your money."

But Shiloh backed away from his reaching hand and the envelope he held.

"It's not charity. I want you to—to earn it."

"Earn it?" he repeated slowly. "What do I have to do? Murder somebody? Your old man, maybe?"

"No. I just want you to sell—" No, that was the wrong approach. So what in the world was the right one? she wondered. "I want to buy something."

He frowned, puzzled. "I know this can't be about my horse, so I don't—"

She snapped her teeth together and said sharply, "I want to buy *you*, Billy Bob."

As he stared, she flushed a brilliant red. That had not come out right at all.

"It's just for a little while. Nothing permanent. A few months, that's all. Then we can divorce. And I'm not asking for anything but your name. That's all. It's in name only, see?"

He stopped her rambling words. "Are you asking me to—to *marry* you?" His voice rose higher in surprise with every syllable.

"Not exactly. I mean, not asking. I do need you to marry me, but I'm asking to buy it—you—" she stumbled to a halt.

His face had gone unexpectedly white and stern.

"And just why," he demanded harshly, "are you in need of a husband so fast?" Unwillingly, his eyes traveled down her body, lingering on her abdomen.

When she caught his meaning, she jumped back even farther from him. "I'm not pregnant!"

"Then why?" he asked persistently.

"I told you, I can't marry Michael. And if I don't do something, Sam's going to push me into it. This way"— she flung up her head—"I get what I want—no marriage—and he gets what he wants."

"I don't see how Pennington—"

"He wants me to marry 'the judge's son.' His exact words," Shiloh answered defiantly.

She had his attention now. He stared again, then began to laugh, but it was not the laughter of amusement.

"This is no joke," she said heatedly. "I mean it."

"You kill me," he said at last. "You want a husband— why, I don't know, you've turned down two—so you just calmly go shopping for one. You're burned up at your father, but this is just like him."

"My money's as good as his, too," she retorted, both angry and embarrassed.

"I figured this *was* his."

"I got it by selling the Porsche to Randy Tate. What's wrong with it? It's the amount you needed, isn't it?"

He pulled the crumpled envelope back in toward him, and there was a flash of blue fire in his gaze.

"You're awful sure of me, seems like," he said with an edge of distaste.

"No, I'm not," she denied, letting out a long breath. "But I know what I need, and I knew what you needed, and this way, it works for both of us." In her mind she heard Sam's words, and she repeated them now, wryly, "It's good business." Maybe she *was* like him; maybe she could beat him at his own game.

"Good business." Billy Bob repeated the words, too. "So, let me get this straight. I get the money free and clear—mine for good—if I marry you."

"That's right."

Billy leaned even closer to the bars. "I don't reckon it's crossed your mind yet that taking marriage vows ought to be something different."

Shiloh moved uncomfortably. "I know all that. I'm surprised you do. But I've torn myself up over it for the last day, trying to decide, and I mean to marry somebody."

"*Any* body, is that who?" he asked disparagingly.

"I haven't thought of anybody else but you to ask," she told him honestly. "And this will be a pretend marriage. We won't live together. We won't—won't do other things. It'll never be real, so the divorce won't count. And nobody but Sam—and Michael—ever have to know."

"You've got it all figured out, don't you?" His voice was resentful. "And what's your daddy gonna do to me when you throw the wrong judge's son in his teeth?"

"Nothing. And even if he does, you won't care," Shiloh answered shrewdly. "You'd like to get at Sam—and your own father. This is the way to do it."

He didn't like that she knew him that well. "And when do you plan to let them in on this little secret? So I'll know when to run," Billy Bob added.

He was going to say yes, she thought, and she wasn't sure if it was panic or pleasure that hit her.

"I don't know. Just . . . when I need to. And it will be ended the day either one of us wants it to be."

They looked at each other a long, searching moment. Each had reasons and motives.

Then Billy Bob looked down at the money again before turning to pace the little cell once or twice like a caged animal.

"When would we—"

"When do you get out?" She answered his question with her own.

"With this"—he held up the envelope—"in two days. Monday."

"We could—could do it then. We can cross the state line. There's no waiting period in Tennessee. It would all be over and done by Monday night," Shiloh answered hurriedly, and a little tingle of apprehension skated down her spine.

"You've got this all planned," he said angrily, "too planned."

"No, I don't. Just what I had to do. I'm—I'm scared to death. But this time, I'm standing up to Sam. You told me to, Billy," she answered defensively.

"I don't like being bought like so much meat, no matter who you're standing up to, Shiloh," he said quietly. "And I gotta wonder what's going on, because you could'a had me a whole lot cheaper four years ago."

"This has nothing to do with that," she answered, her brown eyes meeting his blue ones for a long time.

"Oh, yes, it does," he murmured at last. "It's got everything to do with it, because if I didn't remember what you were then—what we were—no amount of money could make me say yes now." Then he carefully folded the envelope and slid it in the pocket of the T-shirt.

"You'll do it," she whispered in relief.

"I'd like to be pure and noble and play the outraged virgin," he said, with a glint in his eye, "but we both know it would be a lie. Besides, I need the money. This is so sudden, and all that—but I reckon I can marry you, honey. Yes, ma'am, I do."

# 6

*Rain splattered against* the brick-and-concrete facing of the jail window, spraying through the screen and the bars to fall on Billy's face as he stood like a sentinel leaning into the window, the same way he'd stood every night he'd been here.

The sweet spring shower had begun just as Shiloh left. She had parked in the bank's deserted lot tonight, and he'd stood watching her pull away, water dancing against her white headlights.

He wished he were at home, out on the farm. Rain didn't bother him; he'd have walked in it, wading through high wet grass, not caring when his clothes and his hair got soaked and clung to him, not caring when the wind shook the tall pecan trees and rained even more moisture down on him.

Instead, he was caught here, with nothing to see but the concrete and the brick of this little town—and with his worry that tonight he'd made the biggest trouble of his life for himself.

There was an aching kind of pain down in the vicinity of his heart when he thought how he'd once offered to give his all to Shiloh and it hadn't been enough. Now he was just dollars and cents, and that was what she wanted.

It was probably funny that four years ago, he'd lost out mostly because he was the judge's illegitimate son, but now, that very fact had walked him into this marriage.

A *marriage*. That was a scary word.

But it wasn't really marriage. They wouldn't see each other, and there'd be no emotion involved. "Good business," she'd said coolly, and he'd had a flashing impulse to yank her up, kiss her hotly, and tell her what she could do with her "business."

But he was smarter than that now. He needed the money; he wanted out; and he'd enjoy thwarting the plans of the judge and Pennington. She was right about that, he admitted grudgingly.

He could do all of that, and still stay away from Shiloh. Not that he wanted to go near her. Love gone wrong was the worst medicine of all; it had turned him cold toward her.

And if he ever felt the slightest urge to be with Shiloh, all he had to remember was that Michael must have been with her, too—that ought to kill any longing he'd ever had.

He shut his eyes, blocking out the sight of the two of them together, but took time to wonder what Michael had, or hadn't, done to make her repudiate him. And the evil thought slid in before Billy could stop it: had Michael been the first man Shiloh had been with? Once he'd thought he would be—not just the first, but the last, too.

You big fool, he thought now, in amusement.

Sitting down on the cot, he pulled the money out of his

pocket, examining it again. Not a real honorable way to make this money, but this was life, the real, down-and-dirty thing. Money mattered; ideals, like young dreams, didn't.

His grandpa wouldn't see it that way, and neither would his mother. They'd die of shame if they ever discovered what he had done.

But they weren't him, and their way had left all three of them victims.

He pushed the thoughts of them to the back of his head just as he pushed the money back into his pocket, and let his brain fill with the image of Robert Scwell. The man deserved this, especially if he'd paired Michael off with Shiloh for the reason Sweetwater said he had—to get Sam's money and power behind him for a run at politics. The Sewells might have social standing on their side, but there wasn't as much money as there once had been.

All of that was nothing to him. He was just Billy Bob Walker. Nobody expected too much from him, so if he chose to let Shiloh Pennington use him—if he chose to use her—it was his business.

Just business.

"I reckon you're popular tonight." T-Tommy's sharp words broke into his reverie, and as Billy Bob looked up, the sheriff ushered another female figure into the cell area.

Had Shiloh—

"Hi, Billy. Glad to see me?"

The drawling, sweet voice belonged to Angie Blake. So did the blond hair and the vivid blue eyes.

He swallowed his disappointment and stood slowly.

" 'Lo, Angie. No date tonight?"

"You're in here," she pointed out sassily, laughing.

"When the best isn't available . . ." She let the words trail off suggestively, reaching one hand through the bars to let her fingers run down his shirt.

"Yeah, sure," Billy Bob returned. "What you mean is, you're going somewhere and stopped by here on your way."

"Well, maybe," she answered archly. "But it won't be any fun without you."

He looked her over a minute, seeing the petite curves in the high-belted jeans, the shirt opened casually to reveal the two gold chains that wrapped her throat, the carefully done blond hair, shocking in its ultrashort swirl, the manicured, elegant nails. She looked as out of place in this little backwater jail as anything he'd seen yet.

Angie was a doll, to put it bluntly, and he didn't see why he shouldn't—every other soul in town did.

And she was fun, never still a minute, full of laughter and teasing and flirtatiousness, as heady as the rich Jungle Gardenia perfume she wore.

She didn't expect much, either. She'd been married once before to a brute who roughed her up before she finally threw him out. She made it a point to say that she wasn't looking for a second marriage, and she had other boyfriends once in a while. She was, Billy Bob supposed, perfect for a guy like him. Other men certainly seemed to think he was a lucky dog when he had her.

So it aggravated him to discover that he wished it had been Shiloh back a second time. And he didn't like it one little bit that there was a completely unexpected trace of guilt down inside him because Shiloh had been here first.

A man didn't flirt with one woman and let her run her hands all over him, the way Angie was doing now, and then up and marry another one two days later.

The second the sedate, righteous thought hit him,

Billy Bob got mad. She'd bought his name—that was all.
It was all she wanted. He didn't owe Shiloh anything else.

"I've missed you, Billy," Angie told him huskily.

"I know the feeling, baby," he answered fervently, and
leaned forward to let her press her fingers against his lips.


For the second night in a row, Shiloh refused to go
downstairs for supper. She told Laura that her day had
exhausted her and she wanted to rest. The housekeeper
looked at her dubiously but said nothing, and Sam left her
alone, too.

In fact, they'd been avoiding each other ever since
yesterday morning, when he'd thrown down the gauntlet
with a vengeance, when she'd seen clearly how determined he was.

Hurt and scorching embarrassment bubbled up in her
every time she remembered what he'd said about Caroline—what he had hinted that he might believe about
Shiloh. Maybe nothing could have hurt her more than
that implied comparison to her mother. It wasn't true.
Except for a long-ago night with Billy, she had made sure
nobody could say anything about her.

In fact, she'd had little opportunity to date at all while
she was growing up.

Sam had hovered over her and the boys who'd dared
to show an interest in her from the time she was thirteen,
and when she was fifteen and about to be a sophomore
at the local high school, he'd taken her away from members of the male gender completely: he had sent her sixty
miles away to a private school for girls.

Between classes and sports, Shiloh barely had time to
breathe, let alone think about boys, and that was exactly

the idea behind Mississippi Academy for Young Ladies.

Still, Shiloh didn't mind too much. Sam either came or sent Laura after her every Wednesday afternoon for a night at home, and she came home every Saturday to stay until Sunday night.

The few times she was sick, Sam dropped everything to come and get her.

She learned to love the place with its old graceful white buildings and big columns, with its rich, green rolling lawns and huge, ancient shadowy trees. She made friends there.

"This is the way I want you raised," Sam told her firmly. "Good atmosphere, good friends, good education. You're going to go a long way, Shiloh."

When she was a little girl, she'd thought maybe he meant the places he sometimes took her in the summer— Canada once, Japan once, England twice—when he had to go on business.

Then she began to understand that he meant something entirely different. He meant she was going to be Somebody.

Once she realized Sam's ambitions, she began to get nervous: what if she couldn't climb high enough to please him? And she felt trapped: why couldn't she just live a normal life?

The summer after she graduated, she felt like a bird about to take flight. Life was out there, just waiting. In a few months, she'd be on her own, even if she would be only an hour's drive away. Sam had reluctantly agreed to let her live in the dormitory at Ole Miss. It was close enough that he could still keep tabs on her, he figured.

Then one bright, hot June morning, so early that dew still glistened on the grass, she walked outside, where a truck brimming over with landscaping supplies had pulled into their drive, and she ran smack into Life, not at the university, but in her own backyard.

Its name, she discovered, was Billy Bob Walker.

He was slender and slim hipped; if he weren't so tall, he'd look like a boy. And he moved like a well-oiled machine, his walk easy, sensual in its indolence.

Shiloh, standing on the porch, could see his blue eyes and the way they shone with humor even at this distance. Sam came outside, not even noticing her there in the shadows, and bounded off the porch.

"You're the landscaper?" he questioned. "You look awful young to me. I want this done right."

"I'm gettin' older by the second," the man said humorously. "But if you want, Grandpa can come every afternoon and check what I've done. He's the one who sent me, and he won't mind one bit settin' me straight."

Sam paused, as if startled. "You're Willie Walker's grandson?"

"That's right. Ellen Walker's my mother," the other man answered, a trace of defiance in his voice as he stared back.

Sam answered after a second or two, with a dismissive flip of his hand, "Let me show you what I want done."

As the two of them walked away, Shiloh watched the younger one. She liked him. It was that simple.

After Sam left for work and Laura was busy upstairs, Shiloh took a book and went back out to the porch, and wound up watching the man work. It fascinated her to see him, the way he got right down into the rich, loamy earth, reveling in its texture, completely unafraid of dirt or sweat.

He was whistling to himself when he straightened at

last, turning back toward the truck for something, and just as he lifted his cap off his head to wipe his face with the crook of his elbow, he caught sight of Shiloh. Looking straight at him, she could see now that his eyes were long and slanting, so darkly blue they might have appeared black except in bright light.

She thought all of that in one fleeting second before she pulled back a little more in embarrassment at having been caught watching him.

He hesitated before he spoke.

"Hello."

She said something; at least she made a noise.

"I didn't see you sittin' there. I'm Billy Bob Walker, from Walker Farms. We do landscaping."

"I can tell." This time her voice worked, and it held amusement. He laughed, too, looking down at his clothes.

"Yeah, I guess you can."

When he began to turn away, she remembered suddenly to tell him, "My name's Shiloh."

He stopped. "Shiloh? Like the Civil War?"

"Papa said it meant 'a place of peace.' He named me." Shiloh stood up, coming to the edge of the porch where the sunlight hit her full force. His eyes widened, startled. "But most people hear it, and then look at me and think of Abraham Lincoln."

He grinned appreciatively, letting his eyes linger on her long brown legs under the khaki shorts. "Well, that's not what comes to my mind," he drawled.

When Shiloh caught his meaning, she flushed in hot confusion. "I didn't—I wasn't—" she stumbled.

Then he looked up into her wide eyes, and what he saw there, she never knew. But his expression altered, his gaze darkening from a teasing flirtatiousness to something more intent, and—she still remembered this with a sense of deep, surprised pleasure—his own face burned red.

"Sorry," he mumbled, and turned away to the truck.

That night, she thought about the way he had looked at her. She didn't like it—and she liked it too much.

The next day Laura caught her watching him from a window; she watched for a minute, too.

"There's nothin' like seein' a man get down and work, especially when he's as fine as that one," she observed sagely. "I reckon he makes a lot of women stop and look. You just remember, Shiloh, that's all you do. Look."

Shiloh stomped down the hall in an embarrassed huff. How many times had Sam and Laura drilled it into her head?

But when Laura took her afternoon nap, Shiloh finally went back out to the porch. This time he knew the minute she stepped out, although they pretended to ignore each other. At last, he went to the canteen he had put with his tools, turned it up and tried to get a drink.

It was empty.

Shiloh knew perfectly well that he could turn on the hose; so did he. In fact, he walked over to it and flipped it on.

But she went to the kitchen anyway, filling a glass with ice and cold water; then she took it back to him, walking up behind him.

"Here," she said.

Startled, he turned, hesitated, then took the glass. "Thanks."

She waited as he tilted his head back to drink, aware of the heat pouring off of him, of sweat drenching and staining his muddy T-shirt, making it cling to him like a second skin.

It made her nervous, but when he held the glass out and she moved away, when he called, "Hey, wait," she stopped willingly.

"You don't have to stay inside because of me," he told her brusquely. "Because of yesterday. No more come-ons. I'll shut up."

She had to look up to him, even with her five-foot-seven-inch height, and it struck her again: she liked him, the way his too-long hair under the edge of the cap turned the color of ripe wheat in the sun, the way his voice held laughter, the way his eyes burned blue.

She was eighteen. She could talk to him if she wanted to.

So she laughed and answered boldly, "I came yesterday to try to get you to talk. I thought I got in your way instead."

"Not in mine. And you can talk all day long if you want to. It won't bother me," Billy Bob answered, grinning at her in relief.

So she had. Not all day, but just all afternoon, while Laura slept.

They talked about the work he was doing, about what they had done in the past and wanted to do in the future, about life in her private school and out at Seven Knobs, the tiny community where he lived.

Shiloh looked forward to every afternoon and wondered if Billy Bob felt the same golden, sparkling thread of excitement that ran through her when they were together.

She thought he did.

He made the job last nearly two weeks; on his next-to-last day, she helped him work around the big snowball bushes at the far side of the yard, and when they stumbled over each other, he caught her—and after a second's hesitation, kissed her.

She'd been waiting for it; so had he.

But there was way too much emotion in that one quick kiss, and he pulled away, while she wondered wildly if every kiss was that shattering, or just the first, or just ones with Billy Bob.

"I didn't mean to do that, I swear it," he gasped at last, running his hand back through his hair, leaving a streak of dirt across his forehead.

"Oh." She didn't know what else to say. "I'm sorry."

"What are you sorry about?" he demanded in frustration.

"Because you—you didn't like kissing me," she floundered.

"I didn't say that!"

"It sounded like it to me."

He took a deep, steadying breath. "Look, Shiloh—you're barely eighteen. I'm twenty-three."

"I don't see what difference that makes."

"You don't see because you're a kid. You don't know anything."

Shiloh returned angrily, upset at the way he'd made her feel too much, aggravated by his stubbornness, "Fine, if that's the way you want it. But I've got sense enough to know what I like and what I want. I wanted you to kiss me, and—and I'm sure that I enjoyed it. Wasn't I supposed to?"

He stared at her a moment, his face indecisive, torn—then he reached out and pulled her to him once again, sweat, dirt, and all.

His lips on hers were the sweetest elixir she'd ever known, as addictive as a deadly narcotic. All she could do was reach in a dizzy panic for him, hold on to his wet shirt, while her heart threatened to beat its way into her throat.

Then he jerked himself away, sucking in breath. "I've gotta go," he said desperately. "Now. And I won't be back, either."

"Billy—"

He reached down, grabbed up his fallen cap, and stalked off across the yard, moving so fast she had to run to catch up with him.

"What did I do?" she asked.

He flung himself into the truck, pausing only a second to look at her in frustration. "You're a whole lot like white lightnin'. You know what that is? It's whiskey. Clear and pure and as innocent-lookin' as water—and it'll knock you flat and leave you dead if you mess around with it too much. I learned early to let it alone, and I can learn to let you alone, too. You're plain trouble."

"But—"

He started the engine viciously, and she said in desperation, "Your tools—you're leaving them. And I'm not trou—"

"Grandpa can get 'em tomorrow," he interrupted, and he sounded angry. Shiloh turned loose of the truck abruptly.

"I don't understand you, Billy Bob. But whatever's wrong, you're a coward, or else you'd try to fix it. So go on—leave."

He did.

Shiloh spent the night crying into her pillow, and the next morning, she looked so terrible that Laura thought she was coming down with a summer virus.

But that afternoon, while Shiloh began to think the

tears might start again as she wandered outside, Billy Bob came back. He climbed out of his vehicle reluctantly, stopping cold when he saw her. She faced him slowly, heart pounding.

"I came back for the tools."

"So get them."

He did, but when he was through, he lingered, finally coming up to the back porch, where she'd retreated.

"Is your housekeeper—"

"She's asleep."

"Oh." He looked down at his boots a minute. "You understand why I have to leave you alone, don't you, Shiloh?"

His face was beseeching when he looked up toward her.

"No," she answered starkly. She didn't see why she should make it easy for him.

"Everything's wrong about it," he explained passionately. "And I'm the first guy you've ever been around. You told me so yourself."

"I talk too much," she managed. "What's that got to do with it?"

He braced a hand on the porch column and looked straight into her eyes. "You might like somebody else a whole lot more than me. I'm just here and handy. The first one you've had to experiment with."

The admission hurt him; his face was as flushed as it had been on that first day. And it hurt her, too.

"I wasn't 'experimenting,' " she retorted, backing away from him. "Maybe *you* were."

"Me!"

"If I'm such a baby—"

"I didn't say that!"

"No? You make it sound horrible that I don't know many men."

"I don't think it's horrible. I think—I think it's sweet. I think *you're* sweet. Nice. And . . . wonderful."

"Well, I don't. Think that about you, I mean. I don't like you at all."

There was a long pause while they stared at each other, her angry, him contrite. A fat bumblebee buzzed noisily on the climbing Don Juan roses at the end of the porch, and at last Shiloh dropped her gaze to say in a stifled voice, "That's not true. I didn't mean it."

He twisted away without another word, going down the steps, and stopped three strides down the brick sidewalk. For a moment he stood, his back to her, struggling with himself, and when he turned around again, it was with a mixture of rebellion and resignation.

"I'm crazy for asking, and your old man's liable to kill us if he catches us, but—if you want to, you could meet me down there"—he motioned toward the distant magnolia trees—"around ten tomorrow night. There's a late dance in Martinsville, over in Tobias County. Surely nobody will know you over there—if you want to go, that is."

"T—ten?" she repeated, shakily.

"I won't let anything happen to you, I promise," he concluded, and the promise was written on his face like a banner.

She couldn't speak, so she nodded wordlessly instead, and the tears glistening in her eyes weren't like the ones she'd cried last night. Not at all.

They spent six weeks together, meeting two times a week, three toward the end when they couldn't get enough of each other. Shiloh didn't know how they'd gone from teasing and dancing to these heavy emotions; she just knew she was experiencing the most wonderful time of her life. For the first time, she was on her own. Free, and in love.

Billy Bob didn't seem to understand what had happened either, and there were times when he openly worried about where they were heading. But neither of them seemed able to stop . . . until Sam found out.

Her father confronted her with his knowledge of her fling with Billy Bob in late July—and dragged her down to the magnolias that night to face him.

In thirty minutes, he destroyed a whole summer and a good part of her heart. Billy had finished the job when he'd done just exactly what Sam had predicted.

It hadn't helped her ego any to see Billy Bob with Angie Blake; it had, in fact, hurt like sixty. But it started the final cauterization of her emotions.

When Sam had urged her to reconsider colleges, she knew exactly what he was up to, and still agreed without much resistance, so she wound up in another private school, an expensive, reputable university in Tennessee.

A long way from Billy Bob, virtually under lock and key. Sam would have been completely happy if only the school had forbidden male students to enter. But it didn't, so he checked on her regularly, and then began sending Michael in his place in an obvious matchmaking scheme.

She first met Michael the winter following her summer with Billy Bob, when Robert Sewell and Sam began to get friendly. She had known the first time she ever looked at the judge that he was Billy's father, but Sam had been watching her for a reaction, so she had carefully hidden the hard jolt her heart gave.

She didn't like Sewell, and she never asked herself why. But she got used to his looks, so that by the time she met Michael, she was prepared.

He was everything that Billy Bob wasn't, everything Sam wanted in her husband: successful, socially adept, politically correct.

The first time Sam introduced them, it was almost with an air of triumph. She knew why: He was presenting her with an acceptable male who came packaged almost just like the one he hadn't let her keep.

She didn't tell him that she was over Billy Bob, or that she had dated a few others since at the university without his august permission, just as she didn't tell him how stifled he was making her feel. And if she were honest, she'd have to admit that she had liked Michael in the beginning, before she knew him.

Now here she was back with Billy Bob, despite all of her father's best-laid plans. Maybe because of them. At least she wasn't afraid of Billy. And if it was unflattering to remember how hard she'd had to work to get him to agree to this marriage, it was worth it because she could trust him.

He would do his part.

Shiloh remembered suddenly the animal grace of him as he had paced the cell; it brought back another memory, the way the muscles under his skin once felt to her touch.

Some things hadn't changed, she thought quietly: Billy Bob Walker was still fine to look at. Laura had been right about that from the beginning.

# 7

Sam *was out* of town on Saturday. Shiloh spent the day alone and restless, and finally took the car she'd been using all week and went for a drive. The day was calm and still—everything she wasn't.

On Sunday morning, when she came down to breakfast, her father was dressed to go out and waiting for her.

"I don't want you to do something desperate again, Shiloh," he said sardonically, "so I'll tell you in advance. The judge will be here this afternoon. So will Michael. If you choose not to be, that's your business—this time. But you have a wedding in a few weeks, so you'd do well to get over this fit of nerves in the next day or two."

"Why don't you ask him how he felt when he bit me? That was right after he tore my shirt off."

"Shiloh!" Sam's face flamed red in shocked embarrassment, and she felt her own cheeks blaze at the words that hurt and anger pulled from her.

Then she turned and ran upstairs.

♦ ♦ ♦

"Billy! Billy Bob!"

He came awake with a start, the hot rays of the after-noon sun making his face burn. The jail cell was stuffy and too warm.

"Billy!"

Pulling himself up groggily from the cot, he tried to find the voice. He knew it already, but Shiloh was not at the bars to the cell. Then she called again, and he realized with surprise that she was outside the window.

"Shiloh?"

There she stood, in the empty parking lot, looking up at his window. But this was not déjà vu—there was no red Porsche, and today she had on tight, leggy blue jeans, and her face looked as if she'd been crying. She'd changed her mind—he already knew.

"Were you asleep?"

"Must have been," he answered slowly. "What's wrong?"

"Is it—is it still on for tomorrow?" She swallowed heavily, glancing away.

"You mean—"

"Our getting married."

He took a long, considering breath. Now was his own chance to cut and run.

"If you still want to do it, it is," he answered instead.

"I still want to," she answered resolutely. "But when?"

"I'll give T-Tommy the money first thing in the morn-ing. After he gets over the shock, I guess he'll have to do things—fill out papers, I don't know. I'll meet you as soon as I can." A little rush of effervescent excitement shot through him, a tiny, quicksilver stiletto of anticipation that slid through his ribs.

"But where? I've already told Mr. Parsons I wouldn't be in tomorrow. Family matters, I said. He won't dare question that," Shiloh told him with a trace of irony. "Now, where? We don't want to be seen."

Why not, he wanted to ask. Instead, he pondered a minute.

"Where are we going to do it?" he asked.

"I thought—Memphis. It's a big city. Nobody will notice us."

He frowned. "You've got a point. So, meet me out at the old gin. You can park in the back. Nobody will see anything. I'll come as soon as . . . as I get out."

She nodded, then raked her hair back from her face.

She definitely had been crying.

"Are you sure you want to do this?" Billy Bob asked her roughly.

"I'm sure."

"Then what in the hell have you been crying about?"

Her hands went to her cheeks in confusion, then she dropped them. "All brides cry," she said flippantly.


The deserted old cotton gin leaned precariously to the right, a giant, graying skeleton of lumber nearly hidden from the road by a heavy stand of emerald pine trees. The morning air was pungent with the sharp tang of the pine needles.

Once the two-lane asphalt highway that ran past the gin had bustled with business, but a newer road to the north had since turned this one into a leisurely local thoroughfare, so somnolent that farmers on tractors or pulling hay wagons felt comfortable ambling down it.

When Billy Bob turned the truck off the highway and into the gravel road leading behind the gin, no one saw him. He felt a little silly even checking, but then this whole business had a clandestine feel to it that made him act like James Bond.

She was waiting for him when he pulled in, leaning up against a small blue Cadillac—it was Sam's brand of car—in a pair of dark sunglasses that made her look remote. She wore white, too, though it was hardly bridal. Shiloh's gleaming, snowy suit boasted a jacket whose lapels veed sharply, deeply downward, revealing the hollow between her breasts and making Billy wonder nervously if she was wearing anything at all under it.

Her long legs ended in high white heels that pushed her feet into delicate arches, and his eyes lingered on them before he turned off the motor and climbed out, a sudden dark reluctance in him as he faced the girl who was straightening off her car.

The truth hit him hard: This icy fashion plate with the perfect hair and elegant legs and designer clothes was a stranger. He didn't like the way she looked; she made him feel like a welfare case in his jeans and white shirt. And somehow the contrast between the two of them made it clear that it really was just a business proposition, an ugly one: one rich lady buying herself a commodity—him.

"Sorry I'm late," he told her abruptly, as she took a step toward him. "I gave the money to T-Tommy and his mouth dropped open so far he tripped over it. The old buzzard put me through the wringer tryin' to figure out where I got it."

"Do you think he suspects me?" Her voice eased his tension and took a little of the starch out of him. It was husky and sweet as usual, but there was a little tremor in it.

Shiloh was not as cool and calm as she appeared, thank God.

But he wouldn't apologize for his clothes. "I don't think so. But he made me so late I just got out of the jail and came straight here."

"It's okay. But we'd better hurry."

He nodded, and they both started moving, each to his own vehicle. Then both stopped.

"There's no point in takin' both," he pointed out reasonably. And he didn't add, I'll be damned if I'll crawl in Sam Pennington's Caddy, either.

"You're right. You can ride with me," she offered.

"What's wrong with my truck?" he asked belligerently.

She shrugged. "Nothing, except the car's air-conditioned. And there's more room for those long legs of yours." She glanced downward, and Billy's heart gave a hard jerk of surprise. Shiloh never made personal remarks. Even if this one hadn't been especially provocative, it said clearly that she'd been looking at him.

Billy didn't know whether to be dismayed or pleased. He chose a little of both.

"My legs will be fine in the truck," he answered shortly.

"I don't want to leave the car here. I doubt that anybody would find it, but the whole world knows it's one of Sam's." She gestured toward the license plate with its distinctive "S.P." tag. "If it sits here, and somebody sees it, they'll call T-Tommy again, and this game is over before it gets started."

Then she turned back to the car decisively. "Besides, it's got a full tank of gas."

He'd opened his mouth to argue, but her comment made him shut it abruptly. Billy remembered suddenly that he had exactly $36.00 to his name. If something happened to his truck—and it had one bald tire—he might not have the money to fix it, let alone fill it up with gas.

So it was with extreme reluctance and a tinge of anger that he finally went after the high-handed miss who was already sliding into the car.

The driver seat, no less. She was clearly the one in charge here.

You sell yourself like so much merchandise, and that's the way you get treated, Billy Bob thought bitterly, and without another word, he climbed into the passenger seat.

It smelled of expensive leather and her light perfume; this princess coach with her alligator purse on the carpet at his feet and a folded yellow umbrella on the dash was a foreign world.

And the squealing little buzzer that went off when he opened the door wouldn't shut up until he wrapped the seat belt over himself and snapped it closed. Caught and imprisoned by his own hand.

Then they sat staring at each other in silence.

Billy finally made a sweeping motion that invited her to move on. "It's your party, honey. You gonna get on with it, or sit here all day?"

And without another word, she pulled away from the shelter of the gin.

They drove in silence for a while, while he slid glances over at her and considered the way she handled the car. Smooth. A little too quick to go for the gas, but that was all.

She looked totally in control, so he moved to break her hold, flipping on the radio without asking her permission.

When he found a steel-rich, fiddle-crazy song about women and drinking, he left the dial right there.

Still she said nothing.

"That's the damnedest outfit I ever saw any bride wear," he told her at last.

She glanced over at him in surprise. "What's wrong with it?"

"Nothing, if you want to keep the preacher or the JP or whoever it is who marries us hopped up on pins and needles wondering if you've got on anything under that jacket," he answered bluntly.

Her cheeks flushed. "What's wrong with you these days?" she snapped. "You never used to say stuff like that."

"Don't avoid the question," he retorted. "Do you?"

She opened her mouth as if to spit her anger at him but suddenly seemed to change her mind. Instead, her hand went to the buttons on the coat, twisting them deliberately through the button holes.

"You can see for yourself," she taunted unevenly.

Billy couldn't tear his eyes away from her hand, and when she finally pushed the jacket open, his heart hit several hundred beats a minute.

She had on a cool white camisole top, as deeply veed as the jacket but otherwise completely safe.

His momentary relief wasn't much help. "You never used to do stuff like that," he counter-accused.

"So what's *your* reason?" she demanded, shooting an angry glare at him.

"Why'd I say it, you mean? I guess because I don't like the way you look."

She said derisively, with only a trace of hurt in her voice, "You and Sam. He's out to protect my reputation. Why are you so concerned?"

"You don't look real. You look like—like some ice queen behind those big glasses and in that hot little outfit. You sit on your little throne over there moving the rest of the world around like pawns. Don't you think I'd rather have paid my own way out of jail?" he returned in frustration.

She took a deep breath and her hands tightened on the steering wheel. "Than to marry me, you mean?"

He said nothing.

"We don't have to do this," she told him at last. "We can find a place to turn around."

There was a long, stark silence.

"Do what you want," muttered Billy at last. "I'll pay you back the money as soon as I can."

"I don't want the money," she returned hotly. "It's not important."

"Not important!" His voice was incredulous; then he laughed. "That just shows how little you know about the real world, honey. I bet everything I don't have that you've never been without money, or your charge cards, or a nice little checkbook in your whole life, have you?"

Shiloh bit her lip and kept driving.

"That's what I thought," Billy answered triumphantly. "You buy your fancy clothes that I don't even know you in, you'll buy a new car to replace the one you smashed to pieces, you even bought me. Well, I wish I'd cost you a whole lot more, Shiloh. Thousands more. You should have had to pay enough to make you at least think about me and what you were doing to me when you made that offer."

When she stopped the car, they both sat breathing furiously. Where had all the anger come from, Billy wondered wildly. He hadn't known it was in him until it spilled out on her in a dark, acidic tide.

"Forget it," she whispered, never looking at him. "I'll find another way to fight Sam."

"Shiloh, I'm sorry." The words hung in his throat, but he got them out.

She shook her head wordlessly, swallowing heavily. But as her hand reached for the gear shift, Billy caught it, taking both of them by surprise.

It was warm, her skin smooth to his touch—the first touch since the other night in the jail cell. He'd remembered the brush of her hand every day since.

She looked at him in wary shock and tried to pull away, but he held her fingers firmly.

"I said I'm sorry," he told her huskily. "I don't know why I said it, except I'm feeling pretty low right now. I don't like me much, and I'm takin' it out on you."

She just watched him, like a wide-eyed child behind the dark glasses.

Slowly, carefully, he reached out and pulled the dark shades away from her face. Behind them was the girl he'd spent a night in jail with, not the cool snob who'd come home from college with her nose so high in the air she couldn't see him.

"I don't want to marry you now," she told him defensively.

He was so close to her, he could see the pulses beating in her throat.

"So you'll do what? Find somebody else?"

He shook his head before she could answer.

"It won't be the same. I'm perfect for what you need," Billy told her flatly. "If you'll just quit making me feel like a hobo you've picked up out of the goodness of your heart, we'll be all right. Do you think I like gettin' married lookin' like this"—he gestured down at his old clothes—

"when my—my bride looks like you do? And she's footin' the bill, too?"

Shiloh let her brown gaze slide from his face, down the brown length of his throat to the open collar of the white shirt, down to his waist, and out his long arm where the sleeve was rolled up to his elbow.

"You look all right," she told him in surprise, as if she'd never even considered him worth looking at before.

"Thanks," he said wryly, then let his own gaze travel down to that deep vee again where her white shirt contrasted sharply with her warm skin. "You look . . . too good."

Her face suddenly flushed, and her lips opened a little.

Billy watched them a minute. He knew what he was going to do. He was going to make his peace on her lips, then he was going to shut up and marry this girl.

"Billy—" The word held a panicky protest as his mouth drew near hers. "Billy, if you kiss me, this whole thing is off, and I want my money back."

He stared at her, his face darkening. "What in hell for?"

"I told you, it's business. I'm not getting into anything else. I just want this mess straightened out." Her words were rushed.

They hurt his ego. "I don't think that's why. I think you're scared to death."

"Of you?" She tried hard to sound scornful.

"Of me, and of kissing me, and of being here with me right now," he accused.

"You're crazy. I don't want to kiss you because that's got nothing to do with our deal. And besides"—Shiloh knew she should quit while she was ahead, but her tongue wouldn't obey—"I've heard you spread yourself thin.

You're available to everything in skirts these days. I'd rather have kisses that are a little bit fresher, from a man who's a little more discriminating. Yours are too cheap for my taste."

For an instant she actually thought he might hit her; then his face flushed red as he pulled away from her and faced forward out the window.

At last she reached for the gear shift, and to her surprise, her hand was shaking a little. "We'll go back," she whispered.

"No."

He never looked at her; his jaw was as tight and set as granite. "No, we won't. We'll get this over with, because I don't have the damn money to repay you. And when it's done, and we get back to Sweetwater, you walk on your side of the street and I'll walk on mine."

"But—"

"And when you finally get up the nerve to tell Sam, you send word to me and we'll end it. Then I won't owe you one red cent, and I swear to God I'll never come near you again. So drive on. Have the guts to do what you set out to do at least."

And after a long, long moment of indecision, Shiloh pulled from the little park and headed out—toward Memphis.

She'd paid good money for him, after all.


The Shelby County Administration Building was big and crowded, and they waited for a little while in line.

Then it was simple. Quick. Cold-blooded. Painless.

They proved they were over eighteen with their driver's licenses. They signed the marriage license. And Shiloh paid the fee.

"No," she told him as he reached for his wallet, "it's my party, remember? I'm paying."

"Fine," he said stonily.

And that was that.

The marriage was more difficult.

The judge who married them was easy to locate, just a little way from where they bought the license. He was young, round, and prematurely bald—nothing at all like Robert Sewell.

Billy took time to be grateful for that small mercy, but he tried not to look down past the man's nose so that he wouldn't notice his robe.

They had little or no trouble finding witnesses. The next couple waiting to be married—both barely out of their teens—were pressed into service by the judge.

"Now, I believe we've got everything," he declared at last in relief. "If you will just stand here"—he motioned fussily to a spot somewhere in front of him—"we'll get this started."

He glanced down at the license. "You're William Robert Walker—I always like to get names down properly. And you're Shiloh—what a lovely name—Pennington. No middle name?"

"No," she said, her voice tiny and a little nervous.

"Fine, fine. Let's see, you've got license, witnesses—how about the rings?"

They stared blankly at the judge for a minute.

"Rings," Shiloh murmured helplessly, looking up at Billy Bob, and there was a long waiting pause.

"I think we forgot the rings," he told the judge at last.

The man looked from one of them to the other, his pumpkin-shaped face puzzled. Then he asked slowly, "Is this marriage a hasty one? Something you've only recently decided to do?"

And for the first time he stopped and looked them over—Shiloh in the white suit, Billy in the worn jeans. He couldn't help but notice how Shiloh was standing well away from the man beside her instead of holding his hand or hugging up to him the way the happy two waiting their turn were standing.

"Perhaps you'd like to talk to one another in private," the judge added at last.

"No," Shiloh replied quickly.

"We've done all the talking we need to do," said Billy ironically.

"But both of you seem so unprepared—"

"Reckon we're better at things besides talking," Billy drawled outrageously, reaching out to wrap his big hand around Shiloh's upper arm. "You could say we're sorta gettin' married in a fever."

The judge's cheeks flushed nearly as darkly as Shiloh's. "Marriage is not something to do on a spare day," he said repressively, "or on a whim with a person you barely know, or somebody you've met as a . . . a one-night acquaintance." He could barely get out the last three words.

"I've known him four years," Shiloh interposed, "and here, I'll use this for a ring. He can get me one later, or something." She tugged hurriedly at the gold college ring she wore, and when it slid off, she held it out for the judge's inspection.

"Well, if this is what you want," he said reluctantly, then opened his tiny black book with the civil wedding ceremony in it.

Billy remembered to reach up and pull off the cap,

holding it in one hand. Then he remembered more, that once he had thought about eloping somewhere with Shiloh. It had sounded dangerous, and exciting, and romantic. But the reality was something far different.

The judge's chambers were routine and boring. The paneled walls held recessed shelves full of heavy dark books, volumes of law, no doubt. The desk in the corner by the window was neat as a pin with only a picture of a blond-haired woman and a little girl with her father's pumpkin-shaped face sitting on it. And outside the window were buildings and rows of more buildings against the blue of the afternoon sky. When the sun poured in through the panes, it fell on a commercial tourist painting—a collage of sorts about Tennessee—that somebody had hung on the wall.

He was getting married, Billy thought, not in the eyes of God and friends, but under the watchful gaze of Andrew Jackson and Roy Acuff as they stared down from that collage; even a youthful Elvis sneered at them.

And as the judge began, a loud jet swept over the building on its way to a landing at the Memphis airport, nearly drowning the words.

He wished he'd never done this. He wished he were modern and up-to-date, as casual about marriage as the rest of humanity seemed to be nowadays. He wished he didn't remember that he'd also once thought of marrying this same girl in the little church at Seven Knobs where his mother went, where old Brother Thompson talked about a friendly God and knew Billy Bob the child and Billy Bob the man and loved him anyway, in spite of his predilection for Saturday-night carousing and Sunday-morning sleeping-in.

He wanted to go home, away from this strange judge,

and the two teenagers, and Elvis and Roy—and away from the woman by his side who was repeating her vows calmly enough.

". . . until death do us part." Her voice was so low it was barely audible.

"You may give him the ring as a token of the promise you have made," the judge informed Shiloh gravely, and she nodded jerkily and held the ring out toward him.

He remembered to hold out his hand, and she hesitated a minute, uncertain what to do. The ring was small, his hand large, twice the size of hers. It might, with effort, fit his little finger.

On that thought, Billy took her hand in his right one, catching it along with the cap he still held, and all of a sudden, as if an electric bolt of knowledge had been hooked into him, Billy felt her true emotions: her hand was trembling a little, too warm and too wet with perspiration. She was as uptight as he was, and the knowledge sent a wave of relief through him.

Her dark hair looked nearly auburn in the light from the window, and as he stared down at the top of her bent head, she looked up in one fleeting, puzzled glance at his stillness.

Shiloh had always had the brownest eyes he'd ever seen—as wide as an inquiring deer's. Eyes that led you straight down to her soul, if you only knew how to see it.

Right now, at this minute, they were the same eyes he'd fallen into that afternoon he'd first seen her on the back porch of Sam's house. It didn't matter that this was Memphis, not Seven Knobs, and that all the years had come between them.

For a few seconds, he could forget Sam and Sewell and his brother, Michael, and just remember that he'd once loved her.

He pushed her hand toward the finger he had extended, showing her to slide the ring on it. It hung on his knuckle—he might have to cut the gold band off—but it went on at last.

Her fingers clung to his for a minute, and he wrapped her hand in his and held on.

The judge, satisfied, continued. "And do you, William Robert Walker, take this woman . . ."

He got out the words by watching the judge's face; she was watching his, her head tilted to see him as he spoke. Why?

The judge tried to be gracious. "Since there is no ring, you may kiss your bride as a token of these vows."

He didn't look at her as he bent quickly toward her cheek; in spite of everything, her words burned in his ears. His kisses were "too cheap" for her taste.

But as he laid his lips coolly against her skin, she suddenly shocked him by turning her head, and her mouth found his, pressing against it, clinging for an instant. It was a fleeting touch, but every nerve, every cell, every fiber in him went on red-hot, instant alert.

*He remembered her.*

The scent of her skin. The feel of her face against his. The taste of her mouth.

He thought he'd remembered, but he hadn't. His memories held only a fraction of the reality. *This* was Shiloh. This pounding in the veins. This taste of sweetness. This weight against him.

It hurt, the sudden resurrection of long-buried, intense sensation, so he pulled away in self-preservation, and she dropped her head and cut off the visual link, and then he remembered one more thing: why he hated her. She'd made him feel this alive once before, then walked away and left him trying to find the same fire in the blood with somebody else. Anybody else.

She'd left him half-alive, trying to survive, desperate.

". . . and I pronounce you man and wife," said the judge expansively, beaming at them.

"Thank you," said Billy Bob, and then he dropped Shiloh's hand and turned away.


Shiloh decided to stop and eat out of boredom. The big man in the car with her had been deathly quiet ever since they'd pulled out of Memphis a half hour ago. Now they were well into Mississippi.

What was wrong with him? Still sulking because she hadn't liked his reputation with women? Tough, she thought without much sympathy.

But there was more than that: something had happened in the judge's chambers.

*You* happened, you idiot, she thought to herself. Why did you have to go and kiss him after the fuss you raised? There was no reason for it. *None.*

Except, he'd been close. Too close. And as he stood there beside her, his head and shoulders above her, his hand hard and warm around hers, he hadn't been Billy Walker, the wild man of Briskin County. Instead, he'd been tall and strong and handsome, and solid as a rock. He'd been the man she'd once thought he was, somebody who loved her, not because he needed to control her or because she looked like her mother or because he was afraid of being alone, but because he liked her as she was, because he wanted to be with her.

And there was a strong sexual attraction to Billy, too, something that had nothing to do with love. Shiloh saw clearly now what Laura had once warned her about. It was in the way he moved, in the strong column of his neck, in the lazy, easy way he had of slanting sideways looks at her, in his slow smile.

Billy Bob dripped sex appeal.

As she'd watched his lips as he repeated the vows, she thought with a sharp, tearing pang that it would be paradise to have a man love her the way she wanted to be loved, to have a man with this brand of potent attraction swearing fidelity to her, offering his strength and his loyalty to her, and honest-to-God meaning it.

And that thought made her twist her head a fraction of an inch and touch his lips.

Warmth. The taste of salt. And the realization that he was startled—and wary—and too quick to pull away. She caught all those sensations.

It was nothing like their kisses of old, but there'd been just enough to tantalize and begin a slow swirl around the still, puddled edges of emotions.

But reality had to intrude: Billy kissed a lot of girls. He knew his way around women. Those emotions were old hat to him.

Weren't they?


"Want to get something to eat?" Shiloh asked as she pulled in at a little restaurant called the Rebel Inn.

Billy looked at it and shrugged. "Sure."

"Are you hungry?"

He considered that a minute. "What time is it?" he asked instead.

She glanced at her wrist. "Three-thirty."

"Then I guess I am."

"When did you last eat?"

"Breakfast, at the jail."

"Me, too. Breakfast, that is. But I was so nervous I couldn't eat much."

She opened her door and climbed out, leaving him to follow suit, and he caught up with her at the glass entrance door, which he pushed open for her.

It was a middle-of-the-road place, not too fancy, not too plain, mostly empty at this time of day.

Catfish was the specialty, so they both had it, and when the waitress left, Billy asked abruptly, "What were you nervous about?"

It took a minute for her to remember what he was referring to.

"Oh, I don't know. I just never got married before."

"There wasn't much to it."

"No. I guess, in real marriage, the hard part starts now."

He thought about that for a minute. "Well, things won't change for us. Except, you may wake up tomorrow morning and be sorry. What if you and Michael, you know, patch things up? What'll you do about me?"

She watched him a minute. He was looking down at a napkin that he was methodically tearing in shreds, his long fingers slow and steady. Her gold ring glinted as he worked.

He infuriated her some times, but she wanted him to understand that there was no chance she would seesaw back to Michael. Maybe she had used him handily today; she still owed Billy this much. And she thought he needed to know.

"I won't ever be back with Michael," she said decisively. "So don't think, no matter what you hear, that there's a chance in a million of it happening."

He gave her one of his slanting glances; it was speculative.

"And what am I gonna hear?"

"Who knows? Sam may insist on having a wedding."

"And you'll do what?"

"If I can't make him believe that I'd rather be horsewhipped than look at Michael, I'll tell him that there's a small problem. You," Shiloh said steadily.

He put down the napkin and reached for the iced tea the waitress set down in front of them.

"I'm asking you to let me know before you tell your daddy," he said. "There's people I've got to talk to first."

A sharp little arrow of anger shot through Shiloh. Of course, she thought. "There'll be time for you to break the news to An—to your girlfriends. They'll never notice you're married, it'll be over so fast. I promise."

"I was talking about Mama and Grandpa," he retorted. "And maybe it won't be over so fast. Maybe I'll have to wait a little while for this—this divorce for their sakes. I can't tell 'em about the money. Not without—"

"Billy," she said quietly, a little ashamed, "I never meant to make you feel like, well, like you'd been bought and paid for. You're doing me a favor, really."

"Don't ask me for any more like this one," he answered darkly, and the waitress brought the huge platters of golden, battered catfish and baked potatoes oozing butter.

After they'd been eating a few minutes, Billy observed as he licked butter off his thumb, "You don't eat like a New York model, at least."

"What does that mean?" she demanded, putting down her fork.

"No salads, or fruit dishes, or lemon ice water," he answered, and there was a hint of a grin on his face.

"I happen to like catfish," she informed him.

"That's fine by me. So do I." He slid another look over at her. "Since you're the little wife now," he said daringly, and the word sounded strange to Shiloh's ears, "does this mean you do my cooking and cleaning?"

"I wouldn't want to deprive your mother of the pleasure," Shiloh told him sweetly.

"She won't mind. You can scratch my back every night, too. Mama doesn't do that."

"Neither do I," Shiloh answered primly, reaching for her napkin.

"Well, I'll be liberated about it," Billy offered, and his long blue eyes sparkled with humor and suggestiveness. "I'll come over to your house and scratch yours. Anytime. And once Pennington and Michael get wind of that, you won't need to tell 'em anything."

"Thanks, anyway," Shiloh answered. "But you don't have to give up your spare nights for me. You can just keep on with your life."

He put down the glass and pushed his plate away. His face held little or no humor as he looked at her, and he asked abruptly, "So it's okay if I show up at the Palace Saturday night with whoever. Or at the Legion Hall dance. That's where you meet all the girls like you. The ones who don't go to the Palace, who—"

"That's right," Shiloh interrupted. What had he been expecting? That she had thought today would mean something? "It's okay with me."

He looked at her a minute, then gave a little, under-his-breath laugh. "I'd'a swore you were different from this, Shiloh."

"I understand the rules, that's all," she said, shrugging. "But if this were a real marriage, if we'd really run off and gotten married, I'd keep my husband at home, Billy Bob. I'd make sure he wanted to stay there. And—and I'd skin him alive if I caught him out at the Legion Hall with another woman." She flung her napkin down. "Look, I'm ready to go."

She reached for the check, and he got there first, pushing her hand away in determination.

"You know what?" he said in exasperation. "You and your money are gettin' to be a real pain in the neck. I'm payin' for it. And you know what else? I'd rather be married to some ordinary girl who cared enough to skin me alive than to you and your little rules of the game. She'd be a whole lot more fun."

He towered over her for a minute, his eyes blazing blue, before he reached for the cap and slung it on, then walked away.

Shiloh watched him go and wondered why he had the power to hurt her. Why did it matter what he said? He was probably mad because she hadn't fallen for that line of his. And he needn't pull that "I'd rather be married" stuff on her; he could have had Angie long ago if he had wanted to settle down.

The waitress said something to him at the checkout. He laughed.

And for a second, Shiloh wondered what it would be like if she took him at his word, went over there and slid her arm around his narrow waist and told him—this new husband of hers—that she wanted to go home with him.

He'd change his tune then, but he might take her up on part of her offer, at least for the night.

But outside, she tossed the keys at him, and as he caught them against his chest, she told him casually, "You drive. I'm tired." She was no fool; she'd caught on fairly rapidly that his lack of control over this situation was getting to him, and it seemed to be symbolized by this car. So she would give in to his masculine ego a little—let him drive if he wanted to.

But she watched him on the way home.

"What's the matter?" he asked at last.

"Just wondering what kind of husband you'd really make."

"A damned good one," he answered flatly.

"I don't believe it."

"Wait and see. Someday I'm going to find a woman that I'm crazy about—"

"And reform. Right?" There was a sharp pain in her throat that made it hard to get the words out.

When he looked at her again, his face was serious. "I'm not nearly as bad as you think I am. Nor the town, either. They like to gossip. I hear things I'm s'posed to have done that I never thought of doing. And I'm gonna be some-body . . . have something. I'll do as well as Michael. Wait and see. It's just taking me longer."

A hard blur of tears suddenly rose up in her throat, and she looked down at her clenched hands.

"You're already better than Michael, Billy. Believe me."

He looked at her sharply; she felt it.

"Why'd you get with him, Shiloh?" he asked at last, painfully. "Of all the people."

She couldn't tell the truth, couldn't say after all these years, He reminded me of you for a while. So instead, she shrugged. "It was easy. He was there. Sam liked him. And he's smooth, or he used to be."

"You loved him."

"No. I never did. And I'm no liar, Billy."

He clenched the steering wheel with both hands, his

knuckles turning white. "Then that makes it worse than ever, seems to me."

Shiloh said nothing; it suddenly seemed that way to her, too.

They rode in silence for a while, until at last the old gin came into sight. Behind it, in the late evening shadows, his truck sat parked in a brilliant yellow clump of black-eyed Susans as if nothing had happened.

As if she hadn't left here this morning brash and defiant and single, and returned this evening married and filled with old regrets.

He climbed out of the Cadillac quickly, and she followed more slowly. At the truck, he turned.

"Well." The one word was nearly lost on the dewy air, sweet with fresh-blooming honeysuckle. "You know where to find me if you need me," he said at last. The long afternoon shadows touched his face, made the blue of his eyes and the white of his teeth all that showed up distinctly.

He shoved his hands in the pockets of his jeans and stood looking down at her.

"I once imagined being married to you," Shiloh said suddenly, the words spilling before she could stem them.

A muscle ticked in his cheek. "Maybe this way's better. Now you get to go back to your own little world, with your housekeeper and your Cadillac."

"And you can go back to the Legion Hall," she said flatly, "and the Palace."

"Yeah."

He reached up to rub his neck, and she saw the gold ring.

"My ring," she said, motioning toward it. "You won't need it."

He looked at her a minute, then at the ring. "I can't get

it off," he said at last. "You'll have to wait until I get home and put soap on it."

"Then what? You'll mail it to me?"

"Something like that," he answered quizzically.

She nodded, then started to turn away.

Quick as a flash, his right hand shot out to catch her arm. She looked back at him, startled.

"What—"

"Why'd you kiss me in the judge's office?"

His question threw her completely off balance, into a stammering shock.

"He—the judge told me to."

"And you do everything he told you?" A shimmer of humor lighted his face for a second. "That's good to know—because you made a promise in front of him—something about being faithful to me."

"Don't get any ideas about this marriage being real, Billy."

"I've already got 'em, Shiloh. Ideas . . . and questions. Like, why'd you marry me? Why'd you kiss me? And I've got some for myself: why'd I agree? And why'd I *let* you kiss me after all you'd said? But most of all, I wonder why I liked it. I ought'a hate you."

He was nearly smiling down into her face, such an odd mix of teasing and sobriety in his expression that she could only stare up at him in an uneasy, angry caution.

She tried to wrench her arm free without success. "Is that all?" she demanded.

"Just one more thing," he said mildly. Then he grasped her chin in his left hand and pulled her mouth up to his fiercely.

The kiss took her by surprise, his lips hard and sure, and she felt his tongue as he touched her lips but went no farther. The tips of his fingers warm and tight on her jaw—she felt them, too, and her heart as it thudded up into her throat, under his hand as it wrapped her neck.

Then he pulled away, letting his lips linger, letting his fingers brush through her hair, down to the hollow of her throat, and into the vee of her blouse, and his eyes were bright and vivid as he said huskily, "We may have some kind of weird marriage here that's not for real, but I'm not as big and understanding about it as you are, honey. Everytime I see you in town, I'm gonna think, that woman is my wife. I'm not gonna like it one damn bit if you're off with somebody else, and I'll get plain mad if I see you wearing Michael's ring again."

"I told you," she began hotly, about to argue fair play, about to protest, when he flattened his hand against the warm bare skin of her chest, his palm heavy and deliberate against her breasts.

The insolent touch knocked her off balance, left her gasping, and she grabbed his wrist with both hands, meaning to push him away, but he put his other hand lightly across her lips to cut off her words and said cheerfully, "Yeah, I heard you. All those rules of yours for me. I can do anything, right? But these are my rules for you, baby—you can't. As long as you're my wife, stay away from other men."

Then he pulled away, slid in the truck, and said with a flashing grin, "See you at the Legion Hall."

"Billy!" She got her breath back in time to scream after him as the old truck roared away and left her in a cloud of red Mississippi dust. "Billy Bob Walker—you come back here! Right now!"

# 8

"*Where have you* been?"

Her father's voice came out of the shadows at the side of the porch to take her by surprise. It wasn't dark yet, but here, under the roof and the big trees, it very nearly was.

"You scared me." She caught back any confessions; she couldn't give away her ace-in-the-hole—that swaggering blond devil—just yet. "I took a day off."

Sam rose from the wicker chair to face her as she halted uneasily at the edge of the porch. "Without tellin' anybody?"

"I told Mr. Parsons."

"Family business? That was a lie, Shiloh. Now, where have you been?" His face was contained and stiff; his voice was furious.

"I don't have to tell you everything I do!"

"No? Maybe not, but what am I supposed to think when two days ago you yell at me that you're gonna leave for good, and today, nobody knows where the hell you are?" His voice shook an instant before it hardened into anger again.

"You thought I'd left home," Shiloh whispered at last, as realization dawned.

"It's what you wanted me to think," Sam answered accusingly, and he reached up to unbutton the top button of his shirt, only to find he'd already undone it and loosened the tie. He breathed heavily. "Well, wasn't it?"

"No. I just needed to get away and think," Shiloh offered lamely.

"You don't miss work for such lame reasons as that," he snapped. "You've had Laura worried sick."

"I didn't mean to. It's good to know *you* couldn't have cared less," she snapped back.

He turned, rumpling up his already wrinkled suit jacket to ram both hands into his pockets and stand staring at her. Even in the shadows, she saw the pinched lines around his nose and mouth, the tiredness in his face.

"Papa," she said involuntarily, and he let go of all his breath in a sudden expulsion of defeat.

"I thought you'd gone, Shiloh," he said at last, wearily. "I'm tired of fighting. Why can't we get along?"

She swallowed the emotions choking her and rubbed her forehead where a headache had begun to pound. "You want everything your way," she told him. "We get along when I don't fight it."

"Shiloh." He said her name abruptly. "I'll be damned if I ever understand you, but I'll give a little, if you will."

She dropped her hand to stare at him in surprised wariness. "Give what?"

"I told Michael today to give you time, to leave you alone for a few weeks."

"And—and the wedding?"

"We'll postpone it, a little while," he said evasively. "I think this is nerves, Shiloh, that's all."

"And what will happen when I don't ever agree for the wedding to take place?" she asked carefully.

"We'll wait and see. But you'll get over these feelings, and be glad Michael's still here," he answered with his usual self-righteous bullheadedness. "There's not many men that'd be willin' to hang around. He loves you."

Shiloh looked at him, wanting desperately to make her peace with him, but knowing full well this was a long way from over. Still, here at least was a breathing space.

"I don't like feeling as sick as I did today when I thought I was really gonna have to track you down and bring you home," Sam said huskily, and his face blurred a little around the edges as if he were trying hard to hold on to control.

She took a step toward him. "You could just let me go, Papa. Turn loose a little."

He shook his head. "No. I'm not an old fool yet. I know what I've got in you. You're a pretty good kid. And I know down inside me that you want to do what's right. No matter what I holler when I'm mad, I know you'd never deliberately hurt me, or disappoint me. In the end, you'll do me proud."

Have I mentioned that I got married this afternoon? The guilty words hovered on the tip of her tongue. But no, she knew Sam. She might need Billy Bob yet. Wait, wait, she cautioned herself.

"I'm not a saint," she told him at last.

"You wouldn't be mine if you were," he answered, his mouth twisting in a smile. "A little peace for a while, Shiloh?"

She took two steps closer to him. "Just for a little while."

He laughed in relief, then slid an arm around her shoulders. It had been a long, long time since he'd hugged her; Sam was not a man who believed in physical contact. But Shiloh's whole body felt light; her father and she might stop butting heads for a day or two. She might rest and quit running.

"Good. Good. Now, where in the hell have you been?"

She sighed. There was no getting away from it; she might as well answer. "I drove all the way to Memphis and back."

"To see Michael?" he asked, suddenly hopeful. "Because he was here, meeting with me about you most of the day. Shiloh, he wants—"

"*No.* I drove because I wanted to. And if we're going to get along, you'll have to—"

"Stop talking about Michael. I know. I will, for the time being."

The phone was ringing as they stepped into the kitchen. Sam grimaced. "Probably T-Tommy."

"You didn't send him out hunting for me, did you?" Shiloh demanded.

Sam shrugged guiltily, then picked up the receiver.

As Shiloh watched him talk, she remembered the day.

Sam was going to be furious if the events ever came out. He'd feel hurt and angry and betrayed, and the latter was an emotion he couldn't handle at all. Not since Caroline.

If she'd only waited, she might not have had to marry Billy Bob. If she'd only known Sam was going to give her a little room . . .

She wouldn't have spent the day being jerked around, being kissed and mauled and—and threatened by that overgrown daddy longlegs.

♦ ♦ ♦

On Wednesday morning, Sam installed her at the bank in Sweetwater. Six months in Dover was enough apprenticeship, he announced. But Shiloh knew the truth, that he wanted to keep his eye on her. He realized something was wrong with the Memphis story, and he didn't want a repeat of that day.

It wasn't the most pleasant transition. Somebody had to go to Dover in her place, and she went in at Sweetwater over people who'd been around a lot longer.

Two or three of the women clearly resented her; one, Rita, was an acquaintance, a girl with whom she'd gone to elementary school.

Shiloh ate lunch alone in the rec room for three days before Rita came hesitantly on the fourth and sat down at the same table, smiling.

"She acted half-afraid of me," Shiloh told Laura, confused. "I don't know why. I remember that she bit me in the second grade because I spilled paint on her dress. I've known her a long time. We were friends, even."

"Give her a little time. You're the boss's daughter," Laura pointed out sensibly. "It doesn't pay to get mixed up with you."

"I breathe. I get hungry. I sleep. I'm just like her. And the rest of them, too."

"You don't do the things they do."

"What do they do? Go to the Legion Hall on Friday nights?" There, she'd asked about the place, finally able to get it into the conversation.

Laura looked up in mild surprise from the towels they were folding. "Well, that wasn't what I was talking about, but I guess they do. How'd you come up with the Legion Hall?"

"Rita said she goes sometimes." Shiloh kept her gaze on the towels. "Is it a place I could go?"

"There's nothing wrong with the Legion Hall if you like dancing. Me, I don't hold with it. Nothing good ever came out of that much movin' around between the sexes, that's my opinion. But it's not a good idea to get social with people who work for you in the way those do."

"They work for Sam."

"And someday they're liable to be workin' for Sam's daughter," Laura said implacably. "He stays out of their lives. He expects you to do the same."

"Well, I'm not Sam. I like people, Laura. Real people."

Shiloh got up and turned away. When Laura came into the kitchen a few minutes later, she was staring out the window toward the row of magnolias down on the far side of the yard.

"You know what, Laura? Sometimes I wish I was just one of those girls down at the hall, and nothing more."

"You're crazy, girl. Crazy."


The band at the Legion Hall didn't have a name; it was just Jake Piedrow and his three sons. But they could play the fire out of a fiddle tune or a waltz, and Jake's oldest boy, Aaron, had a baritone voice that let him cover everything from ballads to yodels. Jake himself favored the blues, and he liked a good Sam Cooke tune once in a while.

They were experts.

So was the dancer in Billy Bob's arms. Angie's slight weight nearly floated her off the ground as they shuffled and two-stepped with the rest of the crowd. She was smiling up at him; he kept looking away.

Maybe she thought he was keeping an eye out for the youngsters that wandered through the crowd while their parents and grandparents danced.

She could just keep on thinking it. He wasn't about to tell her the truth, that he was eyeing the door in the hopes that a girl with a wild, thick mane of red-lit brown hair and legs as long as the Natchez Trace would walk through.

Where was she?

She wasn't going to dismiss him now that she'd gotten a marriage out of him; she wasn't going to walk away like she had when she was an eighteen-year-old who really hadn't loved him the way he—the adult—had loved her.

He'd be damned if he wouldn't wring something more out of her this time, even if it was just sex. He'd show her what his "cheap" appeal was.

But she hadn't come.

When he stopped dancing, the music rushed on. So did Angie and the rest of the crowd, and he bumped and jostled several.

"What's the matter?" she demanded. "Tired already?"

Billy shook his head. "I'm thirsty. Here, you don't have to leave the floor because of me. There's Tracy."

Angie caught his hand as he lifted to signal the other man over. "No," she said softly, at least as softly as she could in the laughter and the music. "I don't want to be with Tracy. No more dancin'. I'll go with you."

Billy hesitated, then shrugged. She'd come tonight on her own, apparently looking for him; she could do as she pleased.

"Sorry, kid," he told one of Dale Simcox's little twins as he stumbled over him on the way to the Coke dispenser.

"Whew," said Angie as they picked up the tall red cups full of ice and fizz, "it's hot in here tonight."

She ran a hand up her nape, fluffing the ridiculously short bob out, and sipped Coke as she looked up at him. In the yellow glow of the big bulbs that hung suspended from the ceiling, her hair was spun gold, her skin glowed golden, her jewelry and her sleeveless, cool top with its metallic threads all glinted gold.

Not a touch of earthy red-browns about her.

Where Shiloh's hair swung and bounced and waved, Angie's was as controlled and still as the precious metal it resembled, lacquered and gelled until not even the big fans that extended from the ceiling could stir it when their brown blades swung ponderously. The breeze they spawned could hardly be felt in the crowd of people.

"Let's go cool off on the porch," Angie invited, and took Billy's hand to tug him along. A line of sweat dripped down his back, so he agreed. Once out the big wide doors, he leaned a shoulder on the brick building and looked over the scattered, laughing couples who stood around.

No sign of a Cadillac pulling into the parking lot ahead of them.

Angie took another sip and eyed him. "You're awful quiet tonight."

"Am I? Must be tired. Two weeks layin' around jail, and this week back at hard work on the farm again."

"We could go to my place. You'd get some rest there—eventually," she urged in a teasing voice, but she smiled up at him suggestively. "It's been a while, Billy."

He looked down at the hand resting lightly on his shirtfront, its nails long and manicured, sparkling with some kind of glitter—golden, too. She'd pulled out all the stops tonight.

"I don't know, Angie," he said, lamely. "I'm not . . . not in the mood."

Her cheeks flushed lightly. "You've been that way a lot lately. What'd you do, get religion or something?"

"Look, let's just dance."

"No. I don't want to dance. I want to know what's wrong. You've never treated me like this, no matter how many other girls you ran around with. I'm not gonna stand for it, Billy." Her eyes sparked with frustrated temper.

"I didn't ask you to, did I?" He said it quietly.

She stared at him a long, long moment. "My God. There's somebody else, isn't there? Really somebody else. And big, bad Billy Bob Walker thinks he's in love."

"Just drop it, Angie."

"You're actin' like some junior-high kid."

"I said drop it, okay?"

He pulled away from her clinging hands and strode back into the building trying to get away from her jeering words; they made him—and his big plans for tonight— seem ridiculous. Just plain stupid.

It was gone midnight. He was heading home. And he was going to forget Shiloh Pennington.

He stopped by the back door to wait for a group of chattering women who'd halted in front of it for a conversation. He wanted out, before Angie found him again.

"Shiloh Pennington has Diane's job now."

The name struck his ear at such a timely moment in his thoughts that he jumped. Who had spoken it? Somebody in the group of women. The tall one. The brunette.

"Maybe she's as good at what she does as they all claimed down at Dover," she was saying, "but I say it's not right. Mr. Pennington just moved her in without a by-your-leave."

"It's his bank," another answered, shrugging fatalistically.

And a third, a tiny redhead, put in, "I don't think she likes being there too much. We haven't been too friendly."

"Well, that's tough," retorted the first.

"I went to school with her," the redhead said mildly. "She's nice. I like her."

"Oh, please, don't start with a good-neighbor policy," the first returned, but the redhead didn't answer as a man who'd been waiting for her led her onto the floor.

Billy's eyes followed the brunette. What had Pennington done? And where was Shiloh? He came slowly back into the room, considering.

He might just ask the tall, pretty brunette to dance.

The weekend passed slowly. Shiloh spent most of Saturday sunning in the backyard, reading a book, and drinking Laura's iced tea.

Maybe she should have been worried that she was twenty-two and home alone with a good book on a Friday night, but mostly she just felt relief that she didn't have to worry about fighting off Michael.

Still, by Sunday morning she was ready to do something, and when Sam asked her to go to the golf course with him, she was willing. They drove to Tobias County and ate breakfast with two of Sam's cronies, both old enough to be her grandfathers.

After an hour in their company, Shiloh declined their invitation to play golf and instead spent most of the morning swimming in the club's pool. A slightly overweight mother and her two little girls were there as well, so there was someone to talk to, at least as long as the anxious woman wasn't calling the two. "Autumn! Cody! Don't go near the deep end. Do you hear me?"

And as the midday got nearer and nearer, the three left and Shiloh lay dozing like a well-fed cat in the sun.

It was the brush of fingers along her arm that roused her out of sleep—that and the sudden dark shadow that fell over her. But just as she managed to open her sleepy eyes, an open, warm palm, wet with water, pressed against the hot skin of her bare thigh, and someone laid his lips on hers.

She came awake with a hard jerk, her hands flying up instinctively to push him away, and her heart leaped into her throat as she looked straight up into Michael's carefully blank blue eyes.

"Hello, Shiloh."

In a wild panic, she shoved up, pushing against his bent body, scrambling away, recoiling from the accidental touch of her hand on his skin.

"What are you doing here?" she gasped.

"Dad came for his usual round of golf. I came looking for you." His voice wasn't as smooth as usual, his eyes on her lips.

"Don't waste your time. You just get away and keep away from me." She looked wildly around. There were two waiters setting outdoor tables, laying silverware for lunch around the pool. She wasn't alone; she could scream. The panic that had swirled up through her like dust in a hard wind settled a little, letting her see and breathe more clearly.

"Didn't Sam tell you?" Michael said quietly, and his hand reached out to touch one of the brown curls that lay against her neck, dried now from her swim. She watched him, her eyes wide, startled, terrified. Afraid to move. His hand was trembling, insistent at the side of her throat.

It was broad daylight. He couldn't do anything.

"Tell me what?"

Michael's eyes went back to her mouth.

"This marriage isn't off. It's just delayed. He thinks I should give you time. So to please the old reprobate, I'll do it. But don't think for a minute I won't get you in the end, Shiloh, because I will." His last words were nearly whispers. "God, I love you. I handled you all wrong the other day. I won't make that mistake again. I'll be more careful, I swear it, and the next time I'll be the winner. When I think about you, about how wild you were under me—" His breath rapid, his eyes full of slumbrous passion, he leaned closer and closer, until she could see every eyelash, every pore, and she stood mesmerized, locked into a trance that wouldn't let her move. "I don't think I can wait," he whispered in a hot conclusion to his own words, and kissed her.

With one hand hard against the back of her head, with the other suddenly sliding under her buttocks in a rude intimacy, he had Shiloh paralyzed for an instant.

But she didn't close her eyes. She saw his face pressed against hers, magnified a thousand times, and the same smothering sensation that had choked her before swamped her now. She began to fight, in a panic.

"Michael!"

He turned her loose even as her father's voice roared across the pool, and she stumbled from him in haste and panic.

Sam and Judge Sewell stood watching, her father's face furious, the judge's embarrassed. And behind them, the two waiters had straightened, listening.

"You sent him to me," Shiloh choked out accusingly to her father.

"No. I swear it, Shiloh," Sam answered instantly. "And

as soon as I saw Robert and he told me Michael was here, we came in. I gave you my word. And you"—his glare swung to Michael—"you gave me yours, boy."

"Yes, sir, I did," Michael replied, contritely, but his face was flushed and his lips heavy with the passion he couldn't quite manage to erase, even here in this danger zone in front of her father. "But I walked out here and . . . and there she was." He gestured at Shiloh, who remembered suddenly that she was wearing a high-cut, single-piece black bathing suit—and that was all.

She snatched up her robe, flinging it around her.

Michael looked away. Guilt was written on his face, guilt and regret. "My God, Sam, what do you expect me to do? A few days ago she was going to be my wife. How do you think I feel, seeing her now, loving her like I do, and you tell me not to call her, not to see her, not to touch her. Do you think I'm made of stone?"

He pushed back the heavy swath of blond hair that swung down over his forehead in a gesture of despair, and Sam's face softened for an instant in sympathy.

"I expect you to keep your word to me," he said, but his words were calmer.

Michael took a deep breath, but it was the judge who answered, his voice short.

"I think you're being too hard on him, Sam. From what I saw, he kissed her, that's all. The girl's not made of glass. Have some consideration for my boy."

"It doesn't make any difference. Michael promised to give Shiloh time. I promised her she'd have it. That's all you need, isn't it, Shiloh?"

His sudden question pulled her out of her shock and fear and fury. She could still feel his fingers; each one had burned an indelible mark on her skin.

"I need never to have to see him again. Just keep him away."

Then she twisted, running back toward the dressing area, trying to get away from all three of them.

Blind. Sam was blind.

"Dammit, Sam, she can't keep saying things like that to Michael. Can you see this is tearing him up? That girl of yours—"

She never heard the last of the judge's angry remonstrance. The door slammed shut on it, and she was in too big a rush to pull on her clothes.

But before she did, she yanked open her purse, searching through the side pocket. When she found the paper she was hunting for, she spread it open on the dressing table, her fingers shaking.

The paper that proclaimed her marriage to be legal and binding.

To Billy, not Michael.

The rain that fell Monday and Tuesday hampered work and made the air humid and thick. Billy had meant to dig trees and get them ready for shipment to a small chain of stores across the Arkansas line, but he gave up at lunch. The rain was beating holes in the ground and in him; mud clung in huge clumps to his boots; he couldn't see for the sheet of water that ran off the brim of his soaked cap.

He stopped by the barn on his way in to the house, his feet squeaking in his wet shoes.

"Hey, boy," he told the big stallion that blew at him as he entered. The horse was the color of a red flame under amber, big and broad but with a well-shaped head that said that somewhere in his past was Arabian blood.

Billy ran a hand down the long, sleek neck. "You staying dry? I bet you're hating being cooped up, but I couldn't leave you out in that downpour."

The horse paid no attention to his words, nudging his arm instead so that he could get to Billy's pockets.

"Nope. Sorry. No apples, no sugar, no anything," he told him regretfully. "Maybe I'll go to town this afternoon and bring you back something, okay?"

The horse snorted reproachfully, then nudged his nose up under Billy's hand.

"Settle for a pat, will you?" Billy asked wryly, stroking the horse's nose. "You'd better. Since it's all that's available."

By the time he got to lunch, Grandpa had finished and was sitting in his favorite chair, an old, huge rocker, on the back porch, watching the rain fall in heavy gray sheets.

"You're late," he told Billy Bob as the latter shed his shirt and hat, shaking the water vigorously off his face and hair. "But we left you a little something to eat, I reckon. Ellen!" He raised his voice over the pounding rain. "Billy looks like a drowned rat. He needs a towel or two."

And in a minute, Ellen Walker stepped out onto the gray-painted wooden boards of the porch, a towel in each hand.

"Good gracious, boy," she said mildly, looking up at her wet son, "what'd you do? Take a bath out there? Look at those boots. Reckon you better take them off, too."

"It's only a little dirt and horse manure," he returned.

"Is that all?" she asked dubiously, looking him up and down. "You look so dirty I believe I'll just bring your food out here. There's enough germs on you that if you walk in the house, they could just slide off on everything."

Billy grinned at her. "They wouldn't dare get on your clean floor, Mama."

"Well, if you promise to make 'em behave, and then take 'em right back where you got 'em, I'll feed you," she retorted humorously.

His mother had a warm, wry, understated way of talking, a sort of comfortable, earthy, teasing personality. Billy had never seen her get really, really angry nor be cruel to a single living creature.

Too easygoing for her own good, most of Seven Knobs thought. That was probably how she came to get mixed up with Robert Sewell the summer she was seventeen. After all these years, after the initial gossiping and cattiness were long dead, the little community placed the blame squarely on Sewell. Still, Ellen had paid, spending the better part of the last thirty years staying firmly away from every man except her father and her son.

She'd shut the door—literally—in the faces of would-be suitors who'd shown up at odd moments to court the still-pretty, delicate, blond-haired woman. Now no beaux ever came calling on Ellen Walker, and that was the way she wanted it. It was her atonement for her mistake all those years ago.

Billy often wondered if his even-tempered mother had known how to be sad and how to cry before the judge came along. He thought probably not.

He'd never asked her about the details, too afraid she'd tell him, and he'd learned to be grateful that she loved him instead of hating him.

It was better when he didn't think about Sewell at all.

"It's raining too hard to work," he offered at last, after he'd taken a bite of his fried chicken leg. "I need to pick up some things in town. Anything you need, Mama?"

"I can't think of anything. Except, Mary Haile called and said one of her cats had something wrong with it. I think she was hintin' for you to stop by and look at it. You might do that on your way. Where all are you going?"

"Feed store, hardware store—" Billy took another bite and thought a minute, "and maybe the bank."

He had his account in Tobias County, but it wouldn't hurt to open a small one in Sweetwater.

And, of course, he might check on one of his creditors, too, if she was working today.


Things had been slow. Tuesdays were never too busy; usually only four of them worked on the main level: two tellers, a girl at the window, and an officer—Shiloh.

She was on the telephone, staring out the window at the rain that was pulverizing the red-and-white striped petunias in their square boxes at the edges of the tiny lawn when she saw him pull in the parking lot.

She knew the truck immediately, before the driver stuck one booted foot or one long leg out.

And as he came up the sidewalk, head bent against the downpour, she felt the tiny tingling of nerves—in the base of her skull, in her throat, around her heart.

What was Billy Bob, who never set foot in Sam's banks, as far as she could tell, doing here?

Across the room, Rita noticed him, too.

"Well, Susan," she said meaningfully to the tall brunette who worked at the next window and who was busy on an adding machine, "look who the rain dragged in."

Susan cocked one eye inquiringly, then let her hand fall from her work. And as she began to smile, her cheeks flushed pinkly.

She looked happy—thrilled, thought Shiloh in annoyance, remembering Susan's shortness to her most of the time. Billy Bob's personality must be more interesting than hers.

"Hi, Billy," Susan called to him as he entered, droplets glistening on his shoulders.

He grinned at her, glancing around, but when he saw Shiloh, he held her gaze a second too long. She did her best to put disdain in hers.

"What brings you into town?" Susan asked coyly.

"Nothin' much. I need some checks cashed, and maybe I'll open an account. Checking. Can you help me?"

Oh, please, what a line, Shiloh thought sourly, and tried to shut them out, focusing fiercely on the paperwork in front of her.

But she was too aware of the lanky body leaned sideways against Susan's counter, of the laughing, low, husky quality of the other girl's voice as she leaned close to Billy's blond head, of Billy's easy drawl.

What are you doing in here, she thought furiously.

". . . really enjoyed myself Friday night," Susan was saying. "I've seen you there before. Do you come often?"

"Once in a while," he answered, and Shiloh realized suddenly, he'd gone out with this girl, or done something with her, this past weekend. That's why he was here.

The dirty rotten two-timer.

The furious thought took her breath away with sheer temper.

A week ago he was kissing *her,* laying down laws for *her.*

He never intended to follow even one of them himself.

She shoved her hair back and stood up forcefully. Then her eyes met his across the office.

Susan was still talking, but Billy wasn't listening. He

was watching Shiloh, all blue eyes and intensity. Waiting for her to see him. And he didn't smile when their eyes met. In fact, he looked angry.

He hadn't come to the bank to see Susan, whatever they'd done together. He'd come after her, Shiloh.

". . . and maybe we'll run into each other again at the next dance," Susan was saying, as she reluctantly handed him his money and receipts.

Billy turned back to her, straightening off the window. "Yeah, maybe. I'm there most Friday nights."

Shiloh had to move, had to get away from him and the sweet voice of the girl. Air—she needed air. Or water. That would do. Anything.

But as she straightened from the water fountain, he was behind her, blocking her. She twisted to look up at him.

"Hello."

His body cut off the view of the other two tellers, and he wasted no time on trivialities.

"Outside," he said, his voice low.

"What?"

"I'll be in the truck. Waiting to see you."

"But I can't—"

He lifted one arm and pulled a gold chain from inside his shirt. Shiloh stared at what swung on it, then nodded.

"I'll be there, in a few minutes."

Billy bent to the water fountain as she walked away, ignoring the two girls who'd been watching them. But there was nothing to see. At best she'd appeared to be curt to a new bank customer.

He had her ring. There were a thousand ways to return it—trust Billy to do it in broad daylight, in full view of half of Sweetwater, and right under the nose of his latest girlfriend.

She waited a few minutes before she escaped to the rec room, then slipped out the side door. He'd parked between it and a huge snowball bush, and the only window that had a clear view of his truck was the one beside her desk.

She might be safe.

He was pushing open the passenger door as she ran to it, scrambling up onto the rough, worn truck seat. The minute the door slammed, they were too close, locked here together in this quiet capsule of a world, rain beating down on the roof and their breath fogging the window.

He just looked at her a long second.

"My ring . . . you've got it?" she asked at last, her voice too breathy and quick.

He laid one long-fingered, brown hand on the top of the steering wheel. The other arm he slid along the seat behind her, his fingers brushing the top of her pale yellow cotton shirt.

I won't pull away, she thought.

"I haven't seen you in a while," he answered instead. "I don't know if you're all right, if things have changed, if—"

"They're the same. I would have told you if—"

"I'd like to know when. I don't see you, I don't hear from you, and I damn sure can't telephone you at home. The only way I even found out you were working here was from Susan."

"You mean your newest girlfriend, the one that fell all over herself when you walked in?"

"My newest—look, honey, I danced with her twice at the Legion Hall because I heard her ripping you up— something about your new job—and I wanted to know what was going on. You think I like sitting around wondering when Pennington's gonna come after me?" Billy punched the steering wheel with his left fist for angry emphasis.

"You expect me to believe that?" Shiloh's voice was scornful, but all of a sudden, her anger had begun to dissipate.

"Believe what you please," he said. Then he looked up, and his face lightened a little. "Or come and see for yourself."

"I—I can't. Laura says it's better for me not to—to socialize with people who work for Sam. That it'll make trouble."

"Then come and socialize with *me.*"

His voice had a teasing, husky drawl in it as he leaned toward her a little.

"Somebody—would see us."

"So what? Is it gonna ruin you to dance with me?" The edge of frustration cut into his words.

"If Sam found out, he'd make a terrible scene."

"He did once before and you survived."

He was too close to her, leaning in toward her, his face intense. She could feel the heat from his body, the dampness that rose from their clothes.

She pulled away, looked away.

"I can't. And I've got to go. The ring—"

He sat back in the seat, beating down temper. Then he picked up the ring that hung against him.

"It's got your name inside it," he told her calmly.

"I know."

"If anybody saw this—if I showed it to them—there'd be more trouble than any dance could stir up."

She straightened instantly.

"Give it to me," she demanded, and her hand snatched at it.

But Billy caught her arm, his eyes bright and gleaming. "Uh-huh. If you want it, Shiloh, work for it."

"You can't—"

"I'll be at the Legion Hall this Friday night. You want this?" He held it up in his clenched fist, the chain spilling like a delicate thread of lace across his rough, bare knuckles.

Then Billy leaned closer, his face nearly touching hers. "You want the ring, then you come and get it."

# 9

*Okay.*

She'd had enough.

Sam pushed her around and didn't listen. Michael intimidated her.

Now here was Billy Bob, pulling at her for something. Manipulating her.

And he was good at it, too.

Just this Friday afternoon, he'd come back in the bank again, his shirt opened far enough down the front that Susan had nearly fallen out of the teller's window trying to see clear to his navel. The gold chain had sparkled like danger against his brown skin.

The devil had lazed past Shiloh's desk, one thumb hooked in a belt loop, his cap pushed back on his head, eyeing her.

Daring her.

Urging her.

She didn't know what Billy was up to. Maybe he flirted

with her because she was there, and had drawn his attention to her over the past few weeks. But he had been mad half the time they'd been together. If these were his techniques, they left a lot to be desired.

And they stirred a glimmering rebellion down inside her.

She was tired of doing what she was told; she was tired of being told, in fact. She was tired of doing what she should.

If half the women in town could gawk at Billy Bob, then she could dance with him.

By the time she was through with him tonight, she'd have her ring and he'd have a piece of her mind.

It wasn't until she got to the Legion Hall that she began to have second thoughts.

It was ten minutes past ten o'clock when she finally stepped up on the edge of the shadowy porch.

Late. His expectant heart had been nearly sick with worry that she wouldn't show up, again. But here she stood in jeans, white tennis shoes, and a faded rose-red top.

Her hair was different—partially caught back on one side, curling more than it usually did because of the heat.

Beauty stood there, right on the edge of the porch lights, looking for him. Her eyes were searching the crowd that danced just inside the wide open doors.

He pulled in his breath and straightened off the hard brick wall.

"Looking for somebody?"

She jumped a little, startled by his voice as it came out of the shadows. Then she answered, her voice only a little shaky, "Maybe. And you—are you waiting for somebody?"

His cap was gone, she thought fleetingly, and its absence meant that the light hit his strong profile and his blond hair brightly.

"Maybe," he repeated teasingly. "There's just one problem. If my wife hears about this, we're dead."

"Oh, her. I've heard she's a saint of a woman."

"Yeah? And what does that make me?"

"Nothing short of the devil. You bribe and blackmail people to get your way."

His grin faded. "It's only a dance, Shiloh. It won't kill you."

"You could just give me back my—"

"No. That way is no fun."

"And this way is?"

"Wait and see." He reached out, caught her hand. "Come on, and try to smile. You used to laugh all the time."

Pulling her through the edge of the crowd, he gave her no chance to answer until they came to the nearest corner. Shiloh kept her head turned away; sooner or later, somebody would know her, and she'd rather it be later.

Billy twisted, then held out his other arm for her to step into. She hesitated, half-afraid of the proximity, half-afraid of him.

"I haven't danced like this in a long time. Maybe I won't remember how."

"Since how long?"

"Since I was eighteen and fool enough to try to do everything you did," Shiloh retorted unevenly.

"Good. That's real good. But don't worry. It'll come back to you."

He made that tiny motion with his hand again; still she stalled. "Billy, somebody's going to recognize me here."

"How could they? Most don't know you, especially not dressed the way you are now. You never step out of Sam's shadow."

"Somebody will. Then we're in big trouble."

"Who is? Not me. You, only if you let yourself be. One dance, Shiloh."

"Then what?"

"Then . . . we can go somewhere else."

And that was no comfort at all, she thought, but she went when his arm reached out to haul her into his long body.

There wasn't a whole lot of provocation in the Texas two-step, not if you were doing it with a regular Joe.

But every time Billy bumped against her, every time her face came near enough his chest to feel the beating of his heart, it meant something to Shiloh, reminding her of nights she'd lain against him.

And the way he smelled—she'd forgotten how his very scent could twist her up in knots.

Out of the blue, she wished suddenly that she'd kissed him longer in front of the judge. Did he taste the same?

His arms around her were strong as iron manacles; she could feel his fingers wrapping her side, as hard and determined as they had been when he held her face for his own kiss.

She had come tonight to tease and tantalize, but maybe she should leave as quickly as possible, as soon as she had the ring.

Before the thought barely materialized, the music changed, and the band slid into a slow, aching song. The lights above them went out, until the only thing lighting the hall were big lanterns that burned as decorations in the corners and on the refreshment table.

There was one behind Billy, turning him into a gold-edged silhouette, lighting only the side of his face.

Over the microphone, over the music, came the drawling, gentle voice of an old gray man who held his fiddle at rest for a moment. "This one's for all the sweethearts out there tonight. Slow and easy, and all you have to do is hold on real tight." Then he lifted the fiddle to his shoulder and began to pull the bow across the strings in sweet, piercing, slow strokes.

Shiloh stumbled, then tried to back away. Billy stopped her.

"One dance, you said," she whispered, finding his face in the shadows of the dusky room.

"Until the music stops," he corrected. "Don't be afraid, Shiloh. I'm not gonna hurt you."

His face was so quiet, his long eyes so watchful, his voice so calm, so certain.

It had been so long since she'd let Billy—this Billy, the one she trusted—wrap her up completely and hold her against him. Unafraid of anything. Certain of love.

There'd be no room for even one evil memory of Michael in Billy's arms.

No place for Sam, either.

And after tonight, never again. No excuses left for Shiloh to come to Billy after tonight.

Something in her face changed; her body relaxed. And without another word, he pulled her close.

Here in this warm darkness, nothing mattered. Not who he was, not who she was, not what they'd done.

This one moment was what heaven would be like—no past, no future, just an immediate, choking, unbearable sweetness.

She knew, just barely, when his right arm came up, his

hand grasping her skull compulsively, his calloused fingers tangling in her hair as he pressed her hot face against him, bent his own bright head over her dark one.

It didn't matter.

It would tomorrow, but not now.

Nothing mattered, not while the fiddle pulled them through the song, not while it shivered and cried and moaned.

And when the music faded into nothing, life stopped.

With a gasp for oxygen, Shiloh came off his chest and pushed away. She had to get out. Now.

Quick, before the lights came on, and she had to face him. It was better to be a coward and run.

In and out of the crowd, along the edge, to the doors.

Across the floor, Billy Bob came to his senses. She wouldn't get away, not tonight. Not after that dance. He had been holding the Shiloh who had once begged him to make love to her: that was the only truth he could understand at the moment.

The lights brightened and applause from the dancers went up as he shoved his way after her, taking the faster, direct path that she'd avoided. He couldn't see much or think clearly; his whole body was on fire with the way she had touched him. But he caught a glimpse of her as she reached the doors and ran out into the night.

Once outside he scanned the parking lot under the purply security light.

Trucks, and more trucks. A few cars.

To his right, a car door opened. An interior light flashed on, and he saw the rose-red of her shirt as she got in.

He leaped two vehicles, catching himself with his open-palmed hand on their hoods as he catapulted over them, running until he was close enough to yank open her passenger door as she tried to pull out from the parking space.

Shiloh gave a small scream as he threw himself in beside her. Then he reached for the ignition switch, turned off the engine, and yanked the keys away.

"Are you crazy?" she gasped, and she made a futile grab for the keys.

He pulled them back, breathing hard.

"Give me those keys."

"No, ma'am. And if you keep yanking at 'em, I'm gonna toss them across this parking lot."

"No, don't. I'll quit."

They sat in a pounding silence another moment before he asked harshly, "Why'd you run?"

He heard her shuddery breath, saw the way she grasped the wheel. "I gave you your dance. That's all I was supposed to do. I only did what I had to do to get the ring back. And since you're here, I want it." She thrust her chin up aggressively.

"Shiloh, look at me."

"Will you stop ordering me around?"

His hand shot out, grasped her chin, turned her stiff jaw until she had to face him.

"You did all that stuff in there just to get this back?" he asked disbelievingly, grasping the chain and the ring through the shirt, all in one crumpled hold.

"I don't know what you're talking about."

His arms reached for her, his hands catching her by the shoulders as he pulled her toward him angrily. "The hell you don't. You had your face against me, you had your arms around me, and you didn't want to turn loose. I *know*, Shiloh, because I didn't want to, either."

She was shaking in his hands, but she stayed stubbornly silent.

"If that's the truth, you look me in the face and swear it. Tell me that you touched me like that just for this damned ring."

His passionate face, his hands straining against her—they forced her to look up, to open her mouth.

"Tell me. After all these years, tell me you've changed that much. That I couldn't feel what was in you. Was it for the ring?"

"I—please, Billy—"

"Shiloh."

"No. *No.*" The word shook, her throat catching on it. "Now—are you satisfied? Leave me alone!"

"No, I'm not satisfied. Not yet. But—"

She knew what he was going to do even before he moved; she shut her eyes for the inevitable.

Kissing Billy Bob was like falling, plunging, spiraling off some great height. Her heart shot up in her throat, she felt dizzy. And she was weightless, buoyant, exuberantly free.

But there was danger. It gave this flight a piquancy, and it terrified her out of her mind. It was too easy to crash.

She grabbed at him to stop herself from burning to death in her fiery freefall to earth, and he pulled her up to him, so tightly they were sealed together.

And still the kiss scorched and burned.

When he finally slid away from her lips, she was crying, tears so quiet he didn't know they were there until they wet the hollow of his throat where he pushed her face while he sucked in his breath harshly.

"What are you crying about?" he got out at last. "I said I wouldn't hurt you, and I didn't, did I?"

She shook her head.

"What, then?"

She pulled away, and he let her go. The car was hot, even with the windows down. Both of them were wet with perspiration. If he hadn't wanted to hold her so much, it would have been a relief when she moved, a break in the heat.

"So now we've—we've started this again," she whispered shakily, wiping her wet cheeks with the palms of her hands. "What good does it do us?"

"What good—"

"I mean, I can't trust you. You're with a girl every time I turn around. Or in a fight over one."

He had to breathe, so he reached for the door handle and unfolded himself from the car. It was cooler here, directly in the night air, but nothing could cool his emotions. She'd always done this to him, dammit.

"So it should end here, tonight, before—"

"Before *what*? Before you actually let yourself feel something for me again, if you ever did?" He turned violently, resting his arms on the top of the car. "Let me ask you something, honey. Where do you get off thinking you're so perfect yourself?"

After a long moment's pause, Shiloh opened her door and climbed out, and when she shut it behind her, turned to face him.

"All I've heard about is what I've done," he said savagely. "About how—how cheap my kisses and my body are. Well, what about you?"

"I haven't—"

"I didn't kiss you because of . . . of things, Shiloh. It was in spite of 'em. In spite of the things your daddy said to me—and you let him. Hell, you took his side and went with him. In spite of my brother. I know what you did, Shiloh. You let him take my place. He's me, but different. He's the easy way. And in spite of your money that lets you buy other people's self-respect. But that one's my fault. I could'a said no."

His breath was coming in such jerks it was tearing him apart. He pulled away from the car, shuddering. He meant to walk away before she killed him.

"Billy—"

He turned back toward her, his hair as it brushed thickly back from his face and curled along his collar nearly white in the light of the security lamp, his eyes black.

"Did you make me answer you about the ring and kiss me just to pay me back for everything?" She asked it in one painful rush, and he didn't really answer her.

Instead, he said at last, "That kiss wasn't cheap, Shiloh Pennington. I never gave one that cost me so much."

All of north Mississippi lay under an oppressive June heat wave this Saturday afternoon. Maybe the two of them should have stayed inside, but Shiloh's nervous energy had brought them both out here. Laura sat in the swing, a cushion against her back, cooling herself with a hand-held fan that read Hayes and Borden Funeral Home, Sweetwater, Mississippi, on one side and had a picture of an angelic little girl in an Easter bonnet praying on the other side.

Laura watched Shiloh, who sat silently on the porch steps, moodily turning the rose she'd broken off the trellis.

"This heat's terrible," the housekeeper said at last.

"Looks like you're feelin' it, Shiloh. You don't look good. I hope Sam's cooler in Jackson."

Shiloh didn't answer. She couldn't think now of why she'd wanted to come out to the backyard. It was a bad place to be. The roses that climbed the trellis, the rows of Foster hollies that ran along the drive, the dusty ivy that edged the flower beds—Billy Walker had planted them.

*"Where do you get off thinking you're so perfect?"*

*"You let him take my place."*

*"You let him—"*

Shiloh came up from the steps so fast she nearly fell, clutching the rose so convulsively that a hidden thorn stabbed her. She winced and tossed the flower away.

"What'n the world is wrong with you?" Laura sighed. "You got something on your mind, Shiloh?"

"It's something I have to work out myself," she said at last.

Laura eyed her. "Why do I think this has something to do with Michael?"

"No, not him."

"It's all over Sweetwater that the wedding's been postponed. People want to know why. And Lydia Sewell's lettin' it be known that she's not happy with you right now."

"I don't care. I've got other things to think about that are more important."

Laura raised her eyebrows in surprise, but Shiloh didn't notice. She couldn't escape last night. Billy Bob's words rang everywhere she turned. She'd never seen it his way, nor seen herself in such an unflattering light. She'd always thought she was the one wronged, the one who tried to be a good daughter and a good—whatever it was she'd once been to Billy. Shiloh had meant truly to come back from Mexico with things cleared up; she intended to hold both Sam and Billy. He'd been the one who hadn't waited or called or tried to see reason.

He'd run off to Tupelo—how was she supposed to have found him there?—and he'd taken up with another girl.

*"I know what you did, Shiloh . . . he's the easy way."*

Putting her hands over her eyes, she tried to block out everything—the way what she and Sam had done seemed so ugly now, the anguish on Billy's face for a moment last night. Where was the easy-going, I-don't-give-a-damn redneck brawler he'd always been?

Last night, he had scared her and fascinated her and seemed suddenly capable of breaking her heart all over again without half trying.

"If my wife hears of this . . ." She saw him smiling, laughing down at her—golds and blues and whites.

*His wife.* Married to Billy Bob Walker. If she wanted to, right now she could go hunt him up, pull out that piece of paper, and make demands. Nobody in this world would blame her.

Even Billy himself might not protest too much. She felt his face rough against hers, his lips sweet.

But would she get something worth having from him if she did?

"If you want to do something that involves somebody else," Shiloh said abruptly, startling Laura out of the light doze she'd fallen quietly into, "and you don't know if it's in hi—their best interests, why can't you just be honest and explain the situation to—everybody?"

"Lord, Shiloh," Laura said with a yawn, "you lost me way back yonder."

"Does honesty make things right?" Shiloh persisted. "It always seemed to me it just hurt."

"All I ever saw, it set things straight. Might not make things easy, though. You thinkin' about just tellin' the whole town that your engagement's off for good? Sam won't like it. He keeps hopin'—"

"No." Shiloh cut across her words, then stared out at the tiny lily pond, where something was making the reeds move in the heat of the afternoon.

"I've got to go to town, Laura. Just for a while. I'm going to change my clothes."

"Hel—l—lo, trouble."

Jimmy Mabrey breathed the words through his teeth as he looked up from the long bed of the tractor trailer where he was shuffling freshly dug young trees into place, their roots encased in big balls of canvas-covered dirt. He stopped what he was doing, standing completely still, staring off in the direction of the road, toward Walker's Fruit Stand.

Billy Bob, operating the loader that was lifting the trees up to the flatbed, finally twisted to see what had stopped Jimmy's labors. He wiped the sweat out of his face, hardly able to see out of his steamy aviator sunglasses.

But he saw enough.

He nearly went through the roof of the loader.

*What was she doing here?*

The girl who had just climbed out of the Cadillac was tall. She wore cuffed red shorts, and even at this distance, Billy Bob could tell her feet were bare.

She had on some kind of swingy white top that ended

at her waist, sleeveless and low necked, revealing more smooth, tanned skin.

"Good Lord," said Jimmy. "Wonder what color her eyes are behind them glasses?"

"Brown," snapped Billy.

"I say blue. I'm partial to blue. But with legs like that, who cares." His tone was reverential.

"Better close your mouth," Billy advised the seventeen-year-old. "You'll catch flies." He swung out of the loader.

"Where you goin'?" Jimmy hollered after him.

"To see what Trouble wants, that's what. Keep working."

"Someday I'm gonna be the boss," Jimmy murmured to himself.

Shiloh.

*Why?* She'd never come to Seven Knobs before. Was it because he'd made a fool of himself last night and she wanted to rub it in today?

The tall, slender man looked like an advancing dark cloud, Shiloh thought in apprehension, but she kept looking at the fruit baskets displayed. The old man behind the long wooden rows of bushel baskets must be Billy's grandfather.

It was hard to tell what Billy was thinking. Like her, he had on dark glasses, and he was pulling off a pair of heavy gloves.

She jumped into the conversation first.

"I think I want a half a bushel of these," she told his grandfather hurriedly, pointing to yellow peaches splotched crimson by the sun.

"Mighty good choice," the old man told her cheerfully. "They're fresh and sweet."

"They look good." She raked her hair back, running her hand through the top.

"Here, Billy," said the old man, "seein' as how you beat all records gettin' up here from that field, you want to load them in this little lady's trunk?"

Billy didn't say a word. He just stood waiting while Grandpa got things sorted.

No shoes. She really didn't have on any shoes.

The shorts were not nearly as provocative as they could have been, but the feet were a different matter.

His pulse speeded up a little; he hoisted the basket.

"In the trunk, ma'am?" he asked without a flicker of recognition.

She still hadn't looked right at him. She was too scared to, but she nodded, then opened the car door, and pushed some button that made the trunk lid open.

Billy took his time placing the basket with its load of peaches. If she'd come to talk to him, she could come back here. She did.

This close he caught her sweet perfume.

"You must be havin' a party. All these peaches. Too many for you."

She swallowed. "I might have one. A party, I mean. Just for me and—and one other person."

His hands froze where he'd lifted them to shut the trunk.

"My father's in Jackson this weekend. And our house-keeper goes to her house next door and to bed at eight thirty every night."

Had he heard right? he wondered wildly.

Did he understand? Shiloh thought desperately. Maybe she'd done this all wrong.

He slammed the lid, fingers lingering on it. Grandpa was too close for him to grab her up and shake her.

"You better lock your doors if you're all by yourself."

She looked right at him. "I will. All but one. The one in back beside the French doors."

"For your friend."

She nodded, then nearly ran down the dusty road to slide in the car, bare feet and all.

His heart was pounding like a racehorse's, and no amount of water could quench his sudden thirst.

She had come after him. For the first time in his life, Shiloh had come to get him. Why?

"Well, what was her name?" Jimmy demanded as Billy climbed back in the loader.

"You were right, kid. It's Trouble."

Billy was fashionably late, not because he was trying to be but because he spent half an hour trying to get up the nerve to pull in the drive of the closest thing to a mansion that Sweetwater had.

He hoped he wasn't making a stupid mistake as he parked the truck in the paved turn-around in back and wondered what he was letting himself in for. Shiloh had shocked him with that come-on; he didn't know her these days.

He ignored the unexpected pang of disappointment and hurt, reminding himself that a man deserved something for his troubles, and he'd been itching to get his hands on Shiloh Pennington for too long.

*But not this way.*

He brushed the thought aside.

One light was on, behind the door she'd promised to leave unlocked.

Shiloh opened the door before he even rang the bell;

there was no point in pretending that she wasn't looking for him.

He loomed in the silent shadows, then spoke at last. "You better not open the door for just anybody. The big bad wolf's still on the prowl around these parts."

She had been so tense that his wry comment took her by surprise, then she laughed. "You ought to know."

Stepping back, she motioned him in, and after a second's wary hesitation, Billy entered.

He was determinedly casual in his T-shirt and jeans; so was she in the brightly colored madras skirt and blouse, and open-toed sandals.

"You found your shoes," he said ironically, and she flushed. "That's a shame."

Billy looked from her feet to the room. He'd only been in this house once, on the carpet for messing with the great one's daughter. This room was warm and soft, lit by one dim lamp and full of comfortable couches and reclining chairs. There were plants everywhere—red geraniums and ferns—and magazines, and a big-screen television. All along one wall ran French doors opening on to a hedged, shaded alcove in the dark garden beyond.

Not glamorous like the other room he'd seen, but splashed with a sort of well-heeled comfort that made him as uneasy as a high-buttoned shirt.

"You meant for me to come." It was half question, half statement.

"You know I did. Here, sit down. I made a drink—a fruit blend. Lots of peaches," Shiloh told him with a laugh. "You may not like it—no alcohol. I don't drink. But—"

"I don't drink much, either," Billy interrupted. "I don't like the taste of the stuff."

Shiloh said in surprise, "But I thought—"

"Not me. I like to remember my fights."

He wondered if he was supposed to mention the fights. It seemed a little crude for this setting and this girl.

Her skin above the low round top glowed with a rich, warm sheen in the light of the lamp, and if he looked at her lips one second longer, he'd remember exactly how they felt last night.

Abruptly, he fumbled for the chain around his neck. "I've been thinking all afternoon about why you came out to the farm, and I reckon this is it."

But she caught his hand, and he went still, standing there with her hand over his at his throat.

"No, that's not it, Billy. I thought I wanted it back, but you can keep it."

Then she dropped her fingers, and her laugh was husky and nervous. "After all, why give it back now, after all the—the aggravation you've put me through?"

Billy shrugged, confused. "I don't know. Maybe I just wanted to yank you around some, the same way you were doing me. Sort of seemed like fair play."

"I've never yanked you around," she denied indignantly.

"No? Then what do you call what you were doing today?" he demanded.

"That's different. I did that because I didn't know how else to get your attention."

"Oh, you got it all right. There's no red-blooded man in his right mind who wouldn't have noticed—and liked it."

"So, what are you so mad about, Billy?"

"I'll tell you what. It was all a big tease, wasn't it? You got next to me last night, so you decided to do it again today. But now that I'm here, right where you wanted me, you've got your shoes on. Where's all that come-on now, honey?"

"That's not why I did it."

"That only leaves one other reason, Shiloh," he cut in, his eyes as blue as the flame in a hot fire as he dropped his gaze down over her.

She never flinched from his stare, and when he looked into her eyes again, they were straightforward and nearly defiant. But her cheeks burned red.

"That's not the reason, either, Billy," she said quietly. "There's one more."

"I don't know it if there is. What in the hell do you want from me?" He frustratedly raked his hand back through his hair.

"I've got some things that I want to tell you, Billy." He made as if to turn away impatiently, and she reached out and caught him by the arm. "Please."

He might drown in her eyes, so he gave in reluctantly—let her hand push him into the corner of the couch. Then he forced himself to relax, resting back against it, spreading his arms across its back, stretching out his legs.

"Okay. So talk, Shiloh."

When he looked up at her, he was casual and insolent and beautiful, and making it so hard for her to explain.

"When I came to the jail and asked you to marry me, it was to avoid Michael. But it was a whole lot more, too. Sometimes I think it was really to get back at Sam. He's the one who hurt me the most. I know I haven't been too mature about all of this, but I'm willing to admit the truth. Now."

He knew immediately where this conversation was

leading, and it made him angry and mean. "And now you want out of this on the quiet, because last night I lost it and got too intense," he returned. "I forgot those rules, didn't I? I went over the bounds. Well, dammit, so did you, Shiloh—either that, or you needed a man so much that you got turned on by even me."

She sucked in her breath sharply, anger flaming over her, and without thought, slapped him. His head jerked sideways with the force of the blow.

Carefully, he touched his fingers to the hot lash marks of her hand on his cheek before he looked up at her again as she stood over him.

Gasping for breath, her eyes glittering with fury and hurt, she was waiting.

"You can't talk to me like that. I haven't done one thing to deserve it, except be stupid enough to think I could explain my feelings and this situation to you. You don't even listen," she flared.

"Oh, I listen. You think I like what I hear? You just said you married me because it was the worst thing you could do to hurt your old man." He laughed a little. "I tell you, Shiloh, honey, you really know how to make me feel good."

She'd never really thought about Billy as being twenty-seven, nearly thirty. He'd always been teasing and youthful in her memory. But tonight he looked older, his face somber in the shadows. That fact, and the red brand her hand had left on his brown cheek, made her calm down a little, thinking, regretting, considering.

He was anything but happy: wary, cynical, cautious, reluctant. There was a fine edge of control about him, even in spite of her violence, and Shiloh realized now that Billy in his discipline was far more dangerous than Mi-

chael with all his excesses. Shame washed over her: she'd
been the one to lose control.

She should let him go. She should let this end.

"I don't want out. I want time." She didn't know how
else to say it without being blunt.

"Time! For what?"

"Time with you, to find out if there really was another
reason you were the one I asked to marry me."

He was as still as a stone statue, his eyes intense and
blinding.

"I don't know what's happening to me, Billy," she
whispered painfully, twisting her hands together as she
stood in front of him. "You scare me to death—you make
me do things—but when you touch me, everything in me
lights up."

She turned away in confusion and embarrassment.
"Then you walk away. So maybe it's only me. Tell me,
Billy, before I make a fool of myself."

He felt frozen with shock; whatever he'd been expecting, it hadn't been this, this sweet, stumbling confession.
This girl—*this* version of her—was his. The one he remembered. The one he'd thought was dead and gone.

"No," he said at last, and his voice sounded like a
frog's, "it's not . . . just you."

When she turned back, her eyes glistened with tears.
"You asked me what I wanted. I don't want you to walk
away like you did last night before I can tell you that I
didn't know until you put it into words that I'd done so
much wrong to you, Billy. Even tonight."

She moved, a little uncertainly.

He didn't even hear her clearly. His every molecule
was focused on the girl who stepped lightly across his
legs, her skirt brushing his knees, and dropped to the

couch beside him. He couldn't make a sound as she edged toward him until she had him trapped against the arm of the couch. Her light weight rested against him as she laid one tentative finger on the white cotton shirt, against his heart, and let her eyes close as she strained upward to kiss his lean brown jaw with lips of contrition, just where her hand had scalded him.

His eyes were black with emotion, but he made no effort to touch her.

"You say 'I'm sorry' real sweet, Shiloh," he said haltingly. "But what am I supposed to do? I don't know the rules here, either."

"Maybe there aren't any. Except one—honesty. Can't we tell the truth to each other and try to work out whatever this is?"

He watched her a minute, considering. "You want the truth? I don't believe you do, but I'll give it, anyway. I didn't like the way last night turned out. Whatever kind of bad joke that marriage was, it tied us together a little more. I can't forget it. I want to know how much more. I want to kiss you, and see if this thing between us really can burn me up." He looked at her lips, and in the stillness, he heard her too-rapid breathing. "So I've said it. You can run now, Shiloh. Because I'm tired of joking around and playing it cool and pretending like what we've been and done with each other doesn't matter, like I don't remember when I really do."

Billy pulled away a little more, as far back as the couch would let him go, and laughed. "I was right. That's the one truth you didn't want to hear, isn't it?"

"I told you, I'm ready to hear all of it."

She was so close, right under his hands, her cheeks warm and smooth, her eyes velvet and full of sparkling light from the little lamp, her mouth upturned, opening a little. For him?

"You better get away quick, Shiloh, unless—"

He choked on the words, and it was already too late, because she made a movement toward him. His arms reached for her, pulling her against him in one swift motion, hauling her up into his lap, and his mouth smothered hers, painful for a second in its possession.

But Shiloh didn't turn away, or struggle. She wanted this, and she wanted him to know it, so she went where he pulled her, sliding both arms in a passionate hold around his slender waist, and she opened her mouth the instant before his tongue swept urgently across it.

Inside her heart, the delicate, aching little tendrils of emotion that he stirred in her swelled into one huge wave of sweetness that threatened to wash her away, so she hugged him more tightly, until her hands found the bottom of his T-shirt and slid upward in delight over his sleek skin. Somewhere in the middle of her bursting emotions, she felt him shiver beneath her fingertips, and the sensation so surprised and pleased her that she had no room for any other thoughts at all.

Maybe it was an eternity before he pulled away from her lips, dropping kisses on her face, and down the side of her throat.

"A long time," he was gasping against her skin. "Years . . . since you kissed me . . . like that, Shiloh. I don't—"

But she had no time for words now. She slid both hands around his chest, up his throat, tangling her fingers in the heavy mass of hair at the nape of his neck, pulling him down toward her lips again.

He answered her urging hands, twisting so that she was beneath him on the couch, her legs still across his lap as he bent over her, barely letting her breathe. She felt his hand as it slid past her knee, under the skirt, to caress her thigh.

Too far for one kiss; not far enough for the emotions spiraling around them.

She shaped his head beneath her fingertips, holding him down against her throat as his lips slid to the hollow between her breasts.

It felt good to touch him.

*"Shiloh! What are you doing?"*

The shocked voice cut between them like a knife, slicing through the bonds of pleasure and emotion that wrapped them together on the couch.

Shiloh twisted away from Billy in a daze. Who? Who stood there in the door with her hair in a long dark braid over one shoulder of her pink bathrobe, a gun in her hand? She had a gun.

"Laura!" The word burst from Shiloh, half in dismay, half in fright, like the crack of a bat against a ball.

Too late she realized exactly in what position Laura had caught Billy and her. She was pushed down in the corner of the couch, nearly under him. He had lifted himself up enough to see who had entered, and the distracted, flushed look his face wore when he raised his head would have told the story even without his T-shirt being halfway up his chest and his hands firmly on her.

"Laura, put down that gun," Shiloh said, swallowing hysterical laughter. She pushed against Billy's chest, and when he resisted, looking down at her, she whispered urgently, "Let me up, Billy."

He hauled himself up slowly, sliding his hand from her leg, then pulling his shirt down. Deliberate. Calm.

Laura practically quivered with outrage, but she lowered the gun, pointing it toward the floor.

"I couldn't sleep, heard him pull in, looked out and

saw you let him in. I thought it was Mi—somebody else. That you might need help."

"Oh, Laura—"

"But it wasn't. It was *him*. The Walker boy. And you, Shiloh . . . you were—"

"I know what I was doing."

Laura looked at her accusingly. "I thought this was over before you went to college."

"What are you talking about?"

"Did you think I was blind? I saw the way you watched him that summer. I knew he wouldn't stay away from you. I knew you met him, Shiloh. I didn't have a choice. I had to tell Sam."

Shiloh stared at her in dismay. "You, Laura? *Why?*"

"I told you. Sam needed to know. I didn't tell anybody else, not even T-Tommy. But I was right to tell Sam. If there was anything to Walker—to the two of you—you wouldn't be sneaking around like that, hiding from everybody. You can't be up to any good with him, Shiloh."

"You don't know the first thing about it, or Billy," Shiloh said tightly.

"Oh, yes, I do. I know you can't let him handle you the way you just did without trouble. You can't play around with the likes of Billy Walker and not get caught, one way or the other. And Sweetwater, when it finds out, won't forget it. Neither will Michael, nor whoever else it might be you finally decide to settle down and marry someday."

Behind Shiloh, Billy came to his feet, so close his body brushed hers. But there was no time to think about him; Laura's words hurt like knives.

"That's enough, Laura," she choked out.

"No, it's not. I'm ashamed of you, Shiloh. You're with each other for one reason. I saw you. I know what's going on here, in secret. So what does that make you?"

"Tell her, Shiloh."

Billy Bob's voice was quiet, determined, harsh. His hands came down on her shoulders to grasp them forcefully, his fingers painful in their clutch.

"Don't let her talk to you like this. You're gonna have to tell it sooner or later, aren't you? Tonight was about that, wasn't it? So *tell her*."

She wanted to, but she couldn't. There was too much she didn't know, too much she wasn't sure of.

And there was still her father to confront.

"Billy, I—I can't. Not yet."

It hurt to make the admission, and she was too afraid to look at him, but she felt his hands slowly drop away.

"Laura, this is between Billy and me. I'm old enough that you can't stop me, or him. But if you tell Sam, it'll do nothing but make trouble."

Laura's face was as shattered and disappointed as Billy's hands had felt.

"I never thought you'd do this again, Shiloh. Go behind Sam's back. Doing things God never intended you to do with a man who wasn't your husband."

"You don't know anything about what I've done with Billy. It's my life, anyway."

Laura turned away, dragging her housecoat around herself tightly.

"I interfered once," she told Shiloh. "And I see it did no good."

She glanced sideways one more time at the tall man who loomed silently beside the girl.

"But I won't be keeping an eye on you for Sam anymore whenever he goes somewhere. I'll tell him you're too old for me. I won't lie to him, Shiloh, the way you are."

Laura hesitated, then she spoke directly to Billy. "And you, you'd better be careful with her."

He didn't answer, and finally Laura disconsolately stepped out the door and faded into the night, the gun dangling toward the ground.

She might have made a comic figure if she hadn't been so pitiful.

She left behind two silent people.

It was Billy who moved first, pushing his shirt roughly down into his jeans.

"I'm sorry."

He glanced sideways at her. "I'm not. I learned a whole lot while she was here. More than you meant me to know, I reckon."

"What does that mean?"

He straightened, looking right at her. "You never did tell me why you wanted me to come tonight, Shiloh."

"Because . . . I'm afraid of being without you. I don't understand it—I just know that I feel different with you. It's never been like this with anybody else."

"But." He said the one word harshly.

"But I don't know if I can trust the feelings. Or . . . or you."

"Or me."

"Sam says—"

He almost pushed away from her. "Why don't you figure it out yourself, Shiloh? Does it ever cross your mind that you might know me better than he does?"

"I'm confused, Billy. I don't know if I can face Sam with this yet because it means I'll give up everything. You won't lose your home, your family. I will. And all I've got to go on is that when I'm with you, when you touch me, everything lights up. With Michael I never—"

"I don't want to think about you and Michael. And far as I can see, there's nothing for you to give up everything for. There's nothing between us except . . . what? A few kisses? You're sure not about to tell that you married me, are you? I knew that this marriage was a convenience—the money made that easy to see—but I didn't know until tonight that you were ashamed of it."

He'd meant to hurt her, to return the pain she'd handed out to him in the last few minutes. He succeeded; her face went white. "I'm not. I told you. I'm just afraid. I didn't know what I was asking when I got you to come tonight."

"Yes, you did."

"I'm trying to be honest."

"With who? Not me. You brought me here because you like the way I make you feel. Nobody else makes you feel that way. Oh, I know all about it," he said quietly.

"That's not true. I wanted us to be together for a while without demands. I just wanted—a relationship, I guess. To see if there was more there."

"I hate that word, *relationship*. It's bloodless and gutless. Some word Hollywood came up with because they're scared of the real ones. Like you are. And we know already that we can't be together without demands."

He looked away, then back at her.

"We're married, Shiloh. That's our relationship."

"It's just a piece of paper."

"A paper's all it ever is until two people make it more. Come with me. Walk out of here, and come with me."

"I can't, Billy. Not until I'm sure. You don't want to be married. And we did it for the wrong reason. You resent it."

"Then make it for the right ones. I'll get over the resentment."

She shook her head.

"That's what I thought," he said, his voice nearly flippant. "I saw it clear as day when your housekeeper walked in here. You couldn't bear to tell her you'd married me. You'd rather she think you were easy than my wife. And if it's possible, we'll get a quiet little divorce, and maybe you'll never have to tell even Sam about it, if he'll just drop his plans for you without a fuss. You want me to make you feel good, but you don't want to be a part of my life."

"You're making it something it's not," Shiloh whispered. "Making me out to be—and think—things *I'm* not."

"Yeah? Well, you're making me feel like dirt," he answered, emotionlessly. "So we're even. The fact is that you don't want to risk everything on me."

"Give me a reason to, Billy. I want to believe in you."

"Do you? Maybe I feel the same way about you."

His face was so sad in the shadows that Shiloh hesitantly reached out and brushed her fingers down his cheek. He jerked away.

"I don't feel like touching right now, Shiloh. When you get ready to claim me out there, if you do—when you're ready to tell them that I'm your husband—when you're willing to treat me like a man, then you come and get me. But no more meetings in secret. This stopped being fun a long time ago."

Angered by his rejection, torn by her own emotions, ashamed of the motives he'd laid out as hers, Shiloh retorted in self-defense, "What if I never come crawling to you on your high-and-mighty terms?"

He shrugged. "I'll catch on after a while. It won't be much different from what it was before."

But she couldn't stop herself from asking as he turned, "Billy, when will I see you again?"

"Whenever you want to. I'll be around. I always am." He started toward the door, then stopped to pull the chain from his neck. "If this ever means anything to you, if I do—then you can give it back."

And he lifted her hand from her side, dropped it in her palm, and pushed her fingers closed over it, a cold, golden memento of one of the worst nights of her life.

# 10

"*It's a blasted* nuisance, but every Tom, Dick, and Harry at city hall gets his feathers ruffled if we don't participate," Sam told Shiloh as they surveyed the interior of the bank. Miniature flags stood all over the place, little drops of red, white, and blue that echoed the same color scheme in the giant ribbons and streamers that festooned the glass doors.

The Fourth of July was plainly approaching, and all of Sweetwater was getting ready for the annual festivities and parade.

"It looks nice," Shiloh said dutifully. She'd been seeing these decorations every Fourth for years now.

Sam snorted. "Looks like the Republican National Convention. Every place in town does, even the funeral home. But I figure I got off lucky. Sue Ellen Terry has been headin' up the parade committee. She actually tried to get the bank to build a float out of chicken wire. Said it could be green with George Washington's head sitting on it like a dollar bill. She thought that was patriotic."

"Lord," Shiloh said, laughing.

"It gets worse. She wanted you to ride on it."

"Me!"

"Well, she sure knew better than to ask me. But I got you out of it. I told her you'd help give out the prizes after the parade."

Shiloh said in aggravation, "But I don't want to. I don't know the first thing about judging floats."

"You don't judge. You just stand on the platform with a few other dignitaries in the morning and let 'em introduce you. Then you come back in the afternoon and hand out trophies. It's easy."

"Then why don't *you* do it?"

"I have before. But the town's kind of curious about you. And you're easier on the eyes. You'll do fine. Where's Rita? She was supposed to see about a banner for the front of the bank."

Shiloh watched him head off in the unsuspecting Rita's direction. "Why is it," she asked the air, "that I didn't have any courses like Parades 101 back in college when I was studying for this job?"

There was little point in trying to get much accomplished that week. The whole bank—the whole town, in fact—was in an uproar, and would be until Thursday, the Fourth. Sweetwater's parade had been written up in *National Geographic* two years before and now they felt they had a tradition to uphold.

Outside on the square, all sorts of booths were going up around the edges of the courthouse yard. The sound of skill saws and the smell of fresh-sawed lumber cut through the air as Shiloh left for lunch, trying to get away from the hubbub at the bank.

Danny Joe's was packed; he found her a stool near the

back wall by shooing one of his teenaged grandsons off it. And as she ate, Billy walked in.

She'd seen him twice since that night two weeks ago when he'd delivered his ultimatum, and he'd been in her dreams over and over, accusing her of cowardice, of being afraid to come to him.

Once he'd even been in the bank at the end of a hot, dusty day. He had walked in and out without a word to her, but his blue gaze had searched her face for an instant. And he'd pulled in to the service station one Friday afternoon as she and Sam sat in the car at the pumps on their way home. Sam never saw him; he was talking to the station owner. But Shiloh watched Billy park, just on the other side of the gas island, and her heart ached.

His hair had been vigorously brushed, shining like burnished gold against the brown of his skin. His shirt hung open over a T-shirt, and he looked so clean, so cool, so good that Shiloh felt an unreasonable spurt of anger.

Where was he going? She wished that the glittering gold chain was hanging around his neck now, letting her ring dangle against the snowy shirt for all the world to see, instead of lying on her dressing table at home. You're taken, she wanted to cry.

He looked at her a long, long moment, and the demand in her face was answered by the one in his: tell them. Tell the world if you want me. Pride and longing strained silently between the two of them. Then Sam drove away, and they left Billy behind.

She hadn't seen him again until today—and today was somehow different. He'd walked in here deliberately, knowing she was here, and her breath began to come in uneven jerks as he started toward her.

There was no room to sit anywhere except along the

walls; he worked his way around through the greetings and the backslapping until he found a place to stand and wait.

It was directly behind her.

Between the double-time thumping of her heart and the way she could feel his gaze boring a hole through the back of her cream-colored dress, Danny Joe's meal went unappreciated.

"Okay, Billy, what you want?" Danny called out his question over her head.

"A coke and a sandwich."

"Ham, chicken, reuben. That's what we got today."

"Ham, then."

A simple enough conversation, except that Billy stepped up behind her, so close her dress brushed his faded red shirt. She could feel him, hear him, nearly taste him he was so near.

Not daring to look around, she laid down her own sandwich and carefully wiped her mouth with the napkin. She had to get up.

But the wall blocked her on one side, and Billy on the other.

He was looking right down at her as she finally faced him, and he took the words and the thoughts right out of her head.

"Hello, Shiloh."

"B—Billy."

"Miss me?"

She didn't answer his low question. All around them, the world according to Danny Joe's tumbled on; but here in this quiet, intense well there was nothing but her and him.

"Because I sure missed you." He didn't wait for her

answer; he gave his own. "You could invite me to eat lunch with you."

Shiloh was vaguely aware that on the other side of Billy's broad shoulders, on the next seat, was a huge fat man with a New Jersey accent. "There's no room," she said, her voice as low as his.

"Then maybe the next time I'm in here. You could then. People will talk, but you'll live." He said it quizzically, but he was serious.

And his heart was beating under her arm.

In that one minute, she made up her mind. "You think I won't. But I will. The next time I see you here. In front of everybody."

"Even if Sam is here?"

She took a deep breath. "Even Sam."

"We'll see, Shiloh," he said quietly.

"Here's your sandwich, Billy Bob," Danny Joe announced, handing a white paper bag to him. "And I put a doughnut in there for Willie. He's in town with you, ain't he?"

"He won't let me build the booth without him," Billy answered easily.

"You about to get it done?"

"Yeah, maybe this afternoon."

He paid no attention to Shiloh as she stood, too. But after he pocketed his change from Danny Joe, just before he moved away, Billy ran his hand lingeringly down her back, from above her waist down over her hips, in a quick, sweeping, proprietorial move that left her shocked to her toes.

He was gone before she even got her breath back, and nobody in the bakery was any the wiser, except, of course, her.

She couldn't get it out of her mind. Indignant, that's what she was. "No touching," he'd said, but he'd laid hands on her fast enough, in a decidedly personal way.

He was making it easier for her to approach him again if she wanted to. And it wasn't indignation at all that she felt when she thought about that.

She saw him that afternoon when she pulled out of the tiny road that led to the bank parking lot. He was across the street, under the big magnolia tree, drinking from a Coke can.

He must have finished the booth. Most of them looked completed, and most of the workers had either gone home or settled around the courthouse yard to rest.

Billy was in a group with two old farmers, and T-Tommy, and two men Shiloh didn't know, but he wasn't paying much attention to their conversation.

He was watching her drive by.

You devil, she thought, remembering his smooth handwork today. But something had lightened in her heart, and a sudden spurt of pure mischief hit Shiloh.

He thought she was too afraid to do anything as reprisal for that little episode. Maybe she had been until he'd actually done it.

But Billy Walker was in for a surprise.

She parked the car just down the block in the first available space, then got out, the full skirt of the dress with its tiny, cinched-in waist swinging around her calves.

She had Billy's attention the minute she crossed the street. Even from this distance, she could see the blue of his eyes as he stood still, one shoulder propping up the tree, bathed in a ray of sunshine that filtered through the leaves, turning him golden.

T-Tommy's mouth dropped a little in surprise as she approached, and the conversation stopped completely.

"You lookin' for me, Shiloh?" T-Tommy asked in mild confusion.

"No. I was just looking around at the booths. Looking for—something to drink."

T-Tommy stared as if she'd lost her mind. She didn't dare even look at the four other men. Only Billy.

"There's a water fountain on the other side of the courthouse," one of the old farmers offered.

"Not water."

Her gaze dropped to the can Billy held in his hand; he looked from it to her incredulously. And at last, he slowly held it out.

She took it, brushed his long fingers with their rough knuckles, tilted it to her lips, and drank. The liquid was a little too warm, but the stunned look on his face made it delicious.

Nobody moved a muscle as she offered it back to him.

"Thanks." She wanted to run her hand down the opening of the red shirt, brushing the smooth brown skin, but she didn't have that much nerve. Not in front of these staring men.

"Anytime," he returned, but his intended nonchalance came out choked and unsteady.

T-Tommy came to his senses and snapped his mouth shut. "Here, Shiloh, I'll walk you back to your car." His voice dripped disapproval. "Since you quenched that thirst of yours."

She went docilely enough, but not before she heard part of the conversation that erupted in her wake.

"Good God a'mighty, Billy, that was Pennington's daughter. Ain't you got no sense at all?"

And one comment that she didn't like: "Everybody knows she's engaged to Michael Sewell."

T-Tommy stopped by her car, his face grim. "That's the second time I've seen you go after Walker, Shiloh. This will be all over town. Toy Baker was watching, and he's got the biggest mouth this side of the Mississippi River."

"And you think I'm a shameless hussy because I talked to Billy," Shiloh returned tiredly. She was tired, tired of hearing it.

"I don't know why you're doin' it. You're gonna marry Michael. Sam will get mean if this gets back to him. Then he's gonna take it out on Billy Bob. He don't need Sam as an enemy. You think about that the next time you decide to flirt with him. You've got all the aces where Billy's concerned, Shiloh. Be careful how you play 'em."

# 11

*What would Sam* do to Billy? What *could* he do? Shiloh wondered, but she meant to keep her promise to him the next day at Danny Joe's. If she didn't, Billy Bob might not be back for more of this delicious teasing.

But she never got to Danny Joe's. Just before lunch, Noah Ledbetter walked in, freshly arrived all the way from Dover to see her. And by the time she was through with his grievances, it was nearly two.

There was no sign of Billy Bob anywhere when she left to go home, and no time to hunt for him. She had to be at supper early, then back at the square at six o'clock for the kickoff to the next day's festivities. Somehow she'd become Sam's official representative.

Sweetwater lay in a rich, warm glow from the late afternoon sunshine as she headed home; a news crew down from WTVA television station in Tupelo was setting up across the street from the temporary podium and platform that had been erected. This was one of the oldest Independence Day celebrations in Mississippi, but Shiloh wondered when it had grown to be so important that television got involved. Surely one out-of-date *Geographic* article couldn't cause all this.

There was a line of cars in the drive at home. Inside, she stumbled over the mayor and two city councilmen at Laura's kitchen table. She might have asked the housekeeper what was going on, but they'd barely spoken in two weeks, so she said nothing when Laura informed her tersely that Sam needed her in the study.

His voice was gruff on the other side of the door when she knocked. "Come in."

She shut the door behind herself carefully. "Laura said you needed to see me. Where did all these people come from? And why are—"

The words died on her lips as she turned. Judge Sewell sat in the wingback chair beside her father's desk, his face calm, cool, handsome.

Not a hint of the anger he'd shown at the country club.

"Good afternoon, Shiloh," he said courteously as he arose. "It's good to see you. It's been a while."

You'd never know this sophisticated man in the cool gray suit had ever stooped to a messy illicit affair that had produced something as earthy as Billy Bob.

"Judge," she acknowledged, wondering if her dress was clean. He always looked too pristine, too perfect, too together. "I didn't realize you and Sam were in a meeting."

Sam pulled off his eyeglasses and laid them on the desk. "Judge Sewell is here on both business and family matters, Shiloh. He's come to a major decision. He's decided to run for governor."

There was a small, expectant pause. Was she supposed to be surprised?

"I see," Shiloh murmured at last, then held out her hand. "Congratulations, sir."

He shook her hand, then he said humorously, smiling at her, "Or maybe condolences."

The man actually had a dimple, and a sudden charm, all the more disarming because he seemed so proper the rest of the time.

He had bequeathed the charm at least to his illegitimate son.

A sudden insight hit Shiloh. "The news crew from Tupelo—that's what they're doing here."

"Have they already arrived?" The judge frowned, looking at his watch. "They're two hours early."

"Robert is going to make an informal announcement tonight, just for his home county," Sam told Shiloh. "The official one will be next week at the capitol."

Small hometown, patriotic holiday, parades and floats and kids and dogs. Who said Robert Sewell didn't know how to run a campaign? Shiloh thought wryly. Or maybe, Sam knew.

"Are you his adviser?" she asked her father bluntly.

"More like a backer, that's all," Sam demurred. "But I have a stake in this, just as the judge here does, just as you do."

Nobody spoke for a minute. Shiloh knew what was coming; she braced herself for it.

"This needs to be straightforward. Simple. No confusion." Judge Sewell reached out to take her by the wrists, his face kind as he looked down at her. "This mess with you and Michael needs to be straightened out. He's kept his distance for over a month, mostly because Sam has assured him that there are no other men in your life, that you love him, that you only needed time. My son wants to talk to you. All of us—and that includes Lydia and myself and Sam—we want you to be a part of the Sewell family. I hope you've come to the right decision, Shiloh, a mature, thinking, responsible one that will allow Michael to stop worrying himself ill over you."

His voice was gentle, wheedling, pleading, and underneath all that was the sting of reproach, barely felt. His hands were too soft, too wet on her arms.

And over his shoulder, Sam waited, watching her sternly.

I'm just the petted, spoiled little girl who got into a silly lover's spat with Michael and made trouble over it to get attention and my own way. That's what they think of me, Shiloh realized suddenly. They don't take me seriously; they never have.

But they were going to have to.

"It's the right decision for me. I can't marry him."

She wondered where the clear, decisive voice came from; surely not her, the one whose heart was jerking like a jackhammer.

"Goddamn it, Shiloh," Sam swore, his face like a thundercloud. He slapped his hand down on the desk so hard a picture fell—hers. "You're a fool."

The judge dropped her hands like they were hot coals. "You told me she was willing," he said accusingly to Sam, his face dark. No charm now. "She's kept Michael dangling for weeks now. I expected better of your daughter, Sam. And of you."

"So did I."

"There are other girls. Michael won't grieve long. But it would have been better to have the two of them together for everybody to see. I wanted this to be cleared up. Things have been in limbo. Sweetwater's a little town, and it talks. A broken engagement between them is just more fodder for gossip, and that damned news crew is out there, waiting to hear it."

Sam was staring at Shiloh, disappointment etched in his face, but his words were blunt. "It's a minor thing. Who pays any attention to a candidate's grown children? It won't even make a ripple that Michael's engagement was broken. If anything, women'll like him better."

The judge thought about that. "You may be right. We might just stay quiet about everything tomorrow. Let people think what they will."

"No."

Shiloh and Sam spoke simultaneously.

"There's no point in dragging this misery out any longer," Sam snapped. "Shiloh's burned her bridges. She can live with her mistakes. We'll tell it tomorrow. The news people will be gone. And when all this—this election hoopla is over this weekend, me 'n her—we're going to have our own conference."

Her stomach was tied in knots, but her heart felt light, wild, fluttery. She was free, just like that. It was her life and her body, and she couldn't share either with Michael Sewell. She'd known it for a certainty ever since a dance with Billy Bob at the Legion Hall.


The crowd in the courthouse square was boisterous and excited that Wednesday night. Word was out: Sweetwater's favorite son was going to announce. It was such a big occasion that every church in town except a diehard Freewill Baptist over on Houston Road had dismissed services.

Cotton and Jackson sat firmly entrenched on their bench, watching the excitement in the crowds around them.

"I'll lay you ten to one odds that Sewell's the next governor," Cotton offered.

"Not me you won't. He's bound to beat that sorry excuse for one we got now," Jackson retorted. "And the judge has Pennington backin' him. That ornery old man knows things."

"Speakin' of which, there's his girl," Cotton answered, nodding toward the woman who stood hesitantly on the edge of the crowd, scanning it.

"She don't look much like a politician's daughter-in-law," said Jackson doubtfully.

"She ain't never gonna marry into that Sewell crowd. Ain't stiff-necked enough. Did you see the way she sashayed right up to Billy Bob? It's a shame the way women chase men these days."

"I don't know. Billy didn't mind, didn't seem like. But it sure makes you wonder where them two struck up an acquaintance, and what kind of acquaintance it is. Real peculiar, considerin' that Billy's blood kin to Michael."

"She's lookin' for somebody," Cotton observed.

"Michael Sewell?"

"Billy Walker. I'll bet money on it."

"Ain't takin' that bet, either," Jackson returned sagaciously.


She wasn't ready yet to tell Billy everything. Didn't want to talk at all.

But she needed to see him, maybe to touch him in light of this new, exhilarating freedom she'd suddenly found.

He would know without words that she'd taken steps away from Sam. The only thing she was worried about now was if she really wanted to step in Billy's direction. She thought she did, but she needed to see him.

She was a prisoner who'd been cut free, and she had a lot of options.

Where was he?

Not at his grandfather's fruit stand. She could see it from here, through the dusk.

The crackling of a microphone quieted the crowd immediately; the mayor looked a little flustered at the sound, and he blinked in the glare of the big lights the camera crew fixed on him.

"Evenin'," he croaked, then cleared his throat. "We're here tonight in Sweetwater, on the courthouse steps of our fine town, to welcome one of our own. We're real proud of him in these parts; he's come a long way from his raising in the north end of Briskin County. He graduated from the University of Mississippi, then went on to law school there, too. Last few years, he's been a judge that we've all come to respect. But it's time for us to share him and his abilities with the rest of our state. Tonight, ladies and gentlemen, our own Judge Robert Sewell announces his candidacy for the governorship of Mississippi."

A huge roar went up from the crowd, and some man across from Shiloh stuck his fingers in his mouth and gave a wild, shrill whistle.

Robert and Lydia Sewell rose from their chairs on the platform, and Jack Sherrill, the songleader at the AME Church, led the crowd in a vigorous, roaring version of "The Star-Spangled Banner."

Bedlam couldn't have sounded worse, but it didn't

matter. Because suddenly Shiloh caught sight of the one reason she'd come down here tonight.

Billy Bob walked across the road opposite her, well behind the range of the cameras. He had one of his grandfather's peaches, tearing it with his teeth, and his lanky form made a long, long shadow as he strolled under one of the streetlights that had just come on. The rest of the world might be impressed with Robert Sewell, not him.

Over at his grandfather's stand, he swung himself up to the counter, letting his legs dangle. Only his white shirt and his light hair showed up distinctly.

She could just walk over there. The chains, whatever they'd been made of, were gone.

She took one step—then stopped.

What did she want from him? He would want to know, and she wasn't sure.

"Shiloh." The low, husky voice came from behind; so did the warm hand that clasped her bare arm.

Michael. He'd walked up right behind her, his eyes hot and excited even in the twilight.

"What are you doing here?"

"Dad wanted me to come. I barely had time to speak to him. He says he's talked with you. That it's settled."

And his other hand reached for one of the wild brown curls that the humidity had created against her neck.

"It's a good day, Shiloh. Dad gets to announce his big plans, and I get you back, right where you're supposed to be," he whispered, his hand on her arm tightening.

"Michael, you don't understand," she said frantically, straining away from him, but he held her still.

". . . and my son Michael is in the crowd. He drove here from Memphis to be with us," she heard Sewell say jovially over the big speakers. "Come on up here, son. This boy and Lydia are my only family."

Shiloh froze as a thousand eyes turned toward them; she hated being in the spotlight, but here she was, caught in it, trapped against Michael by his hands and the rules of polite society. Then the big camera lights swept over them.

She couldn't kick or scream or bite.

"Come on, Shiloh," he said with a laugh that held excitement and arousal, "you belong up there with me."

"No—no, Michael—"

His hand pulled her along after him inexorably—the faces of the laughing crowd danced in front of her eyes— what was she supposed to do?

Billy. Billy would see this. She had to let him know it was wrong, that she didn't want to be here, being dragged like a sacrifice up to the altar of the local politician.

Twisting frantically to look back over her shoulder, she saw him all too clearly. He wasn't sitting on the fruit stand anymore. He'd come out from it only to freeze in a pool of light, and even if she couldn't see his face, his body told it all. Stiff, unmoving, furious. She stumbled, and Michael's hand above her elbow urged her up the steps.

Sewell's face was stunned when he saw his son pulling her up the wooden steps after him. For once, the glib tongue failed him.

Get us out of this one, Judge, Shiloh thought in hysterical despair.

"I just want to say how proud I am of my father," Michael said smoothly. He looked like a young prince in the hot white lights of the camera. "And I wanted to introduce my fiancée, Miss Shiloh Pennington."

The crowd applauded; Shiloh and Robert Sewell never moved.

But things weren't as bad as they could get, after all; Shiloh discovered they could get worse when Michael looked down at her, caught in the crook of his arm, and kissed her full on the lips, bending her head back with his force.

Sweetwater loved it—they screamed and yelped.

When Michael turned her loose, she looked frantically for Billy Bob, searching the shadows.

He was gone.

And he didn't come back.


"I hate you. *Hate* you. I don't know how much more plainly I can say that. You tried to rape me."

Shiloh's face was as white as Michael's cotton polo top. They stood squared off, facing each other across her father's office, and if words were knives, the silver carpet would have been splotched red. She had been brutal during the last fifteen minutes.

They had retreated here at her insistence when the speeches ended; the judge's fear that she was about to explode outside in front of the crowd made him give in with poor grace to her demands that every one of them hear what she had to say.

"I don't know what you're talking about. I've never touched you," Michael blustered. "Not that way. Maybe you misunderstood."

"Now, Shiloh, don't make any more of a scene," Sam said warningly, from where he stood in front of the closed door, a sentinel at guard. "Think of Lydia. No mother wants to hear things about her son."

"*Me*—make a scene? I just got dragged up on a podium in front of half of Mississippi and kissed by a man I don't like. Who made *that* scene?" she demanded.

"There's been a misunderstanding. I didn't have time to talk to Michael," the judge expostulated.

"You said it was taken care of. All worked out," Michael accused, his face blood-red with shock and embarrassment and anger.

"She won't have you, boy."

Sam's words cut across the confusion in the room.

Lydia fairly trembled with rage as she stepped up to take her son's arm.

"She's not worth this, Michael," she said vehemently. "You need a woman who will love you, and behave like a civilized, decent person. Someone who won't make up vicious lies, someone from an impeccable background. Not from—"

"That's enough, Lydia." Judge Sewell cut her short; he knew who had the money in this room, and impeccable backgrounds didn't matter much stacked up to dollars and cents.

"I'm not ashamed of where I came from," Sam said mildly. "But that's got nothing to do with this. The fact is that Shiloh's stubborn as a mule. She won't marry him."

"Michael, are you all right?" Lydia's anxious words fell on deaf ears. Her son's face had two red splotches on each cheek; the vein in his temple throbbed painfully; his eyes burned into Shiloh's. "Nobody will ever believe any of these lies even if she tries to tell them."

Shaking his mother's hand off, he stepped across the carpet toward Shiloh, and he said clearly, "If I could do that night over, I'd be rougher. And you wouldn't get up until I was through with you. You'd remember it for the rest of your life."

The room reverberated with his words; the listeners stood frozen in a slow-dawning horror.

"Here, you've got no call to talk to her like that!" Sam

sounded apoplectic, horrified, outraged, as he walked toward Michael.

But Michael stopped him cold, shoving him away. "And you, old man, and all your money that my father dances to like a trained bear, you can go to hell. I'll meet you there."

He nearly tore the door off its hinges, then vanished down the hall.

Sewell came out of his trance to rush to the door. "Michael, don't do something stupid," he called after his son.

Lydia Sewell was sobbing quietly, but there was pure fury in her voice. "You've turned the best night of my life into a tragedy, Shiloh. This is your fault. Look what you've done to Michael."

"Michael's thirty years old. He did it to himself," Sam said heavily.

At first black rage consumed him. Under its power, Billy Bob made it to his truck and down the road. Grandpa could catch a ride home with Clancy Green.

His head was full of hot, passionate profanities, waiting to tumble off the tip of his tongue. But something held them back, probably the tremendous iron grip he used to clamp down on his emotions. If he ever really let go of them, he was going to hurt, hurt so much he might not survive.

So he burned up the highway in a deadly silence.

Michael Sewell had just reached out and reeled Shiloh back in. He'd laid hands on her as casually as if he were the one married to her. Right there in front of the whole world, he had claimed Shiloh.

But that wasn't what hurt the most.

She had let him.

That made everything she'd told Billy a lie. A damned lie. What had really happened? She'd used him to get Michael to fall in line? To get something from Sam? She had kissed him and danced with him and lain with him on that couch—and it was all a lie. A game. Another one.

She'd gone right up on that stage and let Sewell kiss her. *Kiss* her. They had looked good together, matched in their cool whites, his blond head forcing hers back so that her brown mane of hair fell thickly, freely.

"My fiancée," Sewell had said.

Well, buddy, thought Billy viciously, there's one little problem. She's married. And I had my hands on her yesterday, and two weeks ago, and four years ago. But if I could get my hands on her now, it'd be different. I might kill her.

Pain began to trickle into his rage, lessening it. Then he slowed down so that instead of taking the road so fast it was a dark blur, he saw where he'd come: home. The farm.

It was all right. He needed a hole to crawl into, to lick his wounds. So he pulled off, turning not toward the house but toward the dark barn, where Chase was.

He found the bridle but didn't even look for the saddle. The big horse was sleepy and confused as Billy Bob slipped the bridle on his nose, but he made no fuss when Billy led him outside the barn doors and vaulted onto his bare back.

The night air was hot and humid; mosquitoes were out in force. But the horse snorted with the realization of his unexpected freedom, and eased into a trot, ignoring the heat.

Billy let him go, riding out into the dark night past the

orchards. Far in the distance, way beyond a stretching field, somebody's porch light glowed dimly.

He ran his hand over his face, trying hard to fight away all sensations. Pain, betrayal, loss.

She'd set him up for it all. And it wasn't like it was the first time she'd done it. Once before she'd made him feel things, gotten to him, then walked away. He just hadn't expected her to go so far. She'd kissed him. Just yesterday, she'd teased him with that Coke can, in front of everybody.

She'd asked for time; she'd made him believe there might be more to this marriage than a desire to get even with her father and his brother. More than a thirty-five-hundred dollar jail fine.

It was all a lie.

The Sewells deserved her.

And Billy Walker had learned all over again that he was the biggest, dumbest fool in this county. Maybe in this state.


He didn't go home until nearly midnight, and he wouldn't have gone then except there was nothing else to do and Chase was beginning to tire. He rubbed the horse down carefully, just to occupy time, and stopped to stroke one of the dogs that had run up to him from nowhere.

He kept wondering where *she* was, seeing her on that platform in that white circle of light. But it wasn't that memory that hurt him the most.

No, what stung like hellfire was the one fact Billy finally forced himself to face: she had looked as if she belonged with Michael. Both cool, well-dressed, poised. The up-and-coming country club set.

He kept seeing her walk up those steps, remembering the swing of her hair as she twisted to look back. He'd seen her face clearly in the light—it had been shocked, pleading. For what?

Or had he misunderstood?

He wondered all of that as he climbed wearily up the steps to the white farmhouse that loomed like a ghost under the moonlight, the dog at his heels.

"Will."

He jumped. The voice startled him, coming from the shadows at the swing. Only one person called him that.

"Mama! What are you doin' up this late?"

"There's a girl that keeps calling here. She says her name is Shiloh. And your grandpa claims that's the name of that banker's daughter in town." Ellen was so agitated she could barely get the words out. "She says every time she calls that it's important."

The swing rocked wildly as Ellen stood, her pale cotton robe blowing a little in the late-night breeze. "She's upset. Boy, you've not gone and got yourself in bad trouble, have you?"

Not unless you count the way I hurt right now, he thought.

"No, Mama. But I know what she wants. It's nothing." She'd called. Why? No matter. It was way too late, and it had nothing to do with the clock.

Ellen gazed up at him, eyes disbelieving. "It is to her. She's gonna call one last time at midnight. She asked me if it'd be okay. I told her I didn't know where you were but she—she sounded desperate."

"It'll work out," he returned wearily, dropping into the swing she'd vacated. "I can't tell you any more right now, Mama. Just go on to bed. I'll wait for the call."

"This girl—is she who Grandpa claims?"

"She's Pennington's daughter, if that's what you mean."

"He said . . . she was with . . . with Michael Sewell tonight." Ellen's words were low with distress.

"That's right. She was."

"Oh, Will, what have you got yourself into?"


In the dark kitchen, he picked up the telephone on the first ring with one hard jerk.

"Yeah?"

"Billy?"

His heart stopped. She'd never called him before, and it was meaningless now.

"What d'you want, Shiloh?" he asked brusquely.

He heard her long-drawn breath. She was nervous. That was good.

"I need to talk to you."

"About what? Well, don't worry, honey, whatever it is, you can have it all. I don't want to see you ever again."

"Billy, don't be like this. We need to talk. I need to explain about tonight."

"You mean when I stood there and saw with my own eyes, heard with my own ears, that you're Michael's fiancée? No, I don't reckon I want to talk about that. You can feed your lines to him tonight. Cry on his shoulder about how afraid you are, about how good he makes you feel."

"Billy, please. I'm not engaged to him. I didn't know he was going to do that. I didn't want him to."

"You mean," he drawled in patent disbelief, "that he just dragged you up there and you didn't have a clue?"

"That's right," she cut in, her voice blurry, as though

she'd been crying—or was about to. "Today the judge and Sam wanted me to agree to the engagement again. He said it would be better for his candidacy if things were settled between me and Michael. And you know what Sam wants. So, I settled things. I said no. But Michael barely got here before the speech started. He thought— Michael did—that I'd agreed to take him back. I couldn't say or do anything in front of that crowd. I just had to—to stand it."

"I don't believe you."

"Why would I call you now, trying to explain, if it wasn't the truth, Billy? The judge swore he'd tell the truth about the engagement tomorrow. It'll be on every street corner. And why would I . . . call you to the house and tell you the way I feel, and let you bully me all over town, if I'm not telling the truth?"

"We got married, and that wasn't the truth."

There was a tiny pause while she registered what he said. "Billy, I could be somewhere, the square maybe, at your grandfather's booth, if you'll only come—"

"You stood in light brighter than daylight and let him kiss you, but I'm supposed to meet you in the dark. Just like always. Well, I never liked it before, and I sure as hell don't like it now. Forget it, Shiloh. This time I'm not comin'."

When she spoke again, she was as angry as he was. "You know what? You're as big a jerk as Michael. I couldn't get it through his head that I didn't want him, and now I can't get it through yours that I do—" She broke off the sentence.

He had to know the end of it. "You do *what?*"

"Nothing," she said hotly. "But it's my turn to make

demands, Billy, like you made here the other night. If you don't meet me at the square in thirty minutes, if you won't believe me when I'm telling the truth, don't you ever come flirting around me with your fast hands again."

# 12

She was *actually* stupid enough to cry.

In fact, Shiloh couldn't seem to stop crying, and all the tears were for Billy. Her world was coming apart: Laura had quit talking, Sam was furious, T-Tommy was disapproving, the Sewells—well, they didn't matter.

She'd faced down Sam and Michael both.

She ought to be happy.

Instead, she was tearing herself up over Billy Bob. And he was as hard and uncaring as a rock.

The night was full of a steamy, swampy heat that curled under doors and hit her in the face when she stepped outside. Most of the town was asleep; Sam was still off somewhere with Sewell, probably holed up until dawn, making plans to rule the kingdom of Mississippi even as Shiloh pulled out in the quiet street in the car.

She didn't care if her father caught her in or out; she had to talk to Billy.

She had to make him trust her. She had to trust him.

In the pocket of the white shorts that she wore was her ring on his chain. Something little, but . . . "if I ever mean anything to you, then you can give it back."

It would be her pledge, her peace offering, to make him listen. Her bond of trust.

If only he'd come.


The center of Sweetwater lay quietly under the silver stars in the wee hours of this Saturday morning.

Shiloh parked behind the old depot, then walked one block up and two blocks over, clinging to the shadows, her heart pounding.

An unexpected, blessed breeze rustled leaves as it swept over the dark town. Except for that, there was silence.

The bright circles of light cast by the lamps on each corner didn't intrude into the black shadows of the big trees and the courthouse.

At first she thought he wasn't there; the old truck was nowhere in sight. But she found it parked on the other side—the dark side—of the fruit stand, and her heart began to beat heavily.

He was here.

He'd come.

He was standing in the deepest shadows, leaning against the wall of the stand, one booted foot crossed over the other. She saw that much because his legs protruded from the darkness and a dim light struck them.

They faced each other in silence, until the black night pressed down on them like a heavy, smothering blanket. Shiloh breathed harshly, fighting the sensation. At last, his voice broke the stillness.

"I know how to act and what I'm supposed to say," he said abruptly, his voice controlled and stiff. "It's nothing to me if you're engaged to Sewell again. I earned the money you offered me, and that's all that's between us. That, and a little heavy petting on the side. If you members of the upper crust want to kiss in front of a television crew, that's your business. But so you won't turn up a bigamist, we need a divorce. Tell me how and when, and we'll go get it quick."

She took a quick, protesting step toward him. "I didn't want to be with him. I told you. And I don't want to hear what you're supposed to say. I want you to tell me the truth."

"I've heard that before. Do you really think I'd trust you enough to tell you that? But there's one thing I don't mind saying." He hadn't moved at all, locked in a quiet, unnerving rigidity. "I'm glad I didn't fall into this sweet little trap you've been baiting for me, honey. Because when I think about you and Michael, it makes me sick. I wouldn't like having my brother's leavings."

The harsh words spilled out between them, in an absolute silence.

"I knew you'd say something that would hurt, Billy." Her words shook. "Now you have. Does it make you feel better?"

"I feel fine."

"No, you don't."

"How would you know?"

"Because I know how *I* feel. And most of it's your fault. I got through the fights with everybody else, but I couldn't sleep because I knew I had to try to set things right with you."

"You can't. Go back to Michael. You looked right with him up on that stage. Like you belonged together."

"Don't say that," she said vehemently.

"Why not? It's true."

In the darkness she found his warm, bare arm unexpectedly, her hand catching it. He shuddered at her touch, breaking away, and the terrible stillness vanished as he straightened violently.

"That's the worst part. You looked like you fit with him. I can't ever forget that, or what you've done with him. Tonight, and all the other nights."

"And what have I done?"

He tried and couldn't say the words, so she rushed on.

"I know what you're thinking. And while you're thinking it, you ask yourself how it's all right for you to sleep around with —what, hundreds?—but for me—"

"I've slept with exactly four women since you left," he interrupted bluntly. "I like living too much to mess around with hundreds. I don't want to die of some disease. I'm careful."

"Oh, four. Is that all? And how many times with those lucky four?"

Even in the middle of his distress, Billy had the prudence to stay quiet.

"That's what I thought." She couldn't keep the hurt out of her voice. "And you'd had girls before me, when I was eighteen."

"I was twenty-three. Yeah, I'd had a few. But I'd never been to the Palace, or done half the things I've done since, until after you took off to Mexico. *You never came back, Shiloh.* What was I supposed to do?"

"You never really cared, then. Or you couldn't have touched another woman."

"You don't know men if you believe that," he answered, ironic humor coloring his words.

She gathered everything in her for her admission.

"Maybe you're right. I don't know men. Not any of them. Not a single one—ever."

There was a long, long silence while he registered her words.

"Did you hear me, Billy?"

"I don't believe you." He couldn't seem to speak.

"You never do. But why not? If we ever get to the point where it . . . matters, you'll find out the truth, anyway."

"It matters right now." His voice was strangled as he stepped forward toward her, leaving the shadows, and his face was twisted with a mixture of doubt and hope.

"I did one thing that was wrong—very wrong—with Michael, but I didn't really even understand that it was all that bad until I saw you again."

"I don't want to hear about it. I can't stand to."

"You already know it. I let him take your place. Like you said. He has this unfortunate tendency to look like you, and for a while it felt like he brought back a part of me that was gone." She rubbed her hands over her cheeks in tired defeat. "You don't deserve to know this, Billy Bob, but I'll tell you anyway. When he touched me, it wasn't right. Maybe it was because I was afraid of being like my mother, or because I've discovered that I really do believe that sex belongs with marriage and love and commitment—or maybe it was because I found that he wasn't really you after all."

"Shiloh."

He reached for her and she backed away, her eyes dark pools that shimmered in the moonlight, backing until she was stopped by the side of his truck.

"No, you haven't heard it all yet. Finally, Michael tried to make me. Do you understand? He hurt me. I had to fight him, like an animal, to get away. That's why I was running the night T-Tommy put me in the cell beside yours."

She paused for breath, gasping. Billy was staring at her in shock.

"Well, go ahead," she burst out defiantly. "Say it. It was my fault. I was teasing him, playing games, like I did with you. It's the way I dress, or talk, or breathe air. Be like Sam. Tell me Michael wouldn't stoop to attempted rape."

He moved at last, as jerky as an old man, his face like stone in the starlight. When he got to the other side of the truck, he opened the door and got in under the wheel.

Shiloh said in alarm, "Billy, what are you doing?" Then she fumbled for the handle and slid in the passenger side.

"Get out, Shiloh." His voice was mild, but there was a controlled ferocity in his motions as he jammed the keys in the ignition.

She caught his arm. "Where are you going?"

He went still under her touch, looking down at her. "I reckon," he said calmly, "that I'm gonna go find Michael Sewell."

"Why?"

"You know why."

"No—no, Billy, you can't. You're going to do what? Beat him up? They'll put you in jail again, all for nothing. He didn't rape me. Are you listening? I got away."

She caught him by both arms this time, reaching across him, across the steering wheel.

"Do you understand what I'm saying? Don't go, Billy, please."

This close, she could feel the violence in him, the strength and temper that lay just under her hands. And then the truth swept over her in a warm, rich tide: Billy Walker had believed her, no matter what else was between them. Believed so much that he had meant to fight for her.

There was a long stretching moment filled with her desperate need to hold him, when her face and voice were full of longing and invitation as she looked up at him.

"I reckon if I was you," he said quietly, "I'd be scared to get too close to a man—any man—unless I was sure I wanted him to touch me. Be sure, Shiloh."

He caught her when she flung herself against him, pulling her tightly to his body. The tears threatened again, pushing against her closed eyelids. She wouldn't cry again, not now. The minutes ticked by, marked by nothing but their ragged breaths as his hands held her tightly in place, not turning loose even one fraction.

He said huskily, "I know it's not supposed to matter these days how many men you've been with, but it does. It does, baby."

Under his hands, she shivered.

"Are you—you're not crying again, are you?"

She shook her head, not sure she could speak, then he held her away, trying to see in the darkness. His hand brushed her cheek, then stilled, and he replaced it with the brush of his lips, his skin warm and smooth against her face.

"You're shaking." His voice was as shattered as her own emotions.

"Not because I'm afraid," she managed, her cheek hot from his touch. "Because I thought on the telephone, you sounded like you hated me."

"Maybe I did. At least, part of me did, ever since I saw you—" he broke off.

"I didn't want to be with him, Billy."

"I needed you to call me tonight," he said somberly. "But only if it means something tomorrow."

"Billy, I didn't come here because I needed to. Don't you see? I thought I needed you and that marriage to hide behind, to throw in Sam's face. But I didn't." Shiloh pushed away from him, fumbling for the words to explain. "All of a sudden, I could do it. I felt like an independent person for the first time. It was my life. And if they didn't like what I wanted to do with it, or if they didn't like me, it wasn't important. I had to tell Michael in front of everybody. I told him I hated him—to stay away. And when I looked at Sam, he looked old and angry, and I didn't want to hurt him, the way I wanted to when I asked you to marry me. But I can't live for Sam. Then I knew. I was free. Free, Billy. I've never felt so light, so . . . uncaged in my life. Does that make sense?"

He didn't answer for a moment. But he let his hands slide down the side of the leather-wrapped steering wheel as he looked away from her, out on the still square with its murky, draped booths and the blue-and-white posters proclaiming Sewell for Governor that had already been plastered on everything available. And his jaw tightened.

"So you don't need me, or the marriage."

"Not for the reasons I did before. But I think I want you, and that's better," she whispered, her hand reaching out to trace his ear.

He didn't flinch; he didn't move at all. "You want me. Am I supposed to like that? How many women have told me that? Do you know, Shiloh?" In the shadows as he turned to look at her, his eyes gleamed ferally. "More than I can count. 'I want you to kiss me, Billy. To dance with me. To go home with me. To make me feel good. To hang on my arm and make me look good.' So keep your 'wanting,' Shiloh; I've had a stomachful of it."

She winced, but she spoke determinedly.

"You don't understand. I think I want you as . . . as . . . this is hard for me to say when you're so angry, Billy, but I want you as my real husband. Not because I need you as a buffer or a slap in the face to Sam. But because— well, the question is, do you want me?"

Still as a statue, Billy stared at her while eternity slid by. Shiloh was glad it was dark; her face was on fire. But she didn't flinch from his wide-eyed stare.

Then he moved in one rough lunge to haul her up against him, her face smothered against his chest, her legs tangled with his. Under her cheek, his heart beat as heavily as hers. "I've wanted to marry you for four years, baby. That's how long you've been under my skin."

His raw, passionate words whispered around her head, and she began to laugh—a broken, emotional sound.

His calloused fingers fumbled for her face, forcing her chin up. His own face was intent, his eyes on her lips as his head dropped toward her, and she flushed deeply, as shy suddenly as if he'd never touched her before. His lips on hers were warm—the kiss sweet—his mouth nearly chaste.

This kiss was a vow, a serious, reverent one. There was only the soft sound of their hurried breathing and the sibilant one when their lips parted, lingered, and parted again.

Then a tiny flurry of movement as she drew in breath and looked down, away from his brilliant gaze.

"I'm coming to get you tomorrow, Shiloh." His words were steady and determined. "Get your things ready."

"I want you to give me time." She said it in a rush, dreading his reaction. "You can't come yet."

"Time!" He laughed incredulously. "Not that again. We're married. You just said—"

"There's Sam to think of—no, don't pull away. This isn't like the movies, Billy. I mean, we've got families, both of us do. Neither one of us wants to hurt them. I told you, Sam already feels betrayed. I've thrown away everything he wanted for me."

"Goddamn it, Shiloh, how much am I supposed to take?" Billy flung open the truck door and pulled violently away from her to stand outside. "It's either me or Sam. I told you years ago. No room for both of us."

"Things have changed. Give him a chance. I want to do it right this time, Billy. Like you said, no more sneaking around. Come to the door tomorrow, ring the bell, ask for me. Take me to—to the parade at ten. Let's walk through town and let the whole world see us. If they don't like it, if Sam doesn't, that's too bad. But he'll know. It won't be like us just turning up married." She didn't tell him that she didn't want her father coming down on him, the way T-Tommy thought he would. Maybe her way would prevent it.

He turned to look at her, raking the too-long hair from his neck.

"Ring the doorbell and ask permission to see my wife. That's good, Shiloh, real good."

"You know it'll be easier to tell about this marriage if we do it this way for a few weeks. A month. And it'll give us time out in the open, out from the pressure, to find out if a marriage will work. I've never even met your mother, Billy. Nor been to your house. If we are going to be married, I want it to last."

Her words were logical, sensible, pleading. He stood stiffly, rejecting them for an eon, then he took a deep breath and his whole body relaxed.

"You offered me money for my name—we got married fresh out of a jail cell—and tonight I watched you kiss another man in front of our whole hometown. Now you want me to be proper and reasonable."

He propped his right forearm on the top of the truck, the other pushing against the open door, and he looked at her while she waited for his answer, while that sweet night breeze blew his hair back a little.

"One day," he said abruptly. "Tomorrow. I'll do it one day and see what happens. If you really do step out Sam Pennington's door with me—" His words were intense, doubtful.

And suddenly, she knew what to do. Now was the time.

"I've got something for you, Billy," she said, her words tremulous.

He eyed her dubiously.

"But you have to close your eyes."

"Shiloh—"

"Just do it."

He made an impatient gesture. "My eyes are closed. See?"

She tried to straighten enough to get to her pocket and bumped her head on the top of the truck before she slid the chain out. His face was lifted toward the light, the angle highlighting the thick blond hair brushed off his temples, the smooth, strong planes of his high cheekbones, the straight line of his nose, the strong one of his jaw. For all Billy's good looks, he wasn't pretty; he looked like a man. Hers.

She dropped the chain over his head; it hung for a second on the bridge of his nose before it slipped around his neck.

And before he could open his eyes, she leaned forward and kissed him, the kiss so dark and intense that he forgot what she'd done and just wrapped her up against him, falling forward into the truck, hitting his elbow on the steering wheel.

When at last she pulled away without breath, he looked down at her, unmoving, his eyes vivid. Then Shiloh broke the gaze to touch the ring, and he glanced down to find it and pick it up himself.

He understood what it meant; the blaze of triumph and tenderness that flared in his face told her that. Then he raised the ring to his lips and kissed it.

He didn't reach for her; instead he pushed her away, down onto the seat. She caught at him, but he whispered no, his eyes gleaming like lambent coals as he looked down at her. Then he lifted his hands and brought both of them to the front of her shirt, to the buttons that held the delicate white cotton cloth together.

Her breath caught in her throat as he unsteadily undid the first one, then the next. He raised his intent, absorbed gaze to her startled one as he reached for the third button.

"Billy—"

"I don't have a ring, not tonight," he said with difficulty as he undid the next button, "and maybe you can't wear one from me for everybody to see for a few days yet. But if you meant all you said, then I've got a right to do some claiming of my own."

She lay perfectly still, eyes wide and heart beating visibly in her throat as he opened the last button, reached around her to pull her shirt from the shorts, and spread it open.

He sucked in his breath at the sight of her skin, glowing with a creamy warmth here in the dim darkness. At the edge of the white satin undergarment she wore, her breasts were so smooth he had to touch them, running his hand gently across all that was exposed. She was trembling a little under his touch, each breath lifting her breasts a little.

"Don't be afraid," he whispered. "Nobody will know. And I'll quit if you want me to."

"What are you going to do?" Her whisper was shaky.

"This," he answered, and he bent his wheat-blond head to the curve of her breast, just at the edge of the lace. She felt his tongue brush her skin, then his lips as they settled firmly on her, pulling with a tender suction.

Then she knew, and a hot sweet wave of emotion swept across her. "Billy," she whispered tenderly, achingly, cuddling his head against her breast, pushing her fingers through his hair to hold him to her.

So different from Michael when he'd bent to her breast, she thought in an unexpected, painful insight.

Billy couldn't know—must never know—what Michael had done, but she wished that he could feel how his unwitting action took away the shame of his brother's; that he could know that nothing had shown her more clearly the difference between the two men, and how much she wanted this one, the one with the gentle mouth.

The world was confused and mixed up: it thought Michael Sewell was the better man.

A woman who'd been with both knew the truth.

The two of them stayed like that a long time, even when his mouth finally released her. And in the long, silent moments afterward, her heart stilled to a reasonable beat and his ragged breathing slowed and calmed.

At last he lifted his head to look her in the face, then he looked down at his handiwork, at the mark his mouth had left at the curve of her left breast.

"That's my claim," he said quietly. "And even after the mark is gone, you remember it, Shiloh. It's there, even if nobody else can see it." Then he breathed harshly and said in an attempt at joking laughter, "And honey, they'd better *not* see it."

She couldn't say anything yet, her throat tight and clogged, and finally, Billy pulled her shirt together and began buttoning it again, glancing up at her time after time as he worked.

"You didn't stop me," he said at last. "So, you don't hate it?"

She shook her head, and he slid to the next button.

"What's the matter, then?" he asked at last, fastening the last one and holding her down to look into her face.

She didn't want to come out of the dazed, honeyed splendor where she'd been lost, where speech was a burden and an intrusion. As he propped himself up over her, she reached out and caught the ring as it dangled between them from the chain around his neck.

"This means no more girls for you," she managed, teasingly.

"No more girls. I haven't been with one since before we married, Shiloh." Then the lines of his face shifted into rueful laughter. "Which means I'm a fool to let you go tonight with just—this." His fingers brushed her shirt where the skin still tingled from the touch of his mouth.

"It's all I can stand tonight, I think."

"But there'll be other nights."

"We're going to make it, Billy Walker."

His face darkened. "Just don't walk off with Michael

anymore, no matter how much you look like you belong with him."

"Billy, we'll look better together, me and you. Wait until tomorrow. You'll see. We're going to set this town on its ear."

# 13

*It didn't seem* to matter that Shiloh had not gotten to bed until three A.M.; she was awake at seven, happy and scared and wound tighter than an alarm clock.

Today was the first day of freedom, and the way things went this particular Saturday would determine the immediate future.

Most of all, she had to bite the bullet and face Sam at Billy's side. If she flinched even once, both Billy and Sam were going to be aware of it.

She smiled at herself in the mirror, a secretive, pleased smile. Billy Bob was coming here, today, for her.

A knock on her bedroom door made her jump.

"Shiloh, are you awake?"

Sam. The girl in the blue cotton sleepshirt stared wide-eyed at the one in the mirror. What did he want this early?

So find out, she told herself sternly.

Her father was already dressed for the day, his clothes

fresh and crisp, but his face under the silver hair was old and tired.

"I thought I heard you moving when I walked past," Sam said quietly. "I don't have much time. I have to meet the judge and two of his advisers in an hour. But I wanted to say"—he looked away, down the hall at the oil still life that hung above an antique drop-leaf desk—"that I regret not believing what you told me about Michael." He said it gruffly, rushing over the words, before he glanced back at her, embarrassed.

Shiloh stared; Sam had never apologized to her before, not in twenty-two years.

"I've been remembering it all night, what he said to you. I know that he's disappointed. I still believe that he loves you as much as he can love anybody, but that's no excuse. Not for anything."

"Papa—" Shiloh couldn't seem to get the word out; then Sam cut her off with a quick movement.

"Lydia was out of line to speak to you like she did. And I had words for Michael, but he never came home last night. Just stay clear of both of them. I've got no time to talk now, but I'll tell you this, Shiloh: there's bigger fish than Michael in the sea, and I reckon, better ones, too, even if it took a lightning bolt to make me see it."

Awkwardly, he reached out to touch her cheek.

Now. Tell him now, she thought, but as she hesitated, gathering up courage, Sam turned away, looking at his watch. "I'm late. I'll see you later today. I won't be at the parade, but I'll be at the square at three. Is that the time you're supposed to present the trophies?"

She nodded wordlessly.

"All right." And he was gone, down the stairs.

◆  ◆  ◆

Billy didn't come.

Not at eight, or nine. And at a quarter to ten, Shiloh walked past the phone resolutely; she refused to call him. She'd said what she had to say last night, and done other things as well.

The mark on her breast burned for an instant, and her cheeks flushed at the memory. If he didn't come after that, she couldn't make him. She wouldn't even try.

He should have gotten his hair cut long ago, Billy thought in a near panic as he brushed it back furiously on Saturday morning. He'd started wearing it this way out of teenage rebelliousness, and then it just seemed as he grew older that he never had enough time to go regularly to the barber shop to maintain a neat, short shear.

Sam Pennington might find a short-haired Billy Bob easier to take.

Well, it didn't matter. It was too late now. And if the old scoundrel didn't like him any better today than he had four years ago, all the haircuts in the world wouldn't matter.

What mattered was that Shiloh was waiting for him . . . he hoped.

But just in case, he meant to wait to tell Mama and Grandpa about her. Some tiny doubt in his heart still lingered. She had to prove herself.

Well, he'd done what he could with what he had to work with, he thought, surveying himself critically in the mirror: the summer plaid shirt, the neatly creased jeans, the big belt buckle, the shined-up boots.

He wasn't Michael, and he wasn't going to make even one concession toward his brother's uptown, well-tailored panache.

It was only six o'clock, but he had this gut feeling she was already waiting for him.

"This is a big day," he told Chase and the dogs solemnly as he fed and watered them. "She says she's going to tell the world." It was safe, he figured, to at least tell the three of them. "Reckon I look all right?"

But it was Ellen who answered the question later. She stared as he walked through the kitchen after he'd washed his hands.

"My gracious," she said in surprise at his neatness.

Billy poured himself a cup of coffee and avoided her eyes.

"Gotta go to town," he said casually, sipping the hot liquid as he faced her. "Is Grandpa ready?"

"That girl who called—"

"I told you, it was nothing to worry about," he said quickly.

"But, Will—"

"Mama," he said flatly, setting the cup down, "don't ask me anything else. I don't want to talk about it. Not yet. It's my business, okay?"

She turned away, her feelings hurt. "If you say so."

Billy watched her stiff back a minute as she washed dishes at the sink, searching for something to say.

"Are you coming with us?"

"No." She answered decisively. "Too many politicians in town for me."

They'd never really spoken of it much before, this matter of the Sewells; it was implicitly understood that the less said, the better. So it was a measure of just how upset Ellen was that she even hinted that the judge's actions concerned her at all, and of just how ebullient Billy was that he answered her.

"You can't keep on and on hiding from him," he said abruptly. "It was nearly thirty years ago."

She turned to look at him, her hands still in the soapy water. "And that's *my* business."

"Mama—"

Grandpa stepped heavily through the screen door. "T-Tommy's pullin' in the drive," he said to Billy.

Billy looked at him in blank surprise. "What for?"

Willie eyed his grandson dubiously. "You're usually the one that can answer that."

"Not this time." He crossed to the screen door and stepped out on the back porch, just as the sheriff climbed out of the car, a strange reluctance about his movements.

"Mornin', T-Tommy."

"Mornin', Billy Bob. Willie."

There was a long pause. Billy reached for the porch bannister to lean forward on it, braced with both hands. "You here for breakfast?" he asked humorously.

T-Tommy didn't crack a smile. "I'm here for you," he said somberly.

Billy straightened. "Me! What in hell for?"

The sheriff took several slow, threatening steps until he was staring up into Billy's face in accusation from the ground below.

"You want to tell me where you were and what you did last night, Billy? And don't say you were at home. Clancy Green got in from fishin' before dawn this mornin'—he's already told me he saw your truck out at two A.M."

Billy opened his mouth to speak—then closed it. He couldn't say he'd been making out with Shiloh Pennington, could he?

"No answer?" T-Tommy's voice was a growl of disappointment and anger.

"What d'you want to know for?"

"There was a wreck out on 25 this morning, Billy—not long after Clancy saw you."

"So? It wasn't me."

"No. It was a man from Magnolia, Arkansas. Somebody ran him off the road. He don't remember much after that—either the other driver hit him nearly head-on and forced the collision, or he forced him to run off the road and wreck that way."

Billy straightened slowly, his face cool. "Like I said, so what?"

"Then the other driver got out of his own car, opened the Arkansas man's car door, looked in at him, saw him layin' there in his own blood, beggin' for help . . . and walked away. Just pulled off. This man—his name's Juliard—he thinks he begged the other driver for help several times."

The morning was so bright it hurt to look out toward the sun-sprayed, glittering trees in the nearest peach orchard. The breeze was unexpectedly cool, too, like the one that had brushed against him and Shiloh as she stood before him last night.

Those stray thoughts wandered into his head in the few seconds before Billy made himself face what T-Tommy was getting around to saying.

Willie had frozen beside him; he thought Ellen had done the same at the screen door.

"I didn't," he said clearly, "hit another car, then walk off and leave the driver."

T-Tommy reached up to pull off his sunglasses before he squinted up at Billy. "Juliard says you did."

His flat words broke the peculiar silence. Ellen gave a sobbing intake of sound; Willie swore. Billy came off the porch in two long, angry strides, right down face-to-face with the sheriff.

"How could he? I don't know anybody from Magnolia, Arkansas—and he sure as hell doesn't know me."

"He described you to a T, Billy. You think I'm makin' it up? That I want to believe it? He thought you were drinking. I hope to God you were. Surely you couldn't leave a man bleedin' to death from somethin' you'd done unless you were drunk, or high. Why, I've seen you work with a sick animal and treat it better than that. But it had to be you. Juliard went on and on about you bendin' over him. He was nearly hysterical. I showed him three different sets of pictures, and he picked you out, over and over, even when the medication that the doctor gave him was settin' in."

"I didn't do it!"

"He's got a concussion. He's cut open here. Hurt bad." T-Tommy put his hands against his own round abdomen. "Some broke ribs, and a compound fracture of his leg. And he laid there for nearly an hour, if we've got it figured right."

"I said, *I didn't do it.*" Billy repeated the words again and again. What had gone wrong with the world? When had it turned upside down?

"Then why did Clancy see you out on the highway?" T-Tommy asked at last, quietly. "What were you doin' at one—and at two—this mornin'?"

"I was . . . drivin'. I went to the—the booth on the square for a while."

"Will!" his mother whispered in dismay. "You went back out?"

What was he going to do? Billy wondered in some distant, cold, logical corner of his mind. Try to straighten this out on his own? Or involve Shiloh? No, first he had to try to work it out. It was a mistake. Surely the truth would show up.

"My truck. Look at it," he told T-Tommy suddenly. "I didn't hit anybody."

"Juliard doesn't know if you did or not. Maybe you just ran him off the road, like I said. Randy Porter's out of town. He could'a told us more if he'd seen the man's car, but he won't be back for three days." T-Tommy fiddled with the glasses a few seconds, then said reluctantly, "I gotta take you in, Billy Bob. You know that."

"But I—" What? What could he say? I'm innocent? I've got a girl waiting?

"He didn't do anything," Willie said angrily, moving toward the sheriff as fast as his cane allowed. "Are you deaf? He said it and said it."

"It's just for questionin', Willie. At least, that's all it is now." T-Tommy walked over to his car and opened the back door. "Some folks would say I should handcuff you, but I don't want to do that. Not in front of your family. So just get on in, Billy. Don't make it hard on everybody."

For a long, horrible moment, Billy thought about what this morning was supposed to have been, and what it had become instead. He was going to jail and he didn't even know how it had happened. Then he felt his mother's agony as she stepped toward him, and he made his feet move.

"All right," he said hoarsely. "Just get it over with, this questioning."

The door with the smooth, empty panel peculiar to patrol cars slammed behind him with a force that jarred; the metal screen between him and the sheriff blurred his vision. He had to blink to clear it.

Just as T-Tommy started to pull out, Ellen ran to his window. "There's a girl. She's in this somewhere, I know. Make him tell you. *Please.*"

"Now, Ellen—"

"Stay out of this, Mama. Go on, T-Tommy. You came after me. You got me. So let's go. *Now.*"

He tried not to look at his mother or his grandfather or the house. He tried not to think of Shiloh, waiting for him, or of what she was going to do when she heard about this. Walk, maybe. Any other woman would, away from him and the trouble that dogged him.

He wouldn't give T-Tommy anything that could lead to her getting mixed up in this mean little nightmare— not unless he had to.

Something was out there, whispering through the crowd, spreading in little concentric circles.

Shiloh didn't notice it at first, too wrapped up in her disbelief and misery. Billy hadn't shown up, even at the parade. What had gone wrong?

Even his grandfather's stand remained closed. Was the old man sick again?

Once or twice, she even thought she caught Billy's name on the wind as she waited on the platform for the parade to begin.

The sun blazed overhead, making her blink and frown.

"I need to get out of the sun," she told the man beside her. She thought he was the principal of the high school.

He grinned at her cheerfully. "Don't worry. It's not that important. The big deal is to be back this afternoon."

A group of men stood in a circle under the trees nearest the fruit stand.

". . . they say he laid there in his own blood."

"Clancy claims that he saw Billy out in his truck at two o'clock this mornin'. Now you tell me, what's he doin' at that hour?"

"Wonder what'll happen if this man dies?"

Shiloh spoke, her voice clear. "Why is Mr. Walker's stand closed?"

They looked at one another. The one with a heavy, hot-looking beard said reluctantly, "He ain't comin' in today."

"He's sick?"

"No, ma'am."

"Then what?"

The black beard hesitated again before he answered. "There's some trouble in his family."

She knew it before she asked. "Billy Bob? It's Billy?" Nobody moved.

"I heard you talking. He's hurt, isn't he? There was an accident?" Icy dread seeped into her heart.

"Nothin' like that," answered another one, soothingly. "He's just—over at the jail, that's all."

"At the jail!" She almost laughed in her relief, except they all looked so serious. "What for? A fight?"

"He was in a hit-and-run accident early this morning. Around two." The black beard spoke abruptly. "They think Walker was DUI and hit some stranger and left him there. The man nearly bled to death."

Shiloh felt her face going white, her body numb. "W—What?" she faltered.

"Now, wait a minute," the second man interrupted testily. "They don't know any of that. They just think it."

"But why? Why Billy?"

"The other driver described him, picked him out of

some pictures. And somebody saw him here around town in his truck this mornin' at the right time."

"But that's because—" She broke off; she would tell it to somebody who could help. She would tell it to T-Tommy.

Even the jail had red, white, and blue banners strung across it, like a beggar that had donned bits and pieces of cast-off finery along with his own ragged clothes.

Inside, they kept Billy waiting while T-Tommy dealt with several phone calls, apparently from Juliard's family in Arkansas. Then he locked Billy in the same cell he'd had weeks ago, while he went to the hospital.

The deputy brought Billy lunch at last, but he didn't talk or tease or tell an ancient joke as he was usually prone to do.

Billy didn't eat. He didn't move.

Where was Shiloh? When was this going to be over? When was the real culprit going to turn himself in?

When T-Tommy got back, he came straight to Billy's cell and unlocked it, Davis hovering in his wake.

"You're gonna need a lawyer, Billy," he said somberly. "J.C.'s outside. He's offered to help you out for a few days, free of charge."

"That's good of him."

"Seems like we ain't doing this right. But I never thought—well, never mind. But Davis here, he's gonna read you your rights. Then we'll do the standard stuff. You want J.C. in here for all of this?"

Billy swallowed. "I guess so. Whatever he thinks."

J.C. took his place in the jail cell, nodding at Davis, reaching out to slap Billy on one shoulder reassuringly, and it made everything horribly clear. I could go to prison for this, Billy thought suddenly as Davis reeled off his rights. The idea shook him so much he was barely aware that Davis searched him as he stood spread-eagled against the concrete wall.

"A pocket knife, a wallet," Davis intoned.

He was going to have to tell about Shiloh.

Then the deputy took matters out of his hands as he slapped his chest and hit the ring. "Here, turn around. Face me," he ordered. "And one—what is this?—one ring. On a chain," Davis added curiously.

"It's got nothing to do with this," Billy told him dangerously. "Leave it alone."

Davis let his hand drop, staring curiously, but T-Tommy spoke suddenly.

"I want to see that, Billy."

"Look, T-Tommy—"

"Are you gonna hand it to me, son, or am I gonna have to get help to hog-tie you and then take it off?"

Billy's jaw clenched, then he gave the chain a hard jerk. It broke in two and the ring went rolling.

"I'm still gonna see that ring," T-Tommy snapped, his temper soaring.

Davis found it, eying it curiously as he handed it to the sheriff. T-Tommy was a little farsighted; he held the golden band out from him a little, frowning.

"What's that say, J.C.?" he asked at last.

J.C. took it, read it, and his jaw dropped. "You're not gonna believe this," he said incredulously. "It's a ring from a college, and—"

"Lawrence Evans University," T-Tommy said, his voice devoid of surprise or any other emotion.

"That's right. There's a name inside it—"

"Shiloh Pennington."

Nobody said anything; Davis nearly choked on his surprise.

Then T-Tommy reached out and pulled the ring from J.C.

"I don't reckon I have to wonder anymore who the girl was that Ellen was talkin' about. Were you with her last night?"

Billy stood indecisively, without answering. "None of your damn business," he managed at last.

"Oh, yes, it is," T-Tommy snarled. "I've had enough of this. Davis, go get Shiloh. I don't care how you do it—"

"There's no need to go get Shiloh." Her voice was husky, but so feminine in the circle of dark masculinity and threatening violence that all four men were startled as they turned.

She stood in the doorway where she had struggled with the state trooper several weeks ago, the vivid blue of her dress a bright foil for her dark hair and wide eyes. They were fixed on Billy.

"Don't say anything," he warned her brusquely. "Just turn around and leave. You don't need to be in the middle of this mess."

"I think I already am. That *is* my ring. And I—I *was* with Billy last night—"

"Shiloh, don't!"

"—or this morning, whatever you want to call it. I met him at midnight at the fruit stand. We were there for . . . for maybe two hours."

There was a long, long pause, full of shock. Davis's mouth hung nearly as slack as J.C.'s.

She bit her lower lip nervously. Billy looked like death, his face grim and hard; he made a tall, stark, towering figure.

"If I'd wanted you to rush in here and sacrifice your

reputation for me, I'd have already said something," he said tightly. "But you've gone and done it, anyway."

She stared at him in confusion. "It's no sacrifice. I wanted—"

"I know what you wanted. Time. And everything done normally. Well, this sure screws that up. Sooner or later, something would have cleared me."

"You can't know that." Her face was white as she clutched at the door facing.

T-Tommy broke the tension between them, his face and demeanor disapproving. "Okay. That's enough. Even if I believe you were with Billy last night—"

"I was."

"—that doesn't explain how Juliard ID'd him. And who's to say this didn't happen after you two got through with your—your meetin'?"

"Don't you know?" Shiloh asked unsteadily. "It wasn't Billy who hit that man. It was—it had to be Michael."

T-Tommy looked at her blankly, his jaw as slack as a dead fish's.

Billy's breath made a shivering hiss as he sucked it in, his eyes too blue, too stunned. Michael. He'd never thought once of Michael, who came to Sweetwater on such fleeting visits and so rarely that he didn't even seem to belong here.

J.C. gave a crack of disbelieving laughter. "I swear to God, I believe she means Michael *Sewell*, the judge's Michael. And not twelve hours ago she was kissing him."

"I didn't want to," Shiloh flashed. "Please, T-Tommy, listen. He drinks too much. Nobody much knows it, but he does. I've been with him when he was way over the line. And he—he stormed out of here last night. We—I broke the engagement. Don't you see? It has to be him."

"You're asking me," the sheriff said slowly, "to bring Sewell in for questionin' in a case like this? He's Judge Sewell's son. If he's not guilty—"

"You brought Billy in," she pointed out angrily. "And he's the judge's son, too."

She had done it: spoken the unspeakable publicly.

Nobody moved for a few seconds.

"Except it couldn't be Billy," she continued more calmly. "He was with me."

"Doing what, now, I wonder?" Davis drawled with a smirk, in an audible aside to J.C.

Billy Bob moved suddenly and his big right hand shot out, shoving the deputy violently. Davis stumbled backward, falling against the wall and down to the ground with a surprised grunt of pain.

"You keep your dirty mouth to yourself. Your dirty mind, too," Billy snarled down at him.

T-Tommy stepped between the two men. "You can't rough up a policeman, Billy, not in my jail."

Davis scrambled to his feet, glaring balefully at the big blond man threatening him. Then T-Tommy put a hand on each one's chest, pushing them apart.

"You, Davis, start calling hospitals in this area. Chances are good that the other driver got hurt in this accident, too. See if somebody answering Billy's description checked in anywhere. Billy, it looks like maybe you've got an alibi. But the law says I can hold you a little longer, and I mean to, until I get to the bottom of this. Shiloh—since you put yourself right in the middle, you can help me, and you damn well better like it hot because we're gonna visit the judge."

"I want to see Billy Bob for a minute. Alone."

She needed to know what he wanted her to do. Was

she supposed to tell all? He'd once said there were people he needed to talk to before they confessed this marriage. And what was he so angry with her about?

But Billy turned away from her. He didn't want her pity and her charity; he didn't want her to have to save him and ruin everything she wanted to hold on to. He didn't want the guilt. Didn't she understand?

"Well, you ain't goin' to," T-Tommy advised her roughly, herding her through the door into the other room. "I can't give you time to talk to him and make sure your stories jibe. It won't help him."

Shiloh stared, hurt. "You think I'd deliberately plan a lie? I'm telling the truth."

T-Tommy sighed. "Yeah, sure. I don't know what to think about you anymore, Shiloh. You're engaged to one man, but you're meetin' his brother on the sly. That's low and dirty."

Shiloh stood still a minute before she moved away. She could tell him, but not until she talked to Billy. "You could try trusting me, T-Tommy," she said coldly. "You're going to find out that I'm telling the truth."

"We're gonna find out, all right. There's gonna be hell to pay at Sewell's."

# 14

"*I just need* to know where your son is," T-Tommy repeated stubbornly.

"And I told you. I don't know." Lydia's voice dripped ice, but there was panic in her gray eyes and in the long, patrician lines of her face.

The room in which the three of them stood was a formal front parlor, far more ornate and elegant than anything Sam owned. It reflected Lydia's excellent—and very expensive—taste, a taste that had whittled away at the Sewell money for years.

The two-story brick Georgian house sat on a fifty-three-acre farm ten miles north of Sweetwater; once the farm had rolled for four hundred acres, but that was before Lydia, too.

And before Michael, who had apparently disappeared off the face of the earth.

"We've called his office in Memphis. We've had his landlord check his apartment. We've called his health club, his country club, his racquet club. Only the country club is even open today. It's a holiday for most people. He's at none of those places. We checked 'em all."

"How dare you! To invade Michael's life like this!" The woman quivered with rage, her nostrils white and pinched. "This—this girl drove him away with her vindictive lies. She broke the engagement and broke his heart. Surely there's no need for her to inflict more damage on my poor son." She glared at Shiloh, who hung behind T-Tommy, needing protection from Lydia's venom. "And I certainly wouldn't tell you anything if I did know, not when you won't even tell me what you want with him."

T-Tommy hesitated, tracing the scrollwork on the baby grand beside him with the fingers of one hand. "Mrs. Sewell, are you aware that Michael has been escorted home on several occasions by personnel from his club because he was drinking too much for them to let him drive himself?"

Lydia paled. "Please leave, before I call somebody, Mr. Farley. You may be the law in this backwater county, but neither you nor Shiloh will be allowed to make unfounded accusations against Michael. *Get out.* Do you understand that language?"

T-Tommy raised his left hand in protest. "There's no need for you to get on your high horse. But the fact is, I need to talk to Michael."

"What for? I demand to know!"

"There was a hit-and-run accident on 25 before dawn this morning. We've got reason to believe the driver who left the scene is someone who looks like Michael. I pulled in Billy Walk—" Too late T-Tommy realized what his words were saying; there was an implicit knowledge of Billy's paternity in them. He hadn't meant to hurt or embarrass this woman if he could help it, but the damage was done now.

Lydia paled further, her skin nearly ashen as she sank slowly into the emerald-and-scarlet striped chair at the corner of the piano. "That name is not spoken in my house."

T-Tommy took a deep breath. "Look here, ma'am, truth is truth and I'm gonna have to speak it. Billy says he didn't do it, and he's got a pretty convincing alibi. That leaves Michael. He's a—he's nearly—they look, ah, hell, they're nearly as alike as two peas in a pod if you really look at 'em, before they talk or move. The other driver described one or the other of 'em to me," the sheriff finished in blunt aggravation.

"The man—the driver—is alive?" Lydia's voice was husky, shocked. And suddenly, she was frightened.

"That's right."

T-Tommy looked back at the silent Shiloh; her eyes had widened at Lydia's words. The older woman stared at the nearby window a long moment, then spoke.

"He'll live, in spite of everything?"

"In spite of the wreck, yes, m'am."

Lydia took a long breath, "I see." Then she stood, impressive in her black sheath dress. "Please go, Mr. Farley. My husband will be in touch with you. But you need to remember two things: my son is *not* a criminal to be pawed over by you, and Robert Sewell *will* be governor in the near future. It behooves you to remember especially the latter."

She was interrupted by the ringing of the telephone. Lydia ignored its shrill sound for a moment, then walked to the tiny table where it jangled insistently.

"The Sewell residence," she said jerkily, then held it

out to T-Tommy. "Someone for you, Mr. Farley." Her words held resentment.

Neither she nor Shiloh looked at each other. Shiloh focused instead on T-Tommy's back and on his suddenly hawkish face as he finished his conversation and turned to them.

"That was Davis," he told the two women. "He says somebody answering Michael's description checked into a clinic on the edge of Memphis this morning. Is that where the judge is now, Mrs. Sewell?"

She swallowed. "You'll have to ask him."

"I mean to."

Judge Sewell beat them back to the jail. His silver Mercedes was in back where he'd entered from the bank parking lot. Discreet. Quiet.

T-Tommy laughed under his breath as he caught sight of the car.

"Well, well, well."

"They already knew what Michael had done," Shiloh said suddenly, a trace of horror in her words. "They thought—Lydia was certain that Juliard was dead. That way he could never have talked."

"You'll never be able to prove it," T-Tommy answered darkly.

"I don't have to. I know." Shiloh shivered, clasping her arms around herself. It wasn't from the chill of the air conditioner; it was from her narrow escape. "Why did you make me go with you? You didn't need me. And I didn't want to go back into that house, not ever again." She accused and condemned with her words.

T-Tommy grasped the steering wheel. "What you

were doing with Billy and Michael, it made me sick
. . . and mad," the sheriff replied haltingly. "And I wanted
to know if you really knew what you were talking about.
You didn't back down, Shiloh, not when you gave me all
those private club numbers, nor told me who to talk to
and the questions to ask. And you hung in there facin'
Lydia Sewell, too." He ran a tired hand over his face, then
the balding top of his head. "Maybe I didn't believe it was
Michael—not him, never him—until you went the distance. By the time we got to the Sewell's house, it was
different. I knew. He was guilty."

"You'll let Billy Bob go?"

"Yeah. But this ain't over. Not for you. There's no way
in paradise Sam won't hear of it. It's all over Sweetwater
now."

"And Billy—what's he so mad at me about?"

"Aw, that's hurt pride and worry talkin'. He stuck up
for you fast enough when Davis put his big mouth in,
didn't he?" T-Tommy patted Shiloh's arm awkwardly.
"Come on. Let's go see the judge. Then I think you and
Billy Walker better face the music. Tell your daddy, the
both of you. An' I'll see you get real nice cemetery plots,
side by side."

T-Tommy's humor, thought Shiloh, left a lot to be
desired. And she was so tired, too tired to find anything
funny.


"Where's Judge Sewell?" T-Tommy demanded the second he and Shiloh reentered the jail office.

Davis and J.C. looked up from the card game they
were playing at a big desk.

"Well, now, it's the strangest sight I ever saw," J.C.

drawled, pulling a stubby pencil from behind his ear to mark a score, then leaning backward in the chair, balancing it precariously on its two back legs. "He's decided he needs to speak to Billy."

Shiloh stared. Had she heard this lawyer correctly?

"Say what?" T-Tommy sounded as incredulous as she.

"Yep. He's in there." Davis nodded toward the next room. The door had been firmly shut between the office and the cells. "He's been in there for—what? fifteen minutes? Just him and Billy Bob."

J.C. came lazily to his feet, his tie hanging limply, the loosened knot near his fourth shirt button. "Nothin' like a father-and-son talk. And Sewell got around to doin' it before his kid hit thirty. Ain't parenthood wonderful?" He swung his suit coat from the back of his chair. "Something tells me that Billy's not in need of a lawyer anymore. Wonder how Michael is fixed in that line?"

T-Tommy looked again toward the doors. "I hope—I hope Sewell's being decent to Billy. What in the world could they be talkin' about?"

"Whatever Billy wants, I figure. He's got this one beat. Davis, here's where the game ends, and you owe me eighty-three cents." J.C. gathered up the cards from under the deputy's nose.

Shiloh was vaguely aware of the conversation between the two of them. Her thoughts were on other things: on the mess Michael was making of his life; on the enmity this was going to cause between her and the Sewells; on Billy's irrational behavior this morning; on the incredible idea that for the first time in his life, his father had come to talk to him.

The thought might have been a catalyst: the second she paused to wonder why Sewell was here, the door between the rooms opened and he emerged. His face was ravaged with anger and worry, and his clothes were unnaturally rumpled. No suit coat, his tie crooked, even some sort of stain on his pocket. It was almost like looking at one of those what's-wrong-with-this-picture scenes, Shiloh thought, surprised.

The judge glared at her, then ignored her presence.

"I worked most of the night on my campaign plans. I've had little or no sleep in forty-eight hours. But on my way home from my meeting, Mrs. Sewell called me on my car phone, Farley, nearly distraught. What did you say to her?"

"I imagine she told you."

"Some wild-eyed story about my son. She says this . . . this man in here"—Sewell's head jerked backward, in the direction of Billy's cell—"could well be the guilty party."

"He's got an alibi."

"If it's some lowlife from that honky-tonk—"

"I'm his alibi." Shiloh couldn't bear the contempt in Sewell's voice. How dare a man like him speak of Billy in that tone? "He was with me."

His body jerked a little in a quickly contained reaction. "At one o'clock in the morning?" he ground out, twisting to confront her.

"And at two."

Exactly what she was confessing turned his face into a red mask of fury. "You little slut. You cheap little tramp. From my Michael, who would've given you anything, to that—that—" he stalled for words.

The words hurt, even coming from him under these circumstances.

"That'll be about all I want to hear of that," T-Tommy said sharply.

"Michael's not guilty of what you're accusing him of. Isn't that what you need to hear? I'm telling you."

"He'll have to stand right here and tell me himself. I mean it, Judge."

Judge Sewell stiffened before he finally said, "For God's sake, Farley, this is an outrage!"

"But maybe he can't come in. Maybe he was hurt in a wreck and he's in a clinic just this side of Memphis. Maybe he didn't get out of this scot-free."

The judge sucked in his breath; his face paled. Then he choked out, "It was a one-car accident. Sheer coincidence that it should happen at the same time as this Arkansas man's. Why do you suppose I wouldn't let Michael talk to anybody here? He hit a . . . a telephone pole, but he was able to drive the car to a Memphis service station. He collapsed there. Some people called an ambulance."

"And he was admitted to a clinic, for all the world to hear about. It's a good thing those people came along," T-Tommy said ironically. "I'm gonna want to see that car, too, and those medical records."

"If there's the least attempt to accuse him, or publicize this, you'll regret it, Farley. It was a simple collision, and he had a simple injury. We both know that Walker is your man, no matter what *she* says." Sewell motioned furiously toward Shiloh. "She hates Michael. She'd do anything to break him."

"Davis, you take Shiloh back there and y'all open that cell. Billy's free to go," T-Tommy said calmly, but his eyes glittered as he focused on Sewell. "And take your time. I got a few things to say to the judge."

♦ ♦ ♦

Billy was lying deathly still on the narrow cot as Shiloh approached the cell; he had a pillow crumpled under his head, and his hand was under that.

Nothing unusual at all about the way he lay.

So why did it seem too quiet here? As though a stupendous explosion had occurred and left behind destruction and a deadly, frozen silence?

A statue might have been on that bed instead of a flesh-and-blood man, but the stiffness didn't come from sleep. His eyes were wide and blue as he stared up at the ceiling. Maybe he hadn't even heard their approach.

Davis felt the blanketing quiet; he was subdued as he unlocked the cell door and barely audible as he spoke. "C'mon, Billy. You can go. Sheriff says so."

Billy made no movement at all; not even his eyes blinked.

"Did you hear me?"

Shiloh stepped through the doors, stopping just inside. "Billy, let's go. It's all right."

He turned his head at her words, the blue, unwavering brilliance focusing on her. "You're still here." The observation was blank.

"Because you are. But we don't have to stay anymore. Come on, Billy. I don't like it in here."

He considered that for a minute, his eyes the only thing about him alive as he scanned her from head to toe. "Maybe I do. Maybe I don't want to go out there."

What was wrong with him?

"They know you didn't do it. They know it was Michael."

He turned his face away to stare at the wall beside him.

Finally alarmed, Shiloh glanced first at the baffled deputy, then stepped closer to look down on him, on the sprawled long legs, on the half-opened shirt, on the taut line of his throat.

Billy.

The unspoken word was full of a sudden longing, of a wild, sweet mixture of compassion and passion; she reached out without thought to touch the heavy rumpled hair and brushed his cheek instead.

"It's Judge Sewell, isn't it?" she asked quietly. "What did—"

But the man under her fingertips exploded into life, as if her fingers had detonated a violent charge inside him. He sat up in a rush and pushed himself off the cot to stand. Shiloh pulled away, hurt by his rejection but unable to say anything in front of the deputy.

"I want my personal things back," Billy said to Davis.

"Okay. They're outside."

"And I can just walk out?"

"Sheriff says so."

"All of a sudden, everybody believes me."

"She's spent most of the day makin' sure they do," Davis retorted, nodding toward Shiloh.

Billy contemplated Shiloh a long moment. Then he bent to scoop up his cap from the bed before going out the open door of the cell. Shiloh moved at last to follow him.

He was acting like a spoiled brat, she thought in a flash of resentment. Hurt pride, as T-Tommy had said?

At the entrance to the office area, Billy stopped cold, blocking the way. Over his shoulder, he shot Shiloh a startled look of warning that was at least an improvement over the blankness of his face up until that moment.

"Are you sure," he asked her ironically, "that you really want to be my knight in shining armor, Shiloh?"

"What?"

"Nothing, except I think we've just met another dragon." With that cryptic remark, Billy twisted sideways in the door and motioned her through. Glancing up at his set jaw, Shiloh didn't see Sam Pennington standing in the office until Billy nodded toward him.

Stopping as sharply as if she'd hit a glass wall, Shiloh had only time to register one thought: her father's expression looked like Billy's.

"You didn't show up at the awards ceremony at three," Sam said tonelessly. The dark red plaid of his cotton sport shirt and its matching solid tie made a hot, vivid splash of color as he stood in the dingy office, like a gash of blood in the tans and browns of the other men. "So I called home, and Laura tells me some things I don't know. Some things that the whole town's talking about."

Nobody moved.

"I want to know"—his voice gained power—"how is it that my only daughter can take up with Billy Walker, and nobody ever breathe a word of it to me? Not one damn word."

"We meant to tell you today."

Sam stared at Shiloh as she spoke, then laughed, an ugly, disbelieving sound. "Well, there's something I had to look forward to and didn't even know it. Big fool that I am, I thought you were gettin' over Michael, that that was why you'd been so quiet. But not you. Laura says you've been runnin' with *him* for weeks. That he came to the house like a sneakin' thief while I was gone."

"That was my fault. I was too afraid to tell you. Billy wanted to. It was wrong."

Sam swallowed, shoving his hands in his pockets. "What are you doin' with him? I said it four years ago. He's not the man for you. And I'm not even going to try to talk about it. You've ruined yourself with Walker today. They're sayin' you were with him most of last night . . . God." He pulled at his collar, then moved abruptly. "Get whatever you've got here. We're leavin'. I don't like airin' my dirty laundry in public." He glared at J.C. and Davis.

Shiloh didn't know whether or not Billy wanted her at this minute, but she did know one thing: if she didn't come through now, she'd never have another chance. Once before, her father had commanded and she'd followed. It had taken four long years and these last few weeks of agony to get back to this point again, but here it was—a second chance.

Billy wasn't speaking or touching or even breathing, it seemed. But she felt it anyway, the dark wave of tension that emanated from him.

This was the moment of truth.

"I'm not going with you."

The clear words dropped into the thickness of the room, as certain as death.

Sam froze.

"What?"

She took a step backward from his furious, stunned glare, until her shoulder brushed the front of Billy's shirt as he stood sideways behind her. But Billy didn't reach for her; this was her fight.

"I'm staying with Billy."

"You either come with me or I swear before God, you'll stop being my daughter. I'll cut you off like I never knew you."

"Please, Papa—" The words clung to her throat; it was hard to speak past the tears and despair that waited in her heart, ready to strike as soon as she stopped fighting them off.

Sam held out his hand; four years fell away. Shiloh loved her father. And she loved Billy with all the passion of a first love, just as she had then, but now she knew the cost of Sam's outstretched palm. No halfways, no compromises.

"It's either him or me," Billy had said all those long days ago.

She blinked back the tears and let her body rest against Billy's, against the heavy thud of his heart, and she shook her head.

Sam's face blanched white, his eyes blazed; he let his hand drop slowly away.

"You don't know what you're doin', Shiloh. I'll cut you off without a dime. Without a home. You'll have no place to go. You don't think you'll live with him, do you?"

She didn't know; she hadn't thought that far.

But Billy's hand was there suddenly, wrapping her waist, pulling her into him a little; she looked up into his eyes, pleading silently with him for help, and she knew what to say.

"Why can't I live with him?" she answered steadily. "He's my husband."

A hard shudder went through him at her words as she gazed steadfastly up at him, into the sudden blaze of promise in his face.

The three men opposite them didn't move. Shiloh thought she'd remember forever the way the lawyer's coat hung from his limp hand. Davis's toothpick dropped from his suddenly slack jaw.

Sam choked out, "What?"

"We got married in Memphis more than a month ago."

Her father's face flooded with a tide of red blood. "All this time, you've been in my house, I've been beggin' you, thinkin' you might reconsider Michael, and you've been *married* to Billy Bob Walker?"

Billy pulled her a little tighter against him; he hadn't said a word until now, but his movement and his still, calm face as he looked Sam dead in the eye spoke it all.

"That's right," he said. "She's my wife, just like I meant for her to be four years ago." For his life, he couldn't keep the tiny touch of triumph out of his voice.

"And you were waitin' for her all this time, weren't you? Like a damned vulture. I could feel it, the way you were watching for her to come home. I should'a run you out of town years ago, Walker."

"It wouldn't have changed the way things have worked out," Shiloh said pleadingly. "Can't you give him—us—a chance?"

Sam pulled himself into order. "You've made your bed, like your mother did. But there's one difference. I wouldn't let Caroline come back the last time. She finally tried to, but you didn't know that, did you? You've lied to me, stuck a knife in my back just like she did. But I raised you. A parent can forgive a lot. The day that you get through with Walker, you come back home. I might forgive you, and we might patch up the mess you've made of your life. Until then, I don't have a daughter."

He had to push J.C. aside to get out the door. His back was straight, his head high, his steps sure. He would live after all, Shiloh thought in misery.

Sam Pennington was tougher than nails.

And she had Billy. She didn't want him to see her cry, so she twisted into his arms, pressing her face against his chest, clutching his waist tightly.

His embrace was hard as he squeezed her against him.

Maybe he wouldn't notice the wetness of her face if she stood here for a minute, wondering if here, in his arms, was really where she belonged.

Sweetwater had been waiting all afternoon to hear what was going on in that jail.

Billy and Sewell and the Pennington girl and Sam himself—it was going to be good, the story that explained this day. The parade had dulled long ago in light of these events.

Luscious tendrils of gossip had already seeped out: Pennington's daughter and Billy Bob had been caught. Or maybe she'd told. Caught doing what? some nitwit wanted to know.

Now rumors floated that it was Michael and not Billy whom the driver in the wreck had identified. There was a terrible irony in that, one which Sweetwater savored on the street corner and the courthouse steps.

But the most shocking piece of news was yet to come.

Cotton was the first to wring anything from Davis as the deputy emerged from the jail in the late, late afternoon, and the news he brought back to the courthouse after that encounter sent an already dizzy Sweetwater reeling again.

"I swear it on a stack of Bibles," Cotton recounted fervently to his listeners. "That girl's gone and married Billy Walker!"

# 15

"*Like I said*, you're free to go," T-Tommy finally told Billy, his voice uneasy.

Shiloh waited for him at the door while Davis returned his personal belongings. Billy shoved the knife and the wallet back into his pocket, then looked at the ring an instant before he slid it on his finger. When he faced Shiloh, he seemed almost confused.

"You need me to drive you home? Since you don't have your truck here?" the sheriff offered tentatively, looking from him to the girl.

Billy hesitated, then he, too, glanced at Shiloh.

"He can ride with me," she offered, and after a moment's pause, Billy nodded.

T-Tommy followed them out to the car and after Billy docilely climbed into the passenger seat, the sheriff caught the door before it closed.

"I'm sorry about this mess, Billy Bob. And you and Shiloh sure knocked me flat with your news. But I want you to know that I wish you well. You be good to her, you hear me?"

Billy answered without looking at the other man. "Yeah. I will."

T-Tommy watched him a minute, then spoke to Shiloh as she buckled herself into the driver seat.

"And you, Shiloh, you take care of him. If you need anything—"

"We'll be fine." Billy's words cut off T-Tommy's admonitions. Neither his face nor his conversation held much emotion.

The sheriff nodded, then reluctantly closed the door.

Shiloh pulled out of town silently, going south, mostly because neither of them had any family in that direction. She'd stood all the family she could today.

They had nowhere to go.

The truth was both painful and embarrassing, but she might have handled it better if Billy Bob had been acting differently. He couldn't seem to shake the dark stillness, the silence, that she'd felt in him when she walked in the cell.

He'd barely said three words the entire time. Even if she understood why he'd waited for her to take a stand before Sam, she didn't understand it now. All she had to go on was the way he'd held her, his arms certain and secure, and the way his face had held reassurance when she'd confessed the marriage.

"Take care of him." T-Tommy's odd words seemed the most appropriate ones she'd heard all day, because Billy—this one sitting quietly beside her in the car— seemed lost, dazed.

Something had happened in that jail cell, something between him and Sewell.

It had left Billy like this, somewhere deep inside himself, thinking. Or maybe grieving.

Shiloh knew Billy Bob Walker, the semibad boy, the teasing flirt. But she didn't know this one, the one that hurt.

"Where are you taking me?" He asked the question uninterestedly, turning his head on the high seat back to look at her, startling her. He *was* alive; he *could* speak.

"I don't know," she admitted. "Do you . . . want to go home?"

He thought about it. "No," he answered at last, shaking his head, his face dark. "I want to get away. Out of this county. Out of . . . out of me."

He shifted his position, gazing out the window, but Shiloh wondered if he saw anything at all.

Okay, she thought in a mixture of anger and compassion. You want to leave everything to me. Well, I don't know what to do, where to go. So, we'll just drive until you decide to talk.

Inside her, the loneliness and the stark anguish grew. Today had been harder than she'd ever imagined; she had harbored a secret hope that Sam would come around.

Now she knew that would never happen.

She needed Billy to touch her, to hold her, to reassure her. Instead, the heart and soul had gone out of him, too.

They were two empty, miserable people speeding down the highway, going nowhere.


Fifty miles down the road, a storm broke. Huge dark thunderclouds had been building overhead for the last hour, turning the early dusk into darkness, and big gusts of warm wind whipped tree branches into wild contortions.

Up ahead, big blue neon letters that said Dreamland Motel glowed against the metallic, heavy gray of the sky. The shy, reserved Shiloh of a few years ago would never have taken Billy there; the hurting, confused, angry one of today pulled the Cadillac under its covered entrance without even asking him.

He glanced at her, his face questioning.

"We can't keep on driving, not in this," she answered him defiantly. "We have to stop."

We have to face each other, and our actions, and our fathers, she wanted to say.

"I'll get the room." He was out of the car before she could speak, and a tiny tendril of relief curled through her. At least he'd come to life a little.

Shiloh watched him stride across the parking area toward the office, the wind molding the shirt against his ribs, making his shirttails flap as they hung outside his jeans. He looked so familiar, so much like the man whom she'd once met in her father's backyard.

It was her wedding night.

Not even that thought had much joy in it, and she sat numbly waiting for his return.

"It's room 20," he said as he opened the car door. A gust of wind blew the smell of rain to her as thunder cracked across the sky. "I'll move the car. Do you want to go on and beat the storm?"

She took the keys from the polite stranger who held them out to her. Even hurrying, she got damp as the fat drops of rain tumbled down on her in the run across the pavement. The lock was stiff, and the motel room smelled stuffy as she pushed the door open.

Two double beds. One for him, one for her? A television. A bathroom and a separate dressing area. A green Bible from the Gideons.

Perfect motel decor.

Inside Shiloh, the depression mushroomed, and when the storm blew Billy in through the door, fear threaded through her as well.

He shook the rain off, his movements rough, shoving the wet hair out of his face. He was too big and too masculine for the room when the door was shut behind him.

Here she was, all alone with two beds and Billy Walker, and this time nobody was coming to pull him away.

He shoved his hands down in his pockets, looking around.

"Not too great, is it?" His words were flippant, casual.

"It's fine."

Her words were swallowed in another booming crash of thunder, and she crossed to the curtain along the back wall. Opening it, Shiloh looked out at the gray dusk and the heavy gray rain that beat against the glass. Homesickness and misery and tension made her whole body ache.

When he walked up beside her, his footsteps were so muffled by the storm that she didn't even realize he was there until her arm brushed his. She jumped violently.

Billy never moved, but just watched her face, gauging her reaction to him before he, too, looked outside.

"Some Fourth of July."

She tried to laugh. "A big one for me. I'm—I'm independent, now."

Billy reached behind her to grip the curtain with its straw weave of greens and pale blues, and he played with it, staring into the rain.

"You can still go back." He said the words clearly, and his voice didn't hold even a tiny amount of emotion. "If you went right now, Pennington would forgive and forget sooner or later."

"Is that what you want me to do?" She watched his fingers on the curtain at her elbow.

"It's up to you."

Hold me, Billy. Tell me you need me, that you want me. Say "I love you." Please. Then it will be worth it.

But he didn't.

"I'll think about it," she managed.

"You don't have long."

She twisted to look up at him. They stood so close that the heat from his body warmed hers—and they were miles apart.

"What's wrong?" she demanded unsteadily.

He never looked down. "Nothing."

"Did you get what you wanted when I told Sam I was going with you? Your own back on him for what happened all those years ago? You won today. I heard it in your voice when you talked to him. Is that all you wanted?"

"I didn't win anything. And I think you'd better go home."

He moved away from her, finally sitting down on the edge of the bed with his back to her. Shiloh watched him, her heart aching and suddenly panicky. She was losing him, and she didn't know why or how. She couldn't seem to hold him.

In the dusky room, his big body, his square shoulders, the tilt of his head—all had a stiff, harsh defiance. So why did her fingers want to reach out to caress him? Why did he seem so forlorn? So abandoned?

"What did Robert Sewell say to you, Billy?"

She had found the right button to push: he visibly

flinched as if he'd been stung. But he didn't turn around.

"Nothing much. And it's nobody's business but mine."

"You're wrong. It's mine, too, because whatever it was, it's taking you away from me." Pushing her hair back with both hands, Shiloh walked to the edge of the bed and looked down on his head, on his hard profile as he turned his head away stubbornly.

"Do you think you're the only one who's had a bad day? The only one who feels anything around here?" Her voice was rising in anger. "I've done everything I know to do for you today—"

"Nobody asked you to."

"I *wanted* to, because I thought you cared. I thought you needed me."

"Yeah, sure. I really needed to hear Pennington come down on you like a ton of bricks. I needed to know that you'd lost a home and your father over me. You know what the whole town's sayin', don't you? It was all over J.C.'s face, T-Tommy's face." He stood in furious memory, his voice no longer calm but cracking under emotion. " 'She married Billy Walker. Threw herself away on that worthless bastard. He's no good to anybody.' And you know what, Shiloh Pennington? They're right. *Right.*"

The words were catching, sobbing, hanging in his throat, and he reached out to shove the Bible off the table in one fierce sweep of his arm.

It slammed against the wall, then hit the floor before silence settled over the room.

"Billy."

"Don't touch me." He jerked away forcefully from her hand on his wrist, backing up against the table to get away from her. "Just leave me alone, Shiloh. You did all any man could ask today. I don't need anything more."

He never even looked at her, keeping his face turned away.

Shiloh stepped back as if she'd been slapped, aching so much she couldn't get her lips to speak.

"I don't understand you," she whispered at last, painfully. "I thought—"

"Maybe I thought the same once. Not anymore. Go on. Leave. *Now.* I want you to get out."

His words were so brutal she gasped, a hand going to her heart as if to protect it. He fumbled in one pocket, finally pulling out the car keys and shoving them at her. She backed away from him, eyes wide and wet. At the door, she hesitated.

"Just where am I supposed to go, Billy?"

"Home. Go to Sam." The words were clipped and jerky as he strained mentally away from her presence, unmoving against the wall. "I'll call somebody to come and get me."

"I trusted you. You said you wanted me." The accusation was unsteady.

"Maybe I meant it at the time. But I know better now. My God, Shiloh, what does it take to get you to leave?" He looked at her at last, and even in the twilight, his eyes looked blank. "Do I have to open the door for you?"

"You don't have to throw me out. I'll walk," she said raggedly.

Rain slapped her in the face as she slammed the door shut behind her, and it blew through the cotton blend of the dress she had on, as cutting as little cold needles against her hot skin and bruised heart.

She bit her lip against the pain, running to the Cadillac.

She wasn't going back to Sam in defeat, not now, not

ever. Her face against the steering wheel, her eyes burning with emotions, she fought away tears. What was she going to do?

More than one woman had made a fool of herself over Billy, even Shiloh Pennington. Well, now Sweetwater had proof that she wasn't like Sam: She was human, capable of grief and pain and shame.

She tried to put the keys in the ignition.

Why did it feel so wrong to leave him here, by himself in this motel while the rain blew and beat all around?

*He needed somebody. He shouldn't be alone.*

The thoughts were so ridiculous Shiloh scoffed at them. He had hurt her.

*Because he was hurting, too.*

Billy's emotions ran deep; they always had, no matter what he pretended. He couldn't walk away from his mother or his past or his crippled grandfather or even a stray animal, not from anything that belonged to him.

And just last night, he had claimed her. She closed her eyes, remembering in agony how his mouth had caressed her, letting her fingers touch the place.

*Grief and pain and shame.* Especially shame. All of that was in him. Why hadn't she recognized it sooner?

Because Billy Bob Walker didn't want her to, probably wouldn't admit to it.

Her father alone had been bad enough. Billy had had his own father to deal with, too.

She climbed out of the car, making herself walk back to the motel, the rain drenching her.

She couldn't bear much more, but she would try one more time to reach him.

The room was nearly totally dark when she slipped into it, and the roar of the air-conditioning unit competed with the pounding rain to hide the sound of her entrance.

Breathing shallowly, shivering in her wet clothes, she leaned against the closed door until her eyes adjusted. He was lying on the far bed, his back to her. Not moving, but she knew he wasn't asleep.

Silently she moved toward the bed, stopping just behind him, hesitating, afraid to speak, afraid to touch. Why was he so still?

Some sixth sense alerted him to her presence. He rolled over just as her hand hovered over his shoulder, his eyes a strange, light shade in the darkness.

"I thought you—" He couldn't say more, his words strangled, torn, choked.

Her wavering fingers touched his face, and for an instant, he let them. Then he pushed her hand away and rolled back over on his side like a scolded child.

Her fingers were wet.

Billy Bob, rough and tough Billy Bob Walker, was crying.

"Will you get the hell out of here?" he pleaded with effort, covering his face with his hands, his whole body outraged.

She couldn't leave. He wouldn't let her near him again if she walked out after seeing him in this condition.

"I won't leave. You can't make me, short of dragging me out. Oh, Billy—" Her hands touched his stiff shoulders tentatively; he was warm under the shirt, alive and hurting.

"Please, Shiloh, leave me in peace," he groaned huskily. "I don't . . ."

But her whole body had come to vibrant life with the feel of him, with the sudden rush of understanding, and she slid both arms around his neck, hugging him fiercely to her, letting the side of her face touch his.

He fought her mentally for a moment, then something

snapped inside him, and his body collapsed as he began to cry, great, tearing sobs that shook his whole frame and terrified her before she tightened her hold on him.

She had once heard Sam cry, but it had not been like this. Her father had never seemed as determinedly masculine as Billy, and his grief had been resigned. Billy's was desperate; it was wrenching him apart.

This was more than today's misery spilling out of him. This was the accumulated passion and anger and anguish of a lifetime, something tied up with Robert Sewell and with Billy's self-worth.

What poison had Sewell poured into him to exacerbate the wound?

Although she'd come to this isolated little motel with every intention of becoming Billy's wife and lover, she could be more. She could hold him, and soothe him, and whisper nonsense phrases of sympathy against his wet face, like a mother tenderly wrapping a child against the harsh world.

She could be his everything.

"He . . . he offered me money," Billy got out at last, his breathing so hard, the tears so heavy she could barely understand him. "Just like you did. I hated him. I hated you. I didn't know I could make such a living, selling myself in Michael's place." His words were jerky, half laughter, half tears—all agonized.

"I'm sorry. So sorry." The whispers on his skin, the way her arms tightened around him. Could he feel her horror? her understanding?

"That's all he wanted to know. Could I be paid to take Michael's place. He said I'd been a mistake. I'd ruined lives. He called my mother a gullible fool. He tried to get her to have an abortion. And she should have. She should have."

Shiloh's hands caught in his long hair, her voice cutting off his terrible words. "*No*. Your mother can't live without you. She loves you. She needs you."

"I always thought . . . he had some kind of feeling for me," Billy whispered jaggedly. "I kept thinkin' someday when I've made it, when I've done something big and right, he's gonna finally admit who I am. He'll stop me on the street, maybe, and—and—" Billy started to laugh again.

"Listen to me, Billy Walker. He's the fool, not you. Never you. He's got no feelings for anybody except himself and the people who make him look good. He's liable to turn his back on Michael if he doesn't straighten up, if he's too big a threat to the things the judge wants."

Shiloh let go of Billy's throat to rise to her knees on the bed behind him, tugging his shoulders insistently until he rolled over on his back, looking up at her.

"You're the only good thing he ever did, Billy." She let her hands soothe his cheeks, wiping away the wetness, let them stroke the hard jawline, the warm neck, the smooth chest under the open shirt. A man and a boy both were here. Her words were for the boy; but her fingers offered an adult, sensual stroke. "You've got all the passion he's never had. Any man would be proud to have you for his son."

His chest heaved. "Don't lie, Shiloh," he whispered, his words more still. The worst of the storm had passed, at least here in this room. "Your own father knows what I am. And he's right. I can't—"

"You're going to stop feeling sorry for yourself," she said angrily, clutching at his open shirt.

"I'm exactly what he called me all those years ago, Shiloh, a hayseed plowboy. I can't do anything for you."

"I don't know what you are, Billy. Neither do you.

You've spent your whole life being Sewell's bastard. Me, I'm the same. I've been Sam's good little girl. But that's over now. I know there's more. Now we're free to find out who we are, and what we can be, all on our own, together."

She bent over him, her heavy brown hair falling to brush his face, her hands on the heavy muscles in his upper arms. She needed the man in him.

"Do you know who I am today, Billy?"

He stared up at her, his throat working, his eyes puzzled. "You're the most beautiful woman I've ever seen, Shiloh. That's all I know."

"I'm your wife. My name is Walker, just like yours. Not Pennington, not Sewell. Shiloh Walker." She'd never said it out loud before; it had an odd taste on her tongue.

Then she followed each of his arms out to his palms, entwining her fingers with his in a warm, intricate lock, pulling his hands up above his head as she hovered over his lips. "You said you couldn't do anything for me, Billy. But you can."

She closed her eyes, her heart pounding too hard for her to look into his face, and laid her lips on his in a searing kiss, opening his mouth, pouring her soul into him. Burning away the memories of the hurt, offering him passion and love.

He was gasping for breath, nearly blind and dumb when she pulled away, his chest under her heaving.

She slid her hands from his despite his belated effort to hold her, then her fingers went to the big, bright, turquoise blue buttons that matched the dress she'd put on this morning with such big plans. One by one the buttons slid through the loops and she peeled the wet dress away until it fell open.

He watched, mesmerized, as she shrugged out of it and it puddled around her waist, a bright sea of color. Then she reached behind herself to unclip the delicate lace and satin that wrapped her breasts, catching it as it fell forward, one strap off one graceful shoulder.

Her fingers touched the mark he'd left last night.

"The man who put this here ought to have the courage to finish what he's started," she whispered. "I waited four long years for the right man, to give him the one thing that's always been mine, and I swear, Billy, if you don't take it tonight, I won't wait anymore. Forget our fathers. I'm here. Think of me. Do the one thing for me nobody but you can—"

He made a lunge upward for her, pulling her down against him, rolling her over on her back, imprisoning her under him.

"I hope to God this is really what you want," he panted, "because this is forever. No going back."

He kissed her throat, her face, her breasts, as he pulled the clothes from her.

"Billy, I—"

"No, don't say any more." He caught her face in his hands, holding her still for his touch. "That mouth of yours is goin' to kill me."

So she told him without words, her hands yanking and pulling at the shirt, pushing it off his shoulders and down to his wrists where he impatiently shook it loose to let it fall on the floor, along with her dress that he dropped.

His hands skimmed her body in the darkness, touching, caressing, feeling.

"I knew you'd be like this," he whispered brokenly. "So many years dreamin' it. Maybe I'm dreamin' now."

Struggling against the pleasure of his fingers, she bit

his shoulder a little, loving the salty taste of his skin; she kissed him, a long line of caresses across his chest. Her hands fell to his blue jeans, to the belt, and hesitated before they fumbled with the loops.

Then his own hands came down to unfasten the belt, and his lips returned to hers as he kicked the jeans away.

Shiloh was nearly delirious with sensation when he came down on her, his legs forcing hers apart. Then she began to shiver under the command and the power of his long, strong limbs. What had she done?

"You're afraid," he whispered, tenderly against her face. "Well, I am, too, baby. Scared of touching you, of ruining your life, of the way I'm hurting inside. It's like trying to keep on talking, but it's over a loud noise that won't go away. All I know is that I want you, Shiloh. I'm certain of that. That, and I love you. Oh, God, I love you."

She'd been waiting for the words for weeks, trying to get up the courage to say them herself. But here, tonight, she'd forgotten her need to hear them in her need to help him.

"I love you," he'd said. Given when she'd least expected them. Maybe given out of other emotions.

But he'd said them, nevertheless.

"Billy," she whispered the word against his face, tangling her fingers in his hair to pull him down to her. "I know it will hurt. It doesn't matter. Because I love you, too."

He laughed against her lips, an exultant, aroused sound.

Maybe it should have been fast and intense and maybe it should have ended in a quick burst of gratified passion on his part; that was what she expected. That would have been in keeping with the rest of the day.

But something in Billy had changed. He had calmed and focused on the here and now. She had his attention. He knew exactly what he was supposed to do. No rushing now. No panic.

Billy Bob Walker was a man with a slow hand—and the patience to use it.

Hadn't she known it? Seen it every time he touched something living?

He meant to prevent any pain, trying so hard she fought back any sound that might have let him know he wasn't entirely succeeding. He was bold, too. Twice in embarrassment, she caught his broad, brown wrist to keep him back. Once he whispered a protest when she pushed his hand away, but he reluctantly obeyed.

And at last, when Sewell and Sam were both long forgotten, when his hair clung to his neck wetly, when his back was slippery with sweat, when her hands had quit digging into his shoulders from hurt and were clinging for another reason, he began to move, his actions strong and purposeful, compulsive, spasmodic, beyond his control.

"Shiloh, I can't . . . wait . . . anymore. Hold me. *Hold me.*"

His desperation fueled what his gentling hands and warm mouth had started. Just as she relaxed against him, expecting nothing more than these pleasurable, tactile sensations, the low-burning fire inside suddenly sparked, and kindled, and exploded in one totally unexpected, passionate blaze of glory.

"Bil—ly." His name was a stunned, broken whimper of sound as she arched against him.

When it was over, she was wrapped around his long body, her face buried in his wet shoulder where he'd collapsed against her. She was shaking so hard she might have had a chill, and the tremors inside her seemed to reach to her toes. His heart thundered against hers.

They lay there a moment, afraid to turn loose of each other, afraid to face each other.

Shiloh was embarrassed at her own emotions. Above her, Billy wondered why she was so still.

Oh, Lord, she felt so good.

Then she moved beneath his heavy weight, and he loosened his hold on her to lift himself and try to see her hot face in the darkness.

"Billy." Her whisper was as shaky as she was on the inside. "I'm not sure . . . what happened—"

He felt relief spreading to his heart. Out of all this rotten, horrible day, he'd done one thing right. He'd given pleasure to his virgin bride.

". . . and I don't know how something that hurt so much in the beginning could end feeling like—like that," she whispered, her voice shy and flustered.

"Good," he said huskily, rolling on one side to cuddle her against him. "Good."

After all these years, he knew what it was like to make love to Shiloh Pennington. Shiloh *Walker*.

It was choking tenderness and roaring passion and peace. Peace, unfurling inside him like the leaves of a plant when it was left in the moisture of the greenhouse.

Outside, the rain burst from the sky in another torrential downpour, slapping the windows of the Dreamland Motel where two lovers lay wrapped in a warm bed, protected for a while from the storms of the world.

# 16

*Shiloh watched his* face as he lay sleeping, this man to whom she had tied her life, and wondered with a panicky sense of fright how she could have known him so little.

Had she married a stranger?

She'd spent countless nights wondering—consumed with curiosity and something far deeper—about what it might be like to have Billy Bob.

Well, now she knew, and he was far more than she'd ever expected, even not knowing exactly what to expect. The lazy drag of his tongue across her skin, the shocking touch of his hands in a hundred places at once, the strength of his body—they were proof that Billy had the deeply sensual nature she'd always sensed without really understanding it.

It made him nearly a threat to Shiloh, unless he was willing to give his everything, just as he'd been demanding from her without words from the first second he'd touched her tonight. He'd allowed her no halfway measures, had somehow gotten her to act and react in ways that were not like her at all.

She had behaved like somebody new. She *felt* like somebody new. Freshly born, sprung out of the heat and the wetness of the lush night.

Not Shiloh anymore.

Somebody different, somebody whose skin stung and tingled from the feathery web in which he had spun her, a web of kisses and caresses and whispered endearments.

Almost afraid, she touched her fingertips delicately to the skin of her stomach, exploring, trying to find the source of the torching flame he'd created within her, the fire with which he branded her.

So ferociously dangerous to lie here like this, her nude body brushed only by the tangled sheets in the darkness of the room. So strange.

Then her fingers struck his as his hand rested heavily on her, daring even in his sleep. His palm was rough against the slight swell of her lower abdomen, and the calloused fingertips were spread open upon her, each hard pad leaving its own tiny imprint in her blood.

A wave of fiery heat swept over her, radiating from his fingers, part remembered passion and part pure embarrassment.

She had stripped her clothes away for him, begged him to make love to her, trapped his hands above his head to try to hold him captive.

She rolled her head away from his sleeping face, from the strong line of his cheeks and his nose, from the sight of his hair as it capped his face instead of being brushed severely away, as it usually was.

Shiloh wondered if she'd ever be able to face him

again. What she'd done—what he'd done to her—
seemed suddenly too forward and too intimate to be
borne.

How had her reckless act of rebellion—her joke of a
marriage—brought her to this strange room, this motel,
this bed, this act?

Billy Bob Walker himself was a confusing mass of
contradictions.

A bruiser in a fight, but a coaxing, tender lover.

A careless goodtimer who cried harsh, racking tears.

Shiloh twisted in the darkness to look at him, her legs
brushing his.

This close, his nose was not perfect after all. There was
a tiny bump at its bridge that made it strictly masculine.
She traced it tenderly with her finger.

He had made her see him in a new way, forcing a
respect for him as a man out of her, forcing her to give
way to his dominance for a while.

But it had been a gentle dominance.

It didn't matter that she'd bought him straight from
jail, that he'd taken her forcibly out of herself during that
painful, wonderful first lovemaking, or even that she was
going to be embarrassed to face him tomorrow.

Billy Bob Walker belonged to *her,* and she meant to
keep him.

He was sitting in a chair watching her when she awoke,
the morning sun hot on her face as it flooded through the
open, long windows at the back of the room.

Shiloh stared at the lush greenery outside where it still
dripped from yesterday's rain, the drops glittering like
jewels, and tried to orient herself. When she moved, the

soreness of her body, the pain of muscles flexing against muscles—all of that brought memories of the night before.

Sitting up with a start, she met his eyes across the motel room and flushed hotly, scrambling for the sheet to hold up to her bare breasts.

In the silence, her heart pounded in her ears as she stared at him, wide-eyed.

He looked away, his own cheeks flushed. Was Billy—*Billy*—embarrassed by their lovemaking, too? she wondered dazedly before his face broke into a tiny, lopsided smile.

"Won't even let a man enjoy the view, will you?" he asked ruefully, standing to walk to the bedside and tower over her.

"Hello," she whispered, staring up at him.

He laughed. "Hello, baby." Then he raked his hand back through his hair. "I took a shower and got dressed before it hit me—I don't have a comb, or a toothbrush, or a razor."

"There's a comb you can use in my purse," she stammered, then drew a gulping, calming breath as he turned away to look for her bag.

He wasn't all over her, at least—that was good, wasn't it? And in his eyes, there was no hint of triumph nor of the knowledge he'd gained about her last night.

In fact, he seemed nearly reserved.

Billy Bob, reserved? The thought was staggering.

"Are you hungry?" He asked the question as he raked the comb roughly through his hair, not paying much attention to the way it fell.

"I guess so. But I'd rather get up and take a shower myself," she said tartly. He had a scrubbed-clean look;

Shiloh had a horrible feeling she looked like a grub worm.

"Okay."

There was a long pause.

"Billy," she said at last, patiently, "would you turn around? So I can get up?"

"I'm not goin' to jump on you just because I see you without clothes, Shiloh."

"Well, that takes a load off my mind," she retorted weakly. "Billy, please, you're embarrassing me. You've got on all your clothes. I don't. It feels unequal, or something."

His teeth were a flash of white in his brown face as he laughed. "Want me to take off mine, then?"

"*No.*" The thought dyed her cheeks; it had been bad enough to be so vulnerable with him in the dark. Broad daylight had to hold even greater fears. "Oh, never mind," she said in sudden determination, wrapping the sheet tightly to her, coming first to her knees in the bed, then to her feet beside it.

Shiloh winced a little as she moved away too quickly and Billy's laughing face quieted and stilled.

"I'm sorry," he said abruptly, turning from her.

Afraid to ask him why he was apologizing, Shiloh made her way over to the bathroom and into its privacy.

Why didn't he touch her?

She refused to make any more moves toward him today; God knew she'd made more than her share last night.


Like it or not, she was stuck with him.

The frustrated, aggravated thought hit Billy as he

paced the long porch that ran the length of the motel and waited for Shiloh to finish dressing.

He'd acted like a jerk yesterday, and a big fool last night.

He'd broken down and cried—*cried*—like a blubbering baby.

Even his ears felt hot at the thought.

Damn, damn, *damn*.

He wondered how Shiloh could bear to have such a sniveling idiot as he'd been anywhere near her.

Billy Bob was sickened by himself; it stood to reason she was, too.

He'd been awake since before dawn, trying to figure it out; along about six A.M., he'd fitted all the pieces together. She'd let him make love to her for one of two reasons: either she felt sorry for him, or she'd come this far with him, expecting him to behave like a man, that she felt she couldn't go back, and the only thing left to do was go all the way.

Which reason was worse?

He closed his eyes, letting the words she'd said—"I love you, Billy—" swamp him, letting the mad delirium she'd caused with her kisses and her body completely claim him.

So sweet, so wild.

He wasn't sure he believed she really loved him, but he knew that there was something in her, some emotion, for him. She was his wife. He had to try to build this beginning into something lasting, to make their worlds mesh.

Could she live with him and like it?

Could she forget the wallowing mess he'd been last night and remember only the way they'd made love, the way he'd tried his damnedest to go slow?

Could he survive if she walked out on him? She might—that was his nightmare.

He hoped he would; he wasn't going to turn loose of her until he found out all of the answers.

Instead, he was going to take her to Mama, and to Grandpa.

To life the way real people lived it in Briskin County.

And to his own bed, not this one in a rented, sterile room.

Today, he was going to take his wife home.

He was going to be, not Sewell's bastard, but Shiloh's husband.


The blue dress was a little rumpled, and she hated putting yesterday's undergarments back on, but the fact was that Shiloh had no choice, and no other clothes, either.

What in the world was she going to do? There were eighteen dollars in her purse and three charge cards, probably already worthless if Sam had had his way.

She was frowning at her own dilemma when she walked out of the motel and found Billy frowning, too, at the car.

"Is this yours?" he asked without preliminary.

"No. It's my fa—Sam's. I was saving my money to make my own down payment on my next car. He thought I had thirty-five hundred dollars, remember? I couldn't tell him I'd used the money for something else."

"Great. Now we're drivin' Pennington's vehicles." Billy raked his hand through his hair in exasperation. "Well, it can't be helped. We'll take it back to the bank as soon as we get the truck, okay?"

"You think Sam will want this car back?" She hadn't

thought about it much; whatever her father had was hers. *Had* been hers.

Billy laughed. "Honey, I know it. And even if he didn't I wouldn't want you to keep it. You're *my* wife, aren't you?"

He searched her face quizzically for a minute before she nodded.

"Come on. Let's get some breakfast." He reached out his hand for hers, pulling her to the driver's side, letting her slide in before he followed her.


The July morning was unexpectedly cool rather than muggy, as yesterday had been before the rain. Along the two-lane highway that led west to Seven Knobs, late black-eyed Susans bloomed.

The pecan grove was the first sign of Walker Farm. It took up the acreage that bordered the road, and just beyond it was the fruit stand itself. Hanging baskets—fuchsia, begonia, ivy, spider plant, fern—dangling from the extended, wide roof of the stand greeted visitors with a blaze of verdant color.

And all around on tables and in crates was produce of the season; north Mississippi grew it in plentitude: ripe, red tomatoes; their yellow counterparts called Golden Boys; fresh, sweet corn still wrapped in its green covers, still dangling its silky white tassels; two kinds of peaches, spread into bountiful heaps of yellows and reds; baskets of bumpy brown cantaloupes and of crisp green fingers of beans and of sticky, fat, bullet-shaped yellow squash; watermelons sprawled on the floor, one round striped one cut open to reveal its wet, ruby-red sweetness.

And presiding over the harvest was Willie Walker himself, sitting in the rocking chair he kept on the corner porch of the place, under the shade of an overhanging pecan tree, right beside the money box that stayed hidden under an old upside-down washtub where he laid his fan when he got busy talking to visitors and customers.

Billy stopped the Cadillac just past his grandfather, pulling off the road into the shade. Then he looked down at Shiloh.

"Come on. Don't be scared," he coaxed, seeing the nervousness in her face. "Grandpa won't bite."

"Aren't you scared?" she asked.

"Nope. Things will be fine, you'll see," he promised, ignoring his own nagging little apprehension.

"Maybe for you, but what do you think you'd feel if this was my family you were going to meet?" she persisted.

"I've already had the honor, and I was shaking in my shoes. But this is my family. They're different. Now come on."

She let him tug her out of the car, then over to where Willie sat, watching without a word.

A woman and two little boys were thumping watermelons. Shiloh didn't know any of them.

"So you finally decided to come home," Willie drawled, without waiting for his grandson to speak. "Your mama's been worried."

"I'm sorry. I figured you'd hear what happened. And I told her from the beginning I'd be all right."

"We've heard a lot. And it appears to me that there's a whole bunch of things you *didn't* tell us." Willie pushed himself up on his cane, looking at the girl whose hand Billy held tightly in his—the girl who stood so close to his grandson. "So this is Pennington's daughter, is she?"

Billy's hand tightened around Shiloh's. "This is my wife," he said pointedly. "Her name is Shiloh."

"Hmphm." Willie squinted at her. "Pretty as a picture, just like Clancy said. I hope she's pretty enough to be worth all the trouble."

"I hope I'm worth her," Billy returned.

Willie looked from her to him, then back to Shiloh. "Why'd you marry him, girl?"

Shiloh answered steadily, "Because I love him."

"How much is this corn, Willie?" the woman called across the fruit stand.

"Price is marked on each bushel basket, Melinda. You just got to look for it."

"Mama, I don't know how else to tell you, so I'll just come out and say it. This is Shiloh. We got married a few weeks ago."

Billy held her in front of him, his hands on her upper arms, her back pressed tightly to his chest. He wanted Ellen to take to Shiloh, to understand that she was different from all the other girls, and not just because she was his wife. But his mother's face was a little frightened, a little shy, a little angry—probably at him.

"It's nice to meet you," Shiloh said hesitantly, her own hands reaching up to curl around his, as if for reassurance.

Her politeness flustered Ellen even more. She nodded at Shiloh and mumbled, "Nice to meet you," her hands twisting the apron she wore.

Billy's mother was a pretty woman, Shiloh thought, shorter and more petite than she herself was, blond and green-eyed. There was little about her even to suggest that she had mothered him.

Certainly none of his laughter. She looked stern and stiff.

They don't like me, she thought in dismay.

"You never gave a sign you were thinkin' about gettin' married," his mother told him quietly. "I got the news long about dark yesterday. The last to know. Ann McIntyre, the biggest gossip in Seven Knobs, she told me on her way home from Sweetwater. I kept waitin' for you to come and tell me. Waited 'til eleven last night before I went to bed."

"I'm sorry, Mama. But we had a pretty rough day yesterday. I wanted to get away." Billy's face darkened as he faced Ellen over Shiloh's head.

"I need to talk to you, Will," she returned, glancing away from the girl in her son's arms.

"That's fair. But I want to show Shiloh the house, okay? We're married, Mama. Really and truly married. We want to live here, unless there's a reason you've got against us doin' that."

His voice challenged Ellen, and Shiloh turned her face toward his chest. This involvement in the personal, intimate relationships of a family that she didn't belong to was intensely embarrassing.

Ellen moved at last, answering flatly. "The house is more yours than anybody's. I'm not disputin' the facts, Billy. You've put ever' red cent in it that's been put in for the last five years. You can do as you please in it."

"It's part mine, that's all." He moved suddenly, pulling away from Shiloh to drop a kiss on his mother's cheek. She caught at his arm convulsively for a second, then released him back to Shiloh.

"Reckon I'll go down to the fruit stand for a while," she said huskily. "I'll be there when you're ready to talk." She looked directly at Shiloh.

Maybe it was hurt, or doubt, or fear, or even reserve that made her seem withdrawn and her green eyes sad, Shiloh thought as Ellen spoke. "We're real glad to have you in the family, Miss Penn—"

"Shiloh." She smiled tentatively at her mother-in-law, wondering if there would ever be a meeting ground for the two of them.

"Walker," Billy added insistently. "Her name is Walker, Mama."

He had never realized before just how old and even downright shabby the interior of the farmhouse was. The outside of it he had kept painted, just as he kept the lawn mowed and the shrubs and the hedges trimmed.

But it had been years since much time had been put into the house. All three of them had worked frantically on the expanding orchards and on the business.

There was never enough money to stretch to buy new carpets or curtains, and even if there had been, Ellen had always been an outdoors, practical person, not a woman who liked or understood any more about a house than keeping it squeaky clean.

It never mattered to her if the bedroom suites matched, or if the two worn-out recliners in the living room were gray and the carpet a dusty tan.

Or that three different kinds of chairs sat around the heavy oak table in the kitchen.

But Billy saw it now with new eyes and winced, remembering the luxury of the rooms he'd seen at Shiloh's house. But he showed her everything stubbornly—better that she understood things right up front.

The house looked like an L from the front, with long bannistered porches filling in from one gable to the end of the house, both upstairs and downstairs, both front and back.

But in truth, it formed a T. An arm projected backward from the kitchen, as well as forward from it.

The room to the front was an old-fashioned, little-used parlor; the room to the back of the kitchen was a complete surprise, a light, buttery room full of the morning sun. Windows on one side let it flood in; windows along the back revealed a giant hickory tree casting a heavy shadow outside; and a door on the third wall opened onto the back porch.

The room held an old white iron bed with a patchwork quilt, a wooden set of drawers painted blue, and a straightback chair with a cane bottom, painted a horrible brown. There was no carpet, just a squeaky, yellowy, waxed wooden floor.

"Whose room is this?" Shiloh asked, breaking the silence that lay around them as he opened doors and motioned her into rooms.

"Nobody's. I think it was once Grandpa's sister's. The place has been in his family for years." Billy moved away, motioning her after him. "Down this hall is the bathroom. There's only one. Here's the den, and down there"—he pointed to a door at the end of the hall—"that's Grandpa's room."

"Where does your mother sleep?"

"Upstairs . . . here." Billy motioned her to the long narrow stairs that led up between two wall-papered walls. Nothing glamorous about these steps, Shiloh thought, remembering the gentle curve and the deliberately exposed, arched support beams of the stairs in her own home. *Sam's* home. Billy Bob's steps were just to connect one floor to another, that was all.

"Mama's in this room." He showed her the open door

at the top right of the steps, but she hung back, reluctant to look in. "She's right above Grandpa. He can't get up and down stairs anymore, but if he needs her, he just taps on the ceiling with his cane."

That only left one important place to visit.

"This is my room," he said quietly, and stood aside to let her enter. It was beside his mother's room. Too close.

A big bed made of red oak stood in the dead center, its headboard against one wall. A table beside it, a lamp, an alarm clock. One tall dresser with a small mirror above it, shelves on one entire wall that ran from the ceiling down to a long desk.

And books.

They surprised her. She glanced at them, then at him as he watched her face.

He didn't seem like a reader.

She moved to the shelves, reached up, and pulled one off. *Introduction to Animal Husbandry*. Another one above that was entitled *Advanced Studies in Horticulture*.

"Have you read all these?" she asked in amazement, putting down the heavy tome she'd picked up.

He shrugged, his cheeks a little flushed. "Most of 'em. Not because I wanted to. Because I had to, so I could understand things that I needed to know."

"I . . . see."

That was a lie. She didn't see anything. How could she? Her eyesight was blurred from tears.

What had she done? She had taken as a husband a man she had only known briefly four years ago. She didn't know him now, not the first thing about the way he lived, not how he thought, not even what he read.

This was an unknown house that didn't feel or smell like home.

Nobody wanted her here except Billy Bob, and he himself had done things to her that had made her a stranger even to herself.

For one painful minute, Shiloh wanted to go home to Laura and Sam, until she fought down the wave of home-sickness.

"What's the matter?" Billy asked tenderly, coming up behind her to wrap his arms around her, to cuddle her up against him, his chin on top of her head. "Afraid I'm gonna make you read all of these books? Well, don't worry. They'd put a hyperactive to sleep, and I want you wide awake, baby."

His teasing didn't offer much reassurance, but enough for her to say what she wanted.

"The room at the end of the porch downstairs, Billy. Could I—can I have that one?"

He went still behind her, the hands that had been stroking her arms freezing.

"You mean—to sleep there?"

She nodded.

"And just tell me," he said dangerously, pushing away from her, twisting her around to face him, "why you can't sleep here, in my room, with me?"

"It's—it's too close, that's what. To everybody. And it's you. Totally you, Billy. I don't belong in this house. I don't think it even wants me here. All this stuff"—she motioned at the books—"I didn't know you read like this. I don't think I have a chance here."

"What you mean is, you're regrettin' everything we've done already," he said in anger, turning loose of her. "This house—*my* home—it's not good enough for you."

"That's not true. But I have to be alone for a little while."

"In a different room, on another floor from me? Tell me something, Shiloh." He caught her chin in his hard fingers, forcing her to look at him. "Where's the girl who told me we were free, the girl who took off her clothes and gave herself to me, the girl who held me last night and called my name when—"

"You were different, too, last night," she cut in, her face flaming. "You needed me. Today you're a part of your family. Of this house. You don't need comfort."

He turned loose, swallowing, his own face flushed.

"All right." Billy moved away and looked out the window at the shady backyard. "By God, then, you take that room downstairs. You stay there until you're ready to be my wife. I want the Shiloh I held last night, not somebody scared of belonging to me, and my family, and my home."

"It all happened so fast, Billy," she whispered, and the sound of her voice was so forlorn that his shoulders sagged and the temper went out of him.

"Don't you think I know how hard this is for you?" he asked, then let his hand reach out to brush her cheek lightly with his knuckles. "I've gotta go smooth things over with Mama. I'll tell her that you'll be using that room. Get some rest, baby. You didn't get much last night."

# 17

"*You've been with* this girl four years and we've never heard a peep about it?" Willie demanded dubiously. The cane in his right hand pointed straight at Billy, as unnerving as the staff of Moses indicting an uneasy, but unrepentant, young Pharoah.

So Billy explained it again, patiently, except for the part about the thirty-five hundred dollars, which he carefully chose to omit.

". . . and we met again the night she wrecked her car and they brought her to the jail to wait for her father."

"You sure got married quick as greased lightnin'," Willie continued.

Billy sucked in his breath in exasperation. "I knew what I wanted, Grandpa. I wasn't going to let her get away a second time."

"What you wanted," Ellen said slowly, ignoring her son's face, focusing stubbornly instead on the Red Delicious apples she was polishing, "belonged to the judge's other son."

"No." Billy's denial was fast and emphatic. "I know what you're thinkin', that I was after Shiloh to get even with the Sewells."

"I won't be the only one thinkin' it," Ellen returned with regret.

"I can't help that. She was mine first. She's mine now."

"And it's that easy for you to forget the time she spent with him?"

"Mama." She looked up at last, her busy, worried hands stilling on the fruit. "She's never slept with him."

Ellen's face flushed a dark red, and her mouth primmed at his blunt outspokenness.

"Did I ask to know that?"

"No. But you needed to hear it, didn't you? And I needed to say it."

"Did she tell you she hadn't?"

"Maybe there wasn't any need. For one thing, I think I would have married her, anyway. I love her, Mama."

"Don't sell your soul and ruin your life for love, boy. I couldn't bear it."

*"Your mother was a gullible fool."* Sewell's callow, vindictive words sluiced through him like scalding bleach, searing his insides. I hate him, Billy thought, looking down at his mother's pleading face . . . then he shook himself away from the thought. "We're free to be what we can be." Shiloh said that.

"She was a virgin, Mama. Beyond a shadow of a doubt. I was there. I know."

"Oh." Her word was a whispered, flustered moue of sound. Embarrassed, surprised, relieved.

It was Grandpa who broke the awkward silence. "I didn't know they still made them," he said wryly. "Trust you, Billy Bob, to find the last one in the state."

"She's not going to like it that I told you."

"We're not likely to bring it up over the supper table," Ellen retorted with a stab of tartness. "And I don't see that it means a thing, at least, not in some ways. She's still the daughter of a rich man."

"A rich, *mean* one," Grandpa interpolated.

"I don't care," Billy said stubbornly. "She stood up for me at the jail. She's the reason they let me go. There's enough between us that this can work. I had to try. And right now, she's scared to death. I reckon she's back there at the house crying. She sure looked like she was about to." He remembered uneasily the lost, empty look on her face.

"We ain't gonna bite her," said Grandpa, a little indignantly.

"I told her she could take the bedroom off the kitchen. The one that nobody ever uses." He tried to say it diffidently, without showing how the words rankled, looking down the long row of pecan trees that ran beyond the stand.

There was a tiny silence of surprise.

"What's wrong with yours?"

Billy Bob frowned at Willie. Did the old man never show any tact at all? "She likes that room. Nobody says I won't stay there with her, do they? But maybe she needs some time on her own, a place of her own for a few days." His heavy shoulders—too wide for the lankiness of his body—heaved upward, shrugging off the surprised, then pitying, looks of his relatives.

"Don't be a fool, boy." His grandfather levered himself up out of the slat-backed rocking chair, rearing up on the cane to stand pugnaciously before Billy. "You already got two strikes against you with this marriage. If you aim to hold the thing together, you better use any kind of glue you can. You've been keepin' that Blake woman happy for years with just one thing, and she's mighty near an expert on it, I hear. So you better try some of it on this new wife. Don't let her scare you off."

"Daddy!"

"Truth is truth, Ellen."

"I'm *not* scared."

Willie turned from his belligerent stance toward his daughter and focused his wisdom firmly on his recalcitrant grandson.

"Sure you are. This wife of yours is pretty. Fancy. You said yourself you've been thinkin' about her for a long time. And on top of all that, she's what we used to call a good woman. They're the scariest kind, boy, especially when you love them. Pure hell on a man. He's always trying to deserve 'em."

"You'd think he was some kind of expert on women, wouldn't you?" Billy said in exasperation to the sky.

And unexpectedly, Ellen chuckled, her hands moving again, like bumblebees over sweet purple clover as she stacked apples into fat, red potbellied piles. "He reads *Cosmopolitan* every time we have to stand in line at the Bi-Rite. And I guess she can have that room if she wants it. You should remember, Daddy, it's got two doors, one to the inside hall, and one to the outside porch. Surely to goodness Will can talk his way into one or the other of them. He's *your* grandson."

She was asleep when he went back to the house at lunch, lying sideways, nearly turned on her stomach in the middle of the patchwork quilt, the bright blue dress tangling around her long brown legs.

Billy's heart turned over, one, good solid flip, as he stood silently in the door watching his young bride sleep. Her thick, waving dark hair spread like a heavy fan over the quilt and the edge of the pillow, sweeping off the rich healthy brown of her tanned forehead, leaving the clean line of her profile clear to his view. One downy, soft tuft of new growth lay against her temple, clinging damply to her skin, its dark silkiness echoed by the long sweep of the eyelashes on her flushed cheeks. It was too warm in the little room in spite of the long row of windows she'd pushed up.

One hand was up under her, her fingers long and slender at the edge of her body, right where the buttons of the blue dress had opened, as if beckoning him. The palm of her hand pressing against her heart pushed her breasts upward; the shadows between them were rich and dusky.

If she hadn't been so nervy this morning, if Grandpa and Mama weren't coming to the house for lunch in a few minutes, if the little room weren't too hot from the noon-day sun, Billy would have shut the door behind him, stripped off his clothes, and gone to bed with her.

*If* he'd thought he was completely welcome in this room.

As it was, he took a deep breath and went to the kitchen just at the end of the tiny hall.

Grandpa came to join him for sandwiches and iced tea while Ellen kept the stand; the two of them took turns at the stand most days.

"Have we got another window fan?" Billy asked suddenly, his thoughts on the fluff of hair that clung to Shiloh's temple, the way it had cajoled him to brush it away from her skin.

"I don't think so. What you need one for?"

"Shiloh's asleep in the back room." Billy jerked his head in that direction. "It was a little hot back there when I checked on her."

"That room's got windows on the east and north," Grandpa said consideringly. "That means it ought to stay pretty cool. It gets lots of morning sun and afternoon shade. But come next month, ain't no place cool. Not ever, not in Mississippi."

"I swear I thought I'd have the money to have this house insulated again this summer, and central air put in," Billy said, turning up his glass to drain it.

"You needed the tractor-trailer more, to haul the nursery stock. Like you'll need some for this fall, if you've got any left. Where'd you get the money to pay that jail fine?" his grandfather asked curiously.

"I just—had it, all right?"

Willie snorted. "Don't get hot with me, boy. It's just gonna be a shame if you had to use the money you've saved for good purposes to pay a fine for—"

"Grandpa, don't say anything to Shiloh about this, you hear me?"

"You mean you ain't told your own wife—"

"That's right. Not yet, anyway." Billy held his grandfather's stare for a long moment.

"This is the funniest marriage I ever heard of in my life," Willie groused at last, disapproval in his voice.

"I've not got time to worry about that," Billy returned, pushing his chair back to stand. "I don't want Shiloh havin' to sleep in a hot room. She's used to something different."

"She'd better get used to *you,* and you to her."

Willie's words were in his ears when he lingered by Shiloh's room on his way out to the farm. She was awake, sitting up drowsily in the middle of a wedding-ring circle stitched into the quilt, raking her hair back off her face.

As he stood in the doorway, she caught sight of him and smiled, a sleepy, sensual smile that gave him more hope than he'd had all day.

"Feel better?"

She nodded wordlessly, then yawned and stretched, her movements lifting her breasts against the blue dress, lifting her upper body into an innocently erotic pose.

"I'm going out on the farm. Want to go with me?" His voice was careless as he tried hard not to care whether she did or not.

Shiloh moved, then she looked down blankly at her dress.

"I don't think I can," she said, whimsically.

"Why not? If you're hungry, we can get you a sandwich first."

"It's not that. Billy, haven't you noticed? I don't have any clothes."

He pulled his gaze from her rueful dark eyes and scanned her body. "I believe I'd notice if you didn't have on anything, honey. Yes, ma'am, I definitely would," he informed her humorously.

She stood up abruptly, letting the blue dress skim down around her legs. "I put this dress on yesterday morning so I could take the town by storm with Billy Walker."

"We sure did that. I don't know if they'll remember what we were wearin' or not, though."

She sighed in exasperation. "I've been wearing it ever since. I either have to wash it, and wear a sheet while it dries—"

"Sounds like a good idea. Whose sheet?" he interrupted daringly, a glint in his eye.

Her face flushed pinkly as she took a step backward,

but her voice was severe. "This is serious. I have to get some other clothes. I've got closets full at home that I—"

"No."

"Some of them are mine, bought with my own money, Billy. Not his."

He took another step into the room, his hands going to his hips. "If you go back now, no matter for what reason, you'll only get tore up again, Shiloh. Looks like to me that we're having a hard enough time today without that. You're scared to set foot in my bedroom."

Tucking her hair behind one ear, Shiloh ignored the challenge in his words and looked at her bare feet. "So, what am I going to wear? I have a little money with me, and a checking account, if Sam hasn't closed it."

"Don't you think," Billy said tightly, his face angry, "that I might buy you clothes? You're my wife. Most men do."

"But you don't have any—" She clipped the words off sharply, and hastily substituted, "I don't want to take your money, Billy. It would feel funny."

"Tell me about it. It felt pretty funny to me to take yours, too, but sometimes you've got to do things." He took another step closer to her, so close now she could have reached out and touched him; his eyes searched hers. "I'm supposed to buy clothes for you, Shiloh. The sooner you let me, the sooner this will start to feel normal."

"Where are you—where are we going to get the money?" she whispered at last, her eyes luminous.

Billy's face lightened instantly, and he laughed a little as he reached out to graze her face with his knuckles. "I made a deal with a chain of stores over in Arkansas. Sold a whole acre of trees to them last month. Remember when I came to the bank? See, I had more on my mind than just aggravating you." His eyes teased her a minute. "That's the first deal that big I've ever made. I'm due to sell the same amount to them every month right up until Thanksgiving. That's several thousand dollars every time I make a sale, even after I cover my expenses."

"And can you live on that?"

"All winter, if we're careful."

"Oh, good."

Shiloh fumbled for an answer, all too aware that Sam put out not thousands, but tens of thousands, every week, and he brought in double that amount.

They hesitated for a long second or two, then Billy reached out and ran his long brown finger down her throat, to the hollow between her breasts.

"It's Friday. I've got to check on some things around the farm. If you want to use the washing machine, it's beside the bathroom. You could get ready—we could go to town when I get back. I think you'll feel better if it's just you and me for a while, instead of my whole family crammed down your throat."

"Not Sweetwater."

"No. Maybe Martinsville. There's a shopping center there. Then we'll do something—eat, dance, go to a movie."

"Are you asking me for a date?" she asked mischievously, trying to ignore the hand at her breasts. "An honest-to-goodness, public date?"

"There's a first time for everything," he retorted, unevenly. "Isn't this the way we're supposed to do it? Get married and then date?" As his eyes held hers, his big hand flattened slowly across her, his fingers slipping under the blue fabric with the insidious strength of sweet outlaw honeysuckle in a prim garden, to lie heavily, hotly against her skin.

She never looked down, just up at him as she said unsteadily, "I think you're awfully free with your hands for a man who doesn't even know if I've agreed to go out with him or not."

"I'm trying to persuade you."

"And do I get more of *this*"—she caught his marauding hand with hers—"if I say yes? Or will you behave?"

He eyed her face for a minute, then let his hand drop away. "I think I'd better behave." He sighed.

Unexpectedly, she reached out to flatten her own hands against his shirt, rubbing her palms over him sensually. "That's a shame," she said regretfully, stepping up into him, against him, feeling the breath as it caught in his chest. "All of my dates who are also married to me have to fool around"—she reached to rain a kiss into the warm hollow of his throat—"when they take me out, or I don't go." She kissed the side of his throat. "So if you're going to behave—"

"I take it back. It was a lie. I won't," he interrupted fervently, his blue eyes laughing down at her in a combination of shock and delight as he caught her hands and pulled them around himself, locking her to him. "I'll put every move I've ever heard of on you, baby. I'll be a regular octopus."

"Is that a promise?" she teased, just as his lips bent to hers.

"Honey, that's a blood oath," he breathed into her mouth.

So she spent the afternoon wearing a long T-shirt of Billy's that she found folded up in the tiny laundry room, while her clothes washed. No one except her was at the house, and its silence and heat began to wear at her until she finally dared to walk outside on the back porch bare-footed. The shirt came to her midthigh; surely if nobody got close enough to realize she had on nothing under it, it would be all right to walk outside.

In fact, the only person to discover such an embarrassing thing was likely to be Billy, and Shiloh doubted if he would mind it much at all.

The yard had an old, established feel to it, probably because of the size of the trees that shaded it, and it was welcoming in an unassuming way. No elaborate lily ponds or strategically placed brown gravel paths here. Instead, an old well house stood off to the far left, its roof barely three feet out of the ground. Over the years, it had been nearly swamped with ivy and the overhanging vines of forsythia.

A wild rose bush sprawled across the old wire fence that ran down the right length of the yard, and its tiny, dusky pink blooms were so heavy and profuse that the fence dipped slightly under its weight, laden down with its honeyed load.

Old-fashioned, shade-loving impatiens ran wild around the bases of the two spreading oaks at the back of the yard, their vivid, lush blooms even more deeply pink than the roses.

A swing—the biggest one Shiloh had ever seen—hung from a frame suspended between the two oaks, and the way the grass had been worn away until the dirt had been exposed under it told her how often that swing was used.

Besides it, there were only three other chairs in the backyard; one of them, a heavy wooden one, sat near the swing. The other two, both rockers, were here, on the back porch. One held a faded, dented cushion. The other sat near the bannister, and the fronds of the huge Boston fern that hung from the basket near it reached down to brush its high back. Beyond the trees and the fence, the land rolled. Seven Knobs was the one section of Briskin County that dipped and rose a little instead of being nearly flat; it dipped and rose seven times, in fact, in long, slow, graceful sweeps.

Peace lay over this place, as did sunshine that sprinkled through the heavy leaves of the trees. The only sounds were the birds and the occasional blast from a horse, probably beyond the distant barn, and the rumble of a far-off tractor.

Was it Billy?

She closed her eyes and pictured him at work in the hot sun, the ever-present cap covering his thick blond hair; the long, sleek muscles in his back pulling upward as he bent to watch the ground beneath him, the sure, deft, brown hands on the wheel.

Friday night, going into town with Billy Bob, promises of kisses and caresses and fun.

She would make this work, in spite of everything—his family, her uncertainty in this house, the lack of money.

And she would begin tonight.


"Mama, Grandpa, we just wanted to tell you that we're going out, and we'll probably be late getting back home," Billy said cheerfully, as he led Shiloh out the kitchen.

Ellen looked up from the salad she was making at the sink; it was the first time Shiloh had seen her since this morning. Ellen offered a tentative smile; that, too, was a first. "Have a good time."

"No need to stay out until all hours tonight," Grandpa

drawled outrageously from his chair beside a tiny little television where the local news was being broadcast in shimmering images. "This time you can bring the girl home with you. Now if you can just get her in the right bed."

Billy muttered an expletive under his breath, his cheeks red as he pulled Shiloh out the back screen door. "That old man's getting on my nerves."

"I don't know how many Friday nights you've laid out with some girl, Billy," Shiloh said dangerously, as he opened her truck door, "but tonight is different. Tonight is your honeymoon."

"I've told you before about those other girls. And one Friday night not so long ago I watched you climb in Michael's Jag in front of the bank and pull off into the sunset," he said brusquely.

Both looked away; neither wanted to fight. Not now.

Then he opened his own door and slid in beside her.

"Shoot," he muttered, looking toward the garage. "I forgot to take the Cadillac back. Just remembered it." He hesitated, then made up his mind. "It'll have to wait until tomorrow. I'm not ruining a date with you for Pennington's car."

Two miles down the highway, he looked over at the girl in the truck with him.

"I like your dress," he said teasingly. "Have I seen you wear it before?"

She relaxed, then fell in with his mood. "At least it's clean. I loved it when I put it on yesterday. Now I'm beginning to wish I'd never seen it. I wore your T-shirt while I washed this, and even it looked better to me."

Billy considered the vision he had of her wrapped in one of his extra-long, tall-men white Fruit of the Looms.

"You'll have to let me see you in it. That way I can give you my opinion. Of course, it's hard to see much with you sitting way over there." He raised his eyebrows questioningly, patting the seat beside him suggestively with his sprawled, lazy hand.

After a second's pause, Shiloh gave a tiny laugh under her breath and slid over to him. His right arm wrapped around her, squeezing her up tight for a second.

"I can't get too close," she informed him.

"Why not? I don't bite."

"No, but this stick shift in the floor won't let me."

"Next truck I own, I'll definitely go for an automatic," he said regretfully, letting her straighten a little. "So where are we going?"

Shiloh stared at him blankly. "I don't know. The only times I ever came to Tobias County, it was to Greenview Golf Course with Sam. I've never been shopping here."

He'd never been to the golf course, he thought, then reminded her quietly, "You came with me once, to a dance."

She thought for a second. "That night was the first time I'd ever been anywhere with you. I couldn't see or hear anything else *but* you. We could have been on the moon for all I remember of the place."

Her words took the shadows away that had chased across his face.

"If I get real lucky, maybe you won't remember much else tonight, either," he said huskily, and his hand squeezed her arm. "Maybe neither of us will."

But by the time he got to Martinsville, he'd definitely remembered a few things, such as the name of the store where Angie shopped. It was in the Delta Shopping Center, along with a Wal-Mart, which suited him fine: the big department store carried fans.

A fancy Atlanta architect had designed the place, determined to make it look as southern as *Gone With the Wind*. He'd even tried to induce Spanish moss to droop and sway from two oaks that guarded the sweltering, sticky span of asphalt, broken at four-foot intervals by neatly lined boxes marking off Bradford pear trees.

A Dodge Dakota truck was tooling out of a spot directly under one of the oaks; Billy beelined for it.

Then he pointed Shiloh in the direction of the clothing store, which she looked over solemnly. "I've never been here before."

"I hear it's okay." He wasn't about to say, I saw its labels in Angie's clothes. Awkwardly, he took the bill he'd carefully creased and folded earlier, lifted her hand, and pushed it in it. "Spend it all. It's not that much anyway."

Embarrassed, she didn't look down. "Aren't you coming with me?"

He grinned. "If you'll let me help in the dressing room, I might. If we didn't get thrown out of the store." Dipping toward her, his lips caressed her jaw, then his teeth nipped playfully.

"Billy Bob Walker, is that all you think about?" Shiloh demanded, glancing around to make sure no one had heard, nudging his mouth away with a finger.

"I've been married—really married—about twenty-four hours. I've been with you one time. One time, for four years of waiting." His face had gone serious; his hands gripped her shoulders as they stood lost in the rows of the parking lot. "So I'm doing well to walk and talk, Shiloh. Yeah. It's all I can think about. Don't you think about it?"

She remembered the way she'd spent the afternoon mooning over him, imagining him at work, his body controlling the tractor.

"Well? Do you?"

"You know I do," she capitulated hurriedly.

"So let's forget this and go somewhere to be together," he suggested swiftly, pushing her face against the open neck of his shirt. "I can say it a whole lot plainer, what I want to do, if you'll let me."

"I've got to have something to wear," she managed.

He released her reluctantly. "Okay. So go get some clothes that I can yank off you in a hurry." Then he smiled, ending the teasing. "That funny pinky-red color you wore to the Legion Hall—I thought you were the prettiest thing I'd ever seen in it, baby."

"Where will you be?" she demanded.

"There. At Wal-Mart. I've got some things to buy."

"Billy." She caught at his arm as he headed away and worried her lip in embarrassment when he obligingly stopped to listen. "I wasn't expecting us to get together this fast, you know."

"So?" He waited patiently, puzzled, running his hand down her bare arm. So warm, so soft. Wal-Mart was a mighty poor second choice to her wet mouth, her luscious body; and what'd she need clothes for, anyway?

"I never had time to—" She looked away, blushed.

He frowned.

"Oh, good gracious, don't you understand, Billy Bob? I haven't seen a doctor about—"

He sucked in his breath as her meaning hit. "This is a fine time to talk about birth control," he murmured ruefully, glancing around them at the cars and the people hurrying past, his stomach tightening, his hands clenching, his whole body pulling in like a big tiger's.

"I didn't remember it last night," she told the second button on his shirt. "I couldn't think at all. But if we keep on like that, things are liable to happen."

"Not things, honey. They have names—babies."

"I didn't think I should wait until, well, you know, to tell you that we'd have to stop tonight unless you were . . . were prepared. Because I'm not. But I will be, in a few weeks. Is that how long it takes?" She was rambling, babbling, trying to say these extremely embarrassing words in broad daylight, directly to him.

He ran his hand up her throat, nudging her chin toward him. Reluctantly, she looked at him, at the warm blue eyes, crinkling at the corners as he gazed down at her with a slow, hot, pleasurable stare. "I don't want to wait. And I don't think anything on this green earth could make me stop something I've started with you, Shiloh. I don't know how long it takes birth control pills—is that what you're talking about?—to take effect. I'm glad you don't know, either. So I'll take care of it tonight and for the next few days." He bent to kiss her lightly, his fingers still warm around her chin, his face intent. "But if we don't quit talking about it, I'm going to give this parking lot a bigger show than it's getting right now." Another kiss. "And you'd better go get those damned clothes while you still can. Be good, Shiloh."

"Yes, Billy Bob," she said demurely, but she flashed a grin at him as she pulled away and ran across the parking lot, the blue dress swirling around her.

He drew a deep breath and turned toward the big store behind him without really seeing anything except Shiloh's pink-cheeked face.

She was so young, so innocent. Angie had always talked about the subject with ease and nonchalance and a joking flippancy. Not Shiloh. And it made him downright edgy with nerves and a heated anticipation to consider the fact that she was planning their lovemaking on an extended, normal basis. It was pure pleasure to consider it. No shame, no guilt, no remorse—they were married. It was right. It was reveling in freedom.

He could definitely get addicted to this situation.


He had given her a hundred-dollar bill. She looked down at it as she stood in the store, and blinked away sudden tears. She didn't think he could afford it.

Part of her wanted to refuse the money; there was a certain shame in being dependent on another person. But the way Billy had given it, she had felt loved and taken care of, too; he was waiting to see if she was willing to take from him, to let him provide for her.

It was clearly a point of pride with him. So Shiloh would swallow her own pride and buy something he would like.

Just for an instant, though, it crossed her mind to wonder if she'd given him anything in return, any emotion, to ease the sting of her own offer of money. Was this how Billy had felt when she'd held out that thirty-five hundred dollars all those weeks ago?

"I'm not your charity case," he had said.

Well, beginning now, she would erase any doubts he might have about that money; it was no more between them than this bill he'd pressed into her hand.

The clothes at this store were less expensive than any she was used to and far more casual. Most of the shorts and pants relied on odd novelty touches and cuts for appeal, and the tops and shirts were eye-catchingly designed.

No lined linen slacks, no silk blouses, no subtly textured expensive fabrics.

Liz Claiborne didn't live here, not in this department store.

But the neighborhood wasn't bad. She liked cotton blends and cool tops, and if there was one thing Shiloh had, it was an eye for cut and color. Hadn't Sam spent years complaining about it?

So she spent fifteen minutes looking over the other patrons of the shop, trying to catch the mood of these clothes.

When she left the store an hour later, two large sacks in her hands, she was laughing. She definitely thought Billy was going to approve.

He was waiting for her in the truck, one long leg outside the door he'd propped open against the heat, which had dropped considerably since the sun had gone down. He was drinking a bottled Coke while he fiddled with the radio; the humidity made the long hair in back cling to the edges of his neck, curling under just a little.

"Waiting for somebody?" she asked mischievously.

His head came up, startled, and then he stared for a long second. "You'll do," he answered at last, sliding out to take her bags from her and put them in the back of the truck, never taking his eyes off her.

He liked the way the floral print shirt lit up her skin; the way the scooped-neck collar hinted at the swell of her breasts.

He caught her shoulders to pivot her completely around in front of him, as he admired the way the shorts hugged her brown legs and wrapped her slender waist.

*She looked like she belonged to him.*

The thought hung in his throat and he swallowed the heavy emotion that reached to choke him. Maybe she'd done it deliberately, buying these clothes; or maybe she'd liked them because a part of her was like this—casual and easygoing.

But seeing her dressed this way helped scrub out some

of the despair he'd been living with since the night she and Michael had made such a matched set in that expensive spotlight.

"Shoes," he managed at last, looking down at the elaborate leather sandals she was still wearing. "You need white tennis shoes."

"No, Billy, I've already spent—"

"Come on. Let's go get a pair." His fingers shackled her wrist as he headed off determinedly, stalking toward the tiny shoe store nestled between an ice cream parlor and a record barn where Randy Travis's disembodied voice floated through the air.

He liked her in these clothes, Shiloh thought, remembering the way his eyes had reflected first a startled, surprised delight and then a fiery pleasure. An arrow of hot excitement shot through her stomach; Billy had liked her a *lot*.

She could barely concentrate on the earnest shoe salesman who removed one sandal and droned on about his sale on Keds, because of her own rattling emotions and because Billy kept watching her face.

He was paying no attention to the salesman, either, except for thinking once or twice that if the man ran his hand much farther up Shiloh's leg while he was taking off her sandals, Billy was going to break his fingers.

"Here," he said brusquely, his voice thick with emotion, "you go get the shoes. I'll do this."

He dropped to his haunches in front of Shiloh, shouldering the ambitious salesman out of the way. The man gasped indignantly, his eyes behind his wire-rimmed glasses angry.

"But this is my job!"

Billy never answered, just sliding the last sandal off

Shiloh's foot, looking up at her as she sat perched on the stool above him. The salesman opened his mouth to speak again, then eyed the long, square width of Billy's shoulders and their determined set before he shut his mouth and headed off to get the shoes, without another word.

Billy pulled her feet up between his spread thighs, his hard palms wrapping the tops of her feet, his fingers reaching underneath to caress her soles.

"I like the clothes," he whispered huskily, belatedly.

The light in his blue eyes nearly burned her alive, so she looked away from the hard angles of his upturned face to the sturdy brown throat to the width of his shoulders, the muscles beneath the blue shirt.

Passion—that was what she felt flowing from him.

The cap blocked her angle of view as he ducked his head, then she felt his lips warm on the top of her foot. It was a quick flaming caress, one sheltered from the view of anybody who might have been watching by the spread of his legs around her and the breadth of his shoulders above her, and she reached out to pull the aggravating cap from his head so that she might see him better.

"Ahem. Here is the shoe size you requested." The salesman's voice was repressive as he slammed the box down beside Billy, who raised his head and lowered her foot as casually as if he hadn't made her quiver with his touch.

But he didn't trust himself to speak as he threaded the laces through the shoes, his big hands deft, if a little shaky. And he slid one on her foot with his other hand around the silky calf of her leg, his long fingers reaching the back of her knee. He repeated the process with the second shoe.

"She needs to walk in them a little," the salesman pointed out in aggravation.

Billy let his fingers linger regretfully on the back of her leg, then slid his hand away and stood.

She stood, too, still clutching his cap against her, her legs so weak from his fingers that they wobbled a little. A few tentative steps later, she announced, "They're fine. Perfect."

He didn't answer, but the slow slide of his eyes down her legs, the tiny smile that hovered at his lips said enough. "I like them, too," he told her at last.

"You two newlyweds, or something?" the salesman asked, disgruntled, as Billy paid for the shoes.

"How'd you know that?" Shiloh asked in surprise.

The man preened himself a little, mollified. "You don't have on rings, but it shows. Believe me, it shows," he added drily.


They bought a huge bucket of chicken and fixin's at some place called Cajun Joe's.

They argued mildly for a few minutes about where they were going with it.

To the drive-in? No, too hot, he said.

To the park? No, too all-American, she said.

To the tables outside the Legion Hall where all of Sweetwater danced and every curious eye in the world would be on them? *NO*.

They wound up down on the edge of tiny Angel Lake, where it straddled Briskin and Tobias counties, all alone in the dusky night except for the occasional distant light of some fisherman. The water on this finger of the lake was too shallow for speedboating and skiing, and there were no spots for camping, so few people came.

Tonight, just Billy and Shiloh, out on a rocky point over the misty water, shaded by twisting cedars and gangly pines. He spread a blue tarpaulin he had in the big storage chest that sat in the bed of the truck, and they ate there, watching the stars and letting the fog that was rising off the lake cool them.

When he finished, he rose without preamble and began to unbutton his shirt in the inky darkness above her.

She let the chicken leg she'd been eating fall to the tarpaulin. "What are you doing?"

He let the shirt slip from his hand, then dropped to one knee to loom over her, like a threatening cloud. "What does it look like?"

"Like . . . you're taking off your clothes." Maybe she'd swallowed the chicken bone instead of letting it roll away; something prodded nervously in her throat.

"You, Mrs. Shiloh Walker, are one smart cookie." He found her upturned mouth and kissed it lightly. "And you taste like chicken."

She heard the slide of his belt as he unfastened it, then felt the forward, hunching movements of his shoulders as he bent to tug off his boots. First one, then the other thudded on the ground beside her. When the rough sound of denim dragging over his skin brought her with a gasp to her feet, he paused, peering up at her in the shadowy night, trying to see more clearly.

"Where you running to?" he asked mildly. "Don't you want to go swimming with me?"

"Swimming? You're going *swimming?*"

He rose to his full height in front of her. Shiloh wasn't certain, but she thought he was—

"Billy, have you got any clothes on at all?"

His laughter was low. "Why don't you come a little closer and find out for yourself? Scared, Shiloh?"

She swallowed. "Why would I be? I've . . . seen you before."

"Did you, now?" The three words whispered satisfaction across her cheek. "I wondered if you looked—really looked—last night. And if you'd be wanting to look again." His hands reached for her shoulders, guiding her to him inexorably. She resisted briefly, but her hands had a will of their own. They remembered the warmth of his skin from the night before, and they sought it now.

Her breath left her in a rush when her fingers raked him, felt the muscles that sloped from his shoulders down into his chest. And without volition, without thought, her arms slid around him, her cheeks pressed against his hard breastbone, her hands brushed down over his buttocks.

"Billy Walker," she choked out in scandalized arousal, "you really don't have on a stitch."

His arms locked her to him, refusing to heed the momentary struggle she made before she gave it up. "You could scream," he whispered in her ear, taking time to trace it with his tongue. "Water carries sound. Clancy Green and his buddies fish here nearly every weekend. They might come to your rescue."

"Who says I—want to be rescued?" she whispered jerkily. She shook back her hair and pressed back against his arm to gaze up at him, piercing the darkness with her eyes. "This is exactly what I should have expected when I agreed to a Friday night date with a wild man like you."

"I'm as ordinary as I can be, Shiloh," he answered, seriously. "I work, and sweat, and worry about rain, and harvests, and money. And if I was wild, it was because I didn't have you."

"Billy, there's not another man I know who could say that, stark naked," she said, with a sobbing intake of tender laughter, "and make me cry."

Pulling her left hand to his lips, he kissed the back of it, lingering at last on her ring finger.

"That salesman with his prowling hands was right about one thing. You need a wedding band."

"I wouldn't mind putting one on you, either, Billy. A great, wide one so everybody would know that you're definitely out of circulation." Shiloh pushed her fingers through his, their entwined hands between them all that kept their bodies from being glued together.

"We'll get them as soon as I make that next sale, okay? Pure gold—to last us fifty years." His tongue traced the finger delicately.

"Is that all?" Her hand twisted to touch his lips.

"I really did mean to swim, Shiloh," he whispered. "First, before anything else."

She pulled his hand down to the front of the blouse, where its buttons lay, and pressed deliberately closer to him, if that were possible. "You can change your plans, can't you?" she returned quietly. "We can swim—later."

# 18

*He drifted awake* at dawn the next morning, the sound of birds chirping noisily in his ears, a cool, sweet, early breeze fresh with the scent of nasturtiums and roses blowing across his skin.

For a long, slow, hazy moment, Billy wondered why there was so much sparkling sunlight in his room, making the tiny dust motes glitter as they floated in the air above him. And the sun was coming from the wrong angle, too, striking him from the right, instead of his left as it normally did in his room.

Then the pure, heavy, contented peace in his body chugged through him—and memory returned.

He was in Shiloh's room, not his. In Shiloh's bed, not his. In her arms.

She was the weight against his side; it was her hair spilling like silk across him, her hand on his chest.

When Billy moved to look down at her, she moved a little, too, turning her face away. Under the sheet, under the quilt, her bare legs tangled with his.

Here in the clear, bright light of this Saturday morning, he saw the fading shadows of the mark his mouth had made on her three days before. Only three days, and his whole life had changed.

He shifted on his side, groaning a little. They'd come close to an argument after they finally got back home last night, all over where they were going to sleep.

"I want to sleep with you. And I'm going to get damn aggravated if you don't return the favor. It's not right, us sleeping apart. But you said it was your room," he protested on the dark back porch, wondering how they could be squabbling just a half hour after they'd left the lake, where they'd worn themselves out with each other. "I don't want you mad tomorrow because I invaded your space, or whatever you call it. So we'll have to go to my room."

"I never said that you weren't supposed to come in here with me," Shiloh returned, her hands urging him to follow her.

The rest of the house lay asleep, in blackness, but someone had moved a tiny lamp into Shiloh's new room. They saw its dim yellow light through the shades that had been partially drawn over the windows. And when she opened the door from the porch, tugging him along by one hand, she drew in her breath sharply.

Over her head, he saw what she did: Ellen had made the bed with fresh sheets, turning back the covers to reveal their snowy whiteness. Besides the lamp, his mother had filled two vases with wild roses and a fragrant mix of flowers from the greenhouses. The roses made a vivid splash of color on the old blue dresser; the other, smaller bouquet drifted sweetness from the bedside table.

Even Willie had made a contribution: the old cane-bottomed chair had been replaced by his favorite rocker from the back porch, and a cushion from the living room couch was fluffed up in it.

"Billy," she whispered, looking back at him, a sheen of tears in her eyes.

He tried to laugh, ignoring the swell of gratitude in his heart. "This is about as much decorating as we ever do around here, Shiloh. See? I reckon they want you to know you're welcome here. They're kind of funny about saying things, but that's what this means."

"They did it for you, too."

"Well, let's just say that Grandpa had hopes I was going to get in this room tonight. He said it was foolishness to sleep apart, too. But I thought you wanted that."

"No, not to be away from you. I needed to feel like I had a private place, for me and you together. I don't want to hurt anybody's feelings, Billy, but I don't think I could be with you like we were at the lake tonight if we were in the room beside your mother."

He grinned at her in the dim room. "You could have a point. I had my hands full trying to keep you quiet. You said you weren't going to scream."

"I didn't."

"Just because I kept your mouth otherwise occupied," he drawled, running his thumb across it now, where it curved up in guilty laughter.

"I've got something for the room, too. It's not much of a wedding present, but it might cool things down in here. The temperature, that is," he added, mischievously. "It's in the back of the truck. Wait a minute."

When he returned with the big blue fan, she watched him set it up in one of the windows and plug it in. Its gentle whirring sucked in the silver night air, rich with the scent of roses and grass and the pines on the edge of the yard, and it blew the fragrance across the foot of the bed, dusting the quilt with coolness.

"I like a night breeze," he said into the silence.

"Thanks, Billy." Her eyes were luminous as she latched her arm inside his, laying her head on his shoulder. "So you did have plans to stay with me."

"Like you said, this is as close to a honeymoon as we're going to get. I wish things could be different, but—"

She put her hand across his mouth. "No complaining from you, mister. Not after I gave it all I had out at that lake. Come to bed, Billy. You're about to drop from exhaustion."

Her fingers lifted to trace the tired planes under his eyes, across his cheeks.

"I don't know why I'm tired." He sighed as he sank down on the quilt. "Out until near dawn with you Wednesday, and no man's gonna sleep much on his wedding night, and trying to keep you happy tonight. Honey," he murmured, already half asleep as he fell back on the snowy pillow, "you're about to wear me out. But that ain't complaining. No, ma'am."

She must have taken his clothes off of him, he thought now, the next morning, as he came awake; he didn't remember doing it. By the time he'd pulled his pants back on, he was alert with a rushing exhilaration, a crystalline sense of well-being. When he opened the door to step barefoot onto the back porch, he found Willie already there, standing at the far end, smoking his early morning pipe, its rich pungence mingling with the clear air.

Billy avoided his grandfather's know-it-all stare as he

shut the door on the sleeping girl behind him, yawning and stretching, trying to work the kinks out of his back. Then he ran his hands through his hair and over his bare chest.

"Pretty morning," he offered at last to Willie, looking out over the dewy, green yard. It echoed the purity of his own emotions.

"Yep," his grandpa agreed complacently, chewing the pipe stem. "Best one I've seen in a long time."

Alone in the glittering brightness of the room when she awoke, Shiloh lay for a few minutes letting the sensations of this strange land wash over her.

She remembered the night before, too, lying awake long after Billy lay asleep beside her, her hand locked in his.

More than anything else, the window fan had reminded her of just how different his world was from hers.

She'd never slept under a fan before. Its blades seemed to blow in the entire universe: scents and sounds that were raw and exotic. She was out in it, unprotected. Listening to the fan, she had a flashing memory of how Billy handled the earth out in Sam's garden on that first morning, as if he knew it and liked it. In the middle of it, right down in the heart of life. It was the same way she had seen him reach out and grasp animals, sure and caring, but with an iron command in his hands. No escaping Billy Walker.

She'd raised his hand to the moonlight that streamed across the bed. Long-fingered, big-knuckled, rough.

A hand that could set a woman on fire, and then soothe her while she burned.

Immediate, earthy, free—that was Billy. He loved, he fought, he hurt and cried with an ardent intensity. A part of the real life Sam had removed himself from, by way of his money. Her father's house was cool and climate controlled, a comfort zone where the sound of the central heating and cooling system blocked out all others, where doors remained sealed and windows shut. Even his garden had been formal, strictly for looks—and Billy had created even that, not Sam.

No sweat, no heat, no weather in Sam's house.

It was a little frightening to be here with every window open, with only a flimsy screen between her and the night, Shiloh thought, even with Billy beside her. But it was exciting, too, and as if to echo her thoughts, a whippoorwill called suddenly, so close to the house that it was shrill and loud, not gentle as distance sometimes made it sound.

Shiloh listened to it as it sang even over the sound of the fan, caught between a longing for father and home and the lure of life red-blooded, the way Billy lived it, where whippoorwills were closer—but not so mistily sweet.


"I was wondering if I could help you."

Shiloh's words startled the woman at the sink; she jumped a little before she turned to face the tall girl behind her.

"Why, I don't know. I was gettin' ready to cook breakfast," Ellen answered, looking down at the big tomatoes she was slicing, her hands nervous. The smell of coffee permeated every corner of the sunny room.

"I'm not too great a cook," Shiloh offered, turning

toward the table. "Laura taught me a few things, but mostly, she wanted to do it herself. And she said—" Too late, Shiloh remembered exactly what Laura had said: "You'll have somebody to do your cooking for you, honey, so why waste your time?"

"I guess she figured Sam Pennington's daughter wouldn't ever need to cook," Ellen said shrewdly, watching her new daughter-in-law's face.

Shiloh flushed. "Something like that. But she was wrong, wasn't she?"

Ellen made no answer as she turned back to her task.

"Thanks for the room, too. I wasn't expecting it. It was beautiful. It made me happy."

Ellen went still at the sink. Then she turned around, wiping her hands on her apron, her green eyes determined.

"That's all I'm askin' from you, too," she said quietly. "You keep my Will happy."

Shiloh braced herself with a hand on a chair back. "I'm going to try, Mrs. Walker. But that's not a promise that we won't fight." She laughed a little. "He's got a stubborn streak—"

"Will's touchy about some things, you mean," Ellen interrupted. "If you know what he is, then you know why. And you're bound to know. You've spent time with Robert Sewell." The woman across the kitchen looked stiff as a poker, as if she'd braced herself against the hard winds of disapproval.

"I know that Billy is Judge Sewell's son, and that you were never married to him," Shiloh answered at last, unsure of what to say.

"And you'll be happy with him just the way he is? He's not his brother."

So Ellen Walker had already heard about that.

"I loved Billy when I was eighteen, but I was too young to know what to do. We fought and—I'll tell you the truth—my father was dead set against it."

"That's not changed, from what I hear."

"No, but I have. I was engaged to Michael because I thought I couldn't have Billy. Then I discovered I couldn't live with a substitute."

"The question is, can you live with my boy?"

"I'm going to try. I love him."

She didn't know what else to say. Maybe if she could have explained about the fan, and the whippoorwill, but they seemed silly and inconsequential here, in this practical farm kitchen with its row of tomatoes ripening in the window above the sink and the white enamel wash pan full of green beans waiting to be snapped that sat on the beige Formica kitchen cabinet.

So she said nothing, and the serious quality of the silence pleased Ellen, who searched Shiloh's face for a minute, then leaned back against the sink, relaxing a little.

"And I reckon he loves you," she admitted with a half smile. "He acts like it. He says he does. And he sure never said that about that Blake girl."

Shiloh winced.

Ellen moved uncomfortably. "Reckon I shouldn't have said that. Well, here, I was about to fix some fried tomatoes. Daddy loves them. We all work outside the house today, Daddy at the stand, and me in the garden, and Will in the field or at the greenhouse. I fix lunch early, while I'm gettin' breakfast, so we can eat it when we get ready. Think you'd—would you want to help with that?"

"If you'll show me what to do."

"I'm not much used to having another woman around," Ellen offered at last. "Maybe you could tell me if I don't quite, you know, handle things right. I mean for us to get along if we can." She smiled tremulously at her daughter-in-law.

"We both love him, Mrs. Walker. I want to get along, too."

"My name's Ellen. I reckon I would rather have you call me that."

"Ellen." Shiloh smiled at Billy's green-eyed mother. "You already know me. I'm Shiloh."

She spent the day with Billy, beginning in the barn. Two dogs jumped around him, following every step he made.

But it was the horse who caught her attention.

"Is this the colt you talked about that summer?" she asked in amazement. "The one that got caught in a barbed-wire fence?"

Billy grinned up at the big horse, reaching out to stroke his velvety nose. "This is the one. Some looker these days, aren't you, boy?"

"But I thought that horse had damaged himself so much they wanted to destroy him." It was hard to believe that the stupendous horse dancing after Billy in hopes of a touch or his attention—whose summer coat burned like a sleek red flame, whose muscles moved with an oiled precision, rippling under the skin—was the same one Billy Bob had described to her four years ago, when he first got him.

This animal, even to Shiloh's inexperienced eye, was pure delight.

He looked as good as his master, she thought wryly.

"He fooled them all," Billy told her with a glint of pride. "It makes Harold Bell sick. Chase was his colt, see. But Bell can't stand to see a horse ruined or hurt, so when he thought he was going to have to put this one down—when I asked him to give him to me—Bell agreed. That way he didn't have to watch him die."

As Billy turned to open the barn door, to lead Chase into the sunshine, the horse nudged him roughly, playfully in the back with his nose.

"He likes you," Shiloh told Billy.

"Yep. I like him, too. He's a friendly sort. Here, buddy, meet Shiloh." Billy pulled the well-shaped nose down toward her, his big hand spread across it. "Let him get your scent. Put your hand up close to his nose, but not too close to his teeth, and keep your palm flat and your fingers together so he can't bite a finger. He thinks it's real funny sometimes to nip strangers. He'll just have to catch on that you belong here now."

Every touch Billy gave the horse, no matter how it directed or commanded, wound up being a stroke or a caress. It was mixed up together, the mastery and the affection.

"I wish I had more time for him," Billy Bob said wistfully, as Chase pranced out the barn door into the open field for the day.

"He looks happy to me."

"Yeah. But he's from show stock, a good line of it. He was born to be shown, or to work a fancy rodeo. But as long as nobody tells him that, I guess he'll be okay."

Shiloh watched the horse dance across the field, his tail high, his spirits the same—a tongue of fire flame on the green grass.

"You picked a winner, Billy."

He turned back to her, the sun hot over his shoulder on his hair, lighting it to gold.

"I've got a knack for doing it," he said teasingly, touching his finger to her nose.

From there, they went to the wet humidity of the greenhouse.

A high-school kid named Jimmy who apparently worked for Billy kept wandering in and out, ogling Shiloh, until Billy finally got firm and sent him out to spray the orchard once and for all.

"That kid's got a leg fixation," he muttered. "And I'd hate to have to fire him just because he keeps looking at yours. He's a good worker."

She glanced up at him inquiringly, a streak of dirt across one cheek, her hair a wild tangle of curls that she'd tried to knot back from her face.

"I thought he was just curious," she said mildly. "It's not every day that the great William Robert Walker gets married."

"What you mean is, it's not every day that a princess comes to work in the greenhouse."

"I'm no princess."

"Yes, you are. Sam Pennington's little glass doll. He'd have a fit if he could see you now." Billy looked over her slender shape encased in one of his huge T-shirts and a pair of black cotton, boxy, beguiling shorts she'd apparently picked up yesterday on her shopping spree.

"Well, he can't," Shiloh retorted, and before the thought could linger in his head, she asked curiously, "Why does your mother call you 'Will'?"

His long fingers kneaded through the soil in front of him for a minute, cradling the heavy begonias he was transplanting carefully, handling them with confidence and ease. Shiloh watched as he settled one definitely in its place.

Then he spoke, keeping his eyes on what he was doing.

"I was six. Joshua Davidson—this kid in the third grade—called me a bastard at school. I didn't know what it was, but I knew it was bad. So I came home from my first day crying. Mama told me what he meant. And what hurt the most was, it hurt her, too. The next day I took a slingshot to school and nearly cracked his head open with it. Boy, did I get a whipping. That principal nearly wore me out."

Billy's hands stopped a minute, as if remembering, before he finished working the soil down around the plant's roots.

"Lost my slingshot and got a reputation for meanness, the very first week of school. I never told them why I did it. But Joshua knew. He kept his mouth shut after that, at least around me."

With his dirty hand, he lifted a plastic container, a blue mix of water and fertilizer with which he soaked the soil around the plant.

"Mama knew why I did it, too. She said she understood, but that I couldn't go around beating up everybody who pointed out the—the facts of my birth. That a real man controlled his temper until he *had* to lose it. And since she knew I was going to be a real man from then on, she wasn't going to call me by a kid name anymore. She was going to call me Will to remind me. She's been doing it ever since."

He set the finished basket off to the side, leaned over

the work table, and rubbed one dirty finger down her left cheek.

"Now you match. A streak of dirt on both sides," he teased. "Well, aren't you gonna tell me how her plan didn't work? How I never really grew up?"

"You mean because you still fight? At least it's not over being called names. Now you fight over girls."

Her brown eyes flashed as he went still.

"I used to. There was nothing better to do, and I didn't care one way or the other. Now I've got you."

"And you won't fight?"

"Not unless you give me a reason to. Not that I wouldn't like to take a swing at your former boyfriend."

She tried to twist away, but his fingers clamped hard on her chin.

"To tell the truth, I'm kinda wondering how many boyfriends there were," he said softly, nearly nose-to-dangerous-nose with her.

"I never did anything—"

"You mean you never kissed them? Nor held them? Nor slid your tongue over their mouths the way you do mine? Hmmm?"

She blushed.

"Maybe that's no big deal with some girls," he said roughly, his other hand catching at her neck to hold her. "But with you, honey, those things could burn a house, let alone a man."

"My school was strict, Billy. Curfews and the whole bit. You could get expelled for even being seen at a club. Great academics, strictest code in the state. It was a good school—and it was just what Sam wanted. He called three and four nights a week, just to make sure I stayed put."

"Now, see, there's something about Pennington I like, after all," Billy said ironically. "He tried to keep you under lock and key. But the way you look—there had to be somebody. How many, Shiloh?"

"I dated a few." It might do him some good to hear a little factual information, Shiloh thought indignantly. She was sick of hearing Angie Blake's name.

"A few? Two?"

"More than that."

"I thought you said it was a strict school," he muttered, and his voice had a growl in it.

"Not that strict, Billy," she teased, her eyes sparkling with laughter and a touch of temper.

"Four? Five? *Six?*"

"You're getting hot," she whispered, as he pulled her face closer to his, preventing her retreat.

"You're damned right I am."

"How was it I kissed all those boys? Like this?" She surprised him by moving closer, by pressing her lips to his suddenly. Then she raised her hands to touch his face, as streaked with dirt as her own was.

"Or was it like this?" She opened his lips with her tongue. He gasped—and made a heated lunge for her.

" 'Scuse *me*. I didn't know you were, uh, busy, uh, look, Billy, I'll come back—"

The stumbling words broke them apart, and Shiloh surfaced just in time to see a grinning, red-faced Jimmy backing out of the greenhouse.

"I'm gonna kill him," Billy muttered, crooking his arm to push his hair back.

"Guess it'll be all over the county that we were making out in the greenhouse," Shiloh said in mock dolefulness.

Billy grinned unrepentantly. "Business will probably double."

The next morning over an early breakfast—this family did everything at the crack of dawn, Shiloh had already discovered—Ellen offered a little shyly, "I'd like it if you . . . if you wanted to go to church with me this mornin', Shiloh."

At her side, Billy stopped his cup of coffee halfway to his lips, surprise on his face.

Grandpa gave him a knowing wink. "These Baptists are quick workers, son. Your mother's already startin' on her to go to church."

Ellen's face brightened with color. "I was hopin' to have some company once in a while, since neither of you ever see fit to go anymore. But if Shiloh doesn't want to, that's all right."

"Maybe she's not Baptist, Mama," Billy suggested.

"I don't know what I am," Shiloh admitted. "Sam sent me to a Methodist prep school and a Church of Christ college. And now, I've gone and married a Baptist." Her eyes laughed at Billy before she finished speaking. "We never went to church, but Sam had a brother, David, who did. Finally, he gave up everything—the partnership they had, all the money they'd made together—and went to South America to be a missionary. He died there. He was always religious, Sam said. Quiet and good, sort of shy. I don't know. I never knew him."

"You sure this is Pennington's brother?" Billy asked dryly.

"Will!" his mother expostulated.

"Anyway," Shiloh continued, "Sam kept waiting for

religion to hit him like that, to feel it like David always did. And when it didn't, he got angry. No use for church, but he cares enough about it that he won't go for any other reason. He's got no time for people who attend just for business or politics or mixing."

"Sounds like he's waitin' for things to be perfect," Willie commented.

"That's the way he likes everything. Daughters, too." Shiloh's voice was quiet.

Willie shot a look at Billy, who'd gotten still and quiet. "He's gonna live a mighty lonely life, if that's the case. Nothing's ever completely the way we want it," the old man offered.

"He is. Lonely, I mean." Shiloh poked at her bacon and eggs.

"People are people. You're gonna hate some and love some, and some are gonna look up to you and some are gonna try to pull you down. But it's still better to get out and live with them, and put up with their faults and your mistakes, than to live completely alone." Willie rose heavily as he finished speaking to go to the sink.

Billy ran a hand around the back of his neck and took another sip from his coffee cup, eyeing his mother over the rim.

"I reckon Grandpa's lecturing Sam Pennington this time, Mama, not you," he said gently.

"I'm livin' my life the way I want to live it," Ellen told her father.

"So is Sam," Shiloh said, with a trace of darkness in her voice. "But I'd like to go to church with you, unless Billy needs me for something."

He shot her a sideways, wicked look from his long eyes, then buried his nose in the coffee cup to drain it.

"Nothing I can think of, right at this minute," he said meekly. "Maybe later," he added suggestively. This time his fingers raked along the angle of his jaw, fresh shaven from an episode not long after dawn when he'd locked himself in the bathroom with her while she showered. She remembered clearly—very clearly—how his shave and her shower had culminated.

Under the table, she stepped on his foot in a scandalized warning.

"They'll look you over good, honey," Billy drawled. "First off because of who you are, and second, just to make sure I hadn't damaged you in any way." Laughter lurked behind his eyes.

"Now, Billy," admonished Ellen. "Don't scare her. They're good people. I'll be ready at nine thirty, Shiloh. And it pleases me that you'll visit this Sunday."

When she had gone, Billy leaned close to Shiloh, his blond head nearly touching hers, whispering conspiratorially, "Jimmy Mabrey's mama and daddy go there. Wayne Mabrey's a deacon. By now, they know what we were doing in the greenhouse yesterday. There's probably a commandment against it."

Under the table, his hand suddenly slid up under the loose shirt of his that she wore, and his fingers raked her stomach. She jumped, reddening, glancing frantically across the kitchen to where his grandfather stood looking out the window.

"There ought to be a law against *you,* Billy," she muttered, "and those wandering hands. They're *everywhere,* even on Sunday."

"Nope. They're just on you."

◆ ◆ ◆

Billy and his grandfather worked in a companionable silence for a while in the fruit stand, cleaning, restocking.

"Been a real good summer so far," said Willie, just before the white car came over the horizon. He watched it approach as he spoke to his grandson, who was down on his hands and knees with the watermelons.

"Hope you've been keeping the girl close," the old man told him.

"What?"

"You may need another alibi. Here comes T-Tommy."

Billy twisted, rising to his feet as the sheriff pulled up in front of the stand.

"Mornin'."

Neither responded to T-Tommy's greeting. He threw up both hands in surrender.

"Okay. I'll just come out and tell you. I'm bringin' bad news. Where's Shiloh?"

"Gone to church with Mama," Billy answered slowly. "This has got something to do with her old man, right?"

"Have you still got that Cadillac of his?"

"It's sitting at the barn. Nobody's been driving it. I meant to bring it back into town and just hadn't done it. Maybe this afternoon. Shiloh doesn't want it."

"Don't you touch it, Billy. That old bastard's gone and filed a report with the highway patrol, claimin' it's been stolen. If a trooper catches you with it, you'll be in hot water all over again."

"Stolen! He knows better than that! His own daughter was driving it." Billy slammed his fist into the big pole that held up one corner of the porch.

"Well, you know how that goes. He's hurt, and he's madder'n hell. He's after anybody he can get, and he hopes it's you, even if it just stirs up trouble for a little while."

"You let him file that report?" Willie asked T-Tommy grievously.

"Not me. I just found out what he'd done last night. It's a good thing Billy didn't get caught driving it."

"He gave them Billy's name?"

"Nope. He didn't go that far. Just an auto theft report. He wants it back, I think, just so he can make life that much rougher for her. 'Cause you see, he figures she needs it, and deep down inside, he wants her to come crawling home because the two of *them*"— he nodded at Billy—"can't make it."

"She's not coming back. Tell him that," Billy said to T-Tommy fiercely.

"Not me. But I'm gonna pull this Cadillac into town behind my car, right up to his door. Wiped clean of every print on it. Say it's at the barn?"

"Hey, what happened to Juliard and Sewell?" Willie called after T-Tommy.

"Oh, them. Well, it appears Juliard thinks he made a mistake. After Sewell's people got hold of him, that is. Now he can't remember who hit him. It's all hushed up in the media, too. And I heard that Pennington was picking up Juliard's tab at the hospital. Wonder how much else went into some sweet little bank account for the guy, back home in Magnolia?"

T-Tommy shook his head cynically. "I tell you, Willie, I'm thinkin' real hard these last four or five days about retiring."

After the sheriff's car had nosed off toward the barn, Willie said to Billy Bob, "I told you Pennington was a mean son of a bitch. He wants the girl back, just like

T-Tommy said. But you can't tell her about this deal with the car. Let her believe we took it into town, or had it taken."

"It would kill her to know what he's done," Billy said somberly. "She loves him."

"There's more than that to this here situation. You're gonna sound mean and jealous, too, if you ride Pennington too much. Best thing to do is just stay clear of him when you talk. We sent the car back—it's nothing much. Okay? No mention of him."

"I'm not going to let him take her away. She won't go," Billy vowed angrily, then strode off toward the pecan groves, swearing viciously to himself.

That night he made love to her with hard, possessive hands that allowed her little or no room to move, and it wasn't until she protested that he relaxed his hold on her.

Afterward the fan blew across them, cooling their skin and calming their heartbeats.

"We took the Cadillac back to town. T-Tommy came and helped us."

Billy spoke the words in the moonlit darkness of the room, breaking the silence between them.

She shifted her head on his shoulder to look at him. "Did you? I hadn't noticed."

There was such a long silence that he finally relaxed. She hadn't cared enough to ask.

But just as he ran his hand down her arm, she rolled on her side to face him.

"Did you take it to—to Sam?"

"No. Reckon T-Tommy meant to."

"Oh."

"You miss him." His words were slow and accusing.

"I'm not going to lie and pretend I don't, Billy. He and Laura were my whole family."

"They *were*. Now *I* am."

"I've proved that, haven't I? I just wish Sam would understand that I can love you and still love him, too."

"A husband always takes a man's daughter away, even if it's only a little. Most men just get smart enough to understand and let it happen because they can't stop it. It's natural, Shiloh."

"I know. Why can't Sam see that? I just hate that he's disappointed and alone." Her voice caught, as if she were crying.

"It's his own fault," Billy returned, his voice hard.

"I know he doesn't want to see me hurt. If he'd just give in, and understand that I love you, he'd gain so much that he doesn't have now. His daughter back, and a son—"

Billy snorted. "Forget that, baby."

"And someday, he'd be a grandfather, wouldn't he?" she asked wistfully.

Billy raised up on one elbow to look down on her as she lay beside him in a tangle of sheets. "Do you love me, girl?"

"You know the answer."

"I want to hear it, anyway."

"I love you, Billy."

"Enough to last even when Pennington never comes around, and when he refuses even to look at those babies you're talking about?"

"I think he will someday, Billy."

"But if he doesn't?"

"Then yes, I love you enough even for that."

"I hope you mean it, because it's a man's right to expect his wife to stick by him, even over her own family. I'm not in the wrong here, Shiloh, and I swear, I won't back down, even for you. And I damn sure won't for your daddy."

They had days of peace after that, when on the surface things lapped smoothly along.

Billy spent most of his time out on the tractor; he had another lot of trees to get ready for delivery in a week. Shiloh helped Ellen in the mornings; she'd discovered she liked hanging out clothes in the summer sun. Must be the Irish coming out in her, she thought ruefully.

And after lunch, she went out to the fields with Billy until it got so sweltering hot that they had to quit. Then like as not, they'd drive out to their hidden little rock at Angel Lake for a fast swim and a not-so-fast lovemaking session.

Ellen got used to their not coming home in time for supper. Usually they fell asleep out on the moss under the shady, dappling trees and didn't wake until after the sun had set.

It was as comfortable, Billy said, as trying to sleep in her bed, which was too short for his six-foot-three frame, and he swore that as soon as he got these trees sold, he was going to take a day to move his own bed into her room.

It was an idyllic existence; Shiloh felt sheltered from the whole world, yet more people came to Walker Farms than she'd ever seen at home. They drifted in without announcement or fanfare, staying for a cool drink of tea or a slice of watermelon: two or three ladies from the church; a crony of Willie's; and the most vocal of all, friends of Billy. The big one they called Toy was nearly comic. He came mostly to convince himself that his buddy had really bitten the dust and gotten married.

But it was a neighbor, Harold Bell, who strolled into the first serious fight between the bride and groom late one afternoon after a little more than three weeks of wedded bliss.

"Don't you think you could take just a little time and teach me how to drive this truck?" Shiloh asked, her voice coaxing.

"Ah, honey, what for? I'm tired. Let's just go for a swim like always." Billy was already tossing two large towels that he'd vandalized off the clothesline onto the seat of the truck.

"Because I might need to drive this truck someday, that's why. Everybody else can—you, Ellen, even your grandpa if he has to." Shiloh's voice was stubborn as she followed him around to the driver's side.

"So if that many people can, there'll always be somebody here to take you where you want to go." He spoke as if that settled it and climbed into the truck.

But Shiloh caught the door as he tried to pull it shut. "I mean to learn to drive this thing, Billy. If you don't teach me, I'll come out here and do it myself."

He sighed, pushing his cap back on his head, running one hand down his face. "Why?"

"Why do I want to learn? Because I've never been someplace where I—I couldn't go where I wanted. It feels like I'm trapped here."

He straightened his wide shoulders a little, his face stiffening as he looked at her.

"I didn't mean that the way it sounded." Her words

were quiet; she looked down at her own fingers, inter-twining her hands together. "Cars and trucks are just the way people go these days. I don't like knowing I can't operate the only one you've got."

"Where you planning on going, Shiloh?" He propped his right elbow up on the steering wheel and waited for her answer. Too quiet. "Out of this trap?"

She stepped up into him, her hands reaching for his blue-jeaned knees, her eyes searching his. "Don't be silly, Billy Bob. If I wanted out, or away, there are other ways. I'd pick up a phone."

"And call Sam?"

"*No.* I don't want out and I don't want Sam. I want to be with you, you stubborn man. But it's a human right that people get to drive themselves around sometimes, isn't it? I want to know how to drive a straight shift—*this* one. *Yours.*" She pushed him in the chest with her hand for emphasis once or twice, her eyes sparkling with tem-per and daring.

She knew exactly what she was doing, getting this close to him, he thought in resignation. Especially wearing the denim shorts he liked and the cool little top that revealed entirely too much skin from his angle right above her.

And the truth was, he'd feel the same way if he were taken somewhere without transportation. He wasn't try-ing to keep her a prisoner; he wanted her to be happy, to come and go as she pleased.

The problem was he hated to see her drive his truck. It was seven years old, had nearly ninety thousand miles on it, and he'd used it hard, for farm work. It was going to hurt to see her with it instead of one of those expensive numbers she had once tooled around in.

He'd rather teach her to ride Chase. At least they were

worthy of each other, a beautiful animal and a beautiful woman. But she was a little afraid of the big stallion. Billy could sense that, and he guessed Chase wasn't a real practical alternative for travel.

"I mean to buy you a car, Shiloh," he said tightly. "It may not be a Cadillac, but I'm looking. I ought to be—*we* ought to be able to afford something after this next sale."

"Okay," she agreed. "But I still want to learn about this one. Just in case. Please, Billy." She dropped a row of light kisses across one side of his face. "Teach me, okay?" Another row on the other side.

"I can think of plenty to teach you," he retorted, but he slid over in the truck seat, lifting first one long leg and then the other over the gear shift. "Come on. I might as well die young."

She flashed him a dazzling smile before she slid in the seat he'd just vacated.

"What do I do first?" she asked breathlessly.

"That's the clutch. And these are the gears, see? Here in the middle is neutral."

The lesson was not a success.

She ground the gears; she couldn't seem to make things shift smoothly, so they jerked up the gravel road to the barn, the engine dying every third jerk; and when she wound up with the truck finally out at the barn, it was turned sideways, its bed on a downhill slant toward the row of shrubs beside the fence. Every time she let up on the clutch to shift the gear from reverse to first, the truck slid a tiny bit farther downhill, toward the shrubs and the little pond where Billy's horse stood, drinking and watching.

"Okay. Easy—easy—try to keep a foot on the clutch and the brake, then touch the gas with your other foot," he instructed warily, one hand grasping the open window, the other the back of the seat.

It was stifling hot on this muggy afternoon; his face was wet with sweat.

"What do you mean, my other foot?" she demanded, panic stricken. "I've only got two. That's three pedals you're talking about."

"I know, I know," he said soothingly. "Just turn your foot over there sideways, try to press the clutch and the brake with the one foot—no—no, Shiloh!"

They slipped another foot backward; his head slammed the rear window when she stood on the brake.

Then the tailgate brushed Billy's prize shrubs and the back of the truck tilted even more downhill. The pond beckoned, the horse snorted derisively.

"Okay." Billy said it with finality, shutting his eyes to rub the back of his head. "That's enough. Lord, Shiloh, how hard can this be?"

She rubbed the shirt against her skin where rivulets of sweat ran between her breasts. "It's impossible, that's what. How can a normal person get off a hill when they have to mash three pedals at once? You just tell me that, Billy Walker."

"Normal people don't get in this situation," he informed her, opening his door.

"Where are you going? You think I can't drive this, don't you?"

"I *know* you can't get out of this mess," he returned, smugly. "I'm coming around to the wheel. Let me get us off this hill. I don't think I can stand any more driving lessons today."

"I *can* drive this. I *will*," she shot at his back, then peered at the floor to see what to do. Without warning, her foot slipped off the clutch, and the truck gave a quick, long slide backward, hitting some object as it did.

She screamed, then rode the brakes again, and the truck died completely, shuddering into quietness. It was too quiet, in fact.

"Billy!"

She looked around frantically. Where was he? Fumbling with the gear shift, she slid it into first, then pulled on the emergency brake.

"Billy!"

Shiloh's feet met the ground just in time to see Billy Bob picking himself up out of the mud near the pond. What was he doing down there? She hadn't hit him, had she? Looking like a thundercloud, he glared up the hill at her, shaking leaves and grass and mud off of himself. Then he advanced back up toward her, his movements deliberate and threatening.

"What happened?" Her voice shook a little.

"What happened? I'll tell you what—I was stupid enough to leave you in the truck while I went behind it to see if we were stuck on this hill or not," he said furiously. "Next thing I knew, the thing was about to roll over me. You ran through the fence, and I tore down two good shrubs and damn near broke my neck running to get away from you. Are you *crazy?*"

She ran after him as he stomped up to the open door and shoved himself under the wheel.

"It was an accident. My foot slipped off the clutch. I didn't know you were behind me—"

"Get in," he bellowed, then forced himself to calm down for a quieter explanation. "I've got to turn this thing around."

Without a word, she raced in front of the truck and

plunged in, and with a lot of wheel spinning and gear-shifting, Billy swung the vehicle out into the road, pointing in the right direction, back toward the farmhouse.

She gave a nervous huff of laughter. "You've got grass in your hair."

His face angry, his eyes a furious blue, he raked the green leaves out of his thick blond scalp. She didn't dare ask where his cap had gone; she thought it was floating on the pond. Maybe the horse had eaten it.

"I'm sorry," she said contritely. "I didn't mean to run over you."

He let the truck slide into motion.

"I really do have a good reason for wanting to learn to drive this," Shiloh told him hurriedly, angling another look over at his thundercloud face. "I want to look for a job."

That got his attention.

"A *what?*"

"A job. I want to work, to make money, to help."

"You can work here all you want. I don't want you off at a bank all day."

"I don't know what to do here. Mostly I follow you, or Ellen, around. If I had a real job, I could earn a paycheck. It doesn't have to be in a bank."

"If that's all that's worrying you, I'll give you a paycheck. I've left money on your dresser both of these past Mondays, haven't I?"

"I know. I appreciate it, Billy. But I don't think I earned it. And sometimes, it feels like I just sit around."

"I can give you a job. Tell me what you want to learn to do around here. I'll teach you. Or my accounts—you can keep the books if you want. Unless"— his voice rose in pure temper—"you're saying you just can't stand me and the farm anymore. So if that's what the hell this is all about, say so."

"Don't yell at me! And none of that is the reason I wanted a job."

They'd reached the house, where Billy killed the engine without even pausing in the argument.

"Then you tell me what's wrong? What's all this talk about traps, and going places? You just got here." He slammed out of the truck, the motion reverberating the entire cab.

She did the same on the other side, her slam nearly as hard, coming around to him. "I was trying to help, Billy. I thought, I'm not much good at farm things. I don't know what to do. So if I go do something I am good at and make extra money I'll be helping my husband."

She was crying now, and she reached out suddenly to give him a rough push with both of her hands against his flat, hard stomach. "But you don't deserve it, you—you— big jerk!"

He watched in silence as she ran up the old sidewalk to the front porch. Blinded by tears, she didn't see the man who stood on the shady steps and so banged into him full tilt.

He caught and steadied her. "Here now, you're gonna get hurt."

She shook herself free, and the last the two men saw of her was her long brown legs as the screen door slammed shut behind her. Then there was silence.

"Huh." The big man strolled down toward Billy, who leaned disconsolately on the truck. "Hello, Billy Bob."

"Mr. Bell." Concentrating on the other man wasn't easy, not when he really wanted to peel himself off the truck, run Shiloh down, and force her body to soften under his, and her mouth to open for his tongue. "Haven't seen you in a while."

"I hear you've been busy, boy." Bell had a swarthy look about him, sort of a modern Pancho Villa appearance, helped along by the big Resistol cowboy hats he wore. Nearer sixty than fifty, he still had an eye for the ladies; he'd divorced three of them, in fact. But his consuming passion was anything horsey, and he had enough money to indulge himself.

"Who, me?"

"That's right. I heard you got married."

"You just met her. She was the one crying," Billy said ruefully.

"Mighty fine-looking woman. I tell you, I didn't believe it when some of the boys said you'd got yourself a wife, but that was some fight. Yep, you two sure look married to me."

Hot, bruised, and mad, Billy Bob had no intentions of listening to Bell's opinions about marital bliss. He was all too aware that this was mostly his fault, that he'd jumped Shiloh over nothing because he was scared stupid Pennington was somehow going to drag her away.

"Did you need to see me about something?"

"Well, first off, there's the same old thing. I still want that horse awful bad. I went down to the barn while I was waiting for you, to take a look at him, but he must have been out in the pasture."

Billy liked Bell, but he resented the way the man made up to Chase, as if the horse still belonged to him. More than once Bell had come to see Billy and he'd found the older man out at the barn, coaxing the stallion, bribing him into trust with apples and caresses.

Maybe he was getting possessive, but Billy Bob was

plain sick of having everybody's hands reaching for what was his. "The answer's the same. No," he informed Bell without a flicker of emotion.

"That's what I thought. But I won't give up. Chase deserves better than what you can do for him right now, son, but we won't talk about that."

Bell reached out to remove the cowboy hat with a long arm that ended in a big, rough hand sprayed with black hairs. Around his wrist, a gold watch gleamed. "I've got this dog, Rosie. You remember her. Best stock dog I ever owned, and I've had her ten years. She got hit by a car an hour or two ago; I thought she was dead, but she's still breathing. Opened her eyes after we made a litter and carried her to the barn. I was wondering if you could come and take a look at her, Billy Bob."

"Dr. Sanders seen her yet?"

"Nope. He's gone to LSU for some seminar for three weeks. And I'd just as soon you looked her over. You've got healing hands—I've said it for years. Have you got time?"

Billy Bob cast one regretful glance at the towels still lying on the hot leather truck seat and thought of the afternoon he'd planned. Shiloh was nowhere in sight. Probably still crying.

Then he sighed. "I've got time."

Like a lost waif, she was waiting for him when he finally got home, long after dark, sitting in the cradle of the big swing, one bare foot dragging across the worn spot in the backyard.

New-cut grass made the air sweet and pungent, and the more cloying scent of roses weighted it, making it nearly drinkable.

Shiloh scooted over a little to let him sit down, raising one bare knee to clasp her hand around it. The creaking of the swing's chains as they swayed in it warred with the crickets and the katydids' songs. Each waited for the other to speak.

"You've got a right to work if you want to." Husky, contrite, tired—his voice alone would have been enough apology, but he said it all. "So I'm sorry. It just hurts me to think you have to, and to know that right now, I can't get you things you're used to having. Like rings and cars."

"At least you didn't go off and punch somebody," she returned, her voice teasing and unsteady. "You weren't in one of those famous Billy Walker fights."

"I think you were the one throwing the punches." Relief ran through his voice, and he held his stomach as if in some kind of mortal pain, right where she'd shoved him.

"I came back to play doctor and make you well again after I pushed you, but I heard that man asking you about his dog."

"I'm recuperating real slow. You can still work on me." His teeth gleamed as he grinned at her in the duskiness.

But when she edged toward him, he caught her wrist and stopped the motion. "Give me time, though, baby. I'm dirty. I need a shower. I just got home," he said unsteadily, then he tucked her hands down on his lap, cuddling them.

On the distant porch, a screen door screaked as Grandpa came out in the shadows to admire the night and smoke his pipe. Long, dreamy tendrils of its rich cherry scent drifted out over the wet grass.

"We had to put Rosie to sleep." Billy's voice was low, regretful.

Her hands touched his thighs, rubbing them in quiet sympathy.

"It's funny. I could save Chase when Bell gave up on him, but I couldn't save that old dog of his when he believed in me. Nobody could have; her back was broken, her spine was damaged."

"He didn't blame you, did he?"

"No. He offered me a job, if I wanted to travel again with his rodeo," Billy remembered, resigned laughter in his words. Then he said, more quietly, "Rosie was just too old, and it was a lost cause from the beginning. At least she didn't feel anything much. She was paralyzed from her front legs down. All I could do was give her the shot and hold her head."

He'd held Chase's head, too, the same way he touched the plants in the greenhouse, and the trees in the orchard, and her in the white sheets of their bed.

"I've seen the way you hold things." She moved in closer, a butterfly looking to light, and laid her face against his hands, bending to his lap. "I wouldn't mind if you touched me like that right now, Billy, even if you do need a bath."

The words surprised him, and after a hesitation, he pulled his right hand free from the weight of her body and laid it across her bent shoulders, rubbing his palm over her back in warm, soothing circles, the silence around them broken at last by another slam of the screen as Grandpa reentered the house.

"Did you know how much easier it is to fight with you than with Sam? I never win with him. He never says 'I'm sorry.' " Slurred with tears, her words were as sweet as rain on his heart. "But *I* can. I'm sorry, Billy. I said things the wrong way today."

Her hands brushed inward under her, between his legs. His breath slammed out of him; her fingers were too close for him to stay calm.

"Shi-loh." The word broke in two, out of desperation.

But her voice was nearly drowsy. "I heard what he said, you know. He's right. You would have made a great vet, because you do have healing hands. Even on the plants. Even on me."

# 19

The morning was gloomy and overcast as Billy pulled away from the farm. Behind him, the load of trees that rode on the flatbed trailer made a green splotch of color as he rolled out onto the highway that led to the state line.

He had left Shiloh sleeping in the bed; she had barely stirred when he kissed her good-bye at five this morning. With any luck, he could get the load off early at the warehouse and be back home by night.

The venture had been an unexpected success. He'd been raising acres of trees now for years, hoping against hope to find the kind of market for his stock that he had at last located.

This was the first year he'd sold any in mass quantities like this. And for every load he dug and hauled, he had planted replacement trees. It might take years to make money in this business, but there was definitely money to be made by a nurseryman who was consistent and reliable in his growth and delivery of stock.

With care, the money he was going to make from now until Thanksgiving might tide them over until the next crop next spring, and even allow a few extras.

Maybe a down payment on a car. And maybe—he thought back to Shiloh's slender hand on the pillows this morning—a wedding band.

A few sprinkles of rain hit the windshield, and a thin, distant streak of lightning crossed the gray sky.

But this was still a good day.


"I told you once," an ugly, bull-faced man at the chain-link fence outside the big warehouse compound droned, "your name's not on this list. No Walker Farms, no William Robert Walker."

"Look." Billy leaned across the wooden window of the yellow booth in which the guard sat. "These trees are due here today. I've got a paper . . ." He fumbled in his pocket, finally pulling it forth. "Here. This is the contract."

The guard watched as he spread it out, then looked down over his big bulbous nose to read it. When the wind threatened to whip it away, Billy caught it and held it down with both hands.

"All right," the guard said reluctantly. "I'll call the office. Something's not right here."

Billy waited, leaned up against the guard shack, his shirt collar turned up against the light mist. Behind him, he heard the man's mumbled words.

"Okay. Mr. Jensen—he's the big dog in charge here—he's coming down himself." The guard handed Billy back the paper contract and watched as he folded it. "This must be some setup. Jensen, no less."

Billy didn't bother to tell him that he'd never met the man; a purchaser had liked his trees and arranged the deal.

Jensen was a big, untidy man with a huge round barrel of a stomach. His sandy brown hair was cut in a stiff-looking flattop, and his tortoiseshell glasses were pressed firm against his face, nearly imbedded in the bridge of his nose.

He was blunt and rude. "Mr. Walker? I represent the company. I wasn't aware that you hadn't been contacted, but we have made a decision to halt purchase of stock from Walker Farms."

"What?" Billy stared at him incredulously. "But I made a deal with a man named Lewis—"

"Lewis Abrahams. I know. I believe the arrangement was for you to deliver a load of trees—specified types—to this warehouse once a month from June to November. Is that right?"

"That's right. And today's the twentieth, the day set for delivery."

"But the fact is, the contract says that we here at the actual site have to be satisfied with your stock, or the sale is to be cancelled. Having looked over your first load last month, we are not satisfied. So you will need to take this shipment back where you got it."

Jensen turned away, but not before Billy came out of his stupefaction enough to grab his arm.

"What do you mean, not satisfied? This is some of the best stock around. I worked to make it that way. Look at it—just look at it. Then you tell me what it is that's unsatisfying to you," he demanded.

Jensen pulled away from Billy's grasp, just as the guard took a step closer, reaching threateningly for his billy club.

"I don't know, Walker. Maybe it's too short. Too tall. Too green. We'll find something if you insist."

Billy let his hands fall to his sides. "You just plain don't want it."

"That's right."

"And what about my contract with Lewis Abrahams?"

"You'll find it costs money to challenge the default of a contract. Have you got that kind of money? Anyway, like I said, we *will* find something wrong."

Jensen turned away a second time. "Matthews, shut the gates after me. Mr. Walker is not entering."

He finally found a McDonald's on the edge of town with enough room to park the trailer and truck.

At the pay phone outside, as the rain came down harder, he tried to hold the paper that had Abrahams's office number on it and dial at the same time.

"Lewis Abrahams," he told the receptionist. "Tell him—Jensen is calling."

He didn't even sweat over the lie. Abrahams had seemed decent, but he wasn't taking any chances on not getting to talk to him.

His chest felt heavy; his brain was on fire. He *had* to make this sale. He'd been depending on it.

"Yes?" This was his man; Billy remembered the slight midwestern drawl the purchaser had. He was from Kansas, he'd said.

"Mr. Abrahams, I want to know why the stock from Walker Farms got turned down at the warehouse this morning."

There was a slight pause. "Who is this?"

"Billy Walker."

"I see. I thought it was—"

"I told her to tell you it was Jensen. I know something's going on. There was nothing wrong with those trees. I want to know what's the matter?"

Another slight pause. "Look, Mr. Walker, I'm new here. I saw your farm and your stock. What I saw was excellent. Well-tended and sturdy."

"So buy it, for God's sake."

"I'll swear I never told you this if you ever bring it up, but I understand somebody put the ax to the purchase. He had ties to major stockholders. Somebody from your home state."

Billy swallowed once, twice. In front of him, somebody had scrawled on the telephone wall, "For a good time, call Ann." The words danced before his eyes.

"Who?" he choked, already knowing the answer.

"I never got the name, but some joker said it was your father-in-law."


He sold the stock anyway, sometimes for half what it was worth. It took him three days to do it, three days of canvassing Arkansas and Louisiana and even up into West Tennessee, selling wherever he could. To roadside markets, to landscapers, once to a man selling horrible paintings on black velvet at a flea market who decided to try his hand at reselling Billy's trees, instead.

It became a point of honor with him not to go back to Briskin County until every tree was gone.

He called home twice, just to tell Shiloh where he was. "In Arkansas," he said, having "some trouble with the truck." He'd be home soon. "I love you," she said. I love you, too, baby.

Damn your father.

Every night he sprawled in the seat of the truck in some roadside parking area, windows and doors open to cool the heated cab. Mosquitoes were everywhere, but he barely heard them.

Why, why did Pennington have to mess it up? He had everything. He had cars and rings and banks and more money than Billy Walker would ever dream of.

But he'd lost one daughter. And no matter what he did, he wouldn't get her back.

Billy looked over the dwindling bed of trees every night, and he made a vow: Pennington would not beat him. He would fight Pennington and Sewell both. His life would go on.

And somewhere he'd get the money he needed for his family to live and for his plans to go on, too.

Shiloh hadn't married a loser.

Billy Bob came home with something on his mind. Shiloh knew it the instant she touched him, so glad to see him that she could have eaten him alive.

But he couldn't seem to focus on her, and she withdrew a little, hurt.

That night he made love to her convulsively, as if he had to prove she was there, then he slipped away into himself again.

And when she came awake sometime before dawn, when the sky was at its darkest, he was sitting on the side of the bed, his head dropped into his hands.

"Billy?" she whispered.

He lifted his head sharply, twisting to see her.

"What are you doin' awake?"

"Wondering what's wrong with you. Are you sick?"

"No. I just couldn't sleep."

"There's more to it than that." Her hand found his thigh, tracing it gently. "I could feel something wrong when you came home."

"Nothing much. Business, I guess. Thinking about things." He captured her hand in his right one, letting his thumb rub her fingers. "You still need a wedding ring. I'm going to get you one, Shiloh. I promise."

Then he stood, looking down at her for a moment. "Seems like I'm always making promises. I guess you'd like to see me keep some, wouldn't you?"

"Keep that one we made in that funny little judge's office in Memphis," she suggested sleepily, smiling at him.

He found his pants on the rocking chair and stepped into them. "I think I'll stand on the porch a few minutes. Go back to sleep, baby."

Two days later, Robert Sewell was on the morning news when Billy Bob went to breakfast, waving to a crowd at a fund-raiser in Hattiesburg. A favorite son, said the newscaster, who went on to list his accomplishments.

Billy Bob watched the man without a word, his coffee forgotten in his hand, and when Ellen came to stand beside her son, her fingers reaching up to his elbow in a need for reassurance, he pressed her hand to his side. Grandpa got up and left before the broadcast was over.

Men like Sewell and Pennington got away with things because people like Ellen and him never spoke up.

It was that thought that sent him into Sweetwater late that afternoon; the town was as sleepy and dusty as always.

All day long he had been remembering what he'd tried so hard to forget: Sewell's words to him in the jail cell. "You can go to jail for a while and it's nothing. You're not important enough. Nobody cares. But if Michael goes, it's going to be splashed everywhere. So do the time, take the money. What's it to you?"

Billy Bob had spoken one concise sentence in which he'd told Sewell in the most vulgar terms exactly what he could do with his money.

He had survived everything Sewell had said; he figured he could take what Pennington might mete out, too.

He was tired of being shoved around by the greenback dollar and men who had more of it than he did.

The cool blue interior of the People's Bank was nearly empty this late in the day. Rita was the only cashier still on duty, and she glanced up, smiling, from the bills she was counting as the sound of his boots rang on the tiled floor.

Then the smile wavered.

"I want to withdraw the money that's in this account," he said roughly, shoving the bank book at her.

Her eyes wide and startled, she pushed buttons on the computer beside her.

"Seven hundred dollars?" she murmured, questioningly, eyeing the screen.

"That's it."

It took less than three minutes for the transaction, and Billy Bob spent most of the time looking for the door in the corner that opened on the stairs.

Up there, somewhere, was Pennington.

"Tell Shiloh hello," the girl offered hesitantly as he folded the money into his wallet.

He made no answer, but he headed for the door, not to the outside, but to the upstairs.

"Wait. Mr.—Mr. Walker, you can't just go up there—we're closing—"

The steel door shut on her surprised voice.

It was easy to find him; his name was on the door, in gold letters, no less.

And inside were several women—two were leaving, one was still seated at a big center desk, laughing at something another had said. Her face looked strange, unable to stop the motions of laughter soon enough to express her shock as he strode by her.

"That's Mr. Pennington's office. You can't—I'll call the bank guard . . ."

And then he was right there, in the presence of the kingpin himself.

Pennington was in his shirt sleeves and on the phone, one of those fat cigars smoking in his fingers when he caught sight of the man who'd invaded his space.

They stared at each other a long, long moment.

Billy's shoulders were squared and pugnacious, his whole long body vibrating with anger. Pennington was calmer, more collected, but his hand moved jerkily to put down the phone.

Marie Watson burst into the room. "I'm sorry, sir, but he just pushed in. I've called the guard."

Pennington's hand stubbed out the cigar in the heavy ashtray on the big desk. "That's all right, Marie. Looks like Walker's got something he wants to say, and I've got a few words for him, too."

She stalled for a moment, plainly unwilling to leave the two of them together, before she reluctantly turned and pulled the door shut behind her.

"You claimed that car was stolen. You blocked the sale of my trees. We both know why—because of Shiloh. Well, I've only got one thing to say: You stay out of our lives," Billy Bob said in a rush, through clenched teeth, and his right index finger pointed and accused.

"Did you stay out of mine?" Pennington returned swiftly.

"I love her. She loves me. We didn't do it to hurt you. But what you're doing is deliberate—"

"This love—I got to say that your lovin' her is awful convenient. Why couldn't you love, say, the Blake woman? Or some girl from Seven Knobs? Why *my* daughter?"

"I didn't plan it, Pennington. My God, I'd rather she was anybody's girl but yours. It'd be a whole lot easier on her and on me both. And you keep hinting that I married her for your money. We haven't asked for anything, and if you'll keep your hands off my business, we'll make it. Or is that what's wrong . . . you're afraid that we will?"

"What's wrong is that you took Shiloh."

"Any man she married would've done the same."

"Don't you think she deserves more than to be married to a Mississippi dirt farmer? One who has a reputation and is a bastard, to boot?"

"I can change the reputation with time. And as for being a bastard, it's got nothing to do with me. Take it up with your buddy, Sewell. He came to Seven Knobs with a God-almighty charity group. They were going to give opportunities to all those poor people who'd never had them. Well, Sewell saw his opportunity and he took it. She believed every one of his lies, so he kept coming back. She didn't know about his family until Grandpa found out what was going on and told her he had a wife and a son he'd forgot to mention. And even then, Sewell tried to keep coming. That's your partner, Pennington, the next governor. If people are blind enough to vote for him, they deserve him."

"You oughta be a preacher, Walker, you sound downright righteous. But don't be too hard on the judge. At least he didn't take thirty-five hundred dollars from Ellen to pay his way out of jail. How long did it take you to talk Shiloh out of it?"

Pennington was still as a cat about to pounce on a mouse, but his face was triumphant and knowing.

Billy Bob felt his own cheeks blanch, then flush. How did the man know?

"That's between me and my wife."

"She wasn't your wife then. Oh, I've checked you out, boy. I called Memphis. I pulled bank statements—yours and hers. And then I remembered T-Tommy reeling from shock when you paid that fine. Two days before the marriage, she got you out. Maybe she had to." Pennington went to the window, his hands on his hips, his stance nonchalant. But his voice was a different story. "Did you get her in trouble and then she had to marry you, Walker?"

After Billy got his breath back, he laughed in utter incredulity. "You don't even know your own daughter, do you? I didn't touch her until after we were married. Shiloh's the most innocent, the nicest lady I've ever known. I just want to live with her and be happy. You won't let us. You're tearing down everything I've worked for, and you're hurting her."

The man at the window stood silent and still for a long, long time, struggling with himself. He tried twice to speak before he finally managed to say, "She talks about me?"

"Shiloh's not coming back to you, not to be your little girl," Billy answered instead, and he hoped he was right. "But she'd be happier if she could see you. I'm telling you this for her, and now I've got something to say for me. If you keep on taking away the reasons I've got to stay on the farm and work, it's going to backfire on you, because we'll go so far away from here you'll never see her again."

Pennington turned swiftly, his face gray. "Don't threaten me. You're not tough enough to play the game. And you've got a weakness, Walker. You're ambitious."

Billy Bob could read it in the other man's eyes: Pennington knew something.

"There's nothing wrong with ambition," he told him. "I heard you were, too, forty years ago in old man Ledbetter's mill. But it's got nothing to do with Shiloh."

"I say it does. Who she is attracted you. She's part of that mind-set that's determined to prove you're better than your father. You want to beat the rap the Sewells have laid on you all these years. That's ambition, and it's got you by the throat."

He held Billy's gaze as he returned to the desk, fumbling for another cigar. His face now was keen, intent, and he lit the cigar before he spoke again.

"Like I said, I've been checkin' you out, and you are one surprise package, boy. It turns out they know you real well in Oxford, and in the strangest place—at the University of Mississippi."

So Pennington had found him out. It didn't matter, but if he laughed, Billy was going to punch him. It was that simple.

"It's not against the law to take classes at the university."

"No, but you've sure laid low about it."

Billy wasn't about to tell Pennington why, that he'd

been half-sure when he started that he was going to fail. It had been a pipe dream for him—Billy Bob Walker— even to attempt it. And it had been hard to come by the money, too. He'd already spent four years clawing his way through only sixty-plus semester hours. But that was nearly enough for what he wanted.

Pennington blew smoke, then continued, "But it's all about to end, isn't it? All this time, and you're about through that school. What is it? Preveterinary medicine? Pretty soon, you're gonna have to face the facts. You're not goin' to be admitted to the vet program down at Starkville. Only thirty students a year get in, and they've got to be next to God and pure as the driven snow. You're nearly twenty-eight, you're married, you've been in jail. Just one word about jail in the wrong ear, and you can forget studying to be a vet."

"So that's something else you've decided to interfere with?" Billy could hear blood beating in his ears, he was so angry.

"The point is, I can stop you, just as fast as I cut off that contract with the Arkansas warehouse."

"And if I walk out on Shiloh?" He didn't know why his voice was steady; even his legs were shaking.

"You might get those ambitions satisfied someday. But only if you take my suggestion. End the marriage."

Talking to the man had been pointless; but at least now they understood each other.

"I don't know how long I can fight you, Pennington. But as long as Shiloh sticks with me, I will. I'll keep on living with her, talking to her, sleeping with her. Even if you do ever get her back, she won't be the same. She'll have been with me. And if I don't get admitted to vet school, I'll live. I'll do something else. Just remember what I said—I'll take her away."

As Billy Bob got to the door, he turned to glance back at Pennington, who suddenly looked smaller. "In case I didn't make that plain enough, my answer to your suggestion is no."

It nagged at him all that night and the next day, that conversation. More than Pennington's threats, his knowledge of the money ate away at Billy.

He knew Shiloh would never have made that offer and he would never have taken it if there hadn't been more going on with them. But it stuck in his craw that the money had been part of the marriage and that Pennington knew at least part of the story.

He had to come up with the money.

And he had to tell Shiloh about the work at the university. He'd meant to all along, but it never seemed to fit with any conversation, and she had missed all the other clues.

Maybe she didn't think he was capable of it. Maybe he was the wrong type, in which case, she might be right. He'd thought the same thing when he had to take Music Appreciation that one semester. It had felt like time served in hell. He'd been miserable analyzing symphonies, wondering if these people had ever heard of George Strait. What did a common man who'd spent most of his life in a pecan grove have to do with a university, anyway?

And he wasn't crazy about the rest of Sweetwater finding out. All of a sudden they would catch on—like Sam had—that he had dreams, and if he failed, it'd be open season on him.

Being just plain Billy Walker was easier, except that at the first sign of trouble, like that wreck, they hunted him down.

But Shiloh should have caught on by now. It aggravated him that she hadn't, and the money between them stung his pride, and Sam's conviction that there was another, better man for her made things worse.

All of those worries kept him preoccupied, and the thought that he had to make more money kept him anxious. He could go with Bell and his rodeo for a few weeks, but he couldn't take Shiloh with him on the road.

That meant leaving her here, alone, open prey for her father.

How could one man cause so much trouble? And what right did Pennington have to take away his livelihood? He'd even threatened Billy's already slim chances at vet school.

It made him want to punch the walls, and it made him restrained in his dealings with Shiloh.

She loved the old reprobate. Why, Billy didn't know.

A visitor arrived the next day. She was for Shiloh.

The gray Ford pulled up in the drive, and Laura Kershaw climbed out. Surveying the yard and the house, the woman looked decidedly uncertain.

Shiloh at the window saw her, and her heart jumped. *Laura had come.* She ran to the front door, then made herself calm down before she walked outside.

The housekeeper was climbing the steps. She hesitated uncertainly when she saw Shiloh.

"Hello, Laura." Shiloh's voice quivered in spite of her best efforts.

"Hello, Shiloh." Laura looked at the girl in the tennis shoes and black shorts and black V-necked top, her hair caught up in a ponytail so silky that dark strands of it had slipped away to brush her neck and her cheeks. "Marriage must agree with you. You look about sixteen—and happy."

"I am."

"Well, I'm not. I miss you, Shiloh."

Shiloh didn't say the obvious. Instead, she reached out for the other woman and hugged her as tightly as she'd ever hugged anybody in her whole life.

". . . and the town hasn't talked of much else since," Laura concluded as they sat in the big swing.

"But we've stayed away from Sweetwater, just so the talk would die down," Shiloh protested.

"That makes it better. This way they just get gossip. We've heard you were . . . kissing in public in a parking lot in Martinsville."

"Who saw that?" Shiloh demanded in exasperation.

"The whole world, if I got the story right," Laura said disapprovingly. "And that you went to church with his mother. I got that from T-Tommy. And I heard that Walker hasn't been out carousing at the Palace for a long time."

"He's been busy."

"And you've been keeping him that way?"

"Well, it's sort of a mutual thing," Shiloh said mischievously.

Laura made a snorting noise in her throat. "I just hope there's more to him than what he can do in bed. Because that doesn't matter as much as other things do in the long run."

"Whatever he is, he's what I want."

"You're happy here?"

"They've made me welcome, Laura."

"I guess that's good. Because we're not doing too well

at home, Shiloh. Sam's in a pretty bad way. He sits and broods and broods, then sometimes he curses you. But most of the time, it's the Walker boy."

"Billy, Laura."

"Sam's in pure misery, and he doesn't know how to climb out."

"Yes, he does. He just has to accept Billy as my husband."

"He might," Laura said sardonically, "the day they do a brain transplant on him and make him a new man."

Shiloh's hands traced the edge of the swing. "He disowned me. Right there, in front of everybody."

"That's all over town, too."

"Laura . . ." Shiloh had tried to keep from thinking about that day, and she'd tried to hide her emotions from Billy, but one fact kept repeating itself over and over. "Sam said that Caroline came back one last time. Is that true?"

Laura's face held a trace of shock. "I didn't know he'd ever breathed a word of it to you."

"But is it true?"

"It was when you were fifteen. She came to the house while you were away at school. White as a ghost and thin—Lord, she was so thin. She was already dying of cancer—I just didn't know it."

"Did she ask about me?"

"It doesn't matter what she asked for, Shiloh. Just because she wasn't a good mother doesn't mean you're not a good daughter. You were. You are now, if Sam would just admit it. I've never told you, but I guess I love you as much as—as a real mother could." Laura looked away out at the orchard beyond the rose-laden fence. "I always pretended you were mine."

Shiloh nodded, then swallowed. "She never wanted me."

"She was sick. In a different way, she was sick from the beginning. She couldn't leave men alone. I heard that her own father beat her, that he didn't want her. They say that has strange effects on some women. But the funniest thing was, she loved Sam. She needed him. Always coming back to him, lying and deceiving, desperate for him to say it was all right. I think he was old enough for her to see her father in him. But that wasn't what Sam wanted. He wanted a wife. And finally, he got sick, too, sick at heart. He couldn't keep letting her come back."

"She barely noticed me. I remember that."

"Caroline was a child. What child has room—or time—for another?"

"Not even when she was dying?"

Laura didn't answer; her eyes avoided Shiloh's.

"Tell me, Laura, why she came back," she asked insistently.

"She told Sam she'd found which school you were in. If he didn't give her more money—he was already paying her so much every month—she would approach you. She put the fear of God in Sam. Don't you think we knew how much a girl wants a mother, Shiloh? Even when you tried to hide it, it was there, in your face. That look didn't leave until you were a teenager, but I think I see it there today."

Laura stood, smoothing her skirt. "To end the story, he took her away. Gave her more money. Kept her up completely until she died a year later. She never asked about you again. That's hard—but it's truth. Sam was the one who wanted you. And me."

"Are you here . . . for Papa?" Shiloh asked painfully.

"No. He thinks he hates you. He's in the wrong. Whether or not he likes Billy Walker as a son-in-law, you're the one who has to make this decision. And Sam's not bearable sometimes. I came to make my own peace, and to bring you some things. They're in the car. Come on. I need some help."

Her heart gave a warm jump at the familiarity of what was in Laura's trunk. Her jewelry case; her makeup bag; her portable combination CD player and radio and television—and clothes. A huge armload of them.

"I didn't bring anything elaborate. But I thought you might need these," Laura offered.

Shiloh buried her nose in them, in the rich sandalwood scent that floated from the sachets and potpourri in her closets and dresser drawers.

She hadn't gone to Sam for them; they were hers. She would keep them.

They dumped her belongings on the bed; she stood the jewelry box on the dresser.

Laura looked around curiously. The room still had an almost sterile look to it.

"Are you sure you live here? That you like it here, Shiloh?"

"I promise, Laura."

"When I think of what you've been used to, I don't understand it. But I tell you what, we could really fix the room up. Call me someday, Shiloh, and we'll paint and paper everything in sight."

Shiloh looked around, too. "I'd like that. But it's different here, Laura. It's not just a house that matters. It's a farm. I'm outside as much as I am inside. I live out there a lot of the time." She gestured toward the windows.

"Hmph. That explains why you're brown as a biscuit.

But it won't hurt to domesticate that husband of yours a little. Winter comes. You'll be glad for my help then. And Shiloh—" Laura hesitated, "be careful."

"What are you talking about?"

"I'm talking about Sam. I think—I think he means to take Billy Walker down any way he can."

Shiloh, startled, stopped all motion. "What has he done?"

"It's not for me to say. I don't know it all, and besides, I owe Sam too much to tell you if I did. Ask your husband."

Billy knew as soon as he walked into the bedroom.

Shiloh's clothes told him; she was wearing a cool yellow buttercup of a dress. In her ears were matching tiny yellow earrings. On one finger of her left hand was a beaten gold twist of a ring.

In his pocket, another ring that he'd ordered in Martinsville and just picked up felt hard against his skin for a minute.

And her face told him: it was tremulous, hopeful, fresh from crying.

"Pennington came, didn't he?"

She was watching his face, waiting for his words.

"No. Laura did."

Laura. His breathing loosened a little, but not his anger. In fact, Laura might be worse. Shiloh would listen to her without any of the friction between her and her father.

"But he sent her."

"She came on her own."

"Don't think I'm that big a fool, Shiloh."

"What's the matter with you, Billy Bob? You used to be so much fun, and now you're—"

"What? Boring? Worried? All of it? Well, I can't help it. Sometimes you've got to live real life, Shiloh, and it's no fun."

"It's because of Papa, isn't it? What has he done, Billy?"

He went still, watching her warily. "I don't know what—"

"Don't try to protect me like I'm some kind of baby, the way Sam did. Laura said he was going to break you."

Anger washed over his face. "She was wrong. He'll never break me. I may be fighting right now just to keep body and soul together, but I'll hang on. We'll make it. He won't quit pushing, and I won't quit fighting back. Not ever. I swear it."

"Tell me what he's done."

"No."

"If you don't, I'll go to him. Now. I'll drag it out of him."

Billy stared at her face, rigid with determination, but he never said a word.

With a quick, purposeful movement, Shiloh twisted toward the door before he reached out a hand to catch her.

"Shiloh—no."

"Tell me, then. I mean to know, one way or the other."

Billy took a deep breath, then let it out in defeat. "Dammit—have it your way, then. He—he blocked the sale of the trees, for one thing. Everything I'd worked for, and I had to peddle the stock off to roadside dealers because he'd got to the warehouse owners. Why do you think I was gone three days? I was trying to get rid of the stock. I didn't want you to know, but there you are. Are you happy now?"

Her face went white; regret eased through him, under the anger as he released his hold on her. "I shouldn't have told you. It's got nothing to do with you, none of it."

"And how much more has he done?" Shiloh could hear T-Tommy's words even now, in her head. Sam really would destroy Billy.

"Nothing much," he answered evasively.

"I want to see him," she said at last.

"No—no, Shiloh."

"I'm going to."

"I said no. Doesn't it matter to you that I want you to stay away from Pennington until we get this marriage together a little more?" he demanded angrily.

"You're my husband, Billy, not my keeper. I love you, and I love my father. Can't you stop being afraid? I'm not going anywhere. I saw your face when you walked in. Even these clothes scare you. I don't have to wear them if you hate them—"

His face was flushed and tight.

"*Wear them.* Sleep in 'em. Do what you like. I'm not scared, and they're not the problem, anyway. They're the symptom. And talking to Pennington won't work. I tried the other day."

"You—you did? Why didn't you tell me?"

"Because it did no good."

"It will when I talk to him. I can make him quit."

"I don't want you begging for me." His face was as white as hers.

"Nobody's going to beg. But I've got to see him."

He stared at her, shocked. "You're going back, really. To 'Papa.'"

"Just for a little while, Billy. You could take me."

"*No.*"

"Then I'll call Laura. She'll pick me up. I'll be back before bedtime."

"And when he's through, I'll be the man you bought and paid for from the jail with thirty-five hundred dollars, and you'll wonder why you're living with me. I remember what happened once before when you tried to talk to Sam about me."

"If I go to see him, maybe everything will be better. He can't undo the marriage. I'll be back. Then when I come home—"

"You don't mean here, do you? This run-down old farm? Because I'm telling you, honey, don't come back for me tonight; I won't be around. If you can go back to your old friends and your old life, I can go back to mine." He grabbed up his cap off the bed and headed for the door, striding with monster steps off the porch, his long legs swallowing ground.

She ran after him, furious herself—and scared. "You can't threaten me, Billy. I've got a right—"

He slammed the truck door behind him. "You've got all the rights in the world. So do I."

"Where are you going? To the Legion Hall?"

"I don't feel much like dancing, but you don't have to dance at the Palace."

"If you think I'm going to turn you loose to go to the Palace—"

"You're my wife, not my keeper. I'm free—you're free. I'll do what I want. And you have a good time with Pennington."

◆  ◆  ◆

Shiloh admitted it to herself: she had handled the situation wrong. But they'd been living under a strain ever since he'd come back from Arkansas. And he hadn't done more than hold her in bed at night for nearly a week. All of her frustration had gone into the argument tonight. That, and her anger over the way he'd treated like a child by not telling her about Sam.

Why had he mentioned the money again, after all these weeks? She wondered uneasily if her father knew the answer to that question.

No matter what, she wasn't going to let Billy get away with his challenge, because he'd made it more out of fear than anything else. She hadn't been wrong about that. Whether he admitted it or not, he was afraid of Sam's power. Well, he had a right to be.

But Billy needn't think he could just waltz off to the Palace after they'd had an argument, no matter what his reasons.

Sam could wait. Her husband couldn't.

So she changed her clothes and called Laura. "Could I borrow your car for a little while?"

The housekeeper asked ruefully, "If I bring it to you, will I get it back in one piece?"

The Country Palace was in the south end of the county, off the highway in a low, flat spot of land. Pine trees almost obscured it from sight in the daytime, but at night a lurid pink-and-blue neon sign flashed on top of it, turning everything in sight alternating hues of the same colors.

The parking lot was graveled; Shiloh's feet crunched over the little rocks as she slid out of Laura's car. Laura would die if she ever discovered that the vehicle had been parked in front of a joint like this.

Even in the darkness, Shiloh could see that the white exterior needed painting; the place had a hard, desperate look to it that scared her and made her wonder why so many people came here; trucks jammed the lot.

Billy Bob's was here.

Her heart sank like lead when she saw it. Why hadn't he cooled off and come home? What did he get out of coming to a place like this? Even out here, she could hear the jukebox; the music was so loud the walls were vibrating.

Well, she was about to find out. Taking a long, steadying deep breath, she pushed open the door.

Dim lights, cigarette smoke, and even louder music—that was her first impression. And under all of that, laughter and stray, rowdy yells.

The door shut behind her, and she stood pressed against the wall beside it, her hands flat against her stomach, as if to protect herself, waiting for her eyes to adjust to the murkiness of the room.

Men hovered around a pool table in the back; two women stood watching, one of them smoking the longest cigarette Shiloh had ever seen.

Women were here: that was both a relief and an annoyance.

This place was a dive, and Shiloh began to simmer; Billy had no business coming here, not when he had a wife and a home.

Where was he?

It didn't take long to search him out: the woman he was with was by far the prettiest thing the Country Palace had to offer. Delicate, petite, sparklingly blond, she was bent over him at a corner table, right under a blue neon sign that screamed BUD.

Angie Blake.

She was talking in his ear, her tiny hand lost on his wide shoulder, her body practically draped over his side.

As Billy listened to the voice of the siren, he turned the silver can on the table in front of him restlessly between his hands, looking up into her face as she reached over to force his jaw up toward her.

Shiloh's blood pressure shot through the roof; she forgot about being afraid as she advanced like an enraged tigress on this ball of fluff and her low-down scoundrel of a husband.


Either the Country Palace had lost its appeal (it never had been blessed with a whole lot of it) or he had changed. He didn't want to be here.

He wanted Shiloh, at home, happy with him. Why couldn't he be enough to satisfy her?

The women here were hard and brittle. There wasn't a one of them whose arms would have held him while he cried. They would have thought he was a fool.

And he'd never wanted to kiss any woman's foot—not her lips, but her foot—the way he had Shiloh's that day in the shoe store.

On the other hand, none of these women would have run home to Daddy, either, or dished it out like she had.

Billy Bob was miserable, wishing he hadn't shot off his mouth to Shiloh about coming here, wishing he could go home.

Then Angie turned up.

She was all he needed.

He just looked up, and she was standing there, watching him.

"Well. It's been a while, sugar." Her face was immobile, quiet. "So, did you come back to sow some more wild oats? Or did you and your sweet college girl get sick of each other?"

Straightening in the chair, Billy answered, "I don't want to talk about Shiloh."

"Oh, don't you? Well, maybe I do. I love you, Billy."

He jerked, looking up at her in surprise.

"I never told you because I was waiting for you to decide to settle down, and I was gonna be there."

"I didn't—"

"Don't say you didn't know. You did."

"I was about to tell you that I didn't mean to hurt you."

"No, probably not. You're just like most men—I was handy and willin', so you helped yourself. But you got paid back, it looks like. You're one miserable-lookin' hound dog tonight. Why'd you marry her, Billy? To slap Michael Sewell in the face?"

He pushed the can away. "Damn it, Angie, leave me alone. You made me feel guilty, okay? Is that enough?"

Instead, she came to his side, leaning against him, her heavy perfume smothering him, and she put a hand on the far side of his face to turn him to her. "You should'a married me, Billy. We're alike. She's gonna hurt you bad one of these days, and when she does, look me up. I'll be—"

"If you don't get your hands off him," the furious voice snapped, "I'm going to pull those false fingernails off and stick them down your throat."

Angie jumped, instinctively springing away.

Billy stared. "Shiloh?"

She was right in front of him, right in the middle of the

Country Palace, aflame with anger and radiating it like
heat, her hands on her hips. She looked country clean,
nearly boyish in the denim shorts.

"That's right. Shiloh. Remember me?"

"What are you doing in here?"

"I ought to ask you the same thing, you—you double-
crossing, two-timing rat!" She shoved her heavy fall of
thick brown hair back behind her ears with both hands;
her eyes were huge and sparking lightning.

"Now wait a minute—"

"No, you wait. I wanted to go see my father—that's all.
But you came here. You let her hang all over you"— she
shot fire at Angie, who took another step back—"and
touch you. If I'd been ten minutes later, you'd have been
in bed with her."

By now the people around them were listening avidly,
straining to hear them. Even the music seemed to have
gotten a little quieter.

"I was just sitting here," he began again, heatedly.

"Which you had no business doing. You have a home
and a wife—"

"Who had run off to Daddy's," he roared at last, shooting up out of the chair in frustration. He didn't care
anymore who was listening; let the whole county if they
wanted to.

"You should have understood. I've been blind as a bat.
I've spent all these weeks thinking how sweet and kind
and gentle you are—"

Okay, he wasn't ready for the county to hear that. Toy
Baker had already burst into laughter, and Billy struggled
for composure, finding it in sarcasm, knowing it was the
wrong solution even when he used it. "Yeah, well, honey,
I guess I had you fooled."

She looked about eighteen again for a minute, her eyes

hurt, then she struck back. "You know that money you were talking about this afternoon? The thirty-five hundred dollars? Well, I got ripped off. Because, *honey*," she mimicked his sarcasm, *"you're not worth it."*

She walked out in the closest thing to silence that the Country Palace had ever known, slamming the door behind her.

Somebody in the crowd whistled in awe, then spoke. "Brother, did you get told."

Angie grabbed at his shirt as he started purposefully out the door, his face white, grim, furious.

"Billy, listen," she cajoled frantically, "don't do something stupid. Women say things . . . Our tongues are the best way we've got of fighting somebody bigger. She didn't mean it—"

But he tore away from her, getting outside just in time to see Laura Kershaw's car roaring off down the highway.

If she'd turned a knife in his stomach, he couldn't have hurt worse.

She was old man Pennington's daughter, right enough: she went for blood.

# 20

*Shiloh didn't have* a mother to go home to, so she did the next best thing: she went straight to Laura with her car, and she stayed there.

Laura took one look at her tear-stained face and put her in her one extra bedroom, where Shiloh pulled pillows over her head in hot mortification.

She—Shiloh Pennington, no, Walker—who had been well bred and polite most of her life, had caused a public scene in a horrible joint. She had brawled with her husband and, worst of all, she had threatened to do the same with Angie Blake.

She was never leaving Laura's house again, never going out in public, never looking any man in Briskin County in the eye again for fear he'd been in that honkytonk tonight and witnessed the whole embarrassing mess.

She had actually threatened Angie Blake, acting like some heathen, violent and primitive.

But then, she'd discovered she *was* violent and primitive where Billy Walker was concerned.

So here it was at last, the real heart of the matter, the thing she was trying to avoid facing: what she'd said to him.

Well, he deserved it.

She had wanted to kill him when he let Angie drape herself all over him; he hadn't done much more than touch his own wife in a week.

Why couldn't he tell her what was wrong sooner?

She didn't ask, her mind accused. She kept waiting for him to spill his guts, but he kept important things down tight inside him.

She'd had to drag the story of his encounter with Sewell out of him forcibly. And then she remembered the way he had at last collapsed emotionally, the way his wet face had felt against hers.

Why didn't she ask? She already knew the answer: She had been afraid he would tell her something about Sam that she didn't want to hear.

If she could take back words, she'd swallow whole those last ones: "You're not worth it."

Everything could have been patched up right until that moment.

Oh, Billy, what have we done? What have I said? I didn't mean it. You know that, don't you?

If only the whole world hadn't been listening, if only his pride hadn't been involved. If only.

Now there was one thing she could do. Oh, Papa, why couldn't you just leave us alone?


She confronted her father the next morning.

In the huge, gleaming kitchen he sat alone at a table, eating and turning the pages of a highly colored sales booklet from a local hardware store. The rustling of the pages was the only noise in the lonely, beautiful room.

Watching him, Shiloh wondered if he knew how isolated he looked. And as he peered over the top of his reading glasses to gaze down at his plate, she remembered him doing the same thing every night for years as he read tales of Richard Scarry and Judy Blume to her before she went to sleep.

He'd started that habit after Caroline left, and he had done it until Shiloh was twelve. Part of his attempts to give her the perfect childhood, part of his fight to keep her from noticing that her mother had abandoned her without a single glance back.

She loved him. She didn't want to hurt him. But it had come down to her marriage—if she had one left.

"Hello, Papa."

He jerked so hard that his hand hit the china coffee cup and its hot brown liquid splashed on his wrist. He never noticed.

"Shiloh!" And for a dazzling, unguarded moment, there was a blaze of welcome in his face before he remembered and tamped it down.

"I didn't know if you would even admit to knowing my name or not."

He looked around, toward the door. "How did you get here? I didn't—"

"I spent the night with Laura. And no, Billy Bob's not with me. We had a fight, a horrible fight, and most of it was over you."

Sam pushed back his chair, stood, and reached for a napkin to wipe off his hand. "Over me! Well, I'm flattered. It does me good to hear I've caused Mr. Walker some misery. You've been gone a long time, girl. Five weeks and a day."

"You told me I couldn't come back, that you didn't have a daughter anymore."

The delicate line of blood crept from his high cheekbones up to his temples. "That was pride talkin'. You know that. If you want to come home, you can. I'm willin' to forgive, Shiloh."

She laughed a little under her breath and took a step toward him. "Thanks. If I ever do anything that calls for you to forgive me, I'll remember. But I'm not slinking home just yet. I want to know what it is that's going on between you and Billy."

Her father's momentum toward her stopped; his keen blue eyes sharpened and his face went blank. "So that's what you've come for, to run interference for him. Well, what's between me and him is between us, Shiloh. If he can't play the game, he shouldn't have stepped into the ring. And that's what he did when he took you. All the plans and dreams and opportunities—"

"You planned. You dreamed. Me, I got what I wanted."

"Billy Bob Walker? He's what you wanted? Then you're a fool. But I already knew it. Any woman who lets a man talk her out of thirty-five hundred dollars before they're even married—"

Shiloh sucked in her breath sharply. "So I was right. You did talk about it with him. Well, I know he didn't tell you, so I will. I went to that jail and begged him to take it." She couldn't tell it all; she couldn't give Sam another weapon against them. "I wanted him out, I wanted to be married to him—because I was afraid of Michael. I wanted to get away from you. And mostly—" she could see it so clearly now—"I wanted to be Billy's wife."

"To get away from me!" His face was blood-red now, as he came around the corner of the table toward her. "I gave you everything."

"That you wanted me to have. But we've been through this before. So again, I'm asking you. What's between you and Billy?"

"Ask him."

"I already have. I dragged a little of it out of him. Now I'm giving you a chance to tell me all, and you won't. You know why? Because what you're doing is wrong, and you know it. You're breaking a good man just because I married him."

"I'm breaking him because he's using you. I know what he is, an opportunist pulling himself up any way he can. First, all that college work, now you, with your money. Well, he can climb up on somebody else's back. I cut the legs right out from under him twice before, and I'll do it again."

He might have been taking an oath, he was so passionate.

As she stared at her furious father, Shiloh knew only one thing: He wouldn't stop until somebody made him.

"Why do you hate him so much? If I'm happy, why can't you leave us alone?"

"You don't know what's best for you. You're like a wild teenager who runs away from home because she's mad at her parents. I know exactly why you're with him," Sam answered violently, his face mottled with anger. "You're out on that old farm because you're rebelling against me—and because Walker is a good lay." He spit the words out, crude and vicious. "I'm speakin' it plain, girl. You're ruining yourself—just like your mother did—just so you can crawl in bed with a man who's good between the sheets and between—"

"Shut up!" Her hands flew to her face, and behind them, her cheeks flamed and blistered with shocked, outraged embarrassment.

"I'm only tellin' the truth." But his voice shook.

Lowering her hands slowly, Shiloh stared at him through tears, her heart twisting. "You've spent years expecting me to be like Caroline, hiding me from men. And I've spent years trying to prove I wasn't and paying for her sins. Billy is my husband. What I do with him in our bedroom is our business, and it's right. I thought I could talk to you, beg you to make your peace with him—"

"There isn't any peace."

"No. I see that now. You're wrong, but it makes it easier to tell you something that I should have told you years ago." Funny how nothing in her seemed to be working; she couldn't feel her heart or even the rise of her diaphragm. Everything had just shut off, except her tongue. "All this time, I've been your everything. Your family when Caroline left. Your top scholar at school. Your dutiful banker. Because I was trying to be your daughter. Your real daughter. But I'm not. *I'm not.*"

He put his hand to the collar of his soft golf shirt, as if it choked him. "What are you talkin' about?"

"I'm not your daughter. You should have suspected it, knowing Caroline." Her teeth were chattering a little. "Laura told me that Caroline came here. It was the year I was fifteen, the year you sent me to the girls' school. She told you she knew where I was. But she didn't tell you that she'd already come to me, several times. She told me how much she missed me, how girls my age needed a mother, how she wanted me to forgive her and let her be with me. She wanted me to leave the school and go with her. Now I know it was so she could hit you up for money to get me back. She always needed more cash. But she got the money a different way, didn't she? I realized that the other day when Laura and I talked. Even though I wanted Caroline to want me, I couldn't leave you—and when I wouldn't go with her, she turned into a petty, spoiled—" Shiloh shuddered. "Then she told me. I wasn't yours."

"You don't know what you're—you're saying." Sam's words were broken, his face shaded gray, his hands reached like claws for the back of a chair to support himself as he hung to it, sick. "I don't believe this pack of . . . lies! You can't do this to us, you can't."

"I didn't believe her, either, for a long time. I just . . . hate her," Shiloh said somberly. "I told myself over and over that she'd done it to hurt me. And then she died. Remember the funeral? You made me go. I didn't want to look at her, to ever think of her. And I thought, she's going to hell because she lied. But I couldn't forget what she had said. And one day I decided to disprove her if I could. I had my blood typed. It took a while for me to figure how to get the information I needed about you . . . and her. I'm B positive. Not her type and—and not yours, ei—ther." The word broke as she struggled to tell it all. "But his. His name was David." She made herself look right into Sam's staring eyes. "He was your brother."

Sam flinched. "My God—oh, my God—dear God—"

"And when I was twenty-one, an attorney came to Evans to see me. He'd been holding a little money and David's personal belongings for me for years, since David died. There was a letter. He said since I was the only Pennington in the next generation, he was leaving these few things to me and hoped that I sometimes remembered him. Nothing at all to betray the truth. But I knew."

"She would have . . . told . . . me. She would have—" He moaned.

"I don't know why she didn't, except I think she thought you would kill her. And there'd be no more money from you, ever. As for me, Caroline never thought much about me at all until I became her means to an end. I was born; she handed me to Laura. She ruined his life, and yours, but I won't let either of you ruin mine."

He fumbled for the chair, falling into it, his face beaded with sweat, breathing in dry, hard heaves.

"I'm sorry," she whispered painfully. "I never meant to tell you. But you've got to see now that I never was what you wanted me to be. None of your money or your rules will ever make me into it. I tried. I wanted you to be my father so much . . ." The taste of salt was bitter in her throat. "I love you. But then I began to love Billy, too. And finding out finally that he was in public what I was in secret—to me, it felt as if there was always a link between us. For a while, I told myself that was why I couldn't forget him. He doesn't know, not yet."

"What will I do?" Sam's face was wet with tears as he looked up at her dazedly.

She wanted to put her hand on his arm, but he made no move at all toward her, just sitting there like a toy that somebody had forgotten.

"I'll give you the letter if you want to see it. It's innocent enough. But David was sorry, I know. It's why he left." Tears blurred Sam's papery, crumpled face in front of her. "I took all your rules and your strictness because doing it made me your daughter. You loved me so much—the rules were part of the love. And I was afraid that if you knew the truth, you wouldn't love me anymore. Well, now I'm Billy's wife. Your rules don't hold for me now, but the love does, if it's given without them. Without the conditions. You have to love me the way I am, and take everything else along with me—your brother's mistake, Caroline's weaknesses—and Billy Walker. He ought to be the easiest of them all for you to swallow. Let us be happy. If you can't, then let me go. I never was yours, except by love. Because I chose to be. It was a strong enough link for me. Is it for you?"

He never answered, staring at his own hands on the table.

When Shiloh tried to move to the door, her feet stumbled along like wooden blocks.

"I love you, Papa," she told him quietly before she shut the door behind her.

She couldn't go back to the farm, not in this condition, not until she found some peace of mind. So she walked along the sidewalks of the little town, never noticing whether she was in shade or light.

She had been a liar on her wedding night. "We're free to find out who we are and what we can be," she'd said. But she hadn't really been free; she'd just been approximating it, trying to salvage Sam's love at the cost of Billy's.

Today was total freedom, and she didn't like it much, afraid of its price tag, torn apart by the agony it brought. The only compensation was that she felt washed clean. Honest. At last.

Four years ago, Papa thought she'd made her final choice. Billy thought she'd made it on the Fourth of July.

But Shiloh knew: she'd made it today. Two loves pitted against each other—the decision had come down in Billy's favor.

Billy Bob was gone, without a word to her.

"He left this morning with Harold Bell," Willie told her, trying to restrain his curiosity. "He's done it before, but not in such a hurry. I don't know when he'll be back."

"But the farm . . . the nursery . . ."

"It's late in the summer for there to be too much. The next big season is fall, when we gather pecans."

"How—how long will he be gone?" It was hard to ask, to admit that Billy had told her nothing.

"Who knows? He took Chase with him. When he does that, he means to be gone awhile. They change towns— even states—ever' day or two. He rode with Bell—put the horse in one of his trailers. He's not got any way to come home until Bell's ready. He said you'd gone home to your daddy."

"But I came back!"

The bedroom was sunny and bright on this Saturday morning—and completely forlorn without Billy. She felt as empty and confused as she ever had in her life as she lay down on the quilt.

She'd faced Sam, torn herself apart, and for what? Billy was gone. He hadn't cared enough to wait.

Beside her on the table, something shone golden in the rays of sunshine. A ring. It was a wedding band, wide and smooth. And inside, their initials, wrapped together by a fleur-de-lis. Her heart eased a little. When had he gotten it?

He should have put it on her; instead, she slid it over her own knuckle.

Looking at it, she remembered Papa's words: "all those classes at the university."

They'd nagged at her, and now she remembered the books, too. Everything began to fit.

Upstairs, in his old bedroom, she touched the volumes on the shelves, then reached for a notebook, full of scrawled notes. His handwriting. Microbiology.

My God.

Ellen was in the door when Shiloh turned, a flicker of pride in her eyes.

"He's studying to be a vet, isn't he? Why didn't he tell me?"

"I guess for the same reasons he won't tell anybody yet. Only a few know. Most just see him around with Dr. Sanders, and think, there's Billy, hangin' around the vet like he always has. They don't know how hard he's worked to get through the prevet program at Ole Miss. He's almost got it made. Now he has to try to get into a vet school, if he can. He's done it one or two classes at a time. When his grandpa got sick, there was no money for months. He couldn't go at all. It's been nearly five years since he started. Most people do what he's done in two or three."

"Most people give up," Shiloh murmured.

It was frightening, this knowledge about her husband. When he was just Billy, it was easier to put a fence around him.

But then she wouldn't have this surge of pride, the same one Ellen felt.

"He didn't give up on you, either," Ellen returned. "I never told him, but I once found a letter he wrote you and never mailed while you were off at college. I didn't know who Shiloh was then. And it was four years ago, after you left, that he went crazy. Broke out, his grandpa called it. I never knew why, until I found out about you."

"We had a fight last night, right in the middle of the Palace."

"Any fool can see that. It was all over Will when he tore in here. He walked the floor waiting for you. But I've got no sympathy for him. He knows better than to hang around that joint."

"I said some things I shouldn't have."

"You're thinkin' he won't come back. But don't worry, he will, if for no other reason than to tear a strip off of you," she said dryly. "He's not much of one for layin' down and takin' it. And I don't think you are, either."

"I used to be."

"Well, see what a good influence he's having on you?" Ellen said soothingly, laughter in her green eyes. "But look at it this way. Today people figure it's a love match between you two. You don't fight like that unless you care."

"Or you're on the verge of divorce." Shiloh could hear her fatal words ringing between them still.

"Which you are *not*. He'll be back."

It was awkward without Billy at her in-laws that Sunday, and Shiloh veered between worry over her father and despair over her husband, spending the day silent and alone.

On Monday, Laura came after her while Ellen and Willie were out at the fruit stand.

"It's Papa." Shiloh spoke the two words as soon as she opened the door. Laura's face was worn and a little frightened.

"He won't let me in, Shiloh. I went over yesterday afternoon after church to see if he was sick. I knew he didn't go to the golf course. The door was unlocked and the family room was torn to shambles. Pictures burned, lamps broken. He was shut in his study and he told me to go to hell." Laura's mouth trembled. She grasped the door frame so tightly her knuckles were white. "In twenty-five years, in all of our arguments, he's never talked to me that way. Shiloh, what have you done to him? What did you say when you left my house to talk to him?"

"It was something . . . I had to do. I called him yesterday. No answer," Shiloh told her painfully.

"He didn't go to the bank today. The house is locked up this morning completely, but I know Sam's in there. I heard him ranting and raving at dawn. If you don't come, Shiloh, T-Tommy's gonna break in."

"I'll come, now."

She should have stayed Saturday. No matter how cold he seemed. No matter what was going on with her and Billy.

"I don't know when I'll be back," she told the silent Ellen and Willie. "Papa needs me."

T-Tommy had to break the doors down, anyway. Sam had locked and dead-bolted all of them.

He was upstairs in his bedroom, still in the same clothes he'd worn on Saturday. But the once-white golf shirt was wrinkled and splotched brown, his hair was in wild disarray, his face was rough with the beginnings of a silvery beard, his eyes were bloodshot.

Shiloh had never seen him in such a state; he frightened her as he glared at them from the Windsor chair in the corner of the bedroom as they burst in.

"Get the hell out of my house," he shouted hoarsely. "You—and you—and"—he shuddered as his eyes fell on Shiloh—"you."

"Papa—"

"Don't. Not now."

"Why not now? I always think of you as that. I called you 'Sam' because I was angry with you. It's the same reason I wore the clothes you hated, drove the car too fast. Because I was a rebellious daughter. *Yours.*"

"You were never that."

"I was always that. I was fighting myself as much as I was you. All of it was over something deeper. I knew down inside myself, whether I admitted it or not, that I loved Billy Bob. That I couldn't marry Michael. You're closer to me than any other person in the world—you could sense it, too. You've always known that Billy was the real threat because . . . you're my father. You know me."

Sam came unsteadily out of the chair, grasping it for support as he stumbled.

Laura tried to reach for him. "You've not had a bite in three days, have you? Let me—"

But he pushed her away, snarling like a cornered, injured animal. "Don't you touch me. Don't you touch me."

Laura stepped back, fright and hurt blending on her face as she twisted to Shiloh.

"Laura, let me talk to him. Alone."

"Are you sure?" T-Tommy asked dubiously. "Sam, you're in a bad way. Let us—"

"Alone. *Please.*" Shiloh's voice was near desperation, and Laura heard it.

"Come on," she told her brother. "Do as she asks."

Then it was just the two of them—a pleading girl and a broken old man.

"Papa, Laura loves you. We all do."

"You betrayed me," he rasped, hitting his open hand on his chest.

"No."

"You knew all along. And Caroline did. And he—*he* did." His face twisted.

"They're strangers to me. I don't know what they knew. But I know what you're feeling." She wouldn't let him look away from her gaze, trying to press the truth on him. "I was sick to my stomach for four days. Then I hated them and God and everybody else in the world. I hated you because you were such a gullible fool where she was concerned. I wished I'd never been born. But it passed, those feelings about you. And I began to see that what makes a father is something more than biology. It's love and concern and discipline and protection"— she laughed, the tears making her voice rough—"and God knows, you've given me that."

He put both hands to his head, raking his wild hair back with hands that shook. "You just don't take a child from its parent and expect the parent to go on living. To go on being normal. I can't, Shiloh. I *can't.*" His voice broke, then pleaded like a child's.

"Then she'll beat you," she whispered thickly, daring to catch at his wrists. He was sick, burning up to the touch. "She'll take the rest of our lives and ruin them, too. Don't let her have us, Papa."

His mouth quivered, but he didn't shake her off. Tears welled at the corner of his eyes, spilling down onto his cheek, catching in the long furrows of his face.

"I'm not your father."

"Yes, you are. I never even saw David. He's no more to me than—than the judge is to Billy. He's a father, a real, live, biological father, and it's worth nothing. Billy's got nobody if Sewell's all there is. But between me and you, there's all the nights you read to me, and the arguments over how much makeup I wasn't supposed to wear, and the day you went to a board meeting with blood on your shirt because I got hurt on the playground at school and you came to the school from the bank, even though you didn't have the time, to patch me up and let me bleed and cry on you."

Pulling his hand up to her face, she pressed the palm to her cheek.

"Papa," she said insistently. "I love you. I love you. I—"

And he reached out, his movements rusty and uncertain—so unlike himself—and gathered her clumsily against his heart.

"Help me," he whispered shakily. "Help me, Shiloh."

She couldn't leave him, not then. They talked until he fell asleep on the bed while Laura and T-Tommy hovered in the kitchen. Shiloh stood looking down on her sleeping father, and she had the strangest, most topsy-turvy feeling in her life. She was young—nearly twenty-three, that was all—but for just a few minutes, she'd felt older than Sam, as though he were the child.

But she was happy. They would make it.

"You'll stay, won't you?" asked Laura, anxiously. "For a day or two, until he's back to normal."

He won't ever be the same, Shiloh thought, like I never was. But all she said was, "I'll stay."

Relief made the housekeeper sag against the sink. "Thank goodness. I was scared to death. And a week from Friday, whether he remembers it or not, he's got the big bash he holds every year for the people connected with the banks. I don't know what to do. Cancel it? Let it go on? I'm scared to ask him."

"Let it go on," Shiloh said. "He needs to have it to think about, and it would only cause talk if it got cancelled."

Laura laid her hand over Shiloh's. "I don't know what's happened. But if you hadn't come, I believe Sam would've killed himself." The words were quiet.

"We won't let him," she answered.


Two days later, her father went back to the bank. Quieter, more subdued. But he wasn't completely defeated anymore. He had hope.

She called the farm. Billy hadn't returned. Shiloh didn't, either.

She tried to convince herself that Ellen was right, that he would come back and forgive her. But Ellen didn't know the whole story—not about the money or Angie or her own father's schemes.

She couldn't sleep in her room at home without tossing and turning, missing him, longing to reach out and touch him. And the house stifled her until she couldn't breathe. Some nights she opened the French doors and let the breeze blow in, listening for a whippoorwill, longing for the buzz of the fan and the rich smell of the orchards. And mostly, for his hands on her, his husky, teasing laughter in her ear.

Finally, she got up one morning with a headache, a heartache, and a stomach full of righteous indignation. Enough was enough. He'd done as much as she had—

kept things from her, shouted at her, been sarcastic—and he'd had a blond floozy sprawled all over him, to boot.

He'd had a fit when Michael had kissed *her,* and she'd apologized as sweetly as she knew how.

Why couldn't *he* apologize?

If he waited much longer, there was going to be nobody to apologize to.

Shiloh was through mourning. He was probably off at some rodeo with a bunch of cowboy groupies hanging on his every word.

So she called Rita and asked her to lunch.

And she would stay at Sam's a while longer.

# $\overline{2}\overline{1}$

*Bell Rodeo was* in town for one night only.

Under the blazing lights of the fairground arena in this east Tennessee county, the big red stallion which the rodeo had brought with it drew all eyes. Fiery in both looks and temperament, a little edgy out in all the noise and excitement, glittering in the bronze and gold trappings, Chase was clearly unpredictable.

That element lent excitement to his movements, even when he was only on the sidelines.

He was a show stealer, born to be here in the limelight.

Billy slid off his back as the rodeo drew to a close, leading the sweating, twitching animal back to the stalls that ran along one side of the arena.

"You're going to be fine, boy," he murmured to him, running his arm up under Chase's head to stroke him. "You like it, don't you?"

The horse didn't answer as Billy went about his business furiously, stripping off the saddle, pampering the stallion, trying not to remember that this was the last time.

Bell made his way back to them as the lights dimmed in the arena. The hum of the crowd; the scent of cigarette smoke thick in the night air; a loud, raucous burst of laughter; these were the sounds that told of the audience's departure as they swarmed to the parking lot.

"Good show tonight," Bell grunted, reaching to stroke the horse's nose. Chase knew him, snorting at him in a friendly sort of way.

"My last night with you," Billy Bob said flatly, reaching down to remove the leather chaps.

"You sure? I like havin' you with the rodeo."

"I'm sure. That was our deal—two weeks with you, to get Chase used to things." The words were clipped, the tone sparse. If he clung strictly to business, Billy thought, he would get through this.

Bell pulled off the heavy leather gloves he wore. "So you're sticking to it, that deal."

"I gave you my word . . . and my horse."

"Fair enough." Bell fumbled in his inside vest pocket. "I'm prepared to keep my end of it. Here."

Billy dropped the chaps over the high back of the wooden stall, hesitated, then reached for the check. He never looked at it, just dragged out his wallet to push the paper in it.

Bell watched. "You in some kind of trouble, boy?" His black eyes were keen as daggers. "Something's bad wrong, or you wouldn't be selling me this horse."

"Nothing you can help me with," Billy returned shortly.

"It's that girl, ain't it?"

"It's just me." His voice said plainly that it was none of Bell's business.

"No matter. I'm gettin' what I want from the deal," Bell answered.

Billy Bob looked at the horse. "Well, so long, fella. I'll see you in the lights out there." He brushed his hand down the big chest, still heaving a little from Chase's exertions in the arena.

Bell looked at Billy's face. "You know you can always come to see him. You're always welcome at Bell Farm, Billy."

The big blond man nodded wordlessly, then walked away. He got to the edge of the stall area before he stopped sharply, wheeling to return, taking big steps. He wrapped both arms around Chase's neck, hugging him fiercely, burying his face against the hot, sleek coat.

And Harold Bell turned away, understanding exactly.

Billy Bob drove all night.

The brilliant green, thrusting ridges of the Appalachians sloped gradually into rolling, pine-covered hills.

Down through Knoxville, through Nashville, through Selmer, across the state line. Corinth, Tupelo, farther south, then west.

Billy was nearly home when the sun rose, as red as the dirt along the edges of the highway.

A few cotton fields and rice paddies mingled now with pecan groves. The loud tourists, the strange accents, the brash feel of Tennessee—all those irritants slid away as Mississippi flowed around him, soothing and gentle.

Home to the land.

To the farm.

To Shiloh.

He let the thought escape at last, testing his emotions to see what he felt, nearly two weeks after that knock-down-drag-out fight. Anger and hurt and—now he could admit it—a longing to see her.

This time he would face her with nothing, absolutely nothing, between them. The money was here in his pocket, and when he shoved it at her, he meant to begin this marriage again. This time they'd begin on equal terms.

If she'd let him. Remembering how she'd flamed with anger at Angie, Billy had a few doubts.

But he had his own indignation to fuel him.

"You're not worth it."

She was going to eat those words, he swore to himself.

The three or four buildings that made up Seven Knobs rose up over the first rise. The grocery store was already open; so was its post office window at the side of the store. Mary Haile was out sweeping off her front porch, and a cat licked its paws contentedly at the edge of her yard.

When Billy made the turn beside the fruit stand, he could see the white of the farmhouse in the distant bright morning light as it filtered through the leaves of the big trees. When he followed the gravel road around to the back, his eyes went automatically to Shiloh's windows.

She hadn't come back the night of the fight. With a sinking heart, he had faced the facts: she had gone home, to the man who might have the power to take her away, just as he had done four years ago.

But across these two weeks he had hoped against hope that she would return, remembering how she seemed to love the place, reminding himself that Shiloh was a woman now, not Sam's little girl, that she'd married him and lived with him against her father's wishes. But when he called home several times, she was never there.

Maybe he had no right to hope she would be; he had hit the high road and stayed gone for thirteen days. But he'd had no choice, he argued with himself: Bell made the deal that way. For thirty-five hundred dollars, Billy gave him the horse and two weeks of his time.

The fan was not on in the window; his heart stumbled just a little.

"Why, Will!" His mother's shocked voice dragged him out of his reverie as she came out the back porch door to throw away a pan of water.

"I just got home and you're already dumping on me?" he inquired humorously, setting down the big blue duffel bag on the porch steps.

Ellen began to smile, and her mouth lifted her whole quiet face into sudden happiness. "You're back, and you're not raving mad like you were when you left here." Her eyes sparkled like emeralds as she set down the pan and reached out to clasp his arms. "It's good to see you. Daddy!" she called over her shoulder. "Come see what's in the backyard this fine mornin'."

The scent of Willie's pipe preceded him. "Did you say morning' glories are in the back—Billy!"

" 'Lo, Grandpa."

"It's about time." The old man nearly smiled. "You've been two weeks gone. Whose truck is that you're drivin'?"

"Bell's. I'm supposed to take it to his farm sometime this week." He stepped up on the porch, looking toward the door. *Her* door. Then he asked the question beating at the back of his brain. "You haven't seen Shiloh, then?"

"Uh." That was Willie's only answer as he looked anxiously over at Ellen. Billy Bob caught the tail end of the look as he turned from surveying the door, and a weight settled heavily in the pit of his stomach.

"She's gone home, hasn't she? For good."

"She came back on Sunday, after you left, Will," his mother answered soothingly.

"And?" His one word was impatient.

"Her father needed her. He was sick."

Billy opened the door roughly, shoving it open on the quiet, empty room. "He's no more sick than I am."

"Now you just wait," Ellen cut in, her voice sharp. "You two have a fight, then you take off for two weeks. Don't blame her for this completely, Billy."

"It was over him and a lot of other things. She gave me the money to get out of jail. I shouldn't have taken it. It's been between us the entire time. Then he found out about it. What was I supposed to do? Let him keep beating me at every turn?"

Billy hunched his shoulders up around his neck as he gripped the bannister. Then Ellen reached out to lay her hand on his back, as if she might ease the keening agony that tore through him.

"She had a talk with her father. I don't know about what. All I know is, he told her about you going to the university, for one thing. She didn't understand why you'd kept it a secret."

Billy swallowed, then swallowed again.

"That's not enough reason for her to go back to him," he managed.

"I'm tellin' you, there was something wrong," Ellen insisted. "It was in the Kershaw woman's face. And Shiloh has called. She came by two days ago, on her way to Martinsville. She was pickin' up something there for a—a reception of some kind she was helping with tonight. She said she just meant to say hello, but she really wanted to come by to see if there was any trace of you here."

"Don't try to sweeten it, Mama," he said wearily,

straightening. Now that there was no rush of adrenaline keeping it at bay, the night's loss of sleep was beginning to wear on him. "I guess I'll get some sleep . . . in my old bedroom."

She'd meant it when she walked off after the fight. She'd left him.


He dreamed of Chase.

The stallion side-danced across a misty field, cocky and beautiful. And the girl that rode his back was every inch as gorgeous, her wine-streaked brown hair nearly the same color as his gleaming coat.

They belonged out there. He had no right to either of them.

He awoke with the thought in his head and misery in his heart, and lay there for a long time in the hot room, wondering what he would do without her.

Her kiss on his lips that spawned hope in the middle of a horrible joke of a marriage ceremony.

Her arms locked around him in a dance.

Her breast beneath his lips.

Her touch burning away the hurt in a dark motel room.

Her sleepy smile.

*"You're not worth it."*

He winced as those last words jarred on his memory.

She was angry. Maybe she was jealous; Angie had been glued to him.

That was no excuse for her to run home and not come back. She knew how he'd take her actions. He would understand that she'd decided she preferred fine cars and expensive receptions, like the one tonight.

When he couldn't bear his own gloomy thoughts anymore, he got up and went downstairs, opening the door to the room. She was here—everywhere.

He turned on the fan and sat down on the bed, and then he began to burn.

She was *his* wife, by her own choice.

And no matter what people said or thought, he was as good to her as any other man could ever be. Didn't she know he was trying? Couldn't she understand he was reaching for better things?

He loved her, dammit.

He wanted her.

He'd sold his one prize possession to try to show her all of that.

And by God, she loved him, too, if she'd just admit it, completely and wholly.

So why had she gone home? Because she wanted to be back in her own world and she didn't think he could fit there, no matter how hard he tried?

Was love not enough?

He made a sudden motion, nearly knocking off the table lamp, and as he caught it, he remembered: he'd put the ring here.

It was gone. Not on the dresser, not in her jewelry box.

She had to have it. She'd carried it with her to Pennington's house.

He looked at himself in the mirror, and he made up his mind. A poor man can't afford pride, somebody once said, but Billy Walker meant to take his own life by the scruff of the neck tonight and see what shook out of it.

He was tired of being the victim. Tired of feeling inferior. Tired of hiding his dreams because the town might think they were too big for him to aspire to. Tired of being intimidated by Sewell and Pennington and Shi-

loh herself, even if she never understood how she'd made
him feel that way.

And if he lost this gamble, then he would go down
proud as a king.

In his case, pride might be all he had left.


The reception, Billy discovered, was local, an annual
thing Pennington did for his employees and board and
investors once a year at the country club in Martinsville.

He'd get to see the place once in his life, after all.

And it was formal. All right, he'd be damned if he
wasn't formal, too.

But in the middle of his plans, one thing shook him:
When he opened the check Bell had given him for Chase
to cash it, it wasn't for the agreed amount. It was for
more, for five thousand dollars.

Maybe Bell thought he was saving the marriage, Billy
thought wryly, but there was gratitude in him, too.

It took two hours to find something long enough and
big enough for him to wear: a coal black tuxedo jacket, cut
like a gambler's frock coat, and a white shirt with tiny,
crisp, distinct little pleats sewn into it, running up and
down the front. They were nearly invisible, they were so
small, but they gave a richness to the shirt.

The tie—he was going to do this right if it killed him,
and this damn tie just might—was black, too, and it
looped into a knot under the snowy lapels.

But no shop had pants long enough to fit his legs, and
there wasn't enough time to lengthen the ones the shop
did have.

So he'd wear jeans and the big belt buckle and his
cowboy boots. And it'd be better this way: she and her old

man both would see that Billy Bob Walker wouldn't toe the mark completely for anybody, not them or society in north Mississippi, either, such as it was.

He showered and shaved and brushed his blond hair back until it glistened. And still he didn't like it. He was nearly thirty. It was too long. He didn't need it to prove a point anymore. When he got dressed, he counted out thirty-five hundred dollars from what was left of the five thousand, snapped a rubber band around it, and stuffed it into the inside breast pocket of the black coat.

Ellen and Willie hovered anxiously in the kitchen when he came down the stairs. The afternoon had slipped away into dusk. It was seven o'clock according to the timepiece that hung on the kitchen wall.

"Good Lord," Willie muttered in shock as Billy entered the room. "The only time a man oughta look this high-falutin' is when they bury him, boy."

"Then I'm dressed right. I figure I'm going to my funeral, Grandpa."

"I figured you were going to crash a party."

"She crashed mine," Billy answered laconically.

"Will, you've got such a hot temper, and you're hurt right now. Please, don't do somethin' that's pure foolishness. If you've got to go, then at least give her a chance. I know she loves you, and she'll take to you easy and sweet as sugar the way you look now. She's been missing you, I know."

"When did she have the time? And anyway," he tried hard to tease, "you're the mother-in-law. You're supposed to be an old witch to her."

"Just remember what I've said, or I'll be an old witch to you instead."

Leland Ritter was sweeping up his shop when Billy knocked on the door. Leland glanced up, his lined face irritated. "I'm closed," he hollered.

"I'll pay you double, Leland," Billy returned, and the tiny little man straightened. Under the bright fluorescent lights, the white fringe around his bald, shiny head looked like a halo.

"Is that you, Billy Bob?" he asked in amazement, squinting toward the glass doors.

"Yeah."

Leland came to the door, unlatching it and speaking simultaneously. "You must need a trim awful bad."

"I do." Billy sat down in the barber's first chair, before he could change his mind.

"Um-huh-huh, look at you." Leland gazed in awe. "Where you going, Billy?"

"I'm going to Greenview Country Club."

"To Pennington's big party?" His voice rose.

"That's right. And I'm not invited. I want to look real good, Leland, so when they throw me out, and when I get up and walk right back in, I'm going to do it in style." Billy's half-serious, half-joking tone made the barber pause a minute.

"It's your hide," he murmured, "but I can trim this hair fast as lightnin' for you. It ain't like you ever get too much cut," he noted disapprovingly, and reached for his scissors.

"I want it short. I want it cut off—all of it." Billy's steady gaze met the startled barber's in the mirror before them.

"The back?" he questioned weakly. "After years of me beggin', you're gonna let me take off the back?"

"Just hurry and do it, before I change my mind."

"Thank you, Lord," Leland whispered, rolling his eyes

heavenward a minute. Then the scissors poised, took aim, and snipped.

Whatever Leland did, it didn't make him look any more like the Sewells, which he'd half feared. The short, thick layers shaped his skull, and he tried not to feel naked when it was over.

"You'd look like a Memphis lawyer if you'd just—" Leland began.

"No. Whatever it is, no. I've done enough."

And after Billy paid, Leland stopped him. "You're gonna crash your father-in-law's party, right? All the big-wigs in two, three counties gonna be there, I hear."

"So's my wife."

"You've got everything except—" Leland hesitated. "Wait a minute."

He vanished into his back room, and when he returned, he held out a glass bottle with a black label on it. Whiskey.

"You take this. You're gonna need it more'n I do." His grin was a white gash in his face.


He started twice across the dark paved parking lot to the Greenview Country Club, and twice he turned around and walked back.

*Just go in,* the brassy side of his nature screamed. *Go get her.*

But this wasn't his world. What if he made a fool of himself? What if she didn't want to see him? What if that last fight had really been the last fight, and it was over?

He'd locked the fears away all day, concentrating with effort on action.

Now all of them hit him at once, all of his insecurities.

What if when she'd gone back home, she'd realized that they really didn't belong together, that she didn't love a rough-edged farm worker who kept clinging to childish ambitions?

Leaning hard against the truck, bracing himself on its hood, Billy fought with himself. And in that dark corner of the crowded parking lot, he reminded himself: I will not be the victim anymore. I'm as good as any of them.

On the truck seat, the bottle caught the light from a security pole, offering Dutch courage. The two or three stiff shots of whiskey he took straight burned the thoughts into his brain, as well as the back of his throat, and reminded him what he didn't like about the stuff.

Why was he hanging around out here, philosophizing? He wasn't Socrates.

He was William Robert Walker from Briskin County, Mississippi. He wanted his wife. He wanted to prove to her he was worth something.

He was telling himself all of that when he walked through the leaded-glass double oak doors that led to the world of the Greenview Country Club.

Ellen Walker's rowdy son had arrived.


"Go tell Shiloh Walker that her husband is here. I've been out of town. She wasn't expecting me back tonight; that's why my name's not on the list." It sounded good, thought Billy in satisfaction, and the doorman at the entrance marked Banquet Hall must have thought so, too. He hurried into the room deferentially, leaving the doors unguarded, and Billy strolled in leisurely.

There was a throng of people; Pennington owned—or controlled—six banks.

Flowers—big vases of yellow rose sprays, fat bowls of dark purple violets, round trays of pinks—covered every space. Green plants—corn plants, twisted jade, mock orange trees—overflowed every corner.

A well-groomed, elegant piano player and a saxophonist were perched on a dais in a corner, playing "Ain't Misbehavin' " to a talking, perfumed, excited throng of guests who didn't hear them.

And at the bar, four or five accountant types sipped and conversed.

The piano player shifted positions, and then Billy recognized him: Aaron Piedrow, who played bass and sang lead at the Legion Hall.

They better watch us, he thought in sudden quick amusement: we're moving in, us rednecks.

He was making his way to the piano when he saw her, and she stopped him cold in his tracks, his heart shooting straight up into his brain.

She had on a flame-red dress that swirled and swirled and swirled in a million soft layers around her legs, so tight and tiny around the waist he could have spanned her with his hands and had room to spare.

It fit snugly over her breasts, apparently held up by nothing except hope, with a mile expanse of smooth, richly tanned skin sweeping up from it.

Thank God there was a jacket, even if it was only a tiny bolero thing that was never intended to be buttoned and offered only whispers of glittering sleeves. In fact, the whole jacket sparkled with a coppery color, more brown than the dress and more red than her hair. He wanted that girl, and anger and outrage and longing and a double helping of jealousy and old-fashioned lust burned away his hurt.

He'd suffered agonies over her; she looked as if she'd never shed a tear in her life.

He'd worked for two weeks just because she'd hurt his pride, just so he could reclaim it. Shiloh probably didn't even remember the fight—or him.

He'd sold his horse for that woman in red.

Billy Bob's temper began to sizzle.


"What did you say?" Shiloh frowned at the doorman, looping her hair back behind her ear with its sparkling, chunky earring.

"I said," he began loudly, over the noise, "your husband said to tell you he was here."

"My husband!" she exclaimed, then laughed a little. "You've made a mistake. He's out of town."

"No mistake. He said"—the doorman stepped aside for a waiter with a tray full of smoked salmon hors d'oeuvres—"he'd got back in town early."

"But he wouldn't—"

"I don't see him," the doorman said, inspecting the crowd. "He should be easy to spot, as tall as he was."

Shiloh's throat closed up for a minute. "Tall?" she repeated. Was Billy really here—tonight?

Billy was home.

But here—*here?* How had he known? What would he think?

"There he is!" the doorman announced in triumph, pointing toward the piano. Her gaze followed his hand, and ran headlong into Billy Walker's stare.

Oh, Lord. Oh, Lord, Lord.

Was that Billy? *Her* Billy? The one who wore John Deere caps, and came home dirty and muddy from the fields, and spent two weeks in the county jail, and slept sprawled across her, and worried himself sick over money?

"Is that your husband? He said he was." The doorman was looking doubtful now, taking in her wide-eyed, disbelieving stare.

"I—think so." She took a step or two toward Billy.

"She *thinks* so? How long's the guy been gone?" the little doorman muttered before he went back to his post.

He was leaning on the piano, looking for all the world as if he'd stepped out of a fancy magazine. His hair—his short hair—was heavy and thick; its cropped layers brushed back from his face were more golden blond than the length behind his ears, and it made him look ridiculously young.

But the wide, wide shoulders of the black jacket tapering into his slender body denied that initial impression of youth. In the tuxedo coat, he didn't look lanky: he looked—well, gorgeous.

He straightened as she got closer, warily circling him. Blue jeans. Long, long legs. And cowboy boots.

It *was* Billy.

How could anybody ever think Michael was handsomer? If they did, they were crazy.

But this man—he couldn't be her sweet, decent, teasing Billy. No man who looked like this fit those adjectives.

And up close, she saw something else: this man was dangerous. It was in the way he watched her, in the blue fire in his eyes.

She stopped in front of him, uncertain and shy.

"Hello, Shiloh."

"Bi—Billy." Her voice cracked a little in shock.

"Don't look so scared," he said, his voice tight. "I didn't come to drag you back ho—back to the farm."

"You—you didn't?" What was wrong with her? She sounded like a moron. She wanted to throw herself on him, pull off that silky black tie, jerk open the shirt, and find Billy, her Billy, down inside this beautiful stranger with the furious eyes.

"No, you look like you're having a real good time. I just came to bring you something." He found the money inside his pocket, pulled it out, and showed it to her.

"No—Billy—I know what it is. I won't take it."

"You damn well will take it. Every time I think of that sweet little deal you offered me in jail—and I took—it makes me sick. So for the sake of my stomach, here." His eyes skimmed over her skin. "I would tuck it in your cleavage, but that top might fall off, so—" He tossed it at her, and she caught it instinctively.

"You've been gone two weeks—*two,* without a word."

"I called. You were gone."

"And you expect me to sit around waiting for you when you're off having fun with some rodeo," she began dangerously.

"I was working. And getting *that.*" He motioned toward the money. "So you and Pennington could never throw it up to me again."

The saxophonist had quit playing, his mouth dropped open slackly as he watched them.

"I didn't mean what I said that night at the Palace," Shiloh got out at last. "I was angry. And you wouldn't listen."

"I listened, to everything you said. About your daddy, and about me. Then you went home and didn't come back. Well, I'm not for sale anymore." His eyes drifted down over her breasts again, down to her long legs. "But before I walk out of here, I'll take a little something on credit."

He towered over her, his arms engulfing her, his body swallowing hers as he yanked her up against his hard rib cage.

His hand catching in her hair, he pulled her head backward, tilting it up toward his before he crushed her mouth under his.

Sweet and willing . . . her lips were all of that.

And when those insidious thoughts made his mouth gentle and cling to hers in desperation, he dragged himself away. She opened her eyes, breathless.

"Anybody would think," he whispered raggedly, "that you wanted to be kissed, the way you hang to me. It must get real lonesome in your daddy's world. You should'a given me a chance, Shiloh. I might have fit a little in here, too. But maybe I don't want to, after all."

He stood her upright on her own feet. He had to get out.

He practically shoved guests out of the way; behind him he heard Shiloh call his name, but he kept pushing.

". . . he's that Walker man. . . . You know, the one Shiloh ran off and married. . . ."

He heard the whispers, and they didn't matter. What mattered was that he was going to get down on his knees and beg her to let them start over if he didn't get away.

Behind him, Shiloh turned to Aaron. "Do you smoke?" she demanded.

"What? Yeah. I mean, yes, ma'am," he stammered.

"I need to borrow your lighter."

Billy got outside by way of a set of French doors, made his escape, and ran headlong into his worst enemy.

Sam Pennington, with a silent T-Tommy behind him, was arguing violently with a tall, blond man.

Michael. It was Michael.

Cold water thrown in Billy's face couldn't have affected him more. He actually staggered backward a little as Pennington turned impatiently to see who had interrupted his little tête-à-tête.

Billy braced himself, but Pennington just stared, then laughed, a dry, wry sound.

"You clean up real good, Walker. You look damn near respectable."

The man seemed smaller, less invincible, nearly . . . defeated. Billy, stunned, looked from him to T-Tommy.

"I'm leaving," he said stiffly.

"What the hell? Stay." Pennington said it with a shrug. "The whole county came uninvited tonight." Then he turned back to Michael, who was staring at Billy in open dislike.

Billy had never been this close to his older brother before, and it took a minute for him to realize that he just didn't care. Not anymore. Not after all this time.

He hadn't thought of Michael in weeks, and precious little of Robert Sewell.

No longing to be like them. No bitterness that he was the forgotten one.

Shiloh had done that for him, he realized suddenly.

She had given him no time and no room for useless envy or longing.

She had taken away the sting.

Now it was Michael who resented *him*.

And it was Michael who had tried to rape Shiloh.

"If I'd known you were letting just anybody in—" Michael began to Sam, and Billy started to shrug out of his coat.

"I think I owe you something, Sewell," he said, cutting

across his half brother's words. They'd never spoken before, not in all of his twenty-seven years.

"Are you talking to *me?*" Michael said, a sneer in his voice.

"I'll let my fists do the talking," Billy answered, his voice heavy, dark, determined. He tossed the coat at T-Tommy, who wailed, "Aw, Billy, don't hit him in front of me. If he takes you to court, I'll have to be a witness against you. Let me at least get turned around—"

"You put your filthy hands on Shiloh. You tried to hurt her."

"She's told you the same lies she—"

Billy cut off his words with a solid, meaty fist right across Michael's face. The blow made a sodden sound, Michael grunted, blood flew.

And as Sewell staggered upright, grabbing at his nose, Billy hit him in the stomach. It bent him over double.

The third blow, just below his neck and across his shoulders, toppled him to the ground, where he spread-eagled face down.

"You make sure," Billy said, panting, going down on one knee beside the prostrate body and speaking clearly in his ear, "that you stay away from Shiloh and you be careful what you say about her."

No answer from Michael.

When he clambered to his feet, he looked for T-Tommy and his coat. But instead, Shiloh stood there clutching it to her, the money still in one hand, her eyes wide and dark.

Then he remembered: he'd been going to impress her with how civilized he was, with how well he could fit into the proper country club set.

T-Tommy spoke from behind Billy, startling him. "Well, it looks like somebody went a round with Michael.

Sewell just won two major endorsements a few days ago. That means that *somebody* cold-cocked the son of the next governor." His voice was mournful.

"He ran into something in the dark, that's all," Pennington said thoughtfully.

Billy straightened, confused at Shiloh's father's behavior, and he wiped the back of his hand across his face where sweat was blurring his vision.

"My coat," he said, breath whistling through the words.

But Sam spoke. "You did me a favor, Walker." His head motion indicated Michael. "So I'll do you one. Try selling your trees again. That warehouse might be more interested this time. You're right on the verge of making a little money. But don't think I'm getting friendly. I'm not. If you make it, you'll damn well do it on your own."

His voice was brusque.

Stunned, Billy ran a hand back through his hair, remembering only then that Leland had chopped it off.

"I guess you won't be home when this party is over," Pennington said ruefully to his daughter.

"I don't know. It depends on—" She flashed a glance at Billy.

"I'll send one of the waiters to clean him up and get him out of here." Pennington motioned toward Michael, who was beginning to stir a little, and then he walked away, T-Tommy on his heels.

"My coat," Billy repeated at last, and she handed it to him this time.

Was this it? Was he just going to walk away? Shiloh wondered.

Is she going to let me leave? Billy asked himself, panicky.

At the door of his truck, he turned, trying to think of

what to say—or do—that would bring out the fire in her.

She had followed him, at least part of the way. A distant light shone from an ornate metal post designed after the Ionic columns of Southern mansions, and it turned her outline into something ethereal.

"I—" he began.

"You're not going anywhere, Mr. Billy Bob Walker." Her voice slicing across the dark, shadowy parking lot was determined, and, praise God, there was that streak of temper in it that meant she cared.

"I'm not?" he asked hopefully.

"Your keys were in the pocket of your coat."

He clutched the coat.

"You took them," he said in relief. She really wasn't going to let him go. "Where are they?"

She pointed out across the night-laden green, where it sloped into a pocket of pines. "Remember how you threatened to throw mine away? Well, I don't make idle threats, and there's the fifteenth hole."

"You threw my—Lord, Shiloh, how'm I going to find them?" he demanded, giving the coat an exasperated fling onto the truck seat.

"I don't care if you ever do." She headed away from him furiously. "You deserve to be stuck out here."

"Where are you going?" he called after her, confused. "Wait a minute—*wait*."

Then he took out after her, out toward the same pine grove she'd motioned toward. She was talking to herself—to the air—to whoever would listen as she marched.

"Gone two weeks, and I'm sick of hearing about Angie. I walk into the Palace, which is one of the most repulsive dives I've ever been in in my entire life—"

"Been in a lot of 'em, have you?" He couldn't resist the dig as he caught up with her.

She stopped. "About as many of them as you have country clubs. And I didn't knock anybody senseless while I was there."

"No, you just wanted to tear her fingernails off."

"What were they doing on your shoulder?"

"The same thing Michael's hands were doing all over you one night in front of Sweetwater. I didn't ask her to be there, Shiloh, and it wouldn't have gone any further. I got married, remember?" He looked down in her face, his own serious. She looked away.

"And there was Papa. I didn't know all he was doing, but we've talked. It's over, Billy. He knows he has to accept you, or else."

His throat worked; he tried to speak. "And what about you? Can you accept me?"

"Which one of you is asking?" she demanded. "The one from the jail? Or the one who's been going to school without telling anybody, even me? I'm your wife, Billy."

"I was going to. I was afraid to tell you. It sounds ridiculous, me in school."

"You're afraid of me, too. Of where I came from."

"What are you—"

"I'm talking about this." She held up the thirty-five hundred dollars. "I know what it's about. Pride, and the stupid thing I said at the Palace. I should never have offered you the money. I did it because I wanted to marry you. But it's more than that with you. This money bothers you so much that I'm going to have to get rid of it all to satisfy you. If I mean to have you, it has to go. And, Billy Walker"— she raised her other hand then; she had a Bic lighter in it—"I mean to have you. I swear it."

Across the flickering flame, their eyes met. Then she shoved it under the edge of the money. And as it curled around the corner of the green bills, he saw the gold of her wedding band. She was wearing it, right here tonight in full view.

The fire caught.

Let it burn, he thought, recklessly. It would make some kind of romantic, idealistic statement about love.

But this was real life.

That was real money.

And it looked like he had a wife to support again.

"For God's sake, Shiloh," he expostulated, then knocked the bills from her hand to stomp out the flame at the corner with his boot. "If that's not just like you Penningtons," he said, his voice unsteady, as he caught her hand, kissing the ring. "Money to burn."

"Someday, I'm going to tell you a story about us Penningtons," she whispered. "But not tonight. You didn't let the money burn, Billy, because deep down inside you, you know it's not important between us. I just needed it as an excuse to get to you."

Her hands were free now, and she used them to loosen his tie. Right here, in the cool, free air, out in the wide-open world with the whippoorwills, she tugged the tie undone.

In his ears, the blood began to pound.

"I used it, too," he rasped. "For a reason to come tonight. To show you I was as good as any of them. That I could fit in with that crowd. But I screwed it up, Shiloh. I don't know what happened . . ."

The tie hung free now, on either side of his throat. Then she moved to the top button of his shirt, and his hands reached convulsively for her waist. Now the blood beat in little points across his body.

"You threw money at me and kissed me blind," she whispered humorously. "You didn't fit in—you outshone.

There's hardly a woman in that club who didn't notice my wild man tonight. But you just remember one thing, Billy." Her hand finished with the second button, sliding under his new shirt, cool against his heated skin. Up his nape, to the shorn hair. "I love you in your boots and muddy T-shirts and in that old truck of yours, too, not just when you look like this. I love you whether you're growing trees or you're the rising young vet."

"Thank the Lord," he murmured. "Because I may never make it." He hoped he was talking about vet school.

The fourth button was his undoing. He caught her up against him as she spread the shirt open, nudging her head back for his kisses, pushing her down to the short, wet grass in the piney shadows of the fifteenth hole, right here in this dark little cove of the country club green.

"I was trying to be civilized and proper tonight," he panted. "But I'll be damned if you're not wilder than me. Here, Shiloh?"

Her answer was to pull him down to her, to stop his questions and reach for his belt.

"You've been drinking," she managed to say at last, when she came up for air.

"Yes, ma'am," he returned hoarsely, his breath hot on the skin at her ear. "Jack Daniels, to be exact. The barber gave it to me."

"It took whiskey to get you through a haircut?" Her laughing lips tried to reach to kiss him.

"No. To get up enough nerve to come in this cold place after a wife who'd left home." His words were as serious as his face.

"You were gone for two weeks, Billy. I came back, and you weren't there. *Two weeks.*" She bit him sharply on the neck, but her hands had reached his waist again, pulling his shirt free of the loosened pants.

"I had to get the money." He let her push him over on his back, letting go of his breath as she pressed kisses into his flat, bare stomach, her own breath warm on his skin.

Desperate, he reached for her and yanked at the sparkling jacket, twisting her out of it. He'd been right—nothing but hope. Her shoulders were warm and smooth, as fragrant as the grass around them.

"You got it from Bell?"

"I sold Chase to him."

She stopped all movement. "Oh, Billy. I never meant for you to do it."

"I'd do it again, a hundred times over for you, Shiloh." He pulled her face up to his. "For us to be together, like this."

She didn't know when she started crying; the tears dripped onto his chest, onto her hands riding him.

Impatiently, he pushed down the top of the red dress, his lips finding her breasts, lifting her to him so tightly she could barely breathe.

Looking down on his blond head, feeling the touch of his lips on her skin, she remembered everything: the way he'd struggled with the trees, the way he'd pushed with dogged determination to get through the university, the way he loved her, and now, the way he'd been willing to sacrifice for that love.

He'd been trying again, tonight, when he came here.

He'd beaten up Michael Sewell, for her. Maybe that was a little primitive, basic, masculine, but that was exactly what she wanted. He was a man. Not a boy. Will. He was Will. Ellen's name for him was the right one.

She scooted down him, pulling his mouth up to her fiercely, spiraling this slow lovemaking into a hot, fast motion. He caught fire instantly, rolling her over onto the damp grass, cupping her shoulders with his hands, his arms under her back, his body covering hers, pushing away clothes frantically. The rhythm came without volition, the natural give and take of two who knew each other, who loved each other.

And when she hit the top of the night sky, high above the pine trees, holding on to him because he was the only reality, a cool wind swept across their heated, clinging bodies, carrying away her quiet, choking sobs.

"I love you, Shiloh." He got the words out in short, sharp stabs of sound against her throat.

"I love you, Bil—no, Will. I love you, Will Walker," she returned, her voice sweet in his ear.

Not too far away, a whippoorwill called across the dark Mississippi sky.


The stars looked close enough to touch, but the moon was too high, a distant buttery slice in the midnight blue canopy above them when they finally moved.

"So this is what you do on a golf course," he said in mock seriousness as he zipped up her dress.

"It's usually more boring," she returned, teasingly, twisting to find his shirt on the ground.

He slid his arms in it as she held it up for him, hunching his shoulders forward. "I surely do appreciate the lesson." He grinned at her. "If I'd'a known this was what you were dragging me out here for, I'd have run, not walked. And I wouldn't have been half as mad about those keys."

"Oh, those." She looked guilty, even in the moonlight. "They're still in your pocket."

He gave a pleased shout of laughter. "You really did

trick me out here just to have your way with me, didn't you?"

"I wasn't original. The golf pro used to use the pine grove all the time for his lady friends. So you see, you're just as proper as the rest of the crowd here. But civilized? I don't think I want you civilized, Will Walker." Her head drooped against his arm. "I want to go home."

He thought about the name Will, and he liked it on her lips. And he thought about the way she said "home."

"To the farm?" He wanted her to say that, too.

"To our room—off the porch—at the farm. There's this bird there that's expecting us . . ." Her voice trailed off in a yawn.

"You're asleep," he said tenderly, as he finished buttoning most of the buttons on the shirt. Then he bent, lifting her up against him, and her face rested on the rich little folds in the cloth, stained with grass now.

"This is very, very nice," she murmured, lips against his throat as he carried her across the green. The club had long since emptied. Only Billy's truck remained in the black parking lot.

Shiloh reached down and opened the door, and he slid her in on the seat where the black coat lay.

Going home, with him, forever.

But just as he circled the truck to get in himself, a tall, thin shadow detached himself from one of the columns that held up the wide balcony of the club.

"Mr. Walker."

Billy, trying to find the ignition key, looked up, surprised. Inside the truck, Shiloh came awake.

"Yeah?" Billy's voice was cautious.

"I've been waiting for you. I got a tip you were here tonight. Looks like you've been having a real good time," the voice said, amused and knowing. "My name's Paul Jansen. I write for the *Memphis Commercial Appeal*." The man stopped to pull a package of cigarettes from his pocket, tapping one out and lipping it into his mouth.

"So?"

"So I've heard that you've got close ties to Robert Sewell. Very close ties." In the flame of the lighter that Jansen held to the end of the cigarette, he was hazel eyed, brown haired. "And that you might want to talk about Sewell to an interested party."

"Like you?"

"That's right. Like me."

Inside the truck, Shiloh didn't move.

Outside it, Billy wondered what would have happened if this man had approached him a year ago.

"I reckon you've wasted your time. What time is it, anyway? Too late for me," Billy said easily, raking his hand back through his tousled hair. "Somebody sent you on a wild goose chase. My wife's father is a friend of the judge's. But me, I'm not."

Jansen blew smoke and straightened. "I heard you were Sewell's bastard son." His voice was sharp, laced with disappointment.

Billy sat down in the truck, and on the seat between them, Shiloh's hand grasped his, squeezing it reassuringly.

"Who, me?" Billy laughed a little. "My name's Will Walker. And I never knew my father."

He shut the truck door decisively, its loud slam echoing across the still lot. "Come on, baby," he said, smiling at her. "Let's go home."